SHE IS ı
HE IS HER

TRICKY MAGIC

L.L. CAMPBELL

TRICKY MAGIC SERIES
BOOK ONE

TRICKY MAGIC

TRICKY MAGIC SERIES
BOOK ONE

Tricky Magic
Book One of The Tricky Magic Series
Copyright © 2022 L.L. Campbell

Second Edition | Paperback
Publication Date: December 18, 2021
ISBN: 979-8-9854622-5-8

You are reading the revised version.

The characters and events portrayed in this book are fictitious
or are used fictitiously. The settings are inspired by real
locations. Specifically where I grew up in New England. Any
similarity to real persons, living or dead, is purely coincidental
and not intended.

Cover Design | Elizianna@elizianna.the.one
Internal Design | L.L. Campbell
Page Formatting| Books n' Moods
Part Designs: Adobe Stock | geraria, croisy, kssss
Designs: Adobe Stock | Good Studio, mila_okie, vidimages
Published by Lexi L. Campbell @readsbylexi
Copy Editing: Lavender Prose
www.readsbylexi.com

DON'T START READING YET...

This book contains graphic sex scenes, talk of emotional abuse, hint at sexual assault, graphic killing, and a shit ton of swearing.

To stay in-the-know on release dates, giveaways, & more, visit:

w w w . r e a d s b y l e x i . c o m

If you have any questions or concerns with my work, please feel free to contact me:

r e a d s b y l e x i @ g m a i l . c o m

Thank you for reading and giving my debut novel a chance! I hope you enjoy the characters and the world they live in.

xo L.L.

Full TW can be found mid-way down the linked page.

For Chris.
Look handsome! I did it.

al an

portsmouth

rosier's lake

glenover

Playlist

Broken Bones - KALEO
mercy - KiNG MALA
Play with Fire - Sam Tinnesz, Yacht Money
Misery Business - Paramore
High - Whether, Dua Lipa
Take Me to Church - Hozier
Jenny of Oldstones - Florence + The Machine
Crazy in Love - Sofia Karlberg
You should be sad - Halsey
Way down We Go - KALEO
I Feel Like I'm Drowning - Two Feet
Call Me Devil - Friends in Tokyo
Power Over Me - Dermot Kennedy
Lion - Saint Mesa
From Eden - Hozier
I WANNA BE YOUR SLAVE - Måneskin
Beggin' - Måneskin
Castle - Halsey
Dark Side - Bishop Briggs
all the good girls go to hell - Billie Eilish

GLOSSARY

I'm an ass and picked weird names:
Ellea: EHL-iyAH
Jadis: JHEY-DihS
Rosier: ROH-zee-ur
Belias: BEL-iy AS
Asmodeus: az-mo-DEE-uhs
Lughnasadh: LOO-nuh-suh

chamonix

10-21-21

He crested the hill
on top of a proud mare.

Her chestnut coat flared
with Hel's setting sun.

And the black scaled armor she wore,
whispered of devastation and death.

PART ONE

We are each our own devil and
we make this world our Hel.
- Oscar Wilde

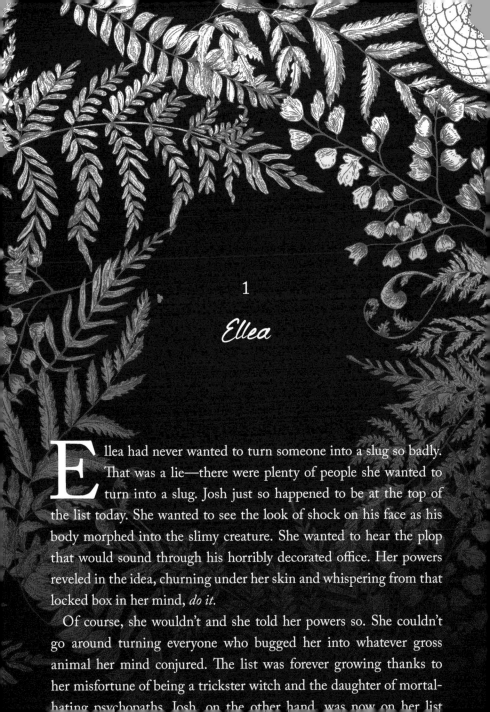

1

Ellea

Ellea had never wanted to turn someone into a slug so badly. That was a lie—there were plenty of people she wanted to turn into a slug. Josh just so happened to be at the top of the list today. She wanted to see the look of shock on his face as his body morphed into the slimy creature. She wanted to hear the plop that would sound through his horribly decorated office. Her powers reveled in the idea, churning under her skin and whispering from that locked box in her mind, *do it*.

Of course, she wouldn't and she told her powers so. She couldn't go around turning everyone who bugged her into whatever gross animal her mind conjured. The list was forever growing thanks to her misfortune of being a trickster witch and the daughter of mortal-hating psychopaths. Josh, on the other hand, was now on her list because he didn't *agree* with the future he'd paid her to look into, and was becoming more irate by the second. And his cologne was gross.

Josh sneered at her from across the desk. He hadn't even given her a comfortable chair to sit in; the hard wood dug into her legs, making her desperate to be finished with this reading. Preferably at home, in an oversized shirt with a book in her lap—she was exhausted. Her week had been filled with one too many bad readings and endless dreams of beasts and monsters.

When was it too early to retire?

"Check the cards," Josh hissed, dragging her from her thoughts. "I know you read for Clint. I can't help but think your vision is false and will help the firm I compete with."

"I've been reading your future for two years," Ellea said with a roll of her eyes. "Why would I start lying now?"

On top of being a trickster, Ellea was also a seer; she'd been reading the futures of the wealthy and famous for the past five years. It was great for her bank account, and another perk of her job was getting a side-eye from the other witches. It wasn't against the rules, but they didn't approve of using your power for personal gain.

Ellea reached for the black velvet pouch that held her favorite deck of tarot cards. The gilded edges gleamed as she shuffled them, one, two, three times. She stopped as her powers pulled at her chest, a feeling that the cards were where they needed to be.

Josh glanced at the stack as she placed it on the left of his desk, and a small drop of sweat escaped his hairline. He had to know Ellea was right. Every session before now had come true, that wasn't about to change. Ellea flipped over the first card, starting at the left. It was the five of pentacles. She didn't bother hiding the smirk that came or the bark of a laugh as she flipped the next card: ten of cups. Josh was fully sweating now, his face even more desperate.

One more card.

Ellea didn't bother looking at the last card as she flipped it. Her magic was right, and she saw his future confirmed as he stared at the last card with horror. He knew what it meant; she usually taught her clients to read the cards.

"The world," he hissed.

Ellea pointed at each card. "Poverty. True happiness and fulfillment. Harmony and completion."

Josh mumbled obscenities under his breath.

"My vision is confirmed. Your current investments will leave you broke, but in the end, you and your family will find peace and happiness—"

"No!" Josh stood quickly and pulled a gun from under his desk. His hand splayed across the mahogany surface, pressing into the cards she had pulled. The gun shook as he held it at her face, and her powers crackled under her skin at the threat before her.

Ellea gritted her teeth, pressing her trickster magic down.

It would be so easy to turn this filthy mortal into a rat.

She forced the thought out of her mind and looked away from the rage in his eyes. Ellea raised her lip as she noted the sweat dripping from his hand onto the cards.

"It's not the end of the world." She blinked slowly at him.

He leaned closer to her, and Ellea's stomach rolled. Josh reeked of alcohol, and his anger mixed with nervousness washed over her. He hadn't aged well in his years as a stockbroker; too many drinks and way too many late-night meetings.

"I have built this empire from the ground up. Why should I believe you? This is impossible!" he shouted, waving the gun around.

Ugh, the dramatics.

With a thrum of her fingers, Josh was tied to his chair and Ellea was across from him, sitting on top of the desk with her legs crossed. The gun dangled on her finger as she leaned back on one hand and glared at him.

"Josh, this could have gone so many ways." She pointed the gun at his forehead with ease and confidence. "I don't appreciate being threatened or shouted at."

"You're a bitch, and you could have warned me sooner." The insult was overshadowed by how much he was shaking.

"You could have called me before you decided to invest all your money." Her smarter clients did.

"It's like you enjoy watching mortals suffer," he hissed, and at that, Ellea was done.

"Let me end your suffering for you," she said, pressing the gun into his forehead.

Josh closed his eyes tightly and whimpered. A stain began forming across his lap as a threatening click sounded through the room, but the gun turned to smoke. Ellea got up and walked toward her things, shaking the feeling of her magic singing at the small use of power. She quickly cleansed the cards with a spell and placed them back into their bag, along with her crystals. Before she turned to leave, she looked toward Josh.

"Instead of reading more into your future and telling you the happy ending of your story," she said, staring into his watery and angry eyes, "I'm going to let you wallow in your piss-soaked self-pity and constantly wonder where your path in life is heading."

"I hope you rot in Hell!" he sobbed and then spat at her.

This ass-hat actually spat at me?

With a cock of her brow, the vile spit stopped before it hit her, rerouted, and splattered right in his dumb face.

"Let me leave you with a curse to close off this *wonderful* session."

Ellea stood fully, intensifying her stare.

Her powers dimmed the lights and conjured smoke that billowed from the corners of his office. She summoned the beasts that had been plaguing her dreams all week. Their scales and feathers gleamed in the lowered light and hissed in languages neither of them knew. Throwing her hands in a woo-woo way her nana would be proud of, she deepened her voice and bellowed out into the room,

"Every door you enter will be closed. Every business deal will be built on lies and ruin." She pointed a steady finger at him. "Your family will always blame you for their woes. You will never feel peace and you will never find happiness!"

In a blink of an eye, the room went back to normal, and she disappeared. Well, she was gone from Josh's sight. She was invisible to him while he crawled across the floor, sobbing and cursing her name. Ellea's heart rate peaked to a new high, and her head began to pound after the use of magic she'd barely tapped into.

I shouldn't have done that.

Rubbing her temples and swearing to herself, she left. Ellea could still hear Josh's sobs as she reappeared and walked past his wide-eyed receptionist. She smiled at the middle-aged woman and placed her dark sunglasses on her face, heading toward the elevator.

It was a scorching day at the end of July, but Ellea decided to walk home. It had been a while since she'd tapped into her trickster magic, and it left her feeling jittery.

Luckily, I didn't waste any of my fancier and more uncomfortable outfits on this fun client.

Josh had been the fourth bad reading this week. No matter how many times she shuffled the cards or looked into a client's future, it was all bad. She scowled and headed toward the historic district of the small city of Halifax. Sporting a light cotton top and a sheer, black skirt, Ellea cursed her heels. She managed half a block before the first dirty look was shot her way. She ignored it, as she had done most of her life. Her parents had made it impossible to be liked by anyone. The magical outbursts in her early years hadn't helped matters either. Her parents had landed themselves in a supernatural prison after killing some mortals, disrupting the order, and several other frowned-upon things. She had zero fond memories of them and was thankful she'd been raised by her uncle and Nana.

Both were seers from her mother's side. Her uncle Felix's mood changed with every equinox or the latest trend, and he'd spent their years together teaching and training Ellea in anything and everything. It had helped to quell the power coursing through her veins. Trickster powers were scary, and was best to be ready for anything without having to tap into that side of her magic.

Jadis, her nana, was the type of seer you saw on late-night psychic commercials. Her favorite pastime was bumping into a mortal on the street and going into a fit about their future or a loved one trying to reach them. Ellea would never dream of doing that. As another dirty look was shot her way, she reached into her bag.

Two books sat in her purse, a brand new one about demons and her old favorite, a shifter reverse harem. She didn't know much about demons; she'd only had one or two glances of the three that sat on the council. The council had been formed over three hundred years ago after the Great Elimination, a time when mortals hunted supernaturals. The battles and hunts ended poorly for both sides, so they'd compromised and formed a council that included supernaturals and humans.

The cover of the book about demons caught her eye. She would read the first chapter and see if it was interesting. Turning to the first page, she dove in while easily navigating her way home. It was a win-win, avoiding glares while reading smut. She managed three pages before she ran into a large and hard body.

"Fuck, watch it," she hissed. People usually navigated around her.

"Hey, kitten," a familiar voice said.

Isaac.

Internally, she cringed at the nickname, but she smiled up at him. They had been fooling around for a few months now after his father, a council member who sat next to her nana, had forced their relationship. She was sure the goal was for it to be serious, but she kept it light. It helped that he had a nice dick and knew how to use it. He was taller than her petite frame. He was blond, lean, and handsome; all witches were handsome or pretty. He always seemed to run into her at the weirdest times, and it made her wonder how much he was investing into their relationship. The other two men she was seeing would hardly ever bump into her on the street.

"Hey, Isaac." He had a paper clutched under his arm, and she caught the headline, "Another String of Vampire Attacks Haunts Eastern Nyrway."

The name of their continent always made her want to giggle.

"More attacks?" She had overheard her nana at a recent brunch discussing ways to stop the increase in vampire attacks.

"Yeah. Nothing your cute little head needs to worry about," he said, brushing her hair off her shoulder. "Want to hang out tonight?"

Ellea suppressed her grimace.

"No. I want to curl up with a book and rest since Lughnasadh is this weekend." She didn't bother to make her smile warm.

He flicked her book, causing Ellea to clutch it to her chest, growing more annoyed.

"I don't know why you don't have one of those fancy e-readers like everyone else," he said with a grin.

"You know I don't like devices." She hated them, and he knew that. She loved the feel of a good book in her hands. Phones were used for calling or to get an all-caps text from her nana. There was no reason for her to be wrapped up in witch social media drama or anything else. It was best to avoid anything that would be said about her. Most of the supernatural community had embraced new technology; some of it made it easier to live peacefully among mortals. But others found it inhibited the old way of doing magic and had been affecting their strength.

"Oh, right, you like the *old ways*," he said with a snigger that had her seeing red.

"Well, it was nice running into you." She gave him a tight smile and tried to walk away.

"What time do you want me to pick you up for Lughnasadh?" he said, grabbing her arm and stopping her retreat.

His father is on the council, he's good in bed, you're just having a bad day, don't curse him.

She took a breath and smiled up at Isaac.

"I'm not sure yet." She patted his hand. "It's been a day; bad reading, you know how it is. Let me get home and I'll call you tomorrow?"

Isaac was also a seer, but he usually kept his visions political, helping his father and the council.

"Of course, kitten." He leaned in to kiss her and Ellea turned her head, forcing him to catch her cheek. "I'll talk to you tomorrow."

Ellea smiled and turned away. The click of her heels was loud in her ears as she took the longest strides of her life.

Three more blocks, you can do this.

Opening her book, she let the words wash away the weird encounter and bad day.

Passing an ancient oak with vines swirling around its massive trunk, Ellea turned onto her walkway. She lived in a stately brick house with a lush front lawn. Creeping fig vines covered the second floor of the home, adding to its historic feel. From the walkway, you wouldn't know how modern the inside was or the magic it possessed. She entered her house and removed her heels, throwing them to the staircase to her right. She paused in her entryway as the sound of someone being killed rang through the home.

"Billy!" she called out to her familiar.

She walked through the plain parlor with its beige walls and cream furniture and headed to the back of the house, following the sounds of a sharp machete and gushing blood.

Fucking beast.

Ellea continued her hunt for Billy, who was a familiar in the form of a fluffy ass, one-hundred-and-fifty-pound, black dog. She was something between a Rottweiler and an American Bull Terrier. It wasn't usual for witches to have familiars at twenty-eight, but their codependency had started after Ellea's parents had been taken away.

"There you are," Ellea said as she crossed into their favorite room.

The dark green walls were accented with artwork in black or gold frames, a tall fireplace, and one too many bookcases. On one of the coziest couches sat her beast of a best friend. Her wide tongue hung out the side of her mouth, and her sharp teeth glinted in the dimmed lights.

25

"That was *awesome*," said the handsome character on the TV screen, Dean Winchester.

Gods, he's so hot, Billy said telepathically.

Billy, in her beast form, could only speak telepathically, but she could communicate with whoever she wanted.

"How many times have we seen this episode?" Ellea asked, rubbing Billy on the head before heading to her room to change.

I could watch him forever and never tire of his tight ass and perfect smile, Billy answered.

Ellea smiled to herself as she reached her walk-in closet that held mostly dark clothing. Throwing her shirt, bra, and supportive boy shorts in the hamper, she reached for her favorite shirt. It was three sizes too big, black, and had a giant silver snake on the front. As soon as the supple fabric caressed her skin, she let out a relaxed sigh. She padded barefoot back to the living room where the home had left her a large glass of water and a margarita next to her favorite reading chair.

How was your day, Bug? Billy asked, turning the volume down with her big paw as Dean yelled "son of a bitch."

"Horrible," Ellea sighed, snuggling into her chair as the two books from her purse floated to her on a phantom wind.

She loved this house.

Ellea chose the demon one.

"Josh had a bad reading, and the fucker pulled a gun on me—"

Billy's growl cut her off, and the lights flickered angrily throughout the house.

"It's fine, I took care of it," she said, then began chewing on her lip.

How did you take care of it? Billy asked.

A smirk crossed her lips before she tapped down the thunder of power that echoed in her mind.

"Just some trickster magic." She flipped through her book and ignored the gaze of her familiar.

She wouldn't see judgment in her eyes, but she wasn't ready for the usual discussion of control, learn your powers—

Good. I'm glad you let that side of your magic help in a scary situation, Billy said, cutting off her thoughts.

"It won't happen again," Ellea grumbled.

She couldn't let it, her magic was volatile, scary, and she didn't know what would happen if she let it out any more than she usually did.

Right, Billy said and turned back to the TV.

Ellea sipped her drink and settled into her book. Her eyes felt heavy, but she fought off sleep.

One more chapter.

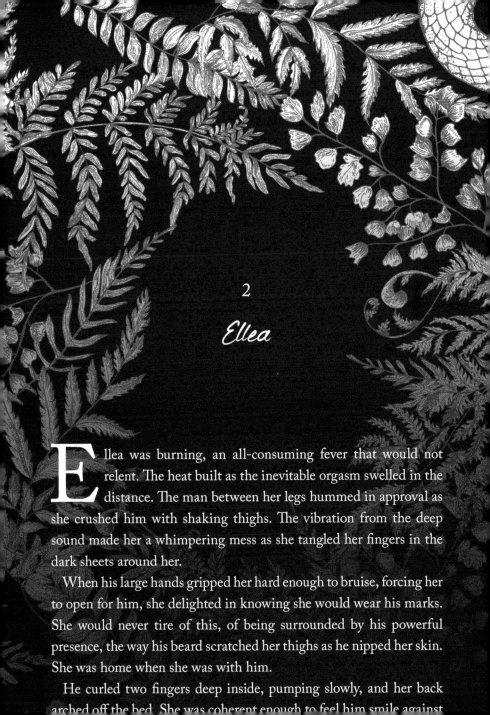

2

Ellea

Ellea was burning, an all-consuming fever that would not relent. The heat built as the inevitable orgasm swelled in the distance. The man between her legs hummed in approval as she crushed him with shaking thighs. The vibration from the deep sound made her a whimpering mess as she tangled her fingers in the dark sheets around her.

When his large hands gripped her hard enough to bruise, forcing her to open for him, she delighted in knowing she would wear his marks. She would never tire of this, of being surrounded by his powerful presence, the way his beard scratched her thighs as he nipped her skin. She was home when she was with him.

He curled two fingers deep inside, pumping slowly, and her back arched off the bed. She was coherent enough to feel him smile against her swollen pussy before he consumed her with his tongue and teeth. A single, sharp bite against her clit had release crashing around her.

Her moan rang through the moonlit room, and he moaned with her as he continued to feast. As she slowly came down from her orgasm, she saw him pumping his arm, finding his own release.

"Let me," she said huskily.

"This was about you," he moaned and nipped at her knee.

He shuddered once more before crawling up the bed, peppering her with heated kisses the whole way. He was so tall and strong; she could feel his powerful muscles as he settled behind her, tugging her in close before kissing her shoulder.

"Feel better, princess?" he whispered before kissing her ear.

"Much better." She settled more into him, unbothered that they were both sticky.

"Will you tell me about your day now?" he asked.

Hadn't she already? She racked her brain, but could only remember him between her legs.

Weird.

"I had to use my trickster powers today on someone who wanted to attack me," she whispered.

"We've talked about this," he said, pulling her in tighter. "You are allowed to use your magic. You need to protect yourself."

Had they talked about this?

Ellea continued searching for a memory, a time when they had met before. All she felt was comfort and freedom. She felt loved and powerful, and that was something she'd never thought she would have. Magic crackled under her skin, and it wasn't scary like all the other times. His own magic answered hers, and she felt warm and settled. This was something she never knew she needed. She feared that if she closed her eyes, it would all disappear.

"I'll see you soon, princess." His voice had become distant.

"But you're right here," she grumbled. "Please don't leave me."

A *thwack* sound jerked her awake, and she winced against Billy's hot breath in her face.

You were drooling, Billy said.

The beast was so close that Ellea's eyes couldn't focus on her large head. Looking around the living room, she found she was still in her reading chair, and her book had fallen to the ground.

"I was dreaming?"

Clearly. Billy sounded amused. *It seemed like you were dreaming of Dean with the grumbling and moaning you were doing.*

"That wasn't Dean," she whispered.

Ellea felt so cold now—cold and empty. She wondered if she would ever feel as content as she did in that dream.

Isaac, then? Billy asked.

"Hel no." Ellea grimaced. "He's getting too clingy. And the man in my dream…"

She couldn't find the words to describe him. She knew he was tall, strong, and had a beard. Ellea looked into the big amber eyes of her beast.

"I don't know who that was," she whispered. "But it was awesome."

Billy gave her a lopsided, puppy grin.

Let's go to bed and see if you can find your new beau, she said before turning and trotting toward the bedroom.

Ellea sat up, rubbing the weariness and sleep from her face. It had definitely been a dream, not a vision. There would never be a time when she was free to use her magic and feel so safe, so loved.

Maybe one day.

She shook the thought. Her magic would stay where it was and that was that. Grabbing her book from the floor, she headed to her bedroom. It was made up of dark paneled walls, high ceilings, and in the middle hung a gold and crystal chandelier. Excessive green velvet curtains blocked out the sun, and there were too many couches for her and Billy to use for reading or napping. The beast was already in the king-sized bed they shared, her large head placed on a pillow. Ellea set her book on the bedside table and removed her shirt to crawl into bed.

Hopefully, her dreams would be more of hot men than the nightmares that usually plagued her. Sadly, they were not. As soon as she closed her eyes, she was greeted with fire and destruction.

Harsh light assaulted her exhausted eyes. Ellea's first thought was about removing her uncle's ability to stroll into her room without her permission. Only he, her nana, and Billy were permitted in her bedroom. No one slept with her except her beast, thanks to the nightmares that had her waking and screaming until Billy could calm her down.

"Good morning, Billy. Glad to see you two are still sharing a bed," her uncle said, and Billy answered with a dramatic yawn and stretch.

"Why are you here so early, uncle?" Ellea grumbled, pulling the blankets over her head.

"Well, it's nine o'clock on Friday, and we've trained on Friday for the past twenty years at this time," he said. "Did you oversleep? I didn't notice any of the boys in the house. Were you up late?"

"No, I didn't sleep well." She sat up and pulled at the blankets before meeting his stare. "Give me fifteen minutes, and I'll meet you in the gym."

Felix gave her a knowing look and headed out of the room. Every

Monday, Wednesday, and Friday, they trained together. They rotated between ancient weapons, martial arts, and marksmanship, along with practicing yoga, meditation, and breathing techniques. All to stay fit, healthy, and in control of her magic. Ellea groaned and looked at her familiar.

"Don't look at me like that," Ellea said.

Are you going to tell him about your dream last night? Billy asked.

"It is nothing new, and there is no need to bother him with it." She also didn't want him to know about the dream she'd had on the couch.

Billy rolled her eyes and headed out of the room. Ellea got up and headed to her closet. Finding some old black leggings, a sports bra, and one of her older band tees, she headed to the bathroom to freshen up. The bathroom was just as dark as her bedroom, and Ellea liked it that way. She had too many terrible memories of crazy colors and unmatched decor from the time she'd spent with her parents. It was calming to have everything simple, elegant, and dark.

Glancing up at herself in the mirror, she sighed. "Looks like I didn't sleep at all last night." She splashed water on her face.

Heading into the gym, Ellea found her uncle already on a yoga mat with one open next to him.

"I thought we were doing weight training today?" she asked.

"With Lughnasadh coming up, I thought it would be best to save our energy. Billy also mentioned something about a nightmare?"

Damn that beast.

"Billy is being dramatic. It was nothing, and I don't feel bothered by it," she lied. Well, she lied about the second part; Billy *was* being dramatic.

Felix arched a brow at her and gestured for her to sit. Ellea plopped down with a huff and sat criss-cross in front of her uncle.

"Now, I'm assuming it is our typical nightmare," he stated.

"Yes," she grumbled at him.

"Let's close our eyes," he said, stretching up and placing his hands gently on his knees. "Go back to the nightmare and try to find if there is anything different."

"I know there is nothing different. It was the same nightmare as always," she said with a sigh.

"Close your eyes and go back," he repeated.

Ellea glared at him, but she mumbled, "Yes, uncle," and closed her eyes with him. Taking a deep breath, she went back.

Ellea pressed her warm body into the man behind her. She felt herself smile as his beard scratched her bare skin.

She snapped her eyes open.

"Too far back," she said as her face heated.

"Who was that?" Felix asked with an amused look.

"Pretty sure he's made up from some book I was reading." She pressed her lips together as heat pooled in her belly.

It had felt so real. It had been extremely disappointing that her dreams didn't bring her back to that moment.

"Try again," he said, and she closed her eyes.

Ellea stood at the top of a steep hill with destruction laid before her. The smell of fire hit her before the feeling of never-ending heat on her skin. Trees were blasted apart around a lake that still burned. Bodies lay before her, lifeless, and her power was crackling like lightning under her skin. Her breathing picked up, knowing what would come next. She glanced down and saw Billy dead before her with her large paws reaching to where Ellea stood. Her uncle and Nana lay on either side, their hands also reaching. The view changed as if she were a bird flying overhead. There was fire everywhere and not a living soul in sight. As the view came closer to Ellea, she saw herself with barely a slip of a linen dress. Black mud and blood covered her up to her knees and elbows. Her hair was limp and wet around her, and her hands were open as if in prayer. With her solid black eyes, she glanced at her shoulder. A hand rested there. Looking up, she found the face of her mother. Her wicked smile was the opposite of her father's solemn expression.

With a gasp, Ellea snapped back to reality. Felix looked at her with such a determined stare. She had never tried to look into minds as he did; it reminded her too much of how her mother used to torture her. But she fully trusted her uncle.

"I told you it was the same, nothing has changed," she stated flatly while trying to even out her breathing.

"But you seem to have forgotten that your parents are gone and can never get to you. We have worked on this all your life," he said calmly, placing a gentle hand on her cheek. "Practice control, calmness, and let go of a nightmare that will not come true."

She leaned into his touch, trying to believe it as much as she could.

"Let's work on some mind work and then thirty minutes of stretching. We'll finish with ten minutes of breath work."

"Yes, uncle." She sighed.

Over the rest of the hour, Felix helped calm Ellea's mind by sharing old and happy memories. She laid on her back with her arms open and her head in his lap. With his hands on either side of her face, he shared memories of them visiting the coast. Billy ran around them and chased seagulls while Ellea held Nana's hand. She could almost smell the sea. He moved on to a different memory. They were bundled up in their cabin during a snowstorm. Her nana and Billy were sprawled on the couch together, their snoring in tune with one another. Snow covered the window behind them, and the lake behind it was frozen. Felix was running around the cabin with a blanket, acting like Professor Snape, while Ellea sat cross-legged on the couch with one of the *Harry Potter* books in her lap. As the memory faded with a whip of her uncle's blanket cape, she felt the tension leave her body. They continued on their plan and went through some stretches and chatted about the upcoming equinox party. Once the breath work was over, they both headed out of the gym and to the kitchen. Two steaming mugs of coffee waited for them on the counter.

Billy was sunning by one of the many windows that looked out on the back half of the property, probably on her fourth nap.

"Who do you plan on bringing to the party, Zaza?" her uncle asked.

Ellea cringed at her uncle's pet name for her, then she cringed at who she would bring. The thought of only going with Isaac bothered her. He was getting too attached. Maybe she could bring Luke and Aiden as a buffer.

"Maybe all of them?" she questioned.

"That is one way to make an entrance," he remarked slyly.

Guests usually only brought a plus one to the celebrations. Bringing three men would earn her some looks. Ellea and the boys had had an understanding for about six months now. She doubted they would mind all going together. It had also been far too long since they'd all shared a bed. Maybe that would help with Isaac as well.

"I will see what they say first, then decide." She paused. "What are your plans?"

"Reece's niece is coming of age," he said with a smile. Reece was his recent boyfriend, the longest he'd had in a while. "I plan on joining his family in their celebration."

Not all celebrations were sexual, even though Ellea always engaged in those types as well. Unlike the others, she never needed the celebrations to help boost her powers, so sex seemed like the best way for her to get something out of it while helping her partner...or partners.

"Mom will lead this time," he said with a small sigh. "It seems Sybil has let her mind go almost completely."

"Can't wait for her dramatics," Ellea mumbled. Her nana would find some way to make this into a show. An elder witch was needed during the celebration to help guide the intentions and goals of the witches; they announced pivotal times of the evening and kept everyone on track. Elders held great power, and it spread to everyone at the celebration.

"You have two days to make up your mind," he said, finishing his coffee and walking it to the sink. "If you want to go alone, let me know and I'll escort you in. If not, I'll see you at the manor."

The manor was the home she'd grown up in after her parents were taken away and where celebrations were usually held. Felix brought Ellea in for a hug and seemed to linger a little longer than usual.

"Jeeze, stop with the smothering. I will see you on Sunday," she said, but squeezed him back.

Felix let go and looked sincerely at her. With a kiss on her forehead, he left.

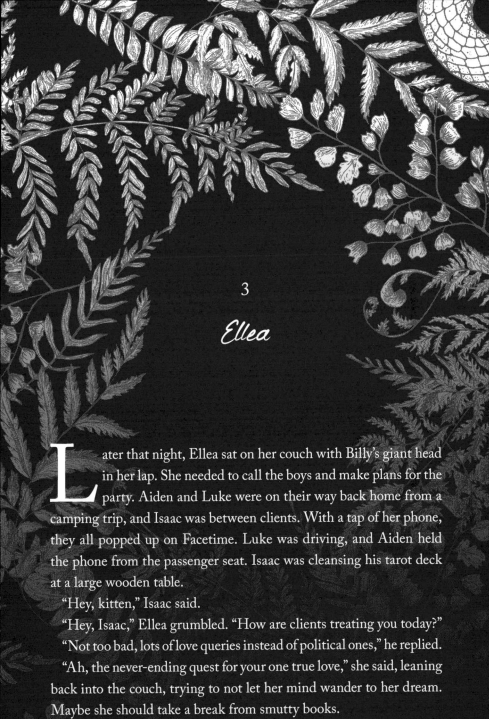

3

Ellea

Later that night, Ellea sat on her couch with Billy's giant head in her lap. She needed to call the boys and make plans for the party. Aiden and Luke were on their way back home from a camping trip, and Isaac was between clients. With a tap of her phone, they all popped up on Facetime. Luke was driving, and Aiden held the phone from the passenger seat. Isaac was cleansing his tarot deck at a large wooden table.

"Hey, kitten," Isaac said.

"Hey, Isaac," Ellea grumbled. "How are clients treating you today?"

"Not too bad, lots of love queries instead of political ones," he replied.

"Ah, the never-ending quest for your one true love," she said, leaning back into the couch, trying to not let her mind wander to her dream. Maybe she should take a break from smutty books.

Never happening.

"Hey boys, how was camping?" she asked.

"A sausage fest, not that we minded, but we are ready to get buried in some witch pussy," Luke said with a wink. Billy made a gagging noise from Ellea's lap.

"Hi to you too, Billy," Aiden said with a smirk.

"Speaking of that," Ellea said while patting Billy on the head, "we need to talk about Sunday."

"What's the plan? Want to kick the sausage lovers to the curb and go with me?" Isaac asked with a shit-eating grin on his face.

"Hel no!" Luke and Aiden said. "Let's leave Isaac out of this and make it the three of us."

That was a good idea, but she wasn't ready to cut ties with him yet. She enjoyed his dominance in the bedroom, and she would have to leave him delicately since his father was on the council.

"I thought we could all go together," Ellea said, trying to speak over the boys arguing. Silence greeted her, and Luke almost swerved off of the road as he gave the phone a husky look. All three of them smiled at her.

"Yes, please," they all said together, and Ellea rolled her eyes.

"Let's chat tomorrow over brunch, and we can determine our intentions," she said.

"I have a better plan," Luke said. "Let's skip out on the party altogether and get started tomorrow after brunch." Aiden agreed with an aggressive nod of his head.

"No, no. We need to keep up appearances, and people already talk too much. Let's put on a show, have some fun, and have some more fun after that," Ellea said with a seductive smirk.

"Whatever you want," Isaac said.

"I will pick you up in the morning, gorgeous," Luke replied. "I will bring the Rover so Billy can join us. I know how much she loves Anthony's waffles."

Billy's head popped up in the video, her tongue hanging out of her mouth. *Luke is now my favorite. Can we keep him?* she said.

"No, you hoe," Ellea mumbled to her familiar. "See you in the morning, boys." With a wink, she ended the call.

Billy rested her head back on Ellea's lap.

Let's put Supernatural on. I want to see my husband, Demon Dean, she said.

It was a nice, overcast day that hid the sun. Ellea was happy about wearing her favorite Slytherin cardigan with her black jean shorts. The three men sat with Ellea under an umbrella at a cafe called Anthony's. Billy was curled in her own chair, refusing to lie on the ground like a regular dog. The cafe sat in one of the wider alleys off of the main road in the center of Halifax. It was set back enough that you could scarcely hear the bustling city street at the opening of the alley. Its many doors were open to the outside, allowing any possible breeze to cool the few patrons waiting for Anthony's famous cooking.

Anthony was about two hundred years old and a very talented kitchen witch. He poured his emotions and energy into anything he created. Even if you had a request for an angry stack of pancakes, he would make them. Ellea was pretty sure a customer had recently made that request; she could hear the heavy metal music and yelling coming from the kitchen at the back of the restaurant. She let her gaze wander around the occupied tables until it snagged on two female witches at a small table inside; they were glaring at her.

"Stop that," Isaac said, tugging on one of Ellea's long curls. "Leave the bitch face at home."

She glared at him, but he ignored her. Isaac was the tallest of the three. He was big, a little over six feet tall, and broad. His light blue eyes and blond hair were so deceiving. He looked soft and kind, but out of the three, he was the roughest, short-tempered and quick to pin you against a wall and fuck you until you forgot your name.

Aiden's long arm reached to her, and a tattooed hand grasped the back of her neck. Bringing her lips close to his with only a breath between them, he said in a husky voice, "I love your face."

Then he pressed a hard, quick kiss to her lips. Pulling away, he gave her a wink and leaned back in his chair, looking smug. She shook her head and smiled. Isaac pursed his lips before giving them a tight smile. Anthony came out, a server on his heels, with a tray of coffees and teas for the table. He slapped Aiden's back and gave a grin to everyone. As soon as his eyes landed on Ellea, it became a strained sort of smile, and his tan skin paled slightly. Luke cleared his throat, causing Anthony's gaze to shift before his sour look could get any worse.

"How are you kids doing today?" the cafe owner asked.

"Good, good, planning for tomorrow. How are things today? Busy?" Isaac asked.

"Yes, busy; mortals seem to be making brunch a 'thing,'" Anthony said while he looked around his restaurant. He looked back at them. "Would you like your usuals?"

"Please, Anthony, and Billy will take your house waffles," Luke said.

"Coming right up," Anthony said with a nod to Luke, completely avoiding Ellea. He headed back inside his cafe.

You would think twenty years would be long enough for people not to treat you like you're about to explode, Billy remarked only to Ellea.

Small spells or unplanned occurrences were common when you

were a toddler, but as soon as Ellea could walk and talk, her mom had begun training her for destruction. When her parents were put in jail, Ellea had refused to touch any part of her magic for months. A few outbursts had happened as Billy and her uncle helped her learn to control her magic, and it had been enough to have the council and other witches constantly watching her.

You aren't like them, Billy said, reading her thoughts. *You need to practice your trickster magic more, it will only—*

"So, what is the plan for tomorrow? Anything you boys want to focus on, or just your typical sexy recharge?" Ellea asked with a plastered smile on her face, ignoring her familiar's grumbling. Luke reached down and placed a hand on her knee. He gave her a knowing look, and she did her best to not be bothered by everything.

"Is there anything you need, El? I know none of us have anything big coming up. We are only interested in spending time with you," he said, staring at her intently.

"Agreed. Luke and I are still free until winter and need nothing special," Aiden said earnestly. Both Luke and Aiden were elemental witches with fire as their strength. They came from old money and mostly saved their powers for the harsh winters since there was no genuine need for work. They would volunteer all over, clearing iced roads and helping in poverty-stricken towns the snowplows wouldn't bother with.

The boys knew Ellea was in no mood to deal with looks or whispers while also manifesting and setting intentions. And she didn't need it for herself; she didn't need to pull strength from the celebration like other witches. They were too good to her—and getting too close. She shook off the thought and nodded in agreement.

"Simple power-up sounds good. Now, what will we wear?" she asked, looking around the table.

"Why not black?" Luke said, and gave her a look that was all mischief. Ellea rolled her eyes at him. Black was a good color, but wearing it *and* showing up to the celebration with a very despised witch would get them a lot of crap, even more than usual. "Silver and gold, too. Yep, that sounds perfect," he finished, mostly talking to himself. It was like he got off on pissing people off. Black was Ellea's staple color in her wardrobe, but it was taboo at celebrations. Almost every other color was acceptable, with witches wearing anything from white to purple to orange—but never black. The silver and gold would be a nice touch, with silver symbolizing the divine feminine and gold the divine masculine. It would really embrace their relationship and give a middle finger to those who would sneer at them.

"I'm in," she said with way more confidence than she'd had before.

"This is going to be fun," Luke said with a grin, rubbing his hands together like a villain.

Saturday was another night for rough sleep. Ellea tossed and turned until Billy nudged her neck to wake her. She woke up with a start, trying to remember where she was. Billy huffed, and the vibration of it rang through Ellea's body, then her weight was on top of her, pressing her into the soft mattress. She looked at Ellea with big amber eyes that glowed in the dark bedroom.

Usual nightmare, Bug? the familiar asked, and Ellea could almost feel her searching her mind.

"No...well, yes." Ellea rubbed her face before she began petting Billy as she tried to remember her dream. "It started at a holiday celebration. I was in the middle of the room and everyone was pointing at me and calling me 'monster.' It was suffocating; so many people were staring at me and closing in." She paused, searching for the details that were already becoming fuzzy. "I was trying to find a way out of there. Then there was a man heading toward the corner of the room. I think it was the not-Dean from my one dream. I pushed through the crowd toward him. I couldn't see his face or anything, only that he was tall and surrounded by shadows. He disappeared through a hidden door while I continued to push through the crowd. I eventually got through and reached for the door, and that's when I ended up on the hill in my usual spot."

That isn't too new. You always dream about people calling you a monster, Billy said, seeming to melt more into Ellea.

"Yeah, but the guy was new."

Just the one?

"Yeah, why?"

Well, I think it would have been three. Have you dreamt about him before? Billy asked.

"Oh, no, it was just the one," Ellea said, thinking about that steamy dream. "I'm not sure; I didn't see his face."

Remember, you are not a monster. Anyone who says that can shove it where the sun don't shine. I think we need to do something. Things are getting worse, and I think your powers are getting restless.

"My powers are fine where they are. I will only use them for emergencies and stick to fortune-telling," Ellea mumbled.

I'm worried you're going to explode like Cas with the Leviathans, the beast said.

Ellea rolled her eyes and continued to pet Billy. "I will not explode, Billy."

We shall see. Want me to tell you a bedtime story to help get you back to sleep? she asked sweetly.

"Yes, please. Make it a good one." Ellea shifted onto her side so Billy could tuck her head under Ellea's chin.

Okay, a good one. A mother of two boys is murdered and it forces her husband to go searching for the killer. Along the journey, he starts to hunt things that creep and crawl in the night. Twenty-two years later, the two brothers have grown up into big, strong, handsome men and have to go searching for their father, who went missing on a hunting trip.

Ellea smiled to herself as Billy continued on. She slowly drifted off to a restful sleep thanks to the big warm body of her familiar weighing her down, replacing the heavy guilt of being a monster.

TRICKY MAGIC

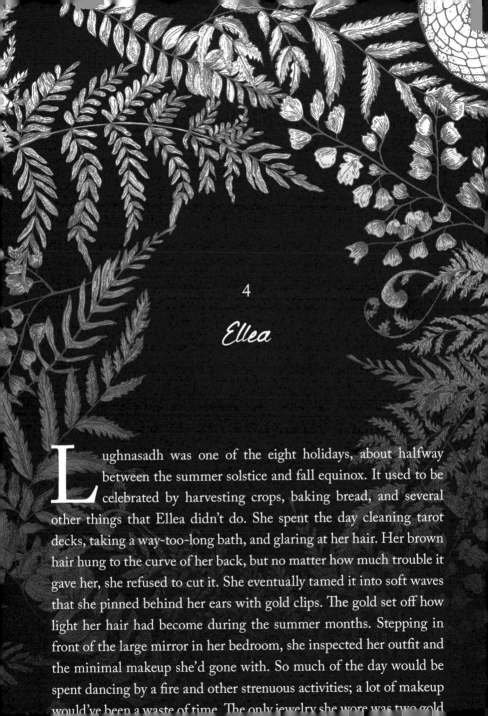

4

Ellea

Lughnasadh was one of the eight holidays, about halfway between the summer solstice and fall equinox. It used to be celebrated by harvesting crops, baking bread, and several other things that Ellea didn't do. She spent the day cleaning tarot decks, taking a way-too-long bath, and glaring at her hair. Her brown hair hung to the curve of her back, but no matter how much trouble it gave her, she refused to cut it. She eventually tamed it into soft waves that she pinned behind her ears with gold clips. The gold set off how light her hair had become during the summer months. Stepping in front of the large mirror in her bedroom, she inspected her outfit and the minimal makeup she'd gone with. So much of the day would be spent dancing by a fire and other strenuous activities; a lot of makeup would've been a waste of time. The only jewelry she wore was two gold cuffs around each wrist.

A tight black bodysuit fastened behind her neck and left her back absolutely bare. Ellea was thankful for her small chest; she could get away without wearing a bra. The skirt was sheer chiffon with gold stars and moons decorating the black fabric. Two slits going all the way up to her hip creases would easily drag any peering eyes up to her scarcely covered front. Thank Hel for permanent hair removal.

Tonight, she would have to embrace her short frame. Heels in the grass would not be good. She didn't mind; her black boots made her feel like a badass. They would help her stroll through the doors with confidence.

Billy came into the bedroom and sat at her feet to look in the mirror. Ellea looked down at her familiar and smiled.

"You look like a regular dog with that collar on," Ellea said, and her grin got wider.

This is not a collar, it is a necklace, and I look awesome. Billy preened, lifting her furry chin.

Billy wore what looked like an oversized gold and silver braided chain. It was as thick as a regular dog collar, but hung elegantly; it finished at the center of her chest with a star pendant. Her black fur set it off beautifully, and Ellea had to admit, she looked pretty cool.

"You do look awesome. You look like a badass," she said, reaching down and patting her soft face. Familiars weren't normally at celebrations, and they were never with their witches for so many years. They arrived in a young witch's life when they needed guidance and left when they were ready to walk the world on their own. Billy and Ellea seemed to have some serious codependency issues, but whatever. Billy was her best friend, no matter how annoying she was, and she wasn't ready to say goodbye. The sounds of three handsome males entering the house pulled Ellea from her thoughts. With a nod at

Billy, they headed out of the bedroom.

"Oh, fuck, Ellea," Luke groaned, covering his eyes with his tattooed hands. He wiped them down his face and gaped at her. "This is going to be a long night with you looking like a sex queen."

"Oh stop, you've seen me in less," she said with a wave of her hand.

"But you look like a badass sex queen," Aiden replied. "Those legs, your curves, those boots…" He came up to her and twirled her.

"Maybe you guys need to leave me for a few weeks more often if I am going to get this kind of reaction out of you," she replied, arching one eyebrow at them. Her eyes landed on Isaac, who had said nothing yet. His face was unreadable, and she felt her smile falter. "You good, Isaac?"

His eyes met hers, and a wide grin spread across his face. "Oh yeah. Let's go show you off."

Luke's SUV pulled up to the manor Ellea had called home for most of her life. It was a sprawling estate with a two-floor mansion sitting in the middle. Vines covered the cracking surface and some of the windows, making it seem like it'd been neglected for ages. This was the house she'd called a friend when things seemed the hardest.

"This place still gives me the creeps," Luke said, peeking through the windshield after he parked near a line of expensive vehicles.

Ellea rolled her eyes and got out of the car. There was nothing creepy about this manor. It had been in her family for well over a millennium, originally built when the first Handleys traveled here from Newhope, the continent overseas. Like most witch dwellings, the house had magic, but it always seemed to have more magic than the rest. Rooms would appear out of nowhere when you needed them the most. Sometimes it would even hide her from whoever she was avoiding. "Hello, old friend," Ellea said as she walked up to the door that opened for her.

The boys followed behind as a gentle wave of music and light chatter led them to the ballroom at the back of the house. They walked past two grand staircases and several entertaining rooms that would be used for private celebrations later. Ellea's heart raced as they neared the entrance of the crowded ballroom. The low murmur of the crowd grew quiet as all eyes gazed upon her and her party. She shoved the anxiety as far down as she could and held her head high, heading straight to her nana and uncle. The boys trailed behind, and the talking quickly picked back up.

"She shouldn't be allowed at public events."
"Such a shame the heir to the most powerful family is a…"
"She can't be trusted."

Ellea ignored the whispers; she had been listening to various versions since she was a small child. Her ability to mask how she felt was almost as strong as her ability to see into someone's future. Ellea came to stand in front of her nana. The older woman's bright sage eyes took in her only granddaughter. Ellea smiled as she admired her nana's emerald dress and the numerous bangles and rings she wore. "You look stunning, Nana."

Her nana smirked, and her eyes glinted as she winked.

"You look perfect tonight, Ellea Elizabeth."

Ellea rolled her eyes. Her nana barely spared a glance for the men behind her before kneeling on one knee to greet Billy.

"Hello, old friend," she said. "You look regal tonight with that necklace. It's very modern of you."

Billy leaned into her, resting her big head in the crook of

the woman's neck.

And you look beautiful as always, not a day over seven hundred, Billy said. With the scoff from her uncle, Ellea knew that Billy had let him hear her too.

"Zaza, I like this look on you," Felix said, kissing her on both cheeks.

Felix had on black linen pants, loafers, and a deep blue button-down shirt that showed off most of his tanned chest. He also had a ring on each finger and one gold hoop in his right ear.

She smiled with thanks and looked for his boyfriend. "Where's Reece?"

"He's helping in one of the other rooms. We have five witches coming of age this year, and they could use all the help."

Ellea grimaced, remembering how a bunch of teenagers could get when it was time for them to step out into the community as full-fledged magic-wielding brats. Her uncle chuckled and motioned to the two women he and her nana had been talking to before she'd interrupted.

"Sybil, Gesa," her uncle said. "You remember my niece, Ellea."

Ellea's lips pursed.

Everyone knew who she was.

Her finishing school lessons took over, and she morphed into the ever-polite council member's granddaughter.

"Hello, Sybil," Ellea said with a bow of her head. "You look lovely."

"You look lovely, Ellea," Sybil replied, her voice rasped with age.

Ellea turned towards Gesa, who smiled, but her eyes were glued to something over Ellea's shoulder. She turned and followed her stare to see Luke and Aiden engaged in a conversation with two older male witches. Ellea smirked. She didn't blame the young witch, and she found that she didn't feel any jealousy. Both men caught them staring and waved with wide grins. She could have sworn she heard

Gesa groan. Ellea's gaze snagged further into the room, seeing Isaac speaking with his father. Both men looked at her at the same time, and it was all Ellea could do to not grimace at their appraising gazes.

"Now, now, Ellea..." Sybil's wavering voice made her turn. "Take my hand and let me have a proper look at you."

Ellea's eyes went wide. What Sybil was implying wasn't a look at her appearance, but her future. She tried stepping back, but the witch grabbed her hand.

"Where is that fearlessness I know and love?" the witch asked in a commanding voice that did not show her age. She pulled her closer with astounding strength. Her free hand pressed against her cheek, and Ellea couldn't help but gasp.

Her blue eyes bore into Ellea's, and time held its breath as the room of witches faded and it was only them standing under the ballroom ceiling. Ellea felt dizzy under Sybil's magic, and she jumped when her voice rang in her head.

"Oh, girl."

"What do you see, Sybil?" Ellea said barely above a whisper. The room began to turn slowly as Sybil's eyes became cloudy.

"Fears evolve and grow, welcoming another, one whose power will balance yours in destruction. You feed his fire as he feeds your chaos. You will turn worlds upside down," Sybil finished in a voice that crept into Ellea's mind, burying itself deep as her vision echoed. The room righted itself, and the ringing in Ellea's ears was replaced with the chatter of the party.

Her stomach turned, but Sybil was calm, a small smile on her face. *Destruction...chaos...fire.*

It was the same as the vision she had always had, but Sybil was implying there was someone else. She almost jumped out of her skin when Isaac inserted himself between them.

"Hello, Sybil, Gesa. You ladies look stunning tonight. Happy celebrations!" He forced Ellea away from them, and she didn't miss the look of distaste on Sybil's face. "Come on, kitten. Let's get you to your nana so she can start the celebration."

She looked up at Isaac as a feeling of dread crept over her shoulders and down her back. Shaking it off the best she could, she searched for her familiar. The large beast was waiting for her at a set of doors that lead to the massive lawn. Ellea had to force Isaac's hand off of her wrist before she could step away from him.

You okay, Bug? Billy asked.

Ellea reached a shaking hand to Billy's large head and let her warmth and soft fur calm her.

This is nothing new. You're fine.

Billy's eyes looked worried, but Ellea nodded and headed out into the night with the boys trailing behind her. They stepped out of the ballroom to the back property, where it was calm and warm. The breeze off of the coast smelled of salt, pines, and fresh air. She inhaled deeply, letting it all calm her as she headed to her family with a small—and very fake—smile placed on her face.

Ellea weaved through the crowd of witches who continued to whisper insults and accusations, but she kept her chin high and walked right past them. Once her eyes met her nana's, she relaxed and let a true smile grace her face. Jadis and Felix stood close to where the extensive property ended at a cliff. A calm sea met a blanket of stars, and a crescent moon hung high in the night sky. Her nana placed her hand on Ellea's face and spoke words she'd said since she was young.

"You need no one but us and the stars. They are nothing but words and mean souls."

Jadis said it so low that only Ellea could hear it, but she'd heard those words so many times that they could be in the middle of a storm and she would know what her nana was saying. She pulled her hand off her face and kissed her palm. Ellea and Billy took their place between her nana and uncle and looked upon all the other witches standing between them in the manor. Ellea raised her chin once more and let her gaze hang over the crowd to focus on the house, separating herself. She wanted to be here for her family, but that was all.

Jadis' voice rang through the crowd, her hands held high, and the calm sea turned with aggression as waves crashed against the rocky shore.

"Lughnasadh blessings, witches."

"Lughnasadh blessings," they repeated.

"As the wheel turns us slowly away from summer, we welcome those that are new, celebrate those who have left, and those who seek power. We bless you with energy. Manifest true. Set strong intentions. Celebrate life. Celebrate death. May your harvest be bountiful and may the universe bless you with warmth." As Jadis finished, the enormous bonfire was lit, casting the field in a sudden, harsh light. The witches all gasped.

Did they not notice the giant s'mores maker on their way out? Billy said with a snicker.

"As above, so below! As within, so without!" Jadis bellowed with a dramatic shake of her arms.

Everyone responded at once, "As above, so below! As within, so without!"

With the final ringing of voices, the sea calmed again, and the band started. Witches embraced each other and went their separate ways, ready to celebrate, some directly to dancing, others to the parlors or smaller music rooms. Ellea turned to her nana and raised an eyebrow.

"Who did you have to pay for the sea and fire, Nana?" Ellea asked.

"A good witch never tells." Her nana smirked. "Go have fun, and try to not ruffle any feathers. Well, don't try too hard." She finished with a kiss on her cheek.

Felix kissed her other cheek before they headed into the house, probably to welcome the witches coming of age. The elders of the night needed to make their rounds to make sure everyone was doing their part or to lend a hand to those who were lost.

Ellea knelt down to say goodbye to her familiar, as they had their own ways of celebrating. Around them, a lot of familiars were saying goodbye to the witches they'd helped since they were young.

Are you sure you're okay? Billy asked. *I can stay if you want.*

She took so much from Billy already; she didn't want to take this. "No, I am okay. Go have fun and creep out some mortals. I will see you later."

She took a deep breath and pulled away from her familiar. Billy looked at her one last time and gave her a nod.

Ellea stood and looked for her boys. Isaac was nowhere to be found and Ellea found herself not at all concerned. Aiden and Luke were standing by the huge bonfire, and she couldn't help but smile as she headed their way. Aiden reached for her first, grabbing her by the waist. He spun her, placing a hand at her back. He dipped her, and his lips hovered above her. He gave her a wicked smile that had her feeling breathless, and the quick kiss made her feel tingly. Her anxiety was easy to forget with these two around her. They straightened, and Luke came at her from behind, snaking his arms around both of them and kissing her on the shoulder.

"Are you ready to dance, gorgeous?" Luke asked, swaying with the music.

"Should we find Isaac?" Aiden asked.

Ellea winced. In the back of her mind, she wished it was just the three of them.

One day I won't have to keep up appearances.

"Let's find the youngest in line to be on the council and get the night started," she said with mock boredom.

Leaving the light of the bonfire behind, the three of them made their way toward the ballroom, looking for their fourth. They stopped in front of a set of doors that led back into the manor, and Ellea saw witches breaking off to head to their own celebrations for the night. She looked over the crowd for the tall blond and was abruptly knocked off balance.

"Watch it, you insolent little witch." It was Isadora, and her nasally voice grated on Ellea's skin. Isadora flipped her long, straight, black hair and glared at Ellea. She was your basic-looking witch with long legs, a small waist, and a face that showed evidence of one too many spells done to it.

"You watch it," Ellea said, stopping herself from rubbing at the sting the witch had left on her arm when she'd rammed into her.

"Looks like Isaac's got some sense to ditch you," Isadora said.

One simple thought and this witch would be screaming on the floor.

Luke reached for her, kissing her cheek and whispering in her ear.

"She's jealous, leave it."

Ellea knew the witch was jealous of her powers, of where her family stood.

"She's probably still mad about the little incident when you were sixteen," Aiden added in her other ear, chuckling.

Isadora glared at their secret exchange, and Ellea was about to leave when she glimpsed blond hair and a strong jawline coming through the furthest door of the long room. Isaac turned as he stepped onto the lawn and headed right for them with a smug smile on his face. Isadora perked up and flipped her hair again right as he passed her. He didn't even notice. Ellea couldn't help but smirk.

"There you are, kitten." Her smirk quickly disappeared. She should have nipped that nickname in the ass before it got this far. He kissed her soundly, making a show of their exchange, and didn't release her until Isadora was stomping away.

Ellea looked back at Isaac. "Ready to dance?"

"Hel yes," all three of them replied at once.

5

Ellea

They danced for what felt like hours, trading kisses, caresses, and never leaving each other. Some witches could be seen coupling off and sneaking into the nearby woods. The magic of the dance was interrupted when three female witches finally found a way to get close enough to break Ellea's bubble. Isadora, Agnes, and Medea had been a thorn in her side since childhood, and tonight was no different. As Luke released Ellea for yet another spin, Isadora jumped on the opportunity. She formed a globe of water in her hand and let it fly into Ellea's face, completely drenching her hair and soaking her top.

"You bitch!" Ellea shrieked in Isadora's smirking face. Agnes and Medea snickered behind her. The crowd of witches around them didn't stop dancing. They only gave them room to work out their years-long hate for one another.

"You were looking sweaty and gross. I thought it would help," Isadora stated. "I think it's time for you to go home."

Ellea rolled her eyes. "You forget, this is my home."

They truly didn't know what she was capable of. Her powers could be destructive and out of control, but when they were directed properly, it was a different type of destructive.

"Thank you. I was feeling hot and worked up. If it wasn't for this lovely distraction, I may have taken all three men on the lawn in front of everyone," Ellea replied serenely, and Isadora's smirk turned into a grimace.

"I wouldn't put it past you, needing to be easy so people can ignore how horrible you and your powers are," she replied, crossing her arms and popping a hip out. "They will learn soon what a wretch you are and they'll regret wasting their time on a worthless witch."

"Worthless and horrible?" Ellea scoffed. "Worthless, no. Horrible? I think I should remind you how horrible my powers are."

"Ellea, don't," Isaac said, stepping near her, but she gave him a scathing look. He stepped away to stand with Luke and Aiden, who were smiling, ready for a show.

The band's music picked up at the perfect time, and the crowd continued to ignore them. Isadora and the others had spent their whole lives sticking a foot out just to watch Ellea fall.

Ellea smiled as the witches' confidence faded. They may have been a few inches taller than her, but that didn't show now. Ellea's powers vibrated through her, and she radiated energy. The magic pulled at her, wicked and raw. Stepping forward slowly, the witches took some quick steps back. Memories seemed to flash before their eyes, all the times Ellea had lost control. They were close to the edge of the lawn now, with the ballroom's open doors to their backs. Almost out of the way.

"I don't think you ever took the time to understand what I can do, Isadora. Your magic is basic, ordinary, and weak. Mine? It creeps and burrows into the mind. You may think it is a trick, smoke and mirrors, but is it?" Ellea slowly cocked her head. Had she even moved her hands? No one would ever know. "I think you have something on your dress."

Isadora looked down and screamed; she screamed so loud that the witches nearby startled and jumped. They didn't jump at what Isadora was screaming about, because they didn't see it. They only saw a witch having a total meltdown, pulling at her dress and swiping at invisible beings. Agnes and Medea tried helping, but they also didn't see what Ellea saw. They tried calming her down with hushed voices and even batted at invisible things to make her feel better. It didn't work. Isadora was having a complete panic attack. She resorted to actually taking her dress off and stomping on it. She continued hitting herself, screaming and jumping up and down with the entire crowd watching her. Ellea's magic reveled in the power, in the madness, and she had to hold back from doing more.

Jadis and Felix poked their heads out of a door. They didn't even look surprised, they only gave Ellea a stern look. She responded with a roll of her eyes. Without even giving a wave of her hand or a snap of fingers, the illusion broke, along with a last scream from Isadora. Panting hard, she looked up at the crowd gawking at her. Then she looked down at her bare body, and Ellea smirked.

The boys closed in on Ellea as Isadora turned and walked into the manor, not even caring to put her dress back on, pretending what just happened was nothing, but she couldn't hide the sobs that shook her body. Medea turned back to grab the dress that was now covered in dirt and grass. She wouldn't look Ellea in the eye as she scurried to catch up with her friends. Jadis gave Ellea one last look before clapping to signal to the band to start back up.

Luke kissed Ellea on the cheek and groaned into her ear. "I love when you are a bad, bad witch."

She shivered and smiled up at him. Would she ever get past the unsettling feeling and guilt after using her powers? She looked back to where the three witches had gone and caught the gaze of Isaac's father, whose face was red with disapproval. Then she caught Sybil's stare, and the look in the old witch's eyes mirrored how Ellea felt. Her smile quickly turned to a frown as she remembered what the seer had said to her earlier in the night.

Fears evolve and grow, welcoming another, one whose power will balance yours in destruction...

"Come on, let's get out of here before I fuck you in front of everyone," Luke said.

Ellea had barely set her feet on the sidewalk outside of her house before Isaac swooped her up and threw her over his shoulder. The thoughts that had haunted her during the short ride home were quickly forgotten as Isaac slapped her ass and then slipped his hand under her bodysuit, finding the wetness that had been gathering all night. Propping her head up on one hand, she glanced up and caught Luke and Aiden trying to make out while walking up the path behind them. She felt herself relaxing into the energy they were all giving off and giggled as they stumbled.

At the sound of her laughing, Luke broke away and rushed up to Ellea. He placed both hands on either side of her face to hold her up so he could kiss her roughly. The coordination that went into Ellea being over Isaac's shoulder while making out with Luke was magic all on its own. Isaac gave her ass another slap, and she yelped into Luke's mouth. It turned into a moan as Isaac found her hot center and inserted a finger, then two. She contemplated starting things on her front lawn under the moon.

The house welcomed them by swinging the door open. The four of them made their way in, and the door closed on its own behind them. Isaac set out on the path to the bedroom they shared for nights like this. He threw Ellea onto the bed, and she laughed as she bounced in the middle of the oversized bed. He sat in the chair in the corner and untied his shoes. With a look at the other two, he gave a nod.

"Go on, let me watch you worship her," he said with a rough voice as he tugged off his shoes and leaned back in the chair. He crossed his foot up on his knee and his eyes bore into her, making her squirm.

"How could we say no to that request?" Luke asked, kneeling to the floor and grasping a booted ankle. He nipped and kissed her calves as he worked on the long laces. Aiden crawled up the bed and laid beside her, trailing his hand over her clothed body and teasing her nipples through the thin fabric of her bodysuit. She let out a groan, and his mouth swallowed the sound. His hand reached up her chest and caressed her neck. She thought he was going to wrap his hand around her throat, but instead, he reached behind her neck and unclasped the top of her bodysuit. He peeled it down, leaving her chest exposed. His hand ran down over her stomach and under the bundled fabric around her waist.

Two fingers slid down to her center. He slowly inserted both of them, drawing out a long moan from her. They all had been teasing each other for hours, and she had been wet and craving this since the beginning.

"You are so wet," Aiden moaned into her mouth between kisses.

Luke threw her boots somewhere, and his large hands were quick to return to her. He ran them up her thighs. Bringing his mouth close to her, he kissed the inside of her knee and worked his way up the inside of her thigh. His hands reached for the gathered clothing around her waist and pulled it down and off of her. She lay there fully naked while Aiden continued toying her wet pussy.

Luke's mouth found its way up to where Aiden was putting in the work. He bit him, and Ellea let out a protest when his hand jerked away. It was quickly replaced by Luke's mouth, and her protest was quickly gone. He feasted on her like he had been starved for weeks. Since Aiden's hand was now free, he teased and pinched her exposed nipples. It was all so much. He moved to her neck, where he bit and licked, causing her to pant and squirm. She turned her head to give him better access, and her eyes met Isaac's. They were dark and he was clearly enjoying the show, his cock straining against his pants. He always liked to watch at first. It got him riled up, and it gave the others a chance to get some time in before he took over.

His eyes watching her was pushing her close to the edge, and the way he looked at her said that he knew it too. Luke inserted two fingers into her, and she almost lost it.

"Not yet," Isaac rumbled. "Look at me, and don't come until I say you can."

Ellea whimpered, and Luke didn't let up to give her a chance to compose herself. Isaac sauntered over to her, never breaking eye contact. She was going to lose it fast if something didn't change. Aiden was still playing with her nipples and now biting at her shoulders. It was too much. She whimpered again. Isaac bent down and grasped her face in his hand with the slightest roughness.

"You are powerful and you are so damn beautiful." He kissed her long and rough. She forgot how to breathe, and when he finally pulled away, reconnecting their deep eye contact, he set her free. "Come for us, beautiful."

With those last words, she did. Luke held her down and never let go as she rode the waves of her climax. He lapped up her release like it was all he'd ever craved. Her body was slick with sweat, but Aiden continued licking and nipping at her neck.

"I've been waiting for that sound all night," Aiden whispered in her ear.

Isaac's eyes still held hers, and when she was finally done shaking, he stood, slowly unbuttoning his pants.

"Now, let's get started," he said.

The moon was bright and high in the sky as everyone's celebrations came to an end. Families said their last goodbyes to their loved ones. Young witches would enter their rooms with big smiles on their faces, knowing they had blessings as they entered a new phase of their lives. All the happiness in the world couldn't stop Ellea from feeling restless.

As their own celebration for Lughnasadh came to its end, it was impossible to not feel the power pulsing between the four of them. Ellea could feel it under her skin, heat and electricity crackling there. Luke and Aiden had curled into each other, and Ellea faced Isaac. She gazed up at him, and she could tell he knew he held a powerful monster, one he greatly coveted and ached for.

The boys' breathing evened with sleep, and Ellea took that as her cue to leave. She slowly detached Isaac's arm from around her waist and slid out of bed as quietly as possible. The house opened the bedroom door for her without making a sound, and Ellea left on silent footsteps.

Once she was halfway across the house, she relaxed and continued heading toward her bedroom. Heavy footsteps sounded behind her. She tried to hurry, hoping whoever it was was only heading to their own room or the bathroom. She would be a liar if she said she hadn't expected what happened next.

"I thought tonight would be different," Isaac said, heading toward her.

Ellea turned, and, without trying to hide her sigh, she answered, "why would tonight be any different?"

"It just felt that way. You seemed different," he said, reaching out his hand. "You used your powers more freely, and I thought you were getting more relaxed. Come back to bed."

"Things haven't changed, Isaac. I'm going to shower and head to bed." She walked up to him and planted a quick kiss on his cheek. "I will see you in the morning." She tried to turn away from him to continue to her side of the house, but Isaac wasn't done.

"Why won't you let us in? Don't you care about our feelings?" he demanded, anger flashing across his face. "How do you think Luke and Aiden feel knowing you can just leave them after a night like that?" He moved towards her while she slowly backed away.

"This is how it is and how it will always be, Isaac. There is no changing how I feel or what I choose to do."

"You aren't being fair, Ellea. We aren't objects you can just use when you feel like it," he said cruelly.

"I'm pretty sure all of us use each other for the same things. Don't pin this on me," she said, crossing her arms across her chest.

"You owe us more, and you need to stop letting your fears get in the way of us." He tried to take another step closer to her, but the house stopped him, throwing up an invisible barrier between them.

"Goodnight, Isaac." She didn't wait for a response. She continued toward her room, letting his words wash over her.

He wasn't completely wrong, and she cared. But she had never slept in the same bed as anyone but Billy. No one needed to be woken up by her nightmares or wonder why she couldn't fall asleep. And where would Billy sleep if someone else was in the bed? She thought about all of this as she headed straight for the shower. It was already running, steam wafting out of the glass doors. She needed to wash off the night and her feelings.

After about thirty minutes under the scalding water, she still felt bothered by the night; not the amazing sex, but what had happened before and after. Sybil's words were mixing with Isaac's in her mind, and she felt a fresh wave of unease creeping in. She couldn't let it suffocate her. She didn't bother drying off and crawled into bed, ready to do her best to forget what had been said tonight.

Billy always knew when she was needed. She bounded into the bedroom. Her new collar was nowhere to be seen, and she had a few leaves stuck in her fur.

I figured you would have still been tied up. Isn't it early? Billy said telepathically.

"No, it's not, and mind your business. How about you? You look like you have been romping around in the forest." Ellea pulled back the blankets to let Billy jump into bed. Billy gave an aggressive shake to rid herself of the leaves and hopped in.

Maybe I was, and maybe you should mind your own business, too.

"Yeah, yeah. Let's go to bed. I really don't want to fall asleep while thinking about you rolling around with a Golem or helhound."

Don't talk about helhounds, Billy snarled.

Ellea let out a nervous laugh at the swift change in mood. Billy's face softened, and the two got snuggled into bed.

6

Ellea

Fears evolve and grow, welcoming another,
 One whose power will balance yours in destruction.
  You feed his fire as he feeds your chaos. You will turn
worlds upside down.

 Fears evolve and grow, welcoming another.
 You will turn worlds upside down.

Ellea woke with a gasp. A sheen of sweat coated her body. *It's just that old bird planting nonsense into my head,* she thought, sliding out of bed for a drink of water. As she disappeared into the bathroom, Billy followed, her paws padding lightly on the tile.

This is getting out of control. You can only go so many nights with no sleep before you turn into a real crazy person.

"It was just a..." She sighed. She couldn't keep calling it a nightmare;

it was more than that. "Go back to bed, I will be there in a minute."

Ellea turned the faucet on, filling a glass of water and gulping it down. Her heart slowly came down to a normal pace. She bent over the sink and splashed water on her face.

I don't know why you think you can lie to me. We need to do something, Billy said in a worried tone that rang.

"I do things, lots of things," Ellea said, drying her face with a towel.

Well, they aren't working. I think things are getting worse.

"You are being dramatic." Ellea groaned.

What was it this time? Something new or the same thing? Billy asked, her tone clipped.

"It was Sybil. That crazy old witch got in my head and it's messing with me." She turned, crossing her arms over her chest.

Do you think it was a real premonition? Billy asked, her tone kinder.

"Real, yes," Ellea said with a sigh. "But she said there was someone else, and I'm wondering if she is crazy or if this is wholly real."

I don't think we could find out. Unless...

"Unless I look into it on my own?" She shouldn't. But she needed answers.

Maybe. But last time you looked into your own future, I found you broken by the edge of a lake, Billy said sadly.

"Well, I am not eight anymore. What's the worst that could happen?" Ellea asked.

I will get the salt. Billy trotted off.

Ellea headed out of her room to where candles floated around the salt circle Billy was creating. It was larger than normal, as if Billy planned on being in there with her. The beast tossed her head, throwing the empty salt container in the corner.

Ready, she said, stepping over the line of salt.

"I don't think you should be in there with me." Ellea chewed on her lip, nervous about what was about to happen. The salt could only keep them so safe. "I don't know what my powers will do."

She didn't trust her trickster powers fully, and she trusted them even less when she planned on doing something that required so much magic and focus. Seers were meant to guide others, and looking into your own future tended to have catastrophic consequences. Regardless of what you saw, you couldn't change it, and trying would upset the balance. Some seers went crazy, stuck on an endless loop of trying to change things and looking into their future again only to see it was worse.

I will keep you grounded, and the house will be here to put out any fires or chaos if needed, Billy said confidently.

"Let's get this over with." She let out a long breath as she stepped into the circle. She sat on the floor with her legs crossed, and Billy settled her head in her lap, her touch grounding.

Placing her hands palm side up on either knee, Ellea attempted to clear her mind. She took a breath in, inhaling the familiar scent of her home—sage, coffee, and books—and let the breath out. A weightless feeling settled over her before a thought tugged her forward.

Show me what is to come.

The smells of burning trees and death came first. Then the soft ringing in her ears faded to the sounds of crackling fire and cries of the dying as she was surrounded by the vision that always haunted her.

Ellea was standing at the top of a hill with destruction laid before her. The smell of burning and death seemed so much stronger than before. Jadis, Felix, and Billy were dead before her. Her limp hair hung heavy on top of her thin dress, and blood and mud coated her arms and legs. There wasn't a living soul in sight except for her parents to her left. The sound of their excited heartbeats crept into her ears, and then a new sound fluttered in. It came from her right. A weight settled on her right shoulder. Her breath quickened as she turned her head to see the large hand of a man. She looked up to take in this new person, but she couldn't. He was so tall, and as her eyes raked up his enormous chest, she was pulled back to the present before she could take in his face.

"What happened, why did it stop?"

I don't know, you kept mumbling, 'Who are you?', then you came back.

"How long was I out for?" It had felt like seconds.

Twenty minutes, Billy said, looking worried.

Ellea's eyes shot to the pools of wax around the salt circle and the floor. *What happened, what did you see?* Billy's weight pressed into her more.

Ellea took a breath and pulled the vision back into her mind, picturing the male standing with her.

"Fears evolve and grow, welcoming another..." It came out in a whisper. She cleared her throat and continued, "there was a guy there. I don't know who he was, and I didn't see his face. But...but I felt calm with his hand on my shoulder. I don't know what it meant, if he helped me destroy everything or.... I felt so calm, so right."

What do you mean?

"How can I feel calm with that amount of death and destruction?" she said, barely hearing her own words. "How could I feel so calm when you were all dead and my parents were beside me?"

And there was no way to recognize him? Billy asked.

"Maybe he was the guy from my dream before? He was so tall, but I only made it to his chest before I was snapped back. It felt like I knew him, though. But I can't place him." She could feel her heart race just thinking about him. "This was dumb, I have no answers."

Billy stood to be eye level with Ellea, still sitting on the floor. *Take a breath. I can feel your powers humming. It could mean anything, Bug. You know how visions can be seen one way and interpreted another.*

Panic crept up her chest as a new fear found her. What if there was a guy out there who would help her destroy all that she loved? The candles, still lit, began floating as the salt vibrated off the floor. A crackling energy floated around her open hands, and the flames of the candles grew tall and aggressive in an instant. Thunder and lightning cracked right outside the house. Her breath came in quick pants, and the room began to blur at the edges of her sight. Who was he? Another crack of thunder and lightning came too quickly to be a storm brought on by nature.

Breathe, Bug, through your nose and out your mouth. Do it now! Breathe, Billy roared in her head.

The house opened the doors suddenly, bringing in a gust of wind and rain. It blew out the candles, and Billy growled, a beastly growl that snuffed Ellea's panic quickly. Her eyes were wide as she took in the sight of the familiar in front of her. Her haunches had risen a few inches, and her lengthened claws had dug into the floor. Her canines lengthened right in front of Ellea's face, and her liquid gold eyes glowed like neon lights.

Ellea took a deep breath in her nose; it shook as she exhaled, trying to find thoughts that would calm her down.

The dream.

The one of the man she didn't know, the man who had listened to her and promised her things she never knew she wanted.

Again, Billy said with a scary, otherworldly voice.

So she did, again and again. Breathing and remembering his hot body, the room came into clearer view, and Billy shrunk back to her normal form.

Ellea stared blankly at the crown molding in her bedroom. Billy's big head was heavy on her shins. Questions swam in her head; they had been since she'd finally calmed down and crawled into bed. Nothing could quell the anxiety that crushed her chest. She felt lost, like she was floating between what was real and what was to come.

When? No one knew. There wasn't a way to tell time in her vision. Next month, next year, a hundred years from now? Only the universe knew.

After a few more minutes of her thoughts spiraling, the home decided it was time to get out of bed; it yanked the curtains open on its own gust of magical wind. The sun shone through the tall windows, and Ellea closed her eyes in protest. Billy raised her head and gave her a gentle nudge to help coax her to get up.

Come on, Bug, we can't do anything about it right now. Let's get up and find you some coffee.

Ellea rolled herself out of bed and grabbed a t-shirt from the floor. She shuffled to the kitchen mindlessly, and as she rounded the corner, a large hand grabbed her right shoulder. Everything came crashing down at once, the vision, the fear, the unknowing, and all the feelings from last night instantly weighed her down. Her magic ignited, and the crackling energy under her skin caused her heart rate to pick up. Ellea whirled around, stumbling back a few steps. Her eyes widened as she looked up into Isaac's curious face. His hand hovered between them, and he looked down at it as if he could feel her energy.

"Rough night?" His face held no concern.

"You could say that," she said, still frozen in place.

"Maybe if you opened up to someone, allowed them to share a bed with you outside of meaningless sex, you would sleep better." He reached for her, grabbing her shoulder again. Her skin crackled and zapped his hand away.

"Don't touch me," she snarled, rearing back from him further.

"Woah, why are you overreacting?" he asked, his hands raised.

"Overreacting?" Her eyes widened.

Fuck all the reasons I continued to sleep with him.

"Look, I'm sorry. Let's talk about this." He began backpedaling, but she was done—so very done. Her magic crackled again, and she struggled to rein it in. *Let's play,* it cooed in the depths of her mind.

"There is nothing to talk about," she said, pinching the bridge of her nose and steadying her breathing and her magic. "I need coffee and need to forget about my horrible night. You should—"

"Horrible?" He said it like a curse. "Everything was fine until you left. You always leave. It's like you don't want to be with me."

"I'm not with you, Isaac! I'm not with anyone—"

"Don't do this. Things could be so much better. We are perfect for each other, all of us. This could be more than just hanging out and hooking up," Isaac said, his eyes pleading. "Think about it. Your powers combined with mine? We would be unstoppable."

Why is he trying so hard to make this work?

An oily feeling crept up her spine, and her powers raged. She could see it, the similarities between him and her parents. Their hunger for power was the same as the hunger he'd shown last night. The same desire shone in his eyes now. She searched for Billy as it became more difficult to suppress her magic. When she couldn't be found, she thought about the man in her dreams. He promised her so much, freedom from her fears and a magic she was comfortable using.

"No."

He reached for her again, and she couldn't suppress the surge of chaos that exploded around them. Isaac threw himself to the floor as her power raged.

"Zaza!" her uncle yelled from somewhere behind her.

No! Why is he here?

Every glass vase broke, every picture frame shattered and fell to the ground, and she sobbed as her magic left her. Something cracked against the wall behind her, and as she slowly turned her head, fighting to control any part of herself, she saw her uncle sprawled on the ground. Blood slowly leaked from his head.

Everything screeched to a stop and then everyone was moving. Luke and Aiden came from the guest quarters, and Billy growled at Isaac until he was sprinting out of her home. She fell to her knees by her uncle, dragging him into her lap as she tried to wake him.

"El, he needs a healer," Luke said, coming to stand behind her.

"I didn't mean to." Her words came out as a sob.

All her life, she'd practiced control. She'd used her magic to mess with someone a few times, but she'd never hurt anyone before.

"I know." Luke reached down, touching her gently on the top of the head. "Aiden is getting the car. Let's get him to the healer's."

The healing center was a short drive from the historic district that Ellea lived in. Every part of the building was meant to be soft and comforting from the high-back chairs to the soft blues of all the decorations. It should have felt more like a home than a hospital, but Ellea didn't feel comforted as she paced the hallway outside of her uncle's room. She didn't feel any ease when the healer said he was fine; her heart only settled slightly when she was allowed into his room.

Her uncle was sitting up in a small bed with several pillows propping him up. She didn't deserve the smile that crossed his face as she threw herself at him.

"I'm so sorry," she cried into the warm blanket that covered his lap.

"Za, I'm fine." He placed his hands around her cheeks, gently forcing her to look into his eyes. "It was an accident."

"It shouldn't have happened."

"Well, it did, and crying about it won't fix anything." His voice was steady and stern as he searched her face.

He was completely healed already, and there was no trace of the gash he'd gotten when he hit the wall. The thought made her chest cave, and tears escaped her eyes.

"I'm so sorry," she whispered.

"So I've heard." He patted the spot next to him. "Sit, tell me what happened."

Taking a deep breath, she told her uncle everything. Ellea started with Sybil's vision, then her own, and then she filled him in on the details he may have missed about Isaac.

"It felt too real. When he placed his hand on my shoulder, it brought me back there. Then when he said 'your powers combined with mine,' I instantly thought of Mom and Dad, and it snapped something in me."

"Did you ever think to explain your fears to him?" Felix asked.

"No; they are mine, and no one should be burdened with them. It is bad enough you, Billy, and Nana have to put up with me," Ellea said quietly. "Plus, I was already over him."

"We don't put up with you; we love you and want you to be free from what your parents created. These fears are genuine, and you are allowed to have them. It is how you deal with them that matters." Placing a hand on her chin, he forced her to see the truth in his eyes.

"I understand. It sounds easy, but it's hard," Ellea said as her bottom lip shook. "My life has been spent looking for ways to change, ways to control this monster that I am destined to become, and I'm tired of it. I'm so tired of being stuck on the path my parents paved."

"I don't think you are on a path at all. I think you are standing still, straddling the line of what our people expect you to be and what your magic naturally wants you to be," he answered. He paused a moment before saying, "The fear your parents created is constantly at your back and you have not taken a moment to look forward."

"Looking forward is a field of destruction with my parents at my side," Ellea said coldly.

"No. That is only one vision. Have you ever thought that your fear is what is driving you toward that outcome?" Felix asked. "What if you embraced things as they are and started living your life, not worrying about what is in the past or the future that isn't here yet?"

"It sounds so simple when you say it. But it's not." The mysterious man from her dream came to the front of her mind. Could she have what he was implying, freedom from fear and control of her magic?

A quick knock came before Luke poked his head in.

"We have a problem," he said quietly as he slipped into the room. "Isaac's dad is here with a couple council members."

Ellea went to ask about her nana, but he shook his head.

"Not your nana. They look pissed, and I think you need to leave."

Ellea's eyes went wide as she looked at her uncle.

"Go, Zaza. You need a break, anyway. Go to our cabin, and I'll come and get you when things quiet down. I don't blame you for anything, but I don't know what Isaac said to the council."

She was half-tempted to let them take her; she deserved it.

Glenover sounds perfect. Maybe I'll meet a wild mountain man to entertain me.

"Aiden is distracting them. If you're going to go—"

"Go," her uncle cut in.

"I love you," she said, swiftly kissing him on the cheek.

She quickly wrapped her arms around Luke, and he kissed the

top of her head.

"Find a mountain man for me while you're at it," he said, squeezing her hard. "I'll miss you."

She couldn't respond. Her heart hurt, but it felt right as she left him and snuck out the door. She caught a glimpse of Isaac and his father before she and Billy rounded a corner and snuck out the back door.

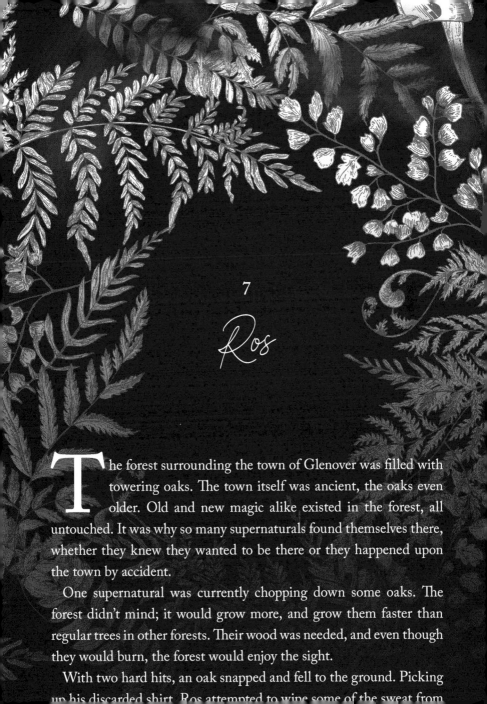

7

Ros

The forest surrounding the town of Glenover was filled with towering oaks. The town itself was ancient, the oaks even older. Old and new magic alike existed in the forest, all untouched. It was why so many supernaturals found themselves there, whether they knew they wanted to be there or they happened upon the town by accident.

One supernatural was currently chopping down some oaks. The forest didn't mind; it would grow more, and grow them faster than regular trees in other forests. Their wood was needed, and even though they would burn, the forest would enjoy the sight.

With two hard hits, an oak snapped and fell to the ground. Picking up his discarded shirt, Ros attempted to wipe some of the sweat from his face. He didn't mind the shards of tree and dirt plastered on his bare and sweaty chest. He would be done soon and would take a much-needed swim in the lake. Ros tucked his shirt into the back pocket of his jeans and bent to grab the newly chopped tree. With one hand wrapped around the trunk and the other propping his axe against his bare shoulder, he dragged it to the hundred others. He would need to triple that number over the next few days in order for the sixty-foot trees to dry in time for Mabon.

Ros couldn't count how many bonfires he'd helped set up for the town. The wolven community had usually been in charge of that task, but with their numbers dwindling, he'd stepped in to help. With one last tug, he lined up the tree with the others. Ros slapped his hands on his dark jeans to shake off the dirt and bark. He stood to stretch and wipe the slight sheen of sweat from his face. Looking up, he noticed his hound staring past him.

Ros perked up and let his breathing slow, calming his beating heart to listen. Zoning out the birds and the forest creatures, he finally heard it: the crunching of the leaves. The sound was too uneven and quick to be one of the forest beasts. He heard a ghastly, wet snarl, and his nostrils flared as a stench wafted toward him. The unwelcome creature was a Drekavac, or what some called a screecher. It was a lower demon that would put the *Walking Dead* zombies to shame. With an eye roll, Ros picked up his axe.

"I got this, Garm," he said to his hound. "It's been a while since I got to make something bleed."

It has been two weeks, Ros, the hound said telepathically while looking up at the sky, asking for strength.

Garm was the size of a small pony, coming up to Ros' hip. He was similar to a black German Shepherd except for his eyes, which were a deep red and would sometimes glow. Garm was one of the first helhounds.

Ros readied his axe and waited. The crunching of leaves got louder, and the stench was becoming overwhelming. As soon as the demon's hot breath was on his neck, he snapped his elbow back, connecting with what would have been the demon's chin. The demon stumbled back and tried to shake the surprise assault. Whoever had sent it clearly didn't warn it what it would be up against. Ros stepped forward and swung his axe, easily chopping one of its legs off.

"Who sent you?" he asked. Annoyingly, the demon just screeched. Ros rolled his eyes again and asked, "Did someone summon you?"

Screech.

"Well, I tried."

Ros swung the axe low, removing the other leg from the demon. Then, with an overhead swing, he chopped its head off; a splattering of black blood sprayed on his already dirty chest.

Hel, those things are gross, Garm said. He walked up to Ros with his flannel shirt clenched in his enormous mouth.

"Haven't seen one of those in a while," Ros said. "Do you mind doing some sniffing around to see if you can track down who summoned it?" he asked, grabbing the shirt from his hound to wipe off the grime.

What if it was sent directly by Hel? Garm asked, looking up at Ros.

"Then I wish you luck," Ros replied with a smirk.

Thanks, he said sarcastically. Garm trotted off a few feet before shimmering into shadows and disappearing completely.

Ros, now happy with his sloppy clean-up job, threw his flannel next to the stacked trunks. He donned his black t-shirt and went to hunt down one of the demon's missing legs. Gathering the parts into a pile, he held his hand over the dismembered demon. Letting his heavy powers rise to the surface, he summoned fire. It burned hot and quickly turned the demon to ash.

"I remember when we used to mess with those things as children," came a voice.

Ros turned slowly. It had not been too long since he'd heard that voice, but long enough to make him wonder why he would be here now. And if he was here, that meant...

"More like they would mess with you, brother," said a soft female voice. "You were always too slow to outrun them."

Carver and Cara came around the gigantic pile of trees and smiled at the towering man standing in front of them. "Hello, cousin," they said together in their creepy twin way.

Two redheads stood in front of Ros, looking as if they'd just left a business meeting. Carver was dressed in a crisp, deep blue suit that accented his deep red hair. He looked like he'd never worked a hard day in his life. His twin, Cara, was dressed in a pair of white, wide-legged pants with a silk blouse to match her twin's suit. They had matched outfits since they were young. "*It helps boost our creepy-twin vibe,*" Cara once said.

"Hello, cousins," Ros replied. They looked so out of place in the middle of the woods. "What brings you to this side of the world?"

"We were in the area on business and wanted to check on you. It has been some time since you sent word home," Carver said.

"We saw your father recently; he seems to think you are still sowing your seed and enjoying life before it is time to come home. Yet, it seems you have actually made this place your home?" Cara asked, looking him up and down. She let her lip curl at his rugged appearance. Where they were crisp and clean, he was every bit the backwoods male. Thick, dark hair hung to his chin, almost blending in with his rugged beard. His outfit was his usual dark Levi's, a faded t-shirt, and a flannel, now dirty and discarded. Ros only raised his eyebrows in reply. He would not give them anything to bring home.

"You would think five hundred years in this place would be enough," they said together, both letting their heads cock to the left.

Ros just bared his teeth in response. Damn, they were creepy—and they got such a kick out of it, too. Ros was sure any of the creepy twins in movies were based on these two.

"I'm sorry if I'm not ready to let our legacy and curse ruin my life." He didn't like many people, but forever was a long time to be alone.

"It seems like you're avoiding the curse pretty well since I don't smell a male or female on you. How much time do you think you have left before your father comes calling?" Carver asked. Cara left her twin's side to examine the pile of ash still smoking behind Ros.

Of course, he didn't have someone's scent linked to him; it was hard to remember the last time he'd bedded anyone, and he would never grow attached. He would never let someone get hurt because of a curse that took anyone who loved the rulers of his family.

"I wonder who sent this lovely creature to say hello to our favorite cousin?" Cara asked, breaking him from his thoughts.

"I wouldn't put it past the two of you," Ros said, raising his chin.

"This wasn't us," they said together. "But someone is clearly trying to get your attention."

"I've heard this has been the fourth demon topside this season," Cara stated with a cock of her head.

"I've heard it was six," her brother replied with the same tilt of his head.

"I have really missed our chats, wonder twins, but I have to finish what I was doing. Please go creep someone else out." Ros walked away from them, heading back to the trees he'd been chopping down.

"Check on Belias," Carver said.

Then together, "we hear he's been topside for a few months now."

Ros' only reply was a middle finger held high over his shoulder.

The sun seemed to drift slowly in the sky as Ros left the one hundred and fifty trees behind. His feet led him up the old path to his home while his mind continued to plan out how many trees would need to be cleared over the next few days. He tried to think about anything other than the visit from his cousins and that demon. The forest parted, and fifty feet in front of him stood his home.

As he approached the deep green structure, his thoughts quickly switched to work he could do on it. He had lived here for the past five hundred years, and it was constant work to keep the old property livable. It wasn't massive like some of the other cabins in the area, but it was perfect for him. One bedroom and one bath were all he and Garm needed. The living area looked over the vast lake through floor-to-ceiling windows he'd installed almost fifty years ago. Not one part of the house was unused; shelves covered every wall, filled with his collections of books and trinkets. Only a few people stepped into his home, and they all said the same thing: "This looks like a hoarder's home."

Ros felt the magic zing around him as he crossed the protection line around his home. Nothing got in without him knowing about it. He headed straight for the fire pit to discard his clothes; there was no need to try and save them with the amount of demon blood caked into the fabric. He stripped down completely and placed his clothes on top of the waiting logs. Fire roared to life with a swipe of his hand, and the heat of the flames blanketed his naked body as if it had been lit for hours.

He looked up at his waiting home, contemplating a shower, then glanced at the lake and thought about a swim. Bringing his hands overhead, he stretched his tall, muscled body. He was slightly sore from chopping trees, but not sore or tired enough to kill the restlessness in him. Swim first and then shower.

Ros left the fire and headed to his long dock. It was a regular occurrence to take laps up and down the lake, no matter the weather; he would be in here until the dead of winter when it would freeze over. The nudity didn't bother him either. There were only three houses on this lake, and even if the residents were home, it still wouldn't stop him.

He glanced at the house to the right of the lake. It had been abandoned for about two hundred years now. Maybe he should check to make sure the structure was still sound, especially since some of the kid gangs in town loved searching through old, abandoned properties. He shook his head, and a small smile graced his lips. Looking at the cabin directly across from him, he wondered if anyone would ever live there again. It had been about fifteen years since the seer and her son had visited the old cabin. His mother would have enjoyed the house to his right. It was higher on the hill and had a massive greenhouse. He had been thinking about her a lot lately. She visited him in his dreams, and he'd started seeing her everywhere, especially in the late summer storms.

As he neared the end of the dock, he shook the memories of his mother from his mind. He was a few flashbacks away from getting to the sad stuff. The demon from earlier had washed away those sad memories, and he was thankful the houses near him were empty. Not only did he hate company, he hated having to explain things even more. Hopefully, Garm would come back with useful news. Ros knew it wouldn't be good news, but at least they could work out a plan.

With a heavy sigh, he pressed off the dock to dive into the chilly lake. The cool water washed over his body as he continued moving underwater. He didn't break to the surface until his lungs screamed so loudly that his mind couldn't focus on anything else.

The lake was about a half-mile wide, and he continued circling it for an hour. He didn't worry about any of the creatures in the water, supernatural or not; he was the scariest thing in the lake. He tried to chase away the concerns in his mind—his cousins' visit, the demons that kept cropping up, and more—while pushing his body. It didn't work as well as he wanted, but he came up with a start to a plan. He would have to call his other cousin and see if he, in fact, was topside. If he was, he would answer some of Ros' questions whether or not he wanted to.

The sun was getting closer to the horizon, and he needed to shower and eat before getting in touch with Belias. Grabbing on to the ledge of his dock, he pulled himself up high enough to place a foot on the wood. He stood, running his hands through his hair to rid it of the lake water.

When the crisp air hit his backside, he wanted to hurry inside, but he also didn't want the forest creatures thinking he was going soft. He settled for a quick walk, refusing to show any discomfort until he was inside his entryway. With a shake of his large body, he allowed his powers to warm the house and made his way to the bathroom. Even the shelves in his mudroom had books tucked between his shoes and gear. "I am not a hoarder," he mumbled for no one to hear as he made his way through the kitchen.

"Oh, I don't know about that, cousin."

Ros paused and then cursed himself.

How did he get in here? he thought while he looked for something to wear. There was nothing, of course. Luckily for him, he wasn't in the habit of being embarrassed. Ros strode naked into the living room and glared at his least favorite cousin.

"Hello, Bel. What brings you to my part of the realm?" Ros said, with no hint of a welcome tone in his deep voice.

"Hel, Rosier, you've gotten…" He paused, looking him up and down. "Wilder and more beastly."

Ros refused to let his surprise show on his features; his magic should have warned him about the intrusion.

"I will ask again, cousin, what brings you here?" Ros asked.

"Do I need a reason to visit my favorite cousin? Did Cara and Carver get the same welcome?" Belias asked with a pout on his face.

"I was more clothed when they popped in," he remarked. He leaned against the door frame, and his cock answered with a small slap against his bare thigh.

Belias twirled his fingers, and strings snaked up Ros' legs, cloaking him in black fabric. As the slithering sound cleared, he was left in too-tight pants that barely covered his long legs and a black button-down with ruffles. Ros growled at the invasion.

"That's better," Belias remarked with a swipe of his hands.

Ros grabbed the front of his new shirt and tore it off his body. His cousin just rolled his eyes.

"No, this is better," he said, throwing the shirt near his fire to burn later. "I am sorry my nakedness embarrasses you, cousin. You should embrace your scrawny stature. Some chicks dig that, Bel."

"I love when you call me that, Rosier," he replied, losing some of his humor. "I have come to talk business. I want to form an alliance with you, only you, and leave the other cousins out of it. I am sure that is why the creepy ones stopped by earlier."

"Did you happen to see them after you summoned that demon to interrupt my work?" Ros asked, getting right to the point of what should have been a phone call.

"No, why would I do such a thing?" he replied with a mock gasp. "I wouldn't try to harm someone I want to form an alliance with." He stood then and brushed off invisible dust from his crisp, black suit.

"Sure, and I am the Queen of Hounds." He turned away from him. "See yourself out. I have no interest in what you are selling."

"Haven't you heard the whispers? Something is brewing in the universe, and it is best we come together instead of hiding away in our dusty holes," Belias remarked, following him.

Ros refused to turn around and face him. "I have heard no such whispers, and I enjoy my dusty hole," he said over his shoulder. "Next time, send word before you muck up my couch and we can grab a drink and catch up instead of you getting an eyeful."

Belias didn't respond, and Ros continued up the stairs to his room and bathroom. He waited two minutes before sending his shadows through the house to see if any unwanted guests still lingered. Nothing came back. He rubbed his face roughly before heading to the shower. It would be quick since he needed to check his boundary spell and figure out how the Hel the oily runt had gotten into his home.

Tangled in dark green sheets, Ros woke with a start. Quickly sitting up, he looked around the room to catch his bearings. It was dark, but he could see the many shelves stacked with various books, weapons, potions, and odd trinkets.

Home. I am home, he thought while looking for his hound. *Right; he's out hunting.*

Taking a deeper breath, he realized he was in his bed, and was not, in fact, being drowned by demons while his mother screamed from the throne she was shackled to. The feel of scales and feathers still danced across his skin. He could still see her long black hair covering her face as she screamed for him, her powers crackling with lightning but never reaching him. Guilt and regret were etched on her beautiful face. She could not reach him. She'd brought him into this world, a world she could not fix.

Ros felt bile creep up his throat. Shucking off the sheets, he went to hunt down water and anything to distract him and his thoughts.

He made his way down the hallway to the bathroom, the only room that was clean and free of clutter. He thought about taking another shower to wash away the sweat and the dreams, but he settled with splashing cold water on his face. Grabbing a fresh towel, he wiped the water from his beard and chest. Grabbing a pair of sweatpants, he decided to do another perimeter check. He had too many unwanted visitors today, and he needed to make sure there weren't any others lurking outside. It didn't matter that he'd checked earlier.

What time is it?

Heading down the stairs to the main floor, he stopped at the landing, listening for anything that he should be prepared for. Satisfied with the silence that answered, he continued to the kitchen. Not bothering with lights, he headed for the fridge for a bottle of water before heading outside.

On silent bare feet, he left his home through the front door. Taking in the large lawn that bled into the woods, he listened again. Nothing but the forest answered back. Feeling himself settle a little more, he ventured off into the woods. Looking up at the moon, he realized he had barely been asleep for a few hours; it wasn't even midnight yet.

With the moon high in the sky and the earth under his feet, his head felt clearer. Ros felt the tether of power circling his property. He continued to follow it all the way until he came to where the woods met the lake. The barrier stopped about fifty feet from his dock. Just as he was about to extend it, he heard something. Well, more like the lack of something.

The forest's noises stilled as he caught a faint whisper on the wind. Pausing, he opened his senses. *What is to come?* whispered back at him, but it was so faint he thought he imagined it. He listened harder, but all he found was silence and the smell of the forest. The noises of beasts and creatures hummed again. Shaking his head, he attempted to continue on until he saw lights. Not from his home, from across the lake. Someone was at the seer's cabin.

Ros crept through the woods on silent feet to get a better look at the house that hadn't been lit in years, stopping at an opening where he had an unrestricted view but was still shrouded in the shadow of the tall trees.

The entire cabin was lit and all the windows opened as if to rid it of any ghosts and years of stale air. He didn't see the seer or her son anywhere in the home that was fully visible with its large windows and the open-floor plan. He inspected the lawn, but there was no sign of anyone or anything. He even tried to scent the air, but the wind was not in his favor.

Ros thought about stopping by tomorrow at a decent hour to say hello—well, to make sure he knew what he was dealing with. He remembered the seer being kind, but knew nothing more about her. Her son was older, but again, he remembered little. They kept to themselves like he did.

Deciding to give up for the evening, he turned toward the forest to head to his unlit home. Looking at it, you could barely take in the details, even with his excellent sight. The wind shifted from behind him, and a powerful gust carried the scent of something. Or someone.

Turning, he followed the scent to a shadow at the end of the long dock. The silhouette was hard to make out with the light being cast behind her. It was definitely female, but he could not make out that supernatural scent. She had a thin blanket clutched around her small frame, making it difficult to make out any features. She faced the moon, and he could make out the deep breaths she was taking. Maybe it was the seer. It seemed to be the right size.

Ros was fully hit with the unique scent as the wind picked up again. She had undertones of sage, like all seers, but then there was an electric scent he couldn't make out. The smell of citrus wove together with something soft.

His eyes grew wide as it all hit him at once.

He whispered to only himself and the forest, "Hello. You are new, aren't you?"

Ros was drowning in a warm bed while his heavy eyes refused to open. He knew he needed to start his day, but he wanted to go back to those dreams. Dreams of a beast finally waking again, pulling itself from the depths of its heavy shadows. This wasn't his usual dream, it was something different. What it was, he didn't know, but he wanted to find out.

His eyes slowly peeled open as hot breath caressed his face. He was greeted by deep red eyes and a wet nose.

You were smiling, Garm grumbled in his head.

"Are you concerned?" he asked in a voice thick with sleep.

It's almost ten. You don't smile like that, and you don't sleep this late, Garm remarked, nudging him in the neck with his cold nose.

"I don't know what you mean by 'like that,' but I do smile." Ros pushed the giant head of the hound away from him. "You don't see it because you're an ass and I never have a reason to smile around you."

Well, I'm about to wipe that smile off your face. Belias is up to something, Garm said, sitting down next to Ros.

"What did you find?" Ros sat up quickly, suddenly very awake.

There is some unrest back home; there are whispers of change, and Belias has been filling the heads of some of the courts. I am not sure what, but they are rallying for something big, Garm said seriously.

"What about the demons? Has he been summoning them?"

Clearly. Not only did I find the types of demons that have been popping up here in his domain, but there is talk about more coming. Directly from his court, he snarled.

"Fucking Belias," Ros said, rubbing sleep from his eyes. "What the Hel is he up to?"

I don't know, but I don't like it.

"I don't need any more surprises," Ros groaned. His gaze drifted toward the window.

What else is surprising? Garm asked, following his gaze.

"We have a new neighbor," he said, looking at the hound. "Or an old one. I haven't figured it out yet, but she is something new."

New? What do you mean?

"I couldn't get a read on her," he said, getting out of bed and hunting down his clothes. "I saw her standing on the dock of the seer's property last night. I was going to investigate more, but I got a message from Weylyn, and I need to head up north and investigate a rogue Vampire clan."

Again? I thought you took care of them already. Garm stole Ros' warm spot in the bed and settled in.

"Same story, different group and different beast," Ros said, pulling on his dark jeans. "I will be gone for at least a week, but I'm only checking things out, no need for backup."

Sure you are, Garm mocked. He settled his large head on Ros' pillow.

You know how to call me when things get out of hand.

"I love the amount of faith you have in me after all these years," he replied, heading for the bedroom door. "Don't have too many parties, please. You know I don't like anyone in this cabin but you and Sam."

Yeah, yeah. Be careful, Ros. Call upon me if you need help, Garm said with worried eyes.

PART TWO

Hel is empty and all the devils are here.
- William Shakespeare

8

Ellea

Monday morning greeted her through unshielded
windows. She could have sworn she shut them before
crawling into bed last night. With a wave of her hand,
the curtains closed, and she burrowed back under her blankets.

It had been a long time since the stars had spoken to her, but they
did last night. While she stood at the end of the dock, they sang a
beautiful melody and welcomed her home. She held onto that sound
as she tried to find sleep once again.

Dreams of walking through the forest, skirting along the lake under
a sky that wanted her to know she was home and safe, were rudely
interrupted. The curtains angrily opened once again, and Ellea glared
at the ceiling through her assaulted eyelids.

"You are not like the other home, are you?" she grumbled. Billy was lying next to her, trying to shove her big head under a free pillow. With a sigh, Ellea tossed her blankets aside and got out of bed. It had taken a four-hour drive to get here, and she was feeling it. After stretching her naked body dramatically, she made her way to the large windows.

From her bedroom, she could see everything. The large lake glittered under the sun that hung above the lush trees. She could easily make out the green cabin across from hers. The third cabin sat high on one of the many hills, but it was barely visible through the dense forest. It had been some time since she'd visited the cabin, and the bedroom had been updated since then. The small bed had been replaced with a king-sized one. Pale green walls were now a soft cream color. The ceiling and floors had been updated with a deep black wood instead of the stone she'd grown up with.

She had lived in many houses growing up, but this cabin was always something more. No matter the color of the paint, she could always rely on this place to settle her. Her uncle and nana had brought her here when her powers needed taming. They seemed calm now, as calm as the lake before her. Her powers opened a crack at the memories of messing with Isadora and attacking Isaac. A single crackle of amusement ran under her skin at the thought of doing it again, but it was smothered as she remembered hurting her uncle. Ellea turned quickly away from the window. She needed a shower, not to stand there thinking of her magic or how she had failed.

Leaving her bedroom and Billy behind, she headed for the attached bathroom. The theme of cream-colored walls stopped at the threshold, and her favorite color greeted her. The skylight was the only source of light, but she could make out the black tiled walls, glass-encased shower, and a deep, black bathtub. At her house in Halifax, the light would have been on and the steam already rolling out of the shower. Here, nothing greeted her.

There was power in this cabin, but it was turning its magical shoulder at her. It seemed she would have to fend for herself.

Once showered and dressed, Ellea headed downstairs, passing the three other bedrooms in the cabin. The top floor was only meant for living space. The open first floor had a large dining room and a library on the lake side of the house. The kitchen and other sitting areas were placed toward the front. She would have to check out the greenhouse on the property to see what state it was in. But first, coffee. Ellea headed straight for the kitchen to hunt it down.

The home may be ignoring her, but thankfully, she'd remembered to bring her fancy espresso machine. Going without cell service was one thing, going without coffee would have been pure torture. Opening the fridge, she grabbed her cream and homemade syrup. Placing it with her favorite black mug, she got to work on her favorite coffee.

She tried not to think about everything that happened over the past few days as she steamed the cream. Life had been moving along fine—normal, but fine. Now she had no lovers, some pissed-off witches, and was in a nowhere town with zero cell service and no easy ways to contact the outside world. Even though it was a drastic change, it felt somewhat right.

Billy padded down the steps as Ellea had her coffee in hand. The beast stretched and yawned while Ellea slipped on her boots.

What is our plan for today, Bug? her familiar asked with a groggy voice.

"I want to check on the greenhouse and property," Ellea said, opening the front door. "Then maybe some reading."

When are we going to get to work on your magic? Billy asked, following after her.

"Don't bring my magic up until I have finished my coffee, Billy," she said a bit sternly. She didn't want to think of it yet. She needed to settle in first and figure out which direction to go. She wouldn't mind some relaxation time with a good book, or a few good books.

Billy and Ellea headed out to the small porch. The cabin itself was a deep gray with wood shutters and a tin roof. Some plants hung over the porch, and a few rocking chairs sat ready to be used. She couldn't wait for it to be cooler so she could sit out here and watch the leaves change.

Gravel and dirt crunched under their feet as they headed toward the greenhouse. Years of weather had turned the glass structure opaque. She was worried about what she would find upon opening the door.

Ellea reached out and turned the rusted handle. An ominous creek sounded as she pulled the door toward her. The musky smell of dirt, old wood, and neglect clung to her nose. Peeking her head through the door, she saw empty flower beds with dried dirt, dead leaves scattered across the tiled floor, a cast iron sink, and old wooden chairs. Billy sneezed dramatically and began walking back to the cabin.

I'm taking a nap, she said with a yawn.

Ellea looked back inside the greenhouse. The dirt and dust sparkled in the rays of light that managed to make their way in. She breathed in deeply, and the memory of a smell tugged at her. The musky, neglected scent reminded her of dark basements and being punished for something she couldn't control. She shook her head to rid the creeping memory of her parents.

She had barely been up for twenty minutes; it was too early for this.

"Yeah, that sounds like a good idea," Ellea said after her. Closing the greenhouse door, she headed back inside. There was plenty of time to explore and work things out—later.

Ellea had been cooped up in the cabin for far too long. She could only read so much smut and deal with so much side-eye from Billy. It had also been a week since she had done any training or exercise.

"I think I should go for a run," Ellea announced to the mush of a dog lying on the sofa.

Good, maybe that will get you to take a shower, Billy grumbled at her.

"I think we should both go for a run," Ellea said, stretching and choosing to ignore Billy's sass. "Let's get out of the cabin and head to town. It's only a couple of miles. Come on! You may meet someone you can entertain yourself with."

Finnnne. I was feeling thicker than usual, anyway, Billy grumbled, getting up and also stretching.

"Well maybe if you acted like regular familiars, your love handles wouldn't get so out of control." Ellea smirked at her beast of a familiar. It was a lie, Billy's size never changed. That comment earned her a snap at her hand as Billy trotted by.

She headed up to her room to change into leggings and a black t-shirt. She caught a glimpse of herself in the mirror and was a little horrified. A week of avoiding life had really done a number to her appearance. She had to do something because lounging around a cabin and feeling sorry for herself was clearly not helping. Grabbing her running shoes on the way down the stairs, she started thinking of a plan.

Billy led the way down the long driveway to the main road as Ellea finished off the last plaits of her braid. They both found a comfortable pace as they headed into town. Instead of feeling stiff and out of shape, her powers steadily increased with each stride. Her mind raced right along with the energy coursing through her limbs.

"I want to swing by the main shop to see what they have in stock," Ellea said.

Billy only chuffed in response.

"It's been a while since I've done basic magic. Maybe I can work on that while I research more about tricksters?"

Another chuff from the beast running beside her.

"You know, we've only gone a mile; if you're already too tired to form a thought, I may be a little concerned."

Bothering with basic magic is not going to help. Research, yes, do that. You need to figure out a way to harness your power, not smother it, Billy stated flatly.

THAT WAS NOT A COUPLE OF MILES!

Billy had been screaming in Ellea's head for about two miles now. Apparently, things were different from when she was a child. A couple of miles had turned into six by the time they reached the main shop. The dog barreled past her and pushed the shop door open. A bell rang as so many smells hit her at once.

There were wall-to-wall shelves with countless objects, some for mortals and some for supernaturals. One section was dedicated to your basic snack needs, while another had jars of animal parts, herbs, stones, and liquids. You wanted any type of crystal, they had it. Need an ice cream and some mugwort? This was your place.

Ellea took a right past a cabinet filled with all types of sea creatures, some alive and others very dead. She came to a halt when she saw Billy had all four legs in the air while getting a very enthusiastic belly rub from a man she didn't recognize. Her tongue was basically on the floor while she was panting dramatically.

"It was only six miles," she grumbled to herself. The guy stood and went back to speaking to the shopkeeper.

Woah, he's tall, she thought. He had to be a shifter with how big and rugged he was. The man wore a worn black shirt under a flannel long sleeve, the sleeves rolled up to his elbows. It was giving off some serious Winchester vibes. Not only was he tall, but he was also big. Like, really big. He ran his hand through his chin-length dark hair, creating a dramatic part and making her zero in on a strong forearm. Her eyes raked up past his wide shoulders to a neck that had her thinking all types of things. Then he flashed a bright smile at the shopkeeper. The sharp points of his canines glinted in the light, and she bit her lip to try and suppress an unnatural sound that wanted to escape her mouth.

Fucking Hel.

Her heart began to race as she realized he looked so much like the man from her dream. His beard reminded her of the man between her legs; the rug burn from it would be so worth it. She groaned inwardly when he finally turned toward her. She caught a glimpse of hazel eyes and dimples before she turned and acted like she was very interested in a jar of dried starfish. What would she even say to him? *"Hey, I dreamt of you and you made me feel things I've never felt before, like one of the best orgasms and feeling like I could accept my magic."* She noticed him bend down to give Billy one last pat and used that as an in.

"Don't mind her, she's being dramatic."

Go away, don't distract him and his big, strong hands, Billy groaned.

"Ew, gross," Ellea mumbled.

"Gross?" the man said, his voice so deep that it should be a crime.

Deep and familiar.

He gave Billy one last scratch behind the ears and stood, his eyes glued to her familiar. Ellea had to crane her neck to look up at him.

"By the looks of it, you had this poor dog run ten miles," he said with a judgmental tone. He tore his hazel eyes from the dramatic puddle of a dog on the floor. She barely held in her gasp when their eyes connected. His nostrils seemed to flare, which had her feeling very self-conscious about the last time she'd showered.

"It was only six, and it wouldn't be so bad if she exercised more," Ellea said, arching a brow and crossing her arms.

His beautiful eyes hardened. It looked like he might just call animal control. Billy would actually have a blast if he did. Her thoughts of her familiar torturing the staff at the pound were interrupted when those judgmental eyes traveled away from her face. Slowly, he seemed to take her in. He clearly didn't like what he saw; he left with a scowl on his face and didn't say another word.

What a way to meet a man from your naughty dreams.

Ellea groaned to herself and continued to explore the shop. Maybe the dream hadn't meant anything; not all dreams were of the future. Maybe she wasn't promised freedom from fear of her magic.

Party pooper! It's been too long since a man like that rubbed my belly in all the right ways, Billy whined from the floor.

9

Ros

Ros let the door slam behind him. He had to physically shake a weird feeling from his body. He hadn't realized that the new person in town would have his powers splintering under his skin. The glimpse he'd had that night was nothing compared to what had been in front of him. She'd looked worn and tired, but those big gray eyes and those pants had done a number to his cock. Leggings on curves like that should be illegal, *and* she'd run six miles here? She had to be in shape. He didn't have time to deal with weird feelings and curvy females with everything else going on.

He glared at Ag's shop door one last time. Shaking his head again, he headed toward his truck. Hopping inside, he gently closed the old metal door, but everything still rattled in response. He threw the newspaper he'd grabbed onto his passenger seat. The headline was from the city of Halifax.

'Council Member's Son Injured in Crazy Accident — His Niece is to Blame'

He would read more later and see if there was anything worth looking into besides crazy witches. The vampires had been keeping him busy as of late, but it was always worth looking into other situations. He turned the key to let his Ford Powerstroke warm up. The old "wait to start' light went out, and he let the beast roar to life. He sat there for a few minutes, contemplating what to do next. Ros decided to visit Sam, the current leader of the local wolven and one of his only friends. They had to talk about Mabon since it was only a month away, and they needed to talk about the vampire issue.

He put the truck in reverse, and as he turned his head, he caught the female leaving the shop. Their eyes locked for a moment. She raised her chin and turned toward the road, beginning her jog back to wherever she had come from. The dog lingered for a moment longer and seemed to smirk at him before catching up with her person.

Crazy witches?

He turned toward the paper again. His mind began piecing everything together as he reversed out of the lot to head to Sam's. It was starting to look like fate had dumped a new mission into his lap.

Ros pulled down the long driveway of the farm. Sam lived on one of the largest properties in Glenover. It had been passed down from generation to generation. Wolven packs on the East Coast had an ancestry hierarchy. The alphas were born, not chosen, unlike some of the West Coast packs. Some said the lack of consistency was to blame for their dwindling numbers. Ros knew that wasn't the issue.

He stopped his truck next to Sam's similar hunk of metal. As soon as the engine turned off, a few of the younger wolven gathered around his truck, yipping and barking with wagging tails. Ros couldn't help but smile as he got out of the truck and kneeled on the ground.

There were five of them, four in various shades of brown and gray and one that was midnight black. One was doing its best to tug Ros' boot off, two were assaulting his neck and face, while the last two sat farther away, only observing.

"Teek!" a booming voice came from the large porch. "Don't let them eat him."

Sam was standing at the top of the steps with his hands on his hips, looking more like a mother hen than an alpha. He was a hair shorter than Ros, and his face was beautiful. Sam kept his beard and hair neat in comparison to the other wolven. His sharp features and angular eyes came in handy when it came time to glare at an out-of-line pup. He wasn't as broad as Ros, but he somehow took up just as much space.

The gray wolven that sat further away with the chestnut one chuffed and snapped its teeth. The three that were all over Ros quickly stopped. As Teek turned and walked toward the back of the house, the rest followed. The smaller one, fully black and wild-looking, was slow to get in line. It paused and looked back at Ros. Teek had to let out a growl to get it to follow. Ros could almost see the black one roll its green eyes before trotting away with the rest. He stood, swiping some of the dirt from his jeans.

"Devika is getting harder to keep in line," Sam said as he watched some of his pack disappear into the woods. Devika had paused again, looking back at the house as if it would rather be there with them.

"I remember when you were younger," Ros said with a grimace. "I doubt Devika will ever wag a tail anywhere near what you were doing at that age."

"I wasn't that bad." Sam grimaced.

"Remember that one Halloween fifty years ago?" Ros raised a brow toward Sam.

"There was only a little property damage and one scared choir group," Sam replied, shaking his head.

"They canceled Halloween for three years after that," Ros said with a laugh.

"What's wrong with you?" Sam asked, searching his face.

"Don't change the subject, Sam," Ros said. "Remember that shifter that held the city meeting in hopes to run you out of town?"

"No," Sam said, shaking his head.

Ros raised an eyebrow at him again, insinuating *how could you forget that?*

"Of course, I remember that, but this is about you. What's up?"

Ros pulled on his shirt and looked down at his hands. Nothing was up besides the usual.

"Nothing?" he said, trying to think of what it could be. "Well, that rogue vampire pack is larger than I thought."

"This isn't work-related," he said, reaching out to grab Ros' forearm. His large hand grasped him gently. Their strength was matched in brute force, but Sam didn't have the same skills as Ros. "Your powers are churning like a storm under your skin."

"You don't need to use your alpha senses on me," Ros said, pulling his arm away and looking into Sam's auburn eyes. "It's nothing."

Ros knew Sam wouldn't push. Sam gestured toward the porch for them to sit. The farmhouse was ancient but sturdy. Its white paint was peeling in a few spots, and the boards creaked under their feet as they walked toward the two large chairs on the side of the house.

"So, these vampires? Are they the same as the ones on the border?" Sam asked.

"No, those ones were old and creepy," he said with a shiver, leaning into the cushioned chair. It was deep and worn, mostly by him. "What is it with old beasts and virgins?"

Sam only sighed. Rogue supernaturals usually fit into two categories: those who liked the old way of doing things—sacrificing virgins, segregation, and feeling superior—and those who refused to follow traditions. They were the worst; unseasoned supernaturals were more likely to cause mass destruction. The creepy old ones picked off their prey in small attacks and stayed mostly under the radar.

Supernaturals and mortals had lived side by side in the realm for ages. There was still unrest, especially when mortals started disappearing or a rogue group killed off a whole building of people. The supernaturals had a council, and it worked to keep things in order. Those like Sam, Ros, and others cleaned up the mess. It wasn't a paying gig, but it helped quell his already damaged soul.

"The ones I watched up north this past week were something else," Ros said, leaning forward and looking at Sam.

"Virgins or riots?" Sam asked darkly.

"Neither," Ros said, rubbing his face, guilt washing over him. "Women and children. But what's weird is that they aren't butchering them; they're collecting them and shipping them off somewhere. It reeked of demons too."

Sam sat up at the mention of demons. "Demons and vamps don't mix," he said as his eyes widened. "This can't be good."

Ros shook his head. It wasn't good, and the worst part was he couldn't take any of them out. "Weylyn has had a few of these groups pop up, but never as large as the one I saw." Ros sagged back into his seat. "I've never been so frustrated. I couldn't save any of them."

Sam leaned over and put a hand on Ros' knee. "We can't save them all," he said as his kind eyes searched his face. "This isn't the first hard mission you've had. What else is going on?"

"Fucking fine, you pushy mutt." Ros dragged his bottom lip across his teeth and huffed a sigh. He didn't get a chance to say what he meant as Sam's nostrils flared and his eyes dilated. *Fucking dog,* he thought.

"You got a chub for"—he sniffed again—"what is that? It smells electric."

Nothing got past a wolven nose. It was almost as good as Ros'.

"There is a new female in town. She seems to be staying at the seer's house on my lake. I got close to her at Ag's before I came here."

Sam wiggled his eyebrows at his friend. "Tell me everything!" he exclaimed and settled into his chair.

"There is nothing to tell," Ros said, ignoring the excitement his friend was showing. "She is this short thing, wild gray eyes, and I can't get a read on her. But this was in the paper."

He handed him the paper, and Sam quickly read through it. It claimed the man had been attacked in his niece's home; there were no names, only that the victim was a relative of a council member and no one was pressing charges.

"For some nothing short thing, you're already getting a hard-on," Sam said with a huge smile, attempting to flick Ros' crotch.

Ros batted his hand away and growled. It was fucking confusing; his powers were angry, his dick was at attention, and he didn't know if he needed to take out the witch.

"So what if I am?" He groaned. "It means nothing, and I need you to keep an eye on her. My powers didn't like being close to her, and it has been a long time since they did that."

"Do you think it's like that one witch?" A grimace spread across Sam's face, and Ros knew what he was thinking.

"The one that was luring men and chopping their bits off to use as a sacrifice?" They both shivered. "No, I don't think it's that. But like I said, something is off, and I could use your help to keep an eye on her. The vampires are enough, especially with my family popping up."

"Mmm," Sam said before a smile spread across his face. "Sure, Rosier, I will keep an eye on the short, little something. I might even keep both eyes on her."

"You're fucking worse than Ags," Ros groaned. "Well, this was fun; I'm going to go before you try and flick my balls again."

"Boo," Sam said with a dramatic pout. He gave yet another eyebrow wiggle. "You love when I flick your balls, and Devon is still overseas. Stay and entertain me."

"I am going to skin your eyebrows off if you don't stop," Ros said as he stood. He turned and adjusted his pants.

"I saw that!" Sam said, standing and slapping his friend on the shoulder. "Maybe she will still be here for Mabon. Maybe she'll strip down and dance around that bonfire you're working so hard on."

"Or she's here to destroy us all." Ros shoved his friend off and stomped to his truck.

"Doubtful! I think you forgot how your cock works and you're getting mixed signals," Sam said, but Ros flipped him off and ripped open his truck door. "You know you love me!"

10

Ros

A bell rang overhead as Ros took a step into the shop. Ag's Apothecary had been a staple in this town for hundreds of years. It had shifted with the times and started stocking more mortal items and trinkets to entice any tourists stopping on their way through town. Agatha herself was an amazing procurer of anything you needed. For Ros, that was a book and Garm's favorite jerky. It had been about a week since he was here last to place an order. A week since he'd run into the new witch in town. He still hadn't made it over to her cabin.

"Ros! How are you today?" Agatha was tall with dark brown skin and straight jet black hair, not a gray strand in sight. Only the faintest wrinkle showed at the edges of her eyes as she smiled at Ros. No one knew Agatha's age, and it was probably rude to ask.

"Not bad, Agatha. How are you?" Ros responded with a smile. She was one of the few Ros let see a different side of him—just a glimpse, but he liked her. She was a witch with no claim to a certain power other than seeking items and knowing what someone needed.

"Good, good. Before I grab your things from the back, I have a favor to ask," she said as a glint sparkled in her eye. Agatha was up to something.

Ros stood straighter. He trusted her, but he didn't trust the favor she would ask for. "Are you going to hold my things hostage if I say no?"

Laughing softly, she grabbed his hand from over the counter. He didn't mind her touch, but worried she would see something in it.

"I would never hold Garm's jerky hostage. Your book, though, I might just hold that if you say no," she said with a wink. Agatha flipped his hand over and looked down at his palm for a moment. His hand was so much larger than hers. "My afternoon girl called in sick, and I won't be able to make my deliveries. Would you mind dropping an order off at the Handley's home?"

She released his hand and looked up at him. There was no worry in her eyes, only knowing. It was hard to hide his grimace.

"Don't give me that look," she said, standing taller and looking a little older. "I figured since you lived on the same street, it wouldn't be an issue."

Ros sighed. Agatha didn't know why he was reluctant to travel to her house. And she didn't need to know. "You're lucky I really want that book."

"Oh, please. Maybe it will be good. Talk to someone other than me, the hound, and Sam," she proposed with a wave over her shoulder as she headed to the back.

"I don't need another witch in my life, you're plenty," he answered with another rare smile.

"Save that flirting for someone your own age. I will go grab the boxes." She walked through the curtains to the back of the store.

"There isn't anyone my own age," he grumbled to himself.

Ros pulled onto his street, one he now shared with someone new. He hadn't thought that he would find himself heading towards the witch's house so soon. His mind raced through all the possibilities of what his magic was trying to tell him. Ros would have preferred more time to learn all he could and figure out what to do with the witch.

He was used to his powers reacting or calling to something that needed to be destroyed before they caused destruction. But something was lingering in the back of his mind. This wouldn't be so simple, and he didn't know what to make of it. For now, he had to deal with the box sitting on his passenger seat.

He could make this quick—drop off the box at the door, knock, and leave. But why were his powers rumbling the closer he got? That beast was crawling to the surface, ready to fight.

Sighing, Ros parked his truck far enough away to take in everything before he approached the large dark structure. Nothing creeped in the woods and the greenhouse seemed empty; all that was left was the cabin. He listened carefully. Nothing. The gravel crunched under his boots as he approached the front door.

Taking a calming breath and begging his powers to relax, Ros listened again. He was greeted with soft moans coming from the back of the house. He perked up at the sound. Not seeing any other vehicles, Ros wondered who was there with her.

His hair lifted on the back of his neck, and he took in the scents. Ros was only greeted with her sweet smell, something soft, and something still unknown to him. Smirking at the door, he realized what was going on.

Any gentleman would come back later, but Ros was no gentleman. Bringing his large fist to the door, he gave a booming knock. His heart matched the heaviness of it, beating hard in his chest.

There was a faint curse and scuffle. Ros only grinned wider. He seemed to be smiling a lot lately.

TRICKY MAGIC

11

Ellea

"This can't be happening," Ellea whispered. This past week had brought her nothing but frustration, and this afternoon had seemed to be the perfect time to take care of business when she'd gotten to a particularly spicy scene in her latest read. Billy was out, what were the chances that her rare alone time got interrupted? She had only met the shop owner and that rude asshole at the shop. Who the Hel would be here? She grabbed a pair of bottoms close by, threw on a t-shirt, and rushed for the stairs.

Another persistent knock banged through the house. "I'm fucking coming!" she couldn't help but yell.

A blush crept up her neck.

How embarrassing.

But whoever was on the other side wouldn't know what they'd interrupted.

"Almost, but not quite yet." The voice that called from the other side of the door was gruff and sounded amused. It halted her steps, and she stood there with only one leg in her pants.

Who the fuck is that?

Ellea finished putting on the horrendous pajama bottoms and tried smoothing her ruffled hair before walking to the door with mock confidence. She opened the door, and right before her eyes was a broad chest and large hands holding a box.

As her eyes traveled up, she scowled, sounding like a hissing cat. Even in her frustration, the smirk that greeted her from across the threshold had her chest caving. This was not the look he'd had when they first met, that was one of judgment. Now there was a sparkle in his eye, and even though it pissed her off, she couldn't help but feel turned on. She needed help and she needed him to leave.

"Whatever you are selling, I am not interested." She went to slam the door in his face, but his large boot stopped her.

"This is already paid for. Agatha asked if I could drop it off on my way home," he said through the small opening of the door. Hearing his deep voice again ignited something low in her belly, its husky tone was speaking to all the parts that never got the ending they wanted. He toed the door open fully and smirked at her.

"You didn't have to go out of your way, I could have grabbed it on a different day," Ellea grumbled.

"I think what you meant to say is thank you." He shoved past her with the box. "You're welcome."

Her scowl hardened at his audacity, and she followed after him, reaching to stop him from getting any further into her home.

"I can take that from you," she said as he dodged her.

"It's quite heavy, I wouldn't want you hurting yourself." He threw a cocky grin over his shoulder and slowly placed the box on the kitchen table before looking around the house.

He was dressed like the last time she saw him, in dark jeans and flannel with perfectly ruffled hair. Scowl lines seemed etched between his thick eyebrows, and he ran the tip of his tongue across a sharp canine as he judged his surroundings. Ellea wondered if other shifters were as massive. It wasn't just his size; his menacing presence took up the whole cabin.

She suppressed a shiver that was more horny than scared and reached for the box.

Too heavy my ass.

As she went to move it just to prove a point, he reached to stop her. His hands grazed hers and he jerked upright, yanking his hand back as though shocked. She could have sworn his eyes blazed brighter. He quickly averted his gaze and looked over her shoulder.

"Is that adorable dog of yours around? I should check on her to make sure you aren't torturing her again," he said while pushing past her. She missed having a home that would stop this asshole from getting across the threshold.

"Excuse me, I don't need strangers barging in my house throwing dog-abuse insults." She headed toward the library and placed the box on the desk, and he followed after her, continuously looking around.

The man stopped abruptly, and his nostrils flared as he looked down at her hands.

Shit, I didn't even think to wash them.

He stepped toward her, and she kept her feet planted, chin raised, refusing to back away. He may be tall and huge, but she was feeling anything but intimidated.

"I take animal care very seriously," he stated, and she rolled her eyes at him. He sneered at her before ripping his gaze away. Maybe he was a wolven; with his attitude and sniffing around, it would make sense.

"That doesn't give you an excuse to barge into my home. Thank you for dropping off my order, but I think you should go." She pointed toward the front of the cabin, and he just stared at that damned hand.

"Your home? I thought an older woman and her son owned this place?" he asked.

She was one minute away from using her powers to kick this way-too-tall and way-too-handsome man out, but her powers didn't rise in angst, ready to explode. Instead, they seemed settled, almost humming at the surface.

"That's my nana and uncle, this is our family cabin," she responded instead of kicking him out. She should kick him out.

"Ah, okay," he said, still not moving.

"Look, buddy, this is getting weird. Thanks for coming all the way out here, but you can go now."

"It was no problem, I live across the lake," he said with a point over his shoulder. Through the open windows, she could see a deep green cabin.

Great, I got a weirdo for a neighbor.

He stuck out his hand. "And the name is Rosier, but you can call me Ros."

Ellea looked down at his hand and bolted back a step. She wouldn't shake it, especially after what she'd been doing with her own hand barely five minutes ago. He followed with a step of his own, as though he didn't want her to get further away from him. This had gone on for too long.

"Ros, I doubt you came here to check on my dog. I assure you she is fine. Please. Leave."

"You're right, I came to drop off the box for Agatha, and to see if you were a threat." He took another step toward her, then paused. He took her in, openly checking her from head to toe. Finally, he headed toward the door. "I'm sorry for the interruption; I will let you get back to it."

He left with a smirk over his shoulder, closing the door behind him. There was no way this man was her savior if he pissed her off this much.

Ellea stood in front of the windows overlooking the lake for far too long. She wasn't admiring the view; she was glaring at the green cabin. What did he mean by "a threat?" She was no threat—well, that he knew of. Did he know something?

She started to pace in front of the long windows. Why would he think she was a threat? They'd only met once before now, and both of those encounters had been brief, if a bit unfriendly. That didn't stop her from thinking about how freaking hot he was. She was very used to the pretty guys from the city, but he was rough, and deep, and so, so big.

Her mind began to wander, and she needed to quickly nip those thoughts in the ass. As a distraction, she wandered into the library to check out the box the very big, very sexy man had dropped off.

"Stop it!" she said out loud to the empty cabin.

Rubbing her face, she pulled the box toward her. There were twelve books with titles ranging from the *Newhope Witch Trials, Fourteenth-Century Encounters with Demons,* and what looked like a fairy tale.

"*Leahpha Fairy Tales and Fables* by B.G. Ash, Illustrations by J. Barnacle," Ellea read out loud. Glancing at the clock and realizing it was already the evening, she settled on the fairy tales and headed up to her bedroom. She'd always wondered how their world came by the name *Leahpha*. It was something she'd regularly asked her tutors growing up, but they would wave her off, saying it didn't matter. She sighed while falling into bed, remembering all she was taught and how it wasn't ever enough to deal with her powers and her curiosity.

Ellea fell asleep after reading only ten pages. The book fell from her hand as she woke from an old nightmare. It was one with her parents, and one she hadn't had in a while. There were too many colors, and her mother's yells rang in her head, ordering her to try again and again, to use more power, always more power. When her mother grew tired of her failures, Ellea had been locked in the dark basement with no food, no light, nothing. The pressure of the darkness felt real, and the desperation to be free had her heart racing. Glancing at the clock, she realized she'd only been asleep for an hour. She angrily tossed the blankets aside and headed for the closet.

Ellea tried to remember to take a breath. It had only been a couple weeks, and thoughts of being on the wrong path were already creeping in. How did she know she was making the right decision? She thought about her uncle, her nana, and what the council thought of her recent outburst. It was only her and Billy right now—and an annoying neighbor. Ellea had spent so long in the city, where there was always someone to entertain her or keep her company.

Now she was stuck in a nowhere town with no lovers, a rude neighbor, and an even ruder home. With Billy gone, Ellea was going to hunt down some entertainment. There may be no way to contact the outside world, but there had to be booze somewhere. Preferably tequila, and a lot of it.

Putting on her favorite shirt, jeans, and her flat boots, she grabbed her keys and headed out to hunt down a distraction.

12

Ros

Ros' truck pulled into the local bar at the edge of town. Sam had called him about fifteen minutes ago to let him know he needed to swing by. There were only a few trucks and cars in the lot, not bad for a Thursday night at Lucky Dogs, a mostly wolven bar until some unsuspecting mortal stumbled in while stopping off of the highway.

Sighing, Ros stomped across the worn parking lot and headed toward the old wooden doors. He didn't know what he was getting into, but his dark powers surged with menace. As soon as he crossed the threshold, he spread his feet and let his hands hang loosely at his sides, ready for anything. He glanced to the right and could see the bartender wiping glasses and glaring at the small dance floor. To the left, he found a few guys drunkenly dancing and laughing. Then he realized he may have read this all wrong. He slowly relaxed, but then he saw her.

Her small frame came into view from behind one of the massive wolven men on the dance floor. She was clad in a deep green tee, dark jeans that hugged her ass, and boots that did nothing to help her height, and she was dancing. She looked so free as the wolven spun her and passed her around.

It had only been half a day since his powers had reached for her. Glancing around the dingy dive bar, he found Sam, and wondered why he'd called. Alone in a dark corner, his friend waved him over with a glass in his hand. Ros kept to the shadows to avoid being seen (not that she would notice) and made his way to the small table.

"Sam," Ros said with a nod. "You called?"

"You asked me to keep an eye on your new toy. Well, I didn't think anything was up until the bartender flagged me over earlier." With a nod toward the bar, he continued, "Milly had to cut her off about thirty minutes ago."

"She isn't my toy," Ros growled, beginning to regret asking Sam to keep an eye on her. "When I said keep an eye on her, I didn't mean about her getting rowdy on a Thursday night."

"Well, it's more than that; she drank over three bottles of tequila. That's enough to knock one of the biggest wolven on his hairy ass, and look at her." He gestured to where she was dancing. "Oh, and when she paid, the cash disappeared when she turned around."

One of the wolven had blocked her from the others on the dance floor, placing his greedy hands all over her small body.

"Well, she is a witch." He nodded to the elderly wolven leaving the floor looking like someone had just stolen his girl. "Old Ernest doesn't seem to be happy at the moment."

"This isn't about some young girl provoking a wolven, Rosier. Clearly, magic is burning up inside her; no one drinks that much with the ability to function," Sam retorted.

"That doesn't look like functioning." Ros watched her push away from the handsy wolven and stumble somewhere to the back, probably looking for a bathroom to throw up in.

Sam grunted. "I am being serious, and you may have a point. I don't remember who her father was, but her mom was a seer, I know that much. It shouldn't be hard to figure out what kind of magic she has. But it's been a while since we've had a strong witch in the area." Sam looked thoughtful, and Ros wondered how dangerous she was. She could be dangerous and malevolent, or she could only be a girl, careless with her powers. Sometimes, that was equally as dangerous.

"Regardless of her parents, you're right. Even a strong witch shouldn't be able to burn with that much power." He looked back at Sam, who had a *no shit* look plastered on his face, and patted him on the back. He was going to go find where the little witch had gone. "Thanks for calling, Sam."

Ros faintly heard a *"good luck,"* muttered to him as he headed away from their dark corner. He quickly picked up the smell of blood oranges, tequila, and...

Fuck, he groaned inwardly. A sweaty wolven scent was mixing with hers. He continued to follow the trail, heading to the back of the bar, and heard words being exchanged as he came to the back door.

"Don't be a tease, we were having fun," a gruff voice said.

"I was having fun, and you were being grabby." Grunts punctuated her words, conjuring up an image of her small body trying to push away the intimidating wolven.

Ros crept through the door and snuck into the shadows of the back alley that ran behind the bar. He didn't like what he saw, but then a smile spread across the witch's face. Why was she smiling at him if he had his predatory hands all over her? She couldn't be into him...

"That's right, sweetheart. I knew you were playing hard to get," he replied, his hands creeping under her shirt.

"No, I remembered, that I'm stronger than you and don't need to take your creeper crap," she said. But she hesitated, his hands still groping her, as if trying to find the strength she spoke of. She shoved him away, but it only seemed to make him mad. He slammed her against the wall.

"Now play nice, and let's have a good time." His lips were too close to her neck. Ros was about to step in when she smiled wider.

"No means no. I think you need to learn to keep your hands to yourself." She shoved him for a moment longer, but it didn't budge him. It seemed she had finally given up, her hands falling back to her sides as she grimaced and turned away from his assaulting lips. She closed her eyes and took a breath, then the man began screaming.

She hadn't done anything that Ros could see, but the six-foot-tall wolven fell to his knees, screaming at his perfectly normal hands. Ros didn't understand. Nothing was wrong.

"My hands!" he screamed.

"Learn to keep them to yourself, and maybe you will get them back." With one final distasteful look, she stumbled down the alley toward the front of the bar.

Ros stood there and watched for a moment as the man's screams seemed to flicker, as though what he was seeing didn't seem real. He got closer to investigate more.

"What's going on?" he asked the man still on his knees. He was panting now, but seemed to be settling. Then he looked up at Ros, and his frightened expression turned to one of anger.

"I'm going to kill that bitch. Putting things in my head..." He tried to stand, but Ros put a firm hand on his shoulder.

"Calm down. What did you see?" he asked.

"Calm down? My hands were ripped off and gone, blood squirting everywhere," he said through clenched teeth. "I will show that bitch who she's messing with."

He tried to get up again, but Ros held firm and grabbed his hands with his free one.

"That's a strange trick," he said while peering down with mock interest, examining the perfectly fine (gross, but fine) hands.

"She is going to learn a lesson," he said to Ros. Ros only smirked down at him.

"Now, now…I don't think *you've* learned *your* lesson," he said calmly. The man only blinked up at him, as if Ros should understand that the girl needed to pay. Ros snarled in the man's face as he gripped his hands hard. The sound of crunching rang through the alley. Flames lit up the darkness, then the wolven was screaming again, but this time it was real. Ros had crushed the man's hands and then lit them on fire. No predatory man deserved to continue to breathe in this realm. If the witch wasn't strong, if he hadn't been there…he couldn't think about it. Ros grabbed him by the face, prying his mouth open, and terror-filled eyes looked up at him. He only smiled and sent his shadows down the throat of the man who had to learn his own lessons. He clawed at Ros' relentless grip as his screams turned into gags. It didn't matter; he would be very dead in moments.

The flames that still coated his hands didn't hurt Ros, they only caressed the skin of their wielder, ready to do any deed he asked of them. A darkness whispered over Ros' shoulder as the man before him slowly gave up the fight. He released his flames to quickly burn up the dead asshole. In moments, a pile of ash scattered across the alley. Ros left it behind, heading in the direction of the witch. He grumbled, "See you in Hel, you piece of shit."

The witch was still on the property, stumbling around with her phone and car keys in the air.

Is she seriously trying to get a cell signal?

"You know there is no service in this town," Ros called out to her. She only turned and glared at him over his shoulder.

"This fucking town and its fucking dense forest... I am trying to call a cab," she mumbled.

"There are also no cabs in this town." He got closer, and she whirled on him with a spark in her eyes, as if this was all his fault. He held his hands up. "Look, I haven't had any drinks tonight, and I'm heading back to our street. I can give you a ride."

Not that he wanted to give her a ride—the thought of being in close quarters made his skin feel tight—but she couldn't be left alone. He didn't trust that some of the wolven in the bar wouldn't find out what had happened and blame her for it. She tried her phone one more time before she hung her head.

"Fine," she said with a sigh. It also seemed like the last thing she wanted to do.

Ros gestured toward his truck, and she gave him an eye roll that he was learning was a signature gesture.

"Yeah, princess, I'm a cliché," he replied and opened the passenger door for her. She bared her teeth at him and his truck, then offered him her keys.

"I would rather take mine home, seems safer than that thing."

Ros glared at her but took the keys; he didn't want to argue, and he wanted to get rid of her as quickly as possible. He opened the passenger door and held out his hand to steady her. She swatted it away and slid in pretty easy for the amount of alcohol she'd had. He breathed in the night air deeply, held it, and then blew it out. Powers churned under his skin, and he told them to calm themselves.

It's only a drive home.

With one last pause and a request to the universe, he opened the driver-side door and got in. Pain instantly greeted him as the steering wheel stabbed him in the chest and his knees slammed into the dashboard.

"Fucking Hel," Ros cursed. "How the fuck do you drive like this?"

She only gave him a bored look as she watched him try and adjust the seat. He reached for any lever he could find, but buttons greeted him instead—it was a new SUV and fully electric. The seat whirred as it slowly freed Ros from the confines of the dashboard.

Ros glared back at her and realized she wasn't buckled in. He reached over and grabbed the seatbelt, trying his best not to touch her, but as his knuckles grazed the skin under her collarbone, the air quickly became thick with electricity. The buckle snapped in place, and his powers began to burn under his skin again. His magic and dick were at odds with each other, and he wondered what she was feeling as she stared straight ahead, eyes wide, her hands on her knees as if she was afraid to move. He took in her profile: a small nose, pouty lips, and freckles that spread across her cheek. How could someone so beautiful have his powers feeling threatened? Chiding himself, he remembered that there were plenty of beautiful and threatening creatures. Maybe he didn't want to believe this one was the evil kind.

She slowly turned toward him, and as their eyes met, her breathing became audible. Glancing down at her lap, thoughts of what he'd interrupted began to creep into his mind. She pressed her thighs together under his hard gaze, and it made him wonder if she'd gone back to the bedroom after he'd left. What would it be like to see her hand disappear under the covers? Did she even use covers? Would she just lay there on full display with no need to hide as she touched herself? He imagined how her hand would travel over her stomach and down her center, parting herself and gathering up the wetness there.

Ros turned the key aggressively, trying to rid himself of the dirty thoughts plaguing him, and the SUV rattled in response. The loud noise broke him out of his vision and hid the low growl that came from somewhere deep inside himself, a place he'd forgotten about. Turning the key again, it started, and he didn't give it time to warm up as he quickly put it in reverse, desperate to get home.

Without looking, he could feel her trying to gather herself. Her head was turned toward the window and he could hear her steadying her breathing.

They arrived on their street within ten minutes without one word uttered. No music, no other looks, only crackling hot energy. Ros was desperate to put distance between them—or not put distance between them. It was so frustrating. The attraction was there, but he didn't know what she was up to. He didn't even know her name.

Her driveway loomed ahead of them, and Ros let out a breath.

We survived.

As Ros pulled up in front of her door, she got out without even waiting for him to put it in park. He turned the SUV off and stormed after her; he wouldn't allow her to be so rude. Ros waited for her to get to the front door. She groaned and turned, scowling as she took three bratty steps toward him. She reached for the keys, but he yanked them out of reach—which was easy with how fucking short she was. She made some sort of screeching bird sound and jumped for them.

"Maybe if you learned some manners, princess, things wouldn't be so hard." He chuckled at her.

"Don't call me that!" She reached for the keys again. He lowered them and let her grasp them in her small hand. Before letting go, he hunched down to her height and smirked in her face.

"I can call you whatever I want. If you need help next time, you know where to find me. And I don't mean for a ride home."

He winked at her and let go of the keys, turning his back without another word.

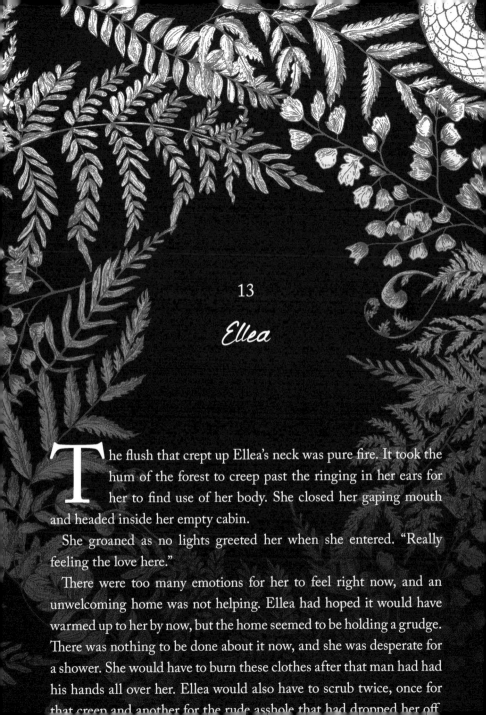

13

Ellea

The flush that crept up Ellea's neck was pure fire. It took the hum of the forest to creep past the ringing in her ears for her to find use of her body. She closed her gaping mouth and headed inside her empty cabin.

She groaned as no lights greeted her when she entered. "Really feeling the love here."

There were too many emotions for her to feel right now, and an unwelcoming home was not helping. Ellea had hoped it would have warmed up to her by now, but the home seemed to be holding a grudge. There was nothing to be done about it now, and she was desperate for a shower. She would have to burn these clothes after that man had had his hands all over her. Ellea would also have to scrub twice, once for that creep and another for the rude asshole that had dropped her off

Whatever had happened during that short drive was beyond anything she had ever felt before, but she couldn't let him get under her skin. Her body tingled with so much energy and her magic was so curious, so desperate to play.

"Fucking traitor."

Ellea leaned against the shower wall, letting the hot stream drown out her anxiety and restlessness. Most people would be more bothered by the assault in a dark alley, but she was more upset at how her body and powers had reacted to *him*—Ros, his name was Ros.

Things were so much easier in Halifax. She worked, went home, hung out with the boys, watched TV with Billy, went to bed, and then did it all over again. Now she didn't know which way was up and why she was getting turned on by some rude forest brute.

Ellea ignored the towel on her way to the bedroom, letting the air cool her wet skin as she headed toward the window. Taking in the moon hanging over the lake, she sighed. Billy was still gone, and she knew sleep would not come easy—why would it? She could count the number of times she had slept without her familiar on her hand. Taking a deep breath, she placed her forehead on the glass. She noticed a moonlit path heading around the lake. Maybe a walk would do the trick. Her body was still humming with energy, and laying in bed would be pointless. Grabbing a clean pair of yoga pants, ignoring a bra, and grabbing her favorite gray sweater, she headed for the back door.

Ellea had never realized that there was such a clear path along the lake. After a short walk, the path forked to the forest, and it was the easy choice to head deeper in instead of back toward the lake. The sounds of the night creatures welcomed her, drowning out the thoughts roaring in her head. Ellea felt her powers slowly quiet with each deliberate breath of fresh forest air.

Ellea's whole body relaxed just in time for a paranoid shiver to run down her spine.

She wasn't alone.

She halted and slid her left foot behind her to avoid the attacker's grab at her shoulder. Her already cocked fist met a thick chest. A whoosh of a grunt came from the attacker—a man. She created distance between them and readied her stance again.

"Ow, that was my sternum, princess," Ros said while rubbing at his chest.

"Stop calling me that. And maybe you shouldn't sneak up behind people walking in the woods." She despised the day her family had decided to build on this land. Would she ever rid herself of him?

"I have nothing else to call you since you still haven't told me your name." He took a step toward her, and Ellea took an equal step back. "Really, you think I am going to attack you? You are the one on my property."

"I didn't see any 'keep out, a crazy man lives here' signs," Ellea said with a smirk.

"Are you here to take me up on my offer? So soon?" he said with a mock bow. "I feel honored."

She was tired of his mouth, and it had been too long since she'd let off some steam. Her magic reveled in the idea, and she didn't have the strength to tell it no.

Or do I want to let go?

Ignoring the thought, she acted fast, pivoting once and delivering a front kick to the side of his bowed head. He was so tall, and this was the only chance he would be at her height. Before her boot landed the blow to his temple, he grabbed her by the ankle and held her there. Slowly lifting his head, he winked and then pulled. She was on the ground in an instant.

"Bastard," she spat at him. She quickly got to her feet, not about to let him think he'd won.

"Is this how you witches flirt? It has been a while, but I'm up for the challenge," Ros said with a grin, readying his own stance.

She didn't need to waste her time on an asshat of a brute who wanted to toy with her. "No thanks, I would rather flirt with…" She couldn't think of anything, so she turned and walked away, with her chin lifted, she called. "Anyone but you."

"You should never turn your back on someone. No wonder you got caught off guard in that alleyway." His insult hit her, and she halted.

How did he know about that?

He must have been following her. That was enough of a reason for her to fully unleash her magic on him. Ellea felt raw power flow from her chest to her hands. She could feel the energy around her as the ground began to vibrate. Slowly looking over her shoulder, she took him in completely. He was tall and big, but she was powerful. Ellea raised her hand, and as she spoke, she barely recognized her own voice.

"Someone should teach you a lesson." She closed her hand, and the two trees by Ros exploded. It was the perfect distraction.

With three long strides, she was in front of him. He attempted to grab her, but she was quicker. Ellea twisted his arm, and he bent over in pain. Using that leverage, she scissor-kicked her legs in the air, wrapping them around his head. With a loud thud, he hit the ground, groaning with the impact.

"Using magic? What a cheater," he said, a hint of pain creeping into his voice.

"I don't need magic to take you. Why don't you shift and we can make this a real fight?" She bent his arm further away from his body, but instead of groaning again, he laughed.

"Shift?" His laughter died down, and she felt his chest heave in a few steady and deep breaths—then she was blind.

The darkness was suffocating. Ros slipped from her grasp, and she shuffled back on her hands and knees. Grasping at the forest floor, she tried to calm her racing heart.

"What is this? Wolven shouldn't have magic," she yelled at him, unable to hide the panic in her voice. As quickly as she'd been blinded, she could see again.

"You think I am a wolven?" He doubled over with laughter and almost ended up on the forest floor again.

Her skin prickled at his husky laugh, but she quickly stood, rallying her magic to try and stop another attack.

"What was I supposed to think? I know nothing about you," she said. His laugh made her angry—well, mostly angry. The richness of the laugh itself was doing something completely different to her.

Ros straightened and the laughter was gone, replaced with a heated look. "Can a wolven do this?"

Shadows began to gather around her and him without even a wave of his hand. He hadn't blinded her earlier; this was shadow magic. Ellea lifted her chin and smiled at him.

"You want to play, big man? Let's play." Her powers begged for more. They caressed her skin and spoke sweetness in her ears. Ellea would let them have a little more freedom for this. An outright attack on her? Yes, they would get to play tonight.

She opened her arms and welcomed the shadows, letting them dance around her body like a lover would. He threw more at her, but he would have to try harder than that to drown her in them. He did, summoning more of them around her...but he missed the illusion.

Ellea was behind him and Ros was fully focused on the other Ellea, the ghost and mirrors version who was now smiling sweetly as the shadows slithered across her face. It was amazing how easy it seemed to cast this illusion. Her powers had never come this naturally. Ellea gasped as he turned on her. She had waited too long to attack.

Ros swiped out a booted foot that left Ellea on the ground below him. She kicked back, bringing him on the ground right next to her, then she shifted and threw her left arm down, striking him in the face. With her right, she punched him in the ribs, allowing her magic to zap him in the process. He took each blow without so much as a curse.

Ros moved quickly for such a large man. He had her pinned with one arm above her head and the other at her side. Ellea snuck her knees up and used her pinned arms as leverage to press him off of her with her legs.

This was nothing like sparring with her uncle, this was rough and raw. She was thankful for her training as she maneuvered to have Ros under her. Straddling his chest, she punched him square in the jaw. He let out a low laugh in response. Ellea was over it, and her powers screamed to end it. Wrapping her hands around his throat, she let her magic come to the surface. Burning his skin with electricity, she brought her face close to him and shouted, "Enough!"

Ros grabbed her wrists. But instead of freeing himself, he held her there and raised his chin, giving her more leverage to hold tighter. As she looked into his eyes, she saw them change, and realized he was no stranger to pain. He wasn't scared or calculating, there was heat in his hazel eyes. As he took the deepest breath allowed, he tightened his grip on her.

Is he into this?

Her powers sang at the contact, the inevitability of it all. Ros must have felt it too. His eyes smoldered. He parted his lips, and words escaped out, "Do it."

Resting his chin on her hands, he bared his teeth at her. That single look had her body and powers fighting and burning. She wanted to throttle him or let him fuck her against a tree—maybe both at the same time. Things were so upside down, all she could do was release his throat and stare at him as she sat there, still straddling his chest. He was massive underneath her, and his heavy breaths moved her up and down.

A low sound came from him and his mouth quirked into a smirk.

"I have to say, I like this view," he said with a groan. As the words registered in her head, his hands slipped up her thighs.

Ellea cocked her fist and punched him square in the jaw—right where a bruise was already forming from the other punch. He slowly turned his head back to her and gave her a full smile. His hands heated through her leggings as he gripped her tighter. In an instant, the hard forest floor slammed into her back, and Ros was above her.

"Oh, I think I like this view too," he said, low and guttural. His face was slowly getting closer to hers.

Did she want this? No, how could she? The tingles she was feeling had nothing to do with him.

Think, Ellea!

Her body unfroze, and she kneed him hard in the balls. He roared and crumbled into a ball next to her. She scrambled away quickly and headed straight for her cabin.

14

Ros

Freckles danced in front of his eyes. They ran delicately along the nose and cheeks of a beautiful face framed with long hair. Ros could feel it tickling his skin, and he wanted to reach out his hand to grip it and pull her mouth to his. But first, he wanted to run his fingers along those freckles, that skin that heated under his touch. He finally reached out his hand, and it felt like nothing… nothing but air.

Waking with a groan, he rolled over to cover his face and pressed his erection into the mattress, trying to rid himself of it yet again. It had been three days since the encounter in the woods, and he had dreamt of her every night. *Her.* The witch. He still didn't know her name.

Who knew letting a witch try and beat the shit out of you would be so motivating? He'd spent every waking hour trying to distract himself. The town had enough wood to last through the year with the amount of trees he'd chopped. His cabin now had new floors and new built-in shelves. The new shelves had led him to reorganizing his library of books and all the items that didn't have a home. He'd also found his love for running again, the laps around the lakes no longer enough to tire him out.

Ros continued to lie there with his face smothered in his pillow, wondering what he could do today. Nothing came to mind. He would have to call Weylyn again. He'd had a blast killing the rogue vampire clan up north, taking his time and making sure they suffered for their crimes. The look of fear on a monster's face as he ripped out their throat with his bare hands was so very satisfying.

No matter how much he did, whatever he killed, his dreams were filled with her. Ros could still feel the tendrils of muscle as he gripped her thick thighs. He could still see the way her eyes had raged at him, then heated in an instant. All the power in her soft hands as she wrapped them around his throat, her magic sparking just below the surface… His cock pressed harder into the mattress, and that was his cue for a very cold shower. He should kill her, end his suffering and stop something bad from happening.

He wasn't going to kill her.

Ros rolled over, cursing his confusing emotions, and got out of bed. As he headed toward the bathroom to shower, Garm appeared. As the hound stepped out of the shadows, he was eye level with Ros' extremely hard and angry erection.

Cheese and rice, put that thing away! What the Hel, boy? the hound yelled in Ros' head. He quickly turned and trotted toward anywhere that wouldn't have a boner in his face.

"Sorry, mutt! Just a little morning wood," he said to his familiar's back.

That thing is not little, and that is way more than morning wood. Get your shit together, Garm shouted.

Ros shook his head and got ready to stand under the cold jet of water, dispelling any thoughts of the way he loved the aggression from that witch. He would have to talk with Garm and figure out what type of powers she possessed. It had been too long since he'd witnessed that kind of strength from someone so small.

After thirty minutes of cold water, thinking about the way a dybbuk demon smelled, Garm in a bikini, Sam in a bikini, and a number of other things, his cock was only slightly hard, and he was ready for the day.

Ros headed straight for the library in search of a book and passed Garm, who was sunning by the large windows, looking exhausted.

What are you looking for? he asked, lifting his head and watching Ros skim his vast collection of new and old books.

"I had an interesting encounter with our neighbor the other night. There is a book that may have a reference to the type of magic she used," Ros replied.

Interesting encounter? Did she use some special magic in the bedroom? Garm asked, sounding almost bored, and laid his head back down on the pillow he was using.

"No, she kicked my ass and used an illusion to distract me," he said, still looking for the small leather-bound book.

She seriously didn't kick your ass. Did she? Garm challenged.

"I mean, yes and no. I let her kick my ass." This enticed the hound enough to leave one of his favorite spots. He got up and walked over to where Ros was looking at the bottom shelves of his many bookcases. Finally, his fingers found it. The book was in the old language and about two hundred years old. "Found it."

That explains the angry boner this morning, Garm said with a deep chuckle. *How long has it been since a female caught your eye?*

"I don't even remember, but her magic..." Ros said while a smile formed on his lips. "The illusion wasn't a spell. I didn't see her conjure it or cast anything. It was simply there, like my shadows. I didn't even realize it until I smelled the actual witch behind me."

Hel, are you going to make it? What are you thinking about right now? Garm asked.

"Citrus, something soft, and how hard she kicked me in the balls." His smile grew wider.

Gross. I bet you deserved it. Do you want me to keep an eye on her while you get your head right? You are creeping me out more than usual, the hound said, looking over Ros' face with mock concern.

"No, I got this. I'm not done with her yet." He flipped through the book, mumbling "illusion" over and over under his breath as he searched for the reference. "Here it is. The deceiver, a witch who creates to meld past and present, to hide, allude, and render destruction. Last known appearance: 1689, Newhope."

We are way past 1689, the hound pointed out.

"I know. There has to be other references," he said while looking up at his books, his brows scrunching in confusion. "I'll head to Ag's later today and see if she can find something."

I don't remember any deceiver witches. What did her power feel like?

If Garm didn't know about deceiver witches, how could Ros hope to learn anything about them? Garm was as old as time; he'd come into the world when the Gods still walked the earth. If he didn't remember them, how could anyone? Contacting anyone in his family about Ellea was out of the question. Garm nudged him, and Ros remembered he had asked a question.

"Fucking strong, and angry. It pulled at my powers. I could feel it under her skin, and the illusion seemed to have a mind of its own. It's some tricky magic." He closed his eyes to let the vision wash over him. A smile crept onto his face. "She was physically strong too. You should have seen the way she punched me."

His smile quickly turned to a frown as he felt his pants getting tighter at the mere thought of her. The hound moved away from him, disgusted.

You males are run by your dicks and small brains. It's disturbing. Turning his back on Ros, he headed back to his sunning spot.

He looked down at his pants and actually agreed with the hound.

"My dick and small brain are going for a swim. I'm just as annoyed as you are," he said, leaving the book on the desk as he headed out the door.

Leaving his clothes behind, he headed toward the lake. A new thought formed in his *small brain,* and he smiled. Maybe the witch was home and could also be disturbed by him. Might as well have some fun while he figured out what to do with her.

15

Ellea

Ellea couldn't get comfortable. It had nothing to do with the couch or the heavy book in her hands. It had everything to do with what had happened three nights ago.

Her powers were still running on an all-time high. The dreams she had were erratic and filled with a strong body and hazel eyes. No one in their right mind would be okay with what had happened, but she would be lying to herself if she said she didn't want it to happen again. Ellea had never felt so strong, putting years of training into a fight like that. And it was over nothing. They'd both overreacted, but it was fun—and hot.

Dammit.

She was going crazy. She brought the book up and hit herself in the forehead.

"Stupid, stupid, stupid." She groaned, then took a deep breath.

Trying yet another spot on the couch and grabbing a pillow, Ellea settled in to finally finish her book, a thick novel filled with dragons, sex, and a fallen kingdom. She could feel the couch sinking into just the right spot, so she turned to her last page. She'd read two sentences before the sound of something dripping stole her attention. Annoyed, she tried to ignore it and keep reading, but it was persistent, grating on her last nerve.

"Billy! Is that you?"

Heavy breathing answered her.

"Billy?" she tried again. "I know it's you. What are you doing?"

Finally getting up from the only comfortable spot she'd found in the past three days, Ellea headed toward the sound of her familiar breathing.

As she came around the corner, she found Billy standing on her two back legs. Her front legs were pressed against the floor-to-ceiling window, and a wet smacking noise escaped her mouth as she licked her own drool off her mouth and began panting again.

"What the Hel are you looking at?" Ellea asked the beast that was almost as tall as her at this angle.

One of the finest asses I have seen in a very long time, she answered, licking more drool off of her lips.

Ellea looked through the window, following the Familiar's gaze. Sure as shit, a butt-ass naked man was walking down the dock across their lake. It was far away, but not too far to see the muscles of his legs leading up to his nice ass. The muscles along his back rippled as he wiped his wet hair away from his face. As if he could feel their eyes on him, he looked back over his shoulder—and smirked. Ellea yelped and backed away from the glass so fast she fell on her butt. "Fucking asshole," she said.

Oh my Gods! It's the hunk from the store! Billy screeched. She didn't move away from the window. "His name is Rosier," Ellea said, standing and rubbing her sore butt cheek.

YOU KNOW HIS NAME? When did this happen? she yelled into Ellea's head. Her nose was still pressed to the glass as Ellea walked back to the window. She didn't get *too* close, hoping he couldn't see her. She was about to explain what had happened when Ros' door opened, and a giant black wolf trotted out.

Ellea whistled at the sight. It was beautiful and huge, but a growl was coming from her familiar. She glanced over as Billy's nails began to grow and her mouth formed a snarl.

That son of a bitch! Billy pushed off the glass and headed for the back door. It opened on her command, and she bolted. "Shit. Billy, wait!" Ellea yelled, running after her. "What's going on?"

Billy didn't answer, and she was fast, so fast. She bounded around the lake at a ridiculous speed; it only took minutes to cover the distance. Ellea kept running as Billy reached the green cabin, and she roared so loud that the surrounding trees shook. Ellea picked up the pace, but she had no idea what she would do when she got there.

Ros and the wolf had retreated into the cabin in the time it had taken Billy to run there. Now the back door creaked open, and the wolf poked its head out. It winced at the sight of Billy. Slowly, it walked out, and Ros was close behind, no longer naked, but only wearing a pair of dark jeans. Ellea's eyes roved from his wet hair, down his chest, and stopped at the button that was not done on the dark denim.

Water droplets were still streaming down his defined abs, traveling toward that dusting of hair poking out of his undone jeans. She suppressed a groan as a painful flutter attacked her heart and stomach.

Hey, Billy. Looking good, sweetness. How long has it been? came a male-sounding voice in Ellea's head, pulling her from her blatant staring.

She paused and shook her head. Looking up at Ros, she realized it wasn't him, but the wolf. She shouldn't be able to hear him.

All I get is a 'Hey' after how long? Five hundred years? Billy growled out.

Six hundred and fifty-two years, actually, the wolf said.

Ellea looked up at Ros, who was staring directly at her. Her mouth went dry at the intensity of his stare. If he could hear their conversation, he wasn't showing it.

You're keeping pretty good track for a mutt that left me high and dry. Billy's growling was feral as she got close to her full beast form.

Billy, sweetness, you know how it is. How it was, he responded with such a quiet tone. He was being submissive, and Billy wasn't having any of it. She snarled and snapped her enlarging canines at him.

"Billy, stop," Ellea tried quietly. Ros just stood there, still staring at her.

She glared at him. "Are you going to help at all?"

He only put his hands up.

Yeah, no help. Typical.

Garm, you have three seconds to get out of my sight, or I'm going to rip off your favorite part. Billy snarled and moved closer to him, circling and moving him away from Ros. *Never mind, I am going to do it anyway.* She pounced, just missing him as she snapped at the air where his tail had been.

The wolf, Garm, booked it toward the treeline, Billy on his heels. Within a minute, trees started snapping. The snarling was deafening. Birds flew and more trees snapped, and Ellea just stood there, not knowing what to do.

"They'll be fine," a deep voice came from right behind her. She turned and stepped back, not trusting herself with Ros this close to her—especially this close, shirtless, and still wet.

"What is he?" Ellea asked quietly, unsure of what else to say.

They hadn't seen each other since she'd left him in the woods with bruised balls.

"A hound who can take care of himself. I doubt he would hurt her." He searched her face and smirked. "If she is anything like you, I worry for him more than her."

Ellea only rolled her eyes at his remark. He was probably right, but she couldn't help but look back at the woods and worry. Billy had only acted like this a few times.

Ellea turned back to Ros.

"And what are you?" she asked with her chin raised.

"We all have our own secrets," he said with a sinister smile and walked away from her.

She grabbed him by the arm to stop him. There was a giant gash at the top of his back, as if something had gone for his neck and missed.

"What happened? That wasn't from me, was it?" Ellea asked, attempting to hide her emotion. She didn't even know what she was feeling right now.

Ros looked down to where her hand gripped him.

"No, princess, you didn't do that." He winked at her. "You aren't the only one I like to play with."

She shouldn't care. They only shared a lake and a few mean words, so there was zero reason for this heavy feeling in her stomach. He was basically a stranger, but she felt...something at seeing him wounded. Even if she'd caused him pain the other night, this felt different. She would have to learn to get her powers and lady parts under control. He was also keeping secrets about his magic. She hadn't met any other witches with power like his, or one his size. Clearly, she had to get out more.

Gods, he was frustrating.

Why did she even care where and how he'd gotten hurt? Why did she have the sudden urge to find out more?

"You should let me know who did that. I can pay them a visit and make sure they don't miss next time," Ellea shouted at him as he continued to walk away. Her legs followed after him, and she didn't know why they felt they needed to do that.

"I'm sure you really mean that," he retorted, not bothering to stop.

"No, but I'm curious," she said, forcing her feet to stop moving.

"Are you worried about me?" He turned and placed his hand on his chest. A stupid smile spread across his lips. "Oh, you are."

"I wouldn't call it worried, more concerned. With that pitiful performance the other night, you may want to sharpen up your skills." Ellea avoided the urge to look below his chin.

"Pitiful?" A low growl emanated from him, and it had her knees wobbling.

"Yes, I kicked your ass!" she snapped, recovering and hiding that the few words exchanged were making her crumble.

"You kicked my ass? Princess, that was foreplay. Next time, stick around and see how fun it can get."

She stood there, speechless. Ros took a few strides with those powerful legs, and she remembered how they'd looked striding down the dock earlier, how he was naked and knew she was watching him.

He was in front of her in an instant and leaned down to her, his breath tickling her ear. "I let you kick my ass. I would have done anything just to have your hands on me, hurting me, caressing me. You could have done whatever you wanted, and I would have thanked you for it."

The roaring in her ears was unbearable as her power raged and her face blazed with fire. His words rang in her head with every desperate step to her cabin. Only a few more minutes and she would be inside and she could figure out how to get control of her magic.

He had left her there and walked into his cabin without another word. The crackling came before the roaring as she'd stood motionless, and when she'd looked down at her hands, her powers were visible. Sparking currents of magic moved around her knuckles and fingers like live electricity. She'd balled her hands into fists and ran.

Now, she stood in front of her back door—it was locked. Quickly running to the front, she found herself still unable to get in. The home had closed all the curtains as if to say, *no, come back when you figure your shit out.* The roaring became louder as she panicked.

The greenhouse.

She ran to the large glass structure and thankfully was let inside. Closing the door, she leaned against it, panting, and covered her ears. She crumpled to the floor, and a wave of fear washed over her. Her parents, her uncle, every magical mistake she'd made flashed before her eyes as she took short, erratic breaths. Minutes passed, and the only change was that Ros consumed her thoughts—how it felt to be so close to him, remembering the night in the woods. It had her magic screaming to be set free. It was begging again to destroy, to play, to be liberated. This was all his fault; he made her feel so many things, and she didn't know how to deal with it. Coming here was supposed to be an escape, a way to figure her shit out.

You can do this.

Ellea reached for the flowerbed to pull herself up off of the floor.

I will get through this.

As her hand touched the weathered wood, it exploded into a thousand pieces, bouncing off the glass walls and coming back at her. She reached her hands out to try and shield herself, but more things exploded in the process. The ringing in her ears was replaced with the splintering of wood and the impact of it on the structure around her. Wood and old dirt rained down and exploded around her, and it felt as though it would never end. A banging came from outside, and Ellea's heart raced even quicker as she pictured Ros coming through that door.

She didn't trust how she or her magic would respond. Could handle his brutish attitude? What did he want with her? Her thoughts stopped as an unfamiliar face poked around the greenhouse door. He was pale with dark eyes that matched his inky black hair.

"I'm sorry, I was up the hill and heard a commotion, and…" His eyes went wide. "Duck!"

Ellea ducked, and the stranger swung out a hand. Everything around her went silent. She braved a look over her shoulder from where she lay on the ground to see wood and dirt frozen around her. With another swipe of his hand, it all fell down around her as though she were in a bubble.

"May I ask what you were trying to accomplish here?"

Ellea eyed the stranger warily. Who was he? Where had he come from, and why had he felt the need to barge in?

"Yes, but I am not going to answer," she said, crossing her arms. "Thank you for the help, but I don't know you, and I am a little concerned as to why you are on my property."

His smile only grew. He didn't look the least bit uncomfortable. "I was touring the house up the hill. When I was walking the property to check it out, I heard whatever you were trying to do in here, and I was concerned." He reached out a hand. "My name is Elias."

Ellea looked at his outstretched hand. His long fingers were pale and delicate. He wasn't a large guy, but still taller than her. She reached out her own and took it.

"I'm Ellea," she said and hid the shiver that came when she touched his cold skin. It was the end of August and still warm during the day. She noticed his outfit: black slacks, a long sleeve button-down, also in black, and shiny black shoes. "How did you keep those clean walking over here?"

"I'll tell you one of my secrets if you tell me one of yours."

"Your shoes and my secrets are not on the same level," Ellea said with a cock of her head. She was growing suspicious of him. "It doesn't seem like an even trade."

"Oh, but you are wrong there," he said, sweeping his hands down at his shoes. "I use a special kind of magic for many aspects of my life."

"And what kind of magic is that?"

"You tell me first," he said. "I think you owe that much since I helped you."

"Look, *Elias,* I didn't ask you to help. I do appreciate it, but I don't owe you jack shit," she said with a raised chin. "I don't have to tell you anything, and neither do you."

"Fine. You keep your secrets, and I will keep mine," he said with a bow of his head. "I will tell you this for free: Whatever you were doing, it wasn't good. I have experience with power growing restless and taking control like that."

How could he hit it directly on the nose?

"I had everything under control." Her words came out quickly. "I would have reined it in eventually."

"Right," he said, clearly not buying it. "Look, I will be in the area for a bit looking at properties. It would be my pleasure to help you in any way I can; it's one of my specialties."

"Thanks for the offer, and thanks again for swooping in and helping," she said sarcastically. "Let me walk you out."

Ellea directed him toward the open door. He went out ahead of her, and as they stood outside, he gave her a bow and headed toward the treeline. He paused and turned to her, a small smile on his face.

"Don't be afraid to ask for help, Ellea. It was a pleasure seeing you again." He turned back to the woods and headed on his way.

TRICKY MAGIC

16

Ros

Ros had woken up over an hour ago after another night of dreaming about the witch. This type of frustration was new. She was something he didn't trust, but that wasn't stopping him from wanting to bury his cock inside her or push her buttons. Being constantly torn between figuring her out, pissing her off, and wanting to get into her pants was exhausting. Her smell also clung to his nose, even in the shower. "Fuck," Ros barked, the sound vibrating through the bathroom.

The constant hard-on was equally exhausting, and he was getting reminders of all the times he'd had to take himself in his own hand— like now. The shower had been meant to rid himself of the pain between his legs; instead, he leaned against the wall as the scalding water beat on his back.

The tile was cold and damp under his hand as he leaned against the wall. His other hand fisted his heated skin, stroking the hard length. Rough pumps sloshed with soap and water. The sound of it played in time with the images of that annoying little witch that had his powers roaring to fight or fuck—or both. He thought about her small hand on him when he'd tried leaving her outside of his cabin. What would that hand look like in place of his, stroking him, toying with him like he knew she would? He looked down as the head of his cock continued to disappear in and out of his fist, wishing it was hers, wishing she was on her knees in front of him with those gray eyes staring at him. He wanted her to look at him the same way she'd looked up at him yesterday, her eyes dilated as he leaned close to her. He recalled the sound of her heart quickening as he whispered in her ear, and the smell of her—Hel, that soft smell reminded him of roses. Roses that were the same shade as her flushed skin, a shade that made him think about that perfect ass, bare and bent over his lap. He groaned as his balls began to draw up tight into him.

Would she whimper and beg for more, or fight, like she seemed to love to do? Would she give in and let him worship her after she took her punishment like a good little witch? A tingle began to crawl up his thighs as he stroked harder and wondered through all the possibilities.

"Fuck..." he said, low and guttural.

His thighs tensed as his strokes became jerky and quick. His orgasm pooled low in his stomach, and with one, two, three hard and final strokes, ribbons of his cum splattered on the wall before him. He leaned his head against the cool tile, his breaths heavy and hard. He groaned as he glared down at his cock one last time, still hard.

Ros rinsed off and crawled back into bed without bothering to dry off. Assuming the position he'd woken up in—angrily staring at his ceiling—he wondered what could be done with all of this.

Garm had never come back after his run in with Billy yesterday. If Ros wasn't so consumed by the small and angry woman, he may have been worried.

Speak of the devil...

The hound's large ears must have been ringing. His giant paws padded down the hall louder than usual.

Are you decent, Rosier? I would like to keep both my eyes, came a gruff voice.

"I'm in bed and all the bits are covered, Garm of Hounds," he said. "And since when are we using our given names?"

Since you started acting like a child, Garm said as he opened the door with one of his own shadows.

"I was worried that dog actually got the better of you," Ros said, sitting up and making sure he was still covered by a blanket. Garm had seen him naked since he was a babe, but one pissed off supernatural was enough.

How dare you? he said, coming to lay in the bed by Ros and taking up the full length of the large bed.

"Well, you are old as dirt." He reached out a hand to pet the hound that was still as jet black as the day he first laid eyes on him. He smiled at the memory.

That dog is a familiar, and one of the originals, he said, sounding very proud.

"I figured she was a familiar; I didn't realize she was an old lady. That poor thing is stuck to that witch's side."

Watch your mouth, boy. And that witch's name is Ellea, Garm scolded.

Ros straightened. "Ellea?" he whispered like he couldn't believe it.

Yes. Are you going deaf, old man? the hound mocked.

"Ellea," he said. Then again, testing out the syllables and liking the way it sounded on his tongue, "Ell-e-ah."

And now you're creeping me out, Garm said.

"What took you so long to come home?" Ros asked, changing the subject but continuing to say "Ellea" in his head.

Well, I had some things to work through with Billy, Garm said a bit slyly.

"Did you find out anything more about Ellea?"

No, we were, ah, busy. A smirk showed on his mouth.

"Gross," Ros said, but with a big smile.

You are one to talk.

"But if Billy is still hanging around her, something must be up." It was uncommon for a familiar to stick around this long—Garm didn't count, not really. He was the original helhound. Their relationship was different. "Maybe it's her winning personality?"

Doubtful. Do you have a plan? Garm asked with a thoughtful look. Ros wondered if he was hiding something.

He took a moment to think about it. Did he have a plan? No, but he never did.

"Woo her, make her fall in love with me, learn all her secrets," Ros said with a sly smile. "I'm still torn between killing her and dragging her to bed."

He groaned and scolded that hunter side of him that was so quick to kill. Yes, she was powerful, but malicious? Probably not. He would have to find out more, which meant more time with her, and that thought made him smile. The thought of not being able to love someone made the smile quickly disappear. That wasn't an option, but he could have fun...for now.

Gods, you males are the worst. I'm serious, Garm remarked, sitting up and taking in Ros' face fully.

"I don't trust her, but she makes me feel so many new things," Ros said, looking into the hound's eyes. All the humor was gone from his stare.

Hel, I feel like you're a kid again, chasing after the ladies in your fathers court, Garm said, letting his head rest on his enormous paws. He looked tired, probably from rolling around in the woods all night.

"That was so long ago. Times are very different now, and the curse means nothing can be permanent when it comes to partners," Ros said. Starting to rub Garm between the eyes, he purred at the contact, then his red eyes snapped open.

Speaking of chasing and partners, Billy mentioned Ellea would be running this morning, he said, then closed his eyes and smirked. *She said she wanted to make sure she was late so she wouldn't get dragged along.*

Ros thought for a moment, but his mind couldn't come to a conclusion. He only knew he wanted to see her again. Not her, *Ellea.* It hadn't been more than a day and he knew her name—he wanted to rub that fact in her perfect face.

"I may not have a fully formed plan, but I'm going to go for a run," he said, stroking the hound's head one last time.

Yeah, I figured. Try to not seem needy, boy. It tends to come off as creepy, Garm said, opening his eyes only to settle higher on the bed, taking up the free pillow.

"Like you know anything about getting a lady," Ros said, getting out of bed. He grabbed a pair of sweatpants, sneakers, and a shirt. He could have left it, but Garm was right, he shouldn't seem too eager.

I got one last night, I know lots of things, the hound said as Ros left the bedroom.

Ros made it down the stairs quickly and headed out the back door. It was still early—the sun was just rising, and the crisp air clung to his skin. Fall couldn't get here fast enough. He hated the time when it was cool in the morning and then burning when the sun was at its highest.

He took a quick look at the property across the lake and noticed the end of Billy's tail going into the cabin. Ellea must already be out if the dog was sneaking in. Ros took a deep calming breath and listened. The even steps hitting concrete came easily to his ears. It had to be her since no one else was in this area. He headed the opposite direction so he would run into her head on. That way it wouldn't seem like he was following her.

"Yeah, Ros, not creepy at all," he mumbled to himself.

TRICKY MAGIC

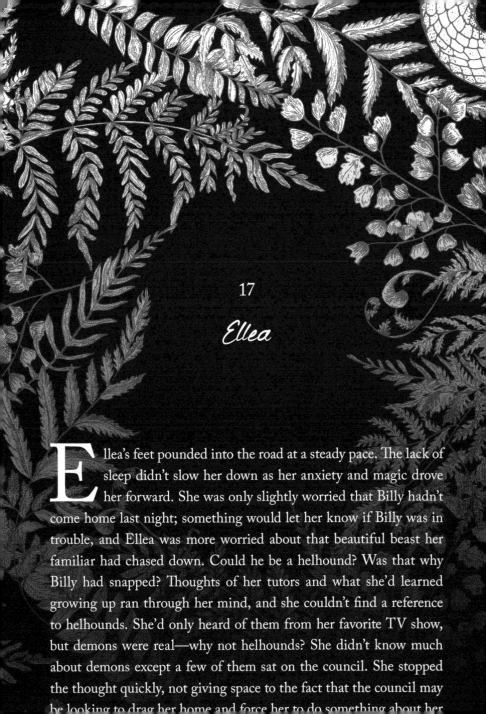

17

Ellea

Ellea's feet pounded into the road at a steady pace. The lack of sleep didn't slow her down as her anxiety and magic drove her forward. She was only slightly worried that Billy hadn't come home last night; something would let her know if Billy was in trouble, and Ellea was more worried about that beautiful beast her familiar had chased down. Could he be a helhound? Was that why Billy had snapped? Thoughts of her tutors and what she'd learned growing up ran through her mind, and she couldn't find a reference to helhounds. She'd only heard of them from her favorite TV show, but demons were real—why not helhounds? She didn't know much about demons except a few of them sat on the council. She stopped the thought quickly, not giving space to the fact that the council may be looking to drag her home and force her to do something about her outburst. Instead, she turned her thoughts to last night's dream. It had been a mix of old nightmares, random men, and chaos. She blamed the guys who had been dropped into her lap recently. Usually she wouldn't mind, but these men...they weren't the fun kind.

She still didn't know what to make of Elias. He'd come out of nowhere, so eager to help, and when she'd needed it. But did she want his help? The little research she'd been doing had gotten her nowhere. What she and her Uncle Felix had always worked on was *not* using her powers. She knew the basics—small illusions and mind games.

According to her research, she should be able to form actual objects, not just the smoke and mirror tricks she could do now. Ellea didn't remember much of what her father could do. Those memories were buried deep, and she would rather start from scratch than stir the crazy pot. Taking a deep breath, she worked on removing the creeping feeling that came with the slightest thought of her early years.

Deep breath in, hold, deep breath out. Let the memory go. She continued this until she noticed something on her left side. *Fucking shit balls.* It was Ros. He was running down one of the cross streets and coming her way. Of course he was. And he just had to be wearing gray sweatpants. Judging by the bouncing between his legs, he was not wearing underwear. *Fucking double shit balls.* She groaned.

Ellea had no way to avoid him, and he already had a shit-eating grin on his handsome ass face. She put on a mask of utter boredom, secretly hoping he would be convinced that her heavy breathing was from the run and not the sight of him.

"Good morning, princess." Ros began to run beside her. "Or should I call you Ellea?"

Ellea almost tripped at her name on his lips. She did her best to hide the breathless sound of her voice as she said, "How the Hel did you learn my name?"

"Your beast told my beast, and my beast told me. The rest is history, princess."

"Don't call me that," she said, scowling at him. "Might as well use my name now that you have it."

Flickers of that hot dream flashed before her. That man had called her princess... She shook the thought and continued to glare at the *not* man of her dreams running next to her.

"Nah, I think I like 'princess.'" A thoughtful look glittered in his eyes. "I will save Ellea for special occasions."

"There will be no special occasions," she said. Her harsh tone only made him smile more. She would just actively ignore everything that he'd said yesterday. "We just happen to share a lake, and for some reason you like to insert yourself into my life."

"Or are you inserting yourself into my life?" He looked at her fully, not breaking his stride. He wasn't even sweating. "I was here first. Plus, *you* were the one that snuck onto my property in the middle of the night."

"Don't worry, I won't make that mistake again."

"Liar! I bet you can't wait to find another reason to come on to my land. Like using your familiar as an excuse." His brow rose.

"That was all her," she replied with her hands up. "I was enjoying my time away from you."

"I doubt that. I know you enjoyed that night in the woods."

"You know nothing about me or what I enjoy." Red dotted her vision. "And you won't ever find out."

How dare he think he knew her or what she wanted, even if it may be true. Yes, she wanted him, but her magic was saying something totally different. She couldn't imagine what would happen if she acted on any of those feelings.

"What are you thinking about right now?" he asked as though he could read her thoughts. Dammit, she didn't know if he could or not. Ellea either needed to learn more about him or stay completely away.

"No, I am not reading your thoughts, if that is what you are thinking. I can smell it on you. The power. And other things." A devilish smile crossed his tan face.

"I am thinking about how fun it was to kick you in the balls, and I'm wondering how soon I can do it again."

"If you want to get close to my balls"—Ros smiled—"you only have to ask."

"The only thing getting close to your balls is my foot," Ellea said. "Or my magic if I learn how to detach them from you."

Ros slowed down, and Ellea took that as an opportunity to pick up the pace, hoping to leave him behind. But she wasn't ever that lucky.

"Could you do that?" he called after her, seeming too curious. "What other things could you do to my manly bits?"

"Ugh." She gagged. "What's wrong with you?"

Ellea had never encountered anyone like him before. He enjoyed talking of violence so much, even receiving it. He'd clearly enjoyed the other night, and her powers tingled under her skin at the memory of it.

"So many things are wrong with me," he said in a way that showed he was fully okay with that statement. "If you're lucky, you will get to learn all of them."

Ellea didn't respond. She didn't know how to. Her responses only seemed to fuel him more, so she just ran, and ran, and ran. Not once did he break pace, and he was barely sweating after forty minutes of running. Her driveway was getting closer, and she couldn't wait to put distance between the two of them. She had so much shit to figure out.

"Same time tomorrow, princess?" Ros asked as she ran down her long driveway. Ellea flipped him off over her shoulder in response, and the deep laugh he answered with went straight to her core. Ellea ran right to the greenhouse; it was time she figured out her magic beyond small illusions.

The mess that she'd left yesterday was completely cleaned up. All that was left were two chairs and an old potting table. The home seemed to care for this building more than it did for her.

"Okay, I can do this," she said to herself. "Start small. An apple. I will form an apple."

Getting herself ready, she imagined it, how it felt in her hands, the taste, and the smell. It would be easy, it had to be. Her power had begun to crackle as soon as Ros appeared on her run, but now she could feel the pull to create. She focused that energy on the small table a few feet in front of her.

An apple, a red, shiny apple will appear on that table.

Pushing that energy out, she kept that image in her mind. Then the table exploded into tiny shards of wood.

"Fuck, this is going to be harder than I thought."

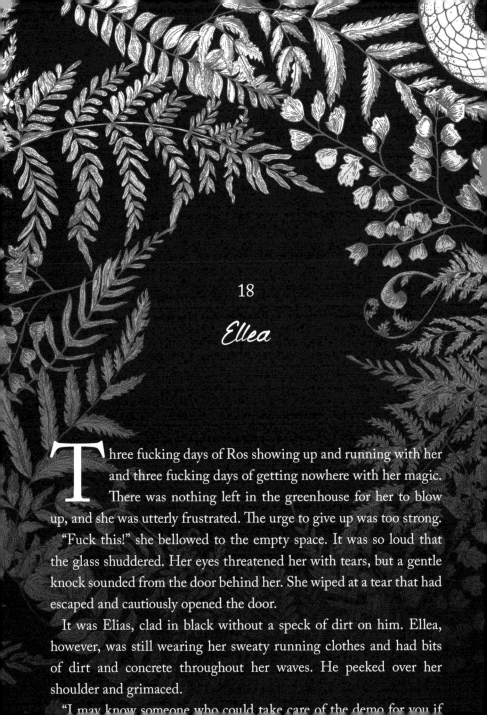

18

Ellea

Three fucking days of Ros showing up and running with her and three fucking days of getting nowhere with her magic. There was nothing left in the greenhouse for her to blow up, and she was utterly frustrated. The urge to give up was too strong.

"Fuck this!" she bellowed to the empty space. It was so loud that the glass shuddered. Her eyes threatened her with tears, but a gentle knock sounded from the door behind her. She wiped at a tear that had escaped and cautiously opened the door.

It was Elias, clad in black without a speck of dirt on him. Ellea, however, was still wearing her sweaty running clothes and had bits of dirt and concrete throughout her waves. He peeked over her shoulder and grimaced.

"I may know someone who could take care of the demo for you if that is what you're trying to do here," he said.

"Thanks, but I think I took care of it." Her scowl was vicious.

"My offer still stands. If you need help with your magic, I can help you, and anytime you want us to stop, we can."

"I don't know you, why would I trust you to help me?"

"It's just magic." He laughed. "I'm not asking you to run off with me."

His eyebrows were raised, and Ellea was so close to giving in. She was desperate for help and didn't know which way to turn. She could ask Ros, but the thought quickly snuffed itself out. There was no way anything good would come from his help. Her shoulders dropped in defeat. More than anything, she wanted this to work, she was so tired.

"Fine," she said exasperatedly. "But if things get weird or I don't like what's happening, we stop and you leave?"

"Yes, of course." His smile was kind.

"I really don't know anything about you," she said, looking him up and down.

"I'm Elias," he said with his hand on his chest. "You need help, and I'm here to help you. What more do you need to know?"

"Right… The dark and mysterious thing only works on some people, you know."

He laughed at that.

"Really, I am only here to help," he said with mock hurt. "I was in your shoes once, it would have been nice if someone offered help when I needed it."

Ellea opened the door fully to let him in. If something went wrong, she could figure it out when the time came.

"So," he said, looking around, "what is it you are trying to do?"

He openly took her in, looking at her from her muddy running shoes to her sweaty t-shirt. How could she tell him without giving too much away?

"I am trying to form an apple," Ellea said, crossing her arms and feeling self-conscious. "I've been able to do small illusions but nothing solid."

There, that wasn't giving too much away.

"Are you going straight to the apple?" he asked. "Or forming what you know first and then attempting to make it solid?"

"I guess I've been going straight to making an actual apple." Saying it out loud made her feel a bit silly. "So I started too big? But it's just an apple."

"Just an apple?" He looked curiously at her. "To some, an apple is so much more. To you, it is the start of something new."

She didn't know how to respond to that. Her mind whirled with thoughts of what he meant. Had it been too long since she'd had a normal encounter with someone? Ros only drove her mad.

"So yes, let's start smaller." He clapped his hands once, and Ellea jumped. He ignored it and continued further into the greenhouse. "Show me an illusion, and we will go from there."

He gave her a warm smile. Yes, it was different talking with someone who wasn't trying to piss you off at every turn.

So she made an illusion of an apple. That was easy, but she was still glad nothing exploded. It was in the palm of her hand, and Elias studied it. He asked her to do it over and over again, never pushing too hard and always keeping his tone warm. They only worked for a short time before the sound of Ellea's growling stomach was loud enough to make him laugh.

"Let's start fresh tomorrow," he said. "I will try to make it here before you start blowing stuff up."

"Sure. I'll see you tomorrow."

They walked out of the greenhouse together, and he headed toward the woods like the first time they met.

"Are you staying close by?" she asked before he got too far, not sure why it mattered.

"Not too far," he said. "I'm still looking at that property on the lake."

He didn't give too much away, which she didn't mind. She was doing the same.

"Okay," she said with a wave. "See you tomorrow, and thanks for the help."

"Of course, Ellea," he said and waved back. Ellea headed toward the cabin in desperate need of food and a shower. When she looked back over her shoulder, he was gone, as if he'd stepped into the shadows and disappeared.

TRICKY MAGIC

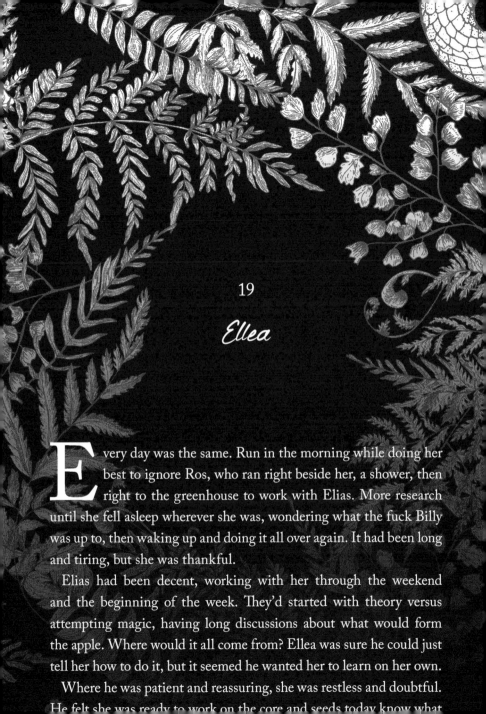

19

Ellea

Every day was the same. Run in the morning while doing her best to ignore Ros, who ran right beside her, a shower, then right to the greenhouse to work with Elias. More research until she fell asleep wherever she was, wondering what the fuck Billy was up to, then waking up and doing it all over again. It had been long and tiring, but she was thankful.

Elias had been decent, working with her through the weekend and the beginning of the week. They'd started with theory versus attempting magic, having long discussions about what would form the apple. Where would it all come from? Ellea was sure he could just tell her how to do it, but it seemed he wanted her to learn on her own.

Where he was patient and reassuring, she was restless and doubtful. He felt she was ready to work on the core and seeds today know what told him this, but she trusted him—and she didn't really have a choice.

"Think about how an apple is actually formed," he said. "They don't just appear one day for a farmer to bring to the market."

"I'm not a child, Elias." There was no harshness in her tone. "This seems like such a long way of doing things."

"I know." His look was encouraging. "But sometimes that's how it has to be. Now the seeds, those come first."

Ellea sat on the floor with her legs crossed under her, the illusion of an apple resting in her palm. Elias had said it a number of times, start with the inside and work your way out.

She could form a few seeds.

Envisioning a tree sprouting the start of an apple, she let out a breath and pushed some more of her magic into the illusion. She waited for the explosion, but nothing came. Elias reached from where he was sitting across from her, his long pale fingers plucking three seeds from the middle of the illusion.

"Step one." He grinned. "You did it."

A wide smile stretched across Ellea's face, and she let the illusion fade away. Another seed landed in her palm, and she marveled at it. It had taken five days to get this far. Trying to not let that discourage her, she looked up from her seed, silently asking Elias for direction.

"Let's go again," he said, crushing the seeds in his hand until they were dust.

20

Ros

Three days into September and fall was already showing her face. The mornings were becoming increasingly crisp along with the nights. Midday still had some heat to it, but nothing compared to the blistering summer. Ellea had been more quiet on this morning's run; not in a moody way, more distracted. Her powers were the same, continuously growing restless under her skin, and Ros often wondered what it felt like for her to have such power coursing through her veins and not releasing it. His own beast rumbled at the thought.

Ros did know what that much power felt like, he had lived with it for centuries, but knowing she didn't do anything with it was the scary part. His research on the little he did know was not helping and neither were their daily encounters. She consumed almost every thought of his. The way her long ponytail bobbed from side to side as she ran. Her curls, like her moods, were never the same; some days they would be relaxed and loose, other days they would be erratic and tight. Her words could have the harshest bites that went straight to his cock. Some days she would be more subdued, almost too tired to fight back, and he hated those days the most.

Where her curls would change, her outfits were always the same. Black leggings and one of three old t-shirts. Those leggings... damn that tight black fabric. They were going to be the death of him. Her ass was fucking perfect, and those short curvy legs held so much power. How could something in such a compact size carry so much magic and strength? She barely made it up to his chest.

The never-ending thoughts distracted him on his drive to Sam's; he was already pulling into the driveway. He had received a call late last night from Weylyn about another vampire clan. This group was further north. Their motive was the same, capturing women and children and using them for a number of things other than blood. Unlike the usual clans, they were still using demons. That's where Sam came in.

He would usually handle these situations on his own, but something was telling him to bring backup. Sadly, this trip also meant he would miss tomorrow's run. They would have to leave now and travel six hours by car, then another hour by foot. He wondered how happy Ellea would be to not have him on the run tomorrow. Honestly, he hoped she would miss him. It made him smile as he headed to where Sam waited on his front porch.

"Ah, I take it the witch is still alive?" Sam asked with a smile.

"Yes." Ros smiled wider. "Very much alive, and very much causing trouble."

"Well, let's go kill some vampires and get you back to her in one

194

piece." He smacked Ros' shoulder. "I would hate for her to have less of you to beat the shit out of."

21

Ellea

Ellea sat in the same spot as yesterday, in front of Elias with her palm up, an illusion of an apple in her hand. It kept flickering, and she cursed under her breath.

"You seem distracted today," Elias scolded. She *was* distracted. Ros hadn't shown up this morning, which should have been a blessing. Yet, the break in routine had thrown her off. The weird part was that her magic was rumbling worse than usual. Ellea thought it should be singing at the break from the giant asshole. The run had also lacked its usual intensity without Ros' unnecessary comments spurring her on.

"I think I'm just tired," Ellea lied with a sigh. "We have been working on this nonstop."

"Well, lucky for you," he said, pausing to place her hand back where it belonged, "I will be gone for a few days."

"Oh? Where are you going?" she asked, thankful for the opportunity of a break but still curious. Ellea still didn't know much about him, only that he was kind and very helpful.

"I have some *family* business to attend to," he said. "It's south of here. I will be gone until Sunday. We can start fresh Monday morning."

"Is it serious?" she asked. His tone had her curious.

"Nothing new. Now, let's work on the apple core. Think about the seeds first and go from there."

So she did, finally holding the illusion steady. She envisioned an apple being created, the seeds being covered by the white flesh, the hardness of it. She directed her powers into that illusion like she had done so many times before. A wet slosh sounded, and her hand was covered in what looked like roughly made applesauce.

"Dammit." She groaned. "The seeds were so much easier."

"I still think you are more distracted today," he said, cocking his head and searching her face. "Let's call it. I want to show you something." He stood and reached out for her clean hand, helping her stand. Ellea looked down at her other hand that was covered in sticky wetness. She pulled away as he tried to grab it, but he was so much quicker. She grimaced thinking of the sticky mess it would cause, but as his cool hand pulled away, hers was clean.

"Thanks," she said, marveling at the magic. "Where are we going?"

They hadn't had too many serious conversations over their time together, but she still trusted him. When they did talk, it was always easy, nothing compared to the conversations she had with Ros.

"I wanted to see what you thought about the other house on the lake," he said, gesturing toward the hilly path behind the greenhouse. "I hope you are up for a walk."

Smiling over his shoulder, he led the way.

Ellea had only seen the property once. She had snuck off with Billy when she was a child. She only remembered that the property had a vastly larger greenhouse and fountains and statues that made you feel like you were stepping into an old movie.

Elias kept stride in front of her, and the conversation was easy, talking about the area, the different trees, and some of their favorite books. His favorite authors were the typical F's—Faulkner, Fitz, and Franz Kafka. He didn't know any of Ellea's favorites. She wasn't surprised; he liked old-school literature, and she favored anything steamy, anything with dragons, or both.

They crested the top of the hill, and Ellea was thankful for all the running she had been doing. She was barely panting, but her legs and butt were burning. She noted to add back in some weight training, or maybe even tackling this hill every once in a while.

Ellea paused as the old structure loomed in front of her. The cabin was so beautiful, even under all the overgrown vines and chipping paint. Its base was jagged stone that made it look like it was built into the hillside. The large back porch sat on tall stilts; she was sure it had an amazing view. The top had several haunting peaks that Ellea loved, and the wood was dark under the greenery. Ellea shivered as she noted the darkness inside.

"I've been here once," she said, rubbing her hands along her bare arms. "When I was younger. I don't remember the cabin, but I remember the—"

"The greenhouse," Elias interrupted. He swept his arm toward the large structure. "That's why I keep coming back to it."

In front of them stood an intricate glass structure. Where Ellea's was simple and rectangular, this one was complicated and beautiful. It had four tall peaks on each corner and a large peak in the center. It was massive and had an ornate fountain to match.

"I've been told a wealthy green witch family built it," Elias said, opening the door. "Most witch's homes have some form of a greenhouse in the north. That way, they can grow herbs and things all year round."

"I didn't realize I was getting a history lesson on this tour." Ellea smirked at him as she walked in. "I have a smaller one at my home in Halifax, but it doesn't get much use. I never had a green thumb."

She wiggled her thumb at him.

"Maybe that will change once you master creating things," Elias said. "I never knew my mother, but my aunt would have loved this. It reminds me of her."

He had never mentioned his family before.

"I'm not sure any of my family had a green thumb," she said, not sure where to go after he mentioned his mother. Ellea wasn't a fan of talking about family.

"What about your mother?" he asked, and Ellea cringed.

"I would rather skip that conversation," she said with a small smile. "Or my father."

"We all have family regrets we carry around with us," he said. "It's how we overcome them that matters."

"I don't have regrets where my parents are concerned," she said a bit harshly. "Only that my grandmother didn't step in sooner."

He studied her face after that comment. "Okay," he said, changing the subject. "If you could grow anything, what would it be?"

"Cheese, chocolate, and coffee, of course," she said with a small smile. "Pasta, too."

"Maybe we should work on one of those when you accomplish the apple," he said, laughing.

She was thankful for the lighter subject. The thought of her parents crept in at every corner of this town. She had never been here with them, and she was thankful they didn't muddy these memories, but that didn't stop them from trying.

Ellea was slow on her run the next morning. She hadn't slept well and cursed her parents for it. The mere mention of them had her dreams filled with some of her worst memories. She was actually hoping to run into Ros for the distraction. *Nope.* She shook her head to rid herself of the ridiculousness of that. Hoping for Ros...*bleh.*

After twenty minutes of running and no sign of the large asshole, she began to worry. Even though she had no reason to worry yet, it was there in her gut. Maybe she could sneak by his cabin and see if he was home. Not talk to him, only to see. Her mind made up, she took one of the forest paths that led to his side of the lake.

Ellea ran by his house twice before she got the nerve to head down his driveway. She jogged until she came up to his old green truck. There was no sign inside the cabin to show if anyone was awake. She stood about a hundred feet from his front door, trying to find any reason to move in closer. Nothing came to her mind other than concern and curiosity, two things she shouldn't have where Ros was involved. She turned, deciding to leave and ask Billy later if Garm had mentioned anything. Ellea stopped as movement at the front door caught her eye. She almost ran until she saw the large black eye that looked through the glass.

The shit-eating grin on the face looking out at her stopped any concern she might have had... *Yep, definitely leaving.* She was about to turn away and give him her back when he swung the door open, only wearing gray sweatpants and looking like he'd been thrown into meat grinder.

"What the fuck happened to you?" she shouted louder than intended. A few birds scattered, and she covered her mouth.

"I knew you would miss me," Ros said, and his smile somehow grew. She didn't know how he was smiling. He limped further onto his front porch, and the morning light made it so much worse.

Ros' right eye was bruised and swollen. His shoulder looked like it'd been used as a chew toy, and bite marks peppered both arms. His ribs were also bruised, and he had a gash across his stomach that continued past his waistband.

"Miss you?" she said, trying to hide her horror. "But seriously, what the fuck happened?"

"Just a little argument," he said, waving his hand. "Nothing that won't be healed in a few days."

"Little argument?" She gaped at him. "You look like a dragon took you for a joy ride."

"Don't be dramatic, princess," he said, smiling. "It warms my heart knowing how much you care."

"Get your ass back in the house before you scare away the forest creatures," came a male voice from inside the cabin. Ellea straightened. She had never seen Ros with anyone but Garm.

"Are you going to just stand there?" Ros asked. "Come inside. I'll take my pants off, and you can help clean up some of my wounds." She scowled at his wiggling eyebrows.

Ellea waited for something to stop her, but there was nothing, and her curiosity had her heading toward his cabin. She didn't know what to expect when she walked through the front door, but it wasn't what greeted her.

Every surface of the rich wood interior was covered. Black shelves lined most of the walls, and they were filled with books, statues, artifacts, and glass enclosures. If there wasn't a shelf, artwork hung in its place. For the amount of stuff, the cabin was extremely clean. It felt like a museum hid its overstock pieces in this place.

The sound of male voices pulled her away from a jar of something's foot or finger. She shivered and followed the voices to a sitting room. A large green couch sat on top of a black wool rug. Sitting on that couch was an extremely handsome man. He stood and was just as tall as Ros. His black hair was neatly shaved on the sides and perfectly tousled on top. Almond eyes crinkled as he smiled at her. One of them was also bruised and swollen. But unlike Ros, he was fully clothed.

"Hi," he said, reaching out a tanned hand. "I'm Sam."

"I'm Ellea," she said, shaking his hand and trying not to stare.

"I know," Sam said with a grin "I've heard loads about you."

"Seriously?" Ros groaned. "He says three words to you, and he gets to know your name right away?"

"Yeah," she answered. "He's a million times better looking, and he didn't scowl at me when he first saw me."

Sam laughed but quickly stopped as if he was in pain.

"I like her," he said, rubbing his chest. "Don't kill her."

22

Ros

Ros wasn't going to kill her, but her magic and power needed an out, needed release. Even now, he could see how the power begged to be set free. Did she even realize it?

Ros often forgot that there was a battle in his head. As soon as he saw her, he completely forgot that she could be the next job, that her powers could force him to do something. Those defiant gray eyes bore into his soul, interrupting those worries. She wouldn't think twice before laying into him, verbally and physically, but she'd come here today, and she was worried about him.

He didn't know what to do with how that made him feel. His thoughts had distracted him from the conversation, and now Sam and Ellea looked at him as if he were a gilled lake beast.

"I'm sorry, what were you saying?" Ros asked. "I was too distracted, realizing that Ellea actually has a heart and cares enough to check in on me."

Ellea raised her gaze to the sky as if begging for patience.

"Sam was going to tell me why you both look like you were thrown through a meat grinder," she said, placing her hands on her hips, looking at both of them with such an intense glare that he felt Sam recoil. How she could stand in a room with two of the largest and most dangerous men and be completely unfazed was unbelievable.

"We had to take care of some rogue vampires up north," Ros answered. "Things got out of hand, but nothing we couldn't handle."

"Out of hand?" Sam said with a raised eyebrow and shook his head. "You had to play the hero and dive into a pile of twenty vamps to save my ass. You should have left me."

"Why, so Devon could come home, find out you're dead, and then hunt me down and feed me to the pack?" His answer was snarky but filled with love.

"Pack?" Ellea asked curiously. "Are you wolven? Ros said he wasn't. He actually almost pissed himself when I thought he was."

"No and yes," Sam answered while Ros began chucking. "I'm a wolven; Devon is actually a witch."

"And Ros?" she said, looking at them expectantly.

"Ros is an asshole," Sam said.

"Well, I knew that." Ellea rolled her eyes. "And a few other things."

"Sam is actually the alpha." Ros said it with so much pride. "He leads all the wolven in the northeast." Ellea whistled at the mention of alpha.

"That seems like a big job. And Devon? What kind of witch is she or he?"

"He," Sam answered, his smile warm. "He is a bit of everything. You may get to meet him one day."

Sam and Ellea continued an easy conversation, and Ros felt the slow creep of jealousy. He enjoyed the banter with Ellea, but he wondered if it would ever be easy. Did he even want it to be easy?

"Mabon is coming up this month," Ellea mentioned. "Do you celebrate it here?"

"We do," Sam answered her. "The town's supernatural population is so large and close-knit that we celebrate together."

"Wow." Her beautiful eyes grew wide. "Everyone? Vampires, wolven, and…"

"Yes, everyone," Sam said. "Even the forest creatures, water beasts, and anyone you can think of."

"It's a real fairytale," Ros said sarcastically.

"Oh, please," Sam said, smacking Ros on the shoulder. "You love the celebrations. Why else would you spend months preparing the wood for the bonfire?"

"I do it for the free alcohol," Ros said, rolling his eyes.

Ellea had gone quiet, and when Ros turned to her, he realized she was staring. He would kill to know what was going through her mind. She took a step back, and her chest began to rise and fall rapidly.

"Well," she said, taking another step back, "glad you are in one piece, and it was a pleasure meeting you, Sam. Umm, I will see you around."

She turned and bolted quickly to the front door. It only took Ros a few strides to catch up with her as she left the front porch. He grabbed her arm, and heat licked at his hand. She whirled on him with her eyes wide, and he shook his hand, trying to get rid of the feeling crawling up his arm.

"I'm sorry about that. This is weird. I should go."

"No," he said, reaching for her again and ignoring the heat. "It's not weird; I'm glad you stopped by and that you got to meet Sam. He has been hounding me to meet you."

She stood there, avoiding his stare. "I'm not sure why I stopped by," she said. "I am glad you're okay, but I should go."

She turned away from him before he could stop her.

"I should be good to run again by Monday," he called after her. But she didn't turn back, only picked up the pace and ran in the direction of her cabin.

Ros felt Sam walk up behind him. He looked toward his friend, and Sam's eyes followed Ellea's retreating form.

"Oh, what I would give," Sam said, smirking, "to see that curvy little sprite kick your ass. Does she always wear those leggings?"

He made a show of adjusting his pants. Ros placed his hands on Sam's shoulders then kneed him right in the balls.

"I'm going to tell Devon you said that," he whispered in his ear as his friend hunched over. "Can't wait to see what curse he puts on your cock when he gets home."

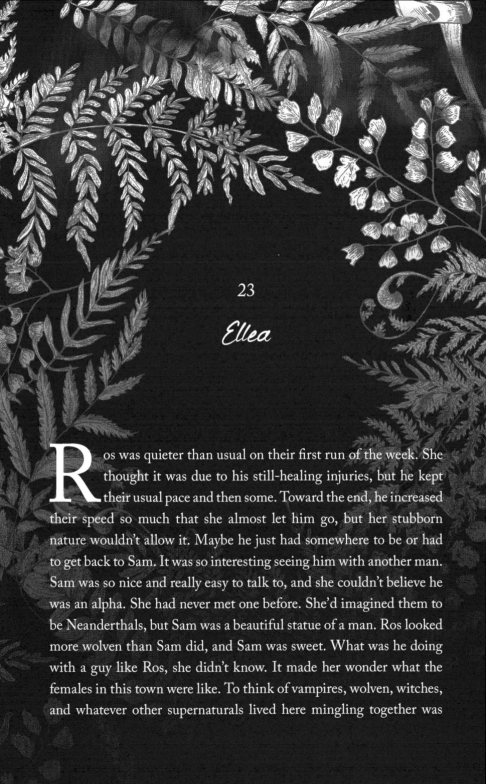

23

Ellea

Ros was quieter than usual on their first run of the week. She thought it was due to his still-healing injuries, but he kept their usual pace and then some. Toward the end, he increased their speed so much that she almost let him go, but her stubborn nature wouldn't allow it. Maybe he just had somewhere to be or had to get back to Sam. It was so interesting seeing him with another man. Sam was so nice and really easy to talk to, and she couldn't believe he was an alpha. She had never met one before. She'd imagined them to be Neanderthals, but Sam was a beautiful statue of a man. Ros looked more wolven than Sam did, and Sam was sweet. What was he doing with a guy like Ros, she didn't know. It made her wonder what the females in this town were like. To think of vampires, wolven, witches, and whatever other supernaturals lived here mingling together was crazy, but maybe she should venture out and explore more.

It was something she thought about as she stepped out of the shower. She'd forgotten that this town wasn't filled with people who knew what she was. She might even be able to go out and not get dirty looks from the locals. She smiled at the thought, and it was decided. After practice this morning, she would head into town and explore. That plan put a pep in her step as she headed out to the greenhouse. Elias was already there, leaning against the glass structure, wearing his usual black. Ros was a pain, Sam seemed like someone she would be friends with, but Elias was something she couldn't put her finger on. He was kind and patient, but they both held a lot close to their chests.

"Good morning," she said, grabbing his attention. He greeted her with a smile that matched her own.

"You seem in good spirits today," Elias said, stepping toward her. "Did you have a good weekend?"

"Yes, it was quiet and restful. How was yours?"

"It was fine."

"Did any of your family give you trouble?" Maybe they could get to know each other more.

"Trouble?" He raised a brow. "It was family, why would I have trouble?"

Sometimes she forgot people had normal relationships with their own family. She only had her nana and uncle, but life with her parents was enough to make her wonder who else had it rough.

"Ah, yes." She shook her head. "I was speaking from experience."

"No trouble," he said with a small laugh. "It was a normal visit to make sure things were in order."

"Do you like things in order?"

"Usually." He paused, seeming to think about his answer. "I like to have a plan and make sure I'm ready for anything. But enough about me. I have a trick for you."

"A trick?" That made her curious and cautious, as the t-word always did. "Will it help with the apple?"

She hoped so.

Ellea always fought with patience, and this felt like it was dragging on.

"It should. I ran into a *friend* during my visit, and they reminded me of something."

"What kind of friend?"

"You are full of questions today. Do you want to learn the trick I have or not?"

"Yes." She rolled her eyes. "Please, all-mighty teacher, teach me your ways."

He chuckled.

"Have a seat," he said, gesturing to the tiled floor. He sat across from her like he always did.

"I still can't believe you let your perfect pants touch a dirty floor," Ellea said, snickering at him.

"You know," he said, "I'm not opposed to taking a ruler to my students."

Her breath caught in her throat. He had such a serious look on his face, and her mouth went dry at the sight of it. He was usually so light and patient.

"Sorry," she said, forcing herself to hold his eye contact. "Show me your trick, please."

"Good. Magic is such a tricky thing. Powers are an extension, not something you force. I believe your magic will create the apple on its own. You can't force it."

He kept saying trick and tricky. It made her wonder if he knew what she was. That worry was overshadowed as she realized what he was implying.

"What do you mean?" The suggestion of letting her magic do something on its own was enough to call this whole thing off. "How am I supposed to control my magic without controlling it?"

"You aren't listening," he said sternly. "You aren't supposed to control your magic. Let it go."

Her heart raced. She couldn't let her magic go. There was no trusting what it would do.

"There has to be another way." She could feel the sweat beginning to gather on her forehead, and her palms felt slick. She stopped herself from rubbing them against her pants.

"Do you trust me?" he asked, holding out his hand.

She looked down at his pale palm facing up at her. It was so delicate, not a callus in sight. Looking up into his dark eyes, she took a breath.

"Kind of?" She was being honest, but she had spent so long fearing her powers.

"Your magic will not harm me or you," he said, his hand still held in front of her. "What is the worst that can happen?"

"I don't know." She tried to think of something.

"Ellea," he said smoothly. "Let's try."

She searched his face, waiting for an excuse to find her. One never came. So she straightened and feigned confidence as she said, "Okay."

24

Ros

Ros paced his cabin, constantly glancing out his windows and across the lake. Where was Ellea? Was she in the cabin, or had she gone somewhere else? He should have had a conversation with her earlier.

He could feel that her powers were raging, and she was as oblivious as she always was. If she wasn't oblivious, she was being careless, which was even worse. But he was also a coward. Getting close to her had been a mistake, and now he couldn't think straight. He couldn't kill her, but something needed to be done. He definitely shouldn't sleep with her, it wouldn't be a one-time thing, and he couldn't make any promises to her. Sam was no help, and neither was Garm; they thought with their dumb hearts instead of their brains. He didn't trust her powers, didn't trust how he felt about her. The thoughts of spending more time with her, getting to know her, fuck her, were becoming harder to push down deep.

Take one step.

Her powers. He would have to figure out what to do about her powers. His biggest fear was that this discussion would lead to the end. Her anger would get the better of her, one thing would lead to another, and it would be over. It would end with her being consumed by her powers, and he would have to step in and take care of it. But where would that leave them?

Only one way to find out.

His cock and his dumb heart would have to get over it. It was time. He would do it now, and whatever happened...well, that would be it.

TRICKY MAGIC

25

Ellea

Ellea left the greenhouse, throwing her fully formed, fully real apple in the air and catching it. With a grin on her face, she looked back at Elias. He had been the one to help her form something real. It had taken a few tries to get her heart to slow and to calm her anxiety. She'd never trusted her magic before, but with Elias there to guide her, it became simple. She felt so free. It had been so simple after she let go. Her powers were still roaring, but maybe a time would come where she could fully let go.

"I can't believe I did it," she said with a grin on her face.

"I knew you could." His grin grew to match hers. "Now take a bite, let's see if it's real."

Ellea brought the shiny red apple to her mouth. Her teeth scraped across the skin, and she bit down. A delicious juicy crunch greeted her, and the taste exploded in her mouth. It was real. She'd actually done it. It wasn't just an illusion, it was a real apple.

"What. Is. This?" a deep voice asked.

Ellea turned quickly toward the voice that rumbled from the edge of the trees. It was Ros, and he was glaring over her shoulder at Elias.

"What are you doing here, Belias?" he said.

Ellea was confused. Belias? Did they know each other? Quickly swallowing and wiping the juice from her mouth, she tried responding, but Elias—or Belias—beat her to it.

"Hello, cousin." An oily grin spread across his face. She almost didn't recognize him.

"Cousin?" Ellea said, looking between them.

"Ellea," Ros said to her in such a serious voice. "What are you doing with him?"

He looked furious. What was she doing with him? Elias—no, Belias—had a smirk on his face that she had never seen before.

"What do you mean?" she answered. He had no right to come here and ask questions. Gaining her confidence, she stood taller. "What are *you* doing here?"

"What am I doing here?" he roared at her. "I will ask you again. What are you doing with Belias?"

"First of all…" She whipped the apple at him, and he easily dodged it. Finding the angry tone that easily came around Ros, she replied, "I was under the impression that this was Elias."

"Elias, Belias…" Belias said, looking as if this was the best day ever, "pretty much the same. You can call me whatever your heart desires, but Ellea and Elias had such a sweet ring to it."

What the fuck?

This was not the same person she had spent almost every day with over the past couple weeks. Ros was fuming where he stood, almost vibrating with anger.

"Wait," Ellea said with her hands in the air. "You two are related?"

"Yes," they answered together. Ros' came out in a growl where Belias came out as gleeful.

"We have been cousins for"—Belias counted on his fingers—"over a millennium."

The world began to sway.

A millennium.

"You aren't witches, are you?" Her words were barely audible over the ringing in her ears. "What are you?"

So many scenarios flew through her mind. She didn't know what kind of supernatural could live over a millennium.

Belias grinned, and Ros' face dropped. A few moments passed before an answer came.

"Demons," Belias said while still grinning.

"You're not witches," Ellea said, putting her hands on her knees. She was going to lose it. "You're demons!"

Bile crept up her throat as she tried to remember the slightest thing she knew about demons. All she did know wasn't good.

"I'm half," Ros said, stepping toward her. "Half witch, half demon."

"Demon princes," Belias added. "That makes it better. Right?"

"No," she said in a harsh whisper, a whisper that quickly turned to a shriek. "That is not fucking better, Belias."

Fucking demons. Demon fucking princes.

Oh, Hel.

She was going to be sick. She had fantasized about fucking a demon. When she looked at Ros and only concern showed in his eyes, she still wanted to.

"I'm going to be sick," she said, swaying toward the cabin. Ros followed after her. "No! Both of you fuck off. I don't know what sick demon game this is, but I don't want you here."

Hurt flashed across Ros' face, and Belias was still grinning. She scowled at both of them before heading inside.

PART THREE

Fucking, demons.
- Unknown

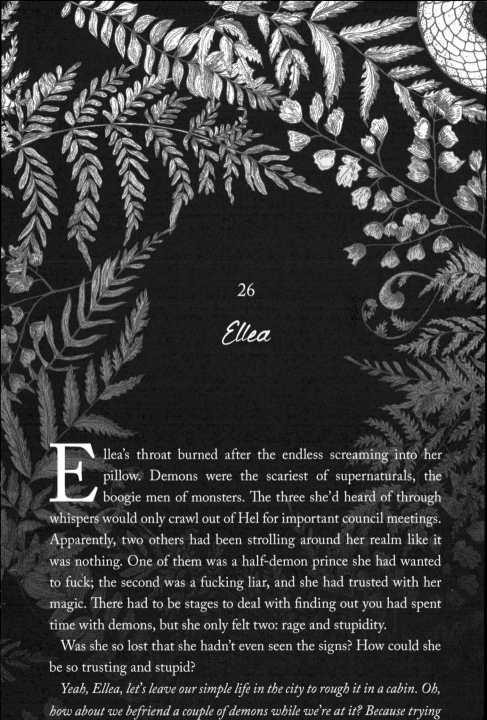

26

Ellea

Ellea's throat burned after the endless screaming into her pillow. Demons were the scariest of supernaturals, the boogie men of monsters. The three she'd heard of through whispers would only crawl out of Hel for important council meetings. Apparently, two others had been strolling around her realm like it was nothing. One of them was a half-demon prince she had wanted to fuck; the second was a fucking liar, and she had trusted with her magic. There had to be stages to deal with finding out you had spent time with demons, but she only felt two: rage and stupidity.

Was she so lost that she hadn't even seen the signs? How could she be so trusting and stupid?

Yeah, Ellea, let's leave our simple life in the city to rough it in a cabin. Oh, how about we befriend a couple of demons while we're at it? Because trying

L.L. CAMPBELL

to figure out what to do with your magic while fantasizing about the big one was so fucking smart.

She wanted to scream again, and of course, Billy was nowhere to be found. Now the day was gone, the moon high, and Ellea found herself needing air. Grabbing a small blanket, she headed out of the cabin. The nights had always been cool here, and it was only September. Maybe the moon and the stars would have some insight into what to do now—they had been so talkative on that first night.

Standing at the edge of the dock, she waited and waited, but no whisper came, only the crunching of footsteps. She knew they were Ros'. He couldn't even stay away for a day. His heavy steps sounded on the dock and stopped right behind her. She didn't need to turn to see the anger radiating off him, she could feel it, but he had no right to be angry.

"I need to know," he said, breathing heavily, "what you were doing with Belias."

"I think you need to sit down, old man." She didn't bother turning. "You sound a bit winded, and that isn't good for a man your age."

How dare he come here asking questions? She should be the one asking questions.

"You don't know him. He could have manipulated you into doing something, and you wouldn't even know."

Ellea turned sharply and glared up at him. The moon was so bright that she could see all of his features, his heavy brow, those beautiful eyes, and that handsome face. She scowled at herself inwardly.

"I may have been dumb enough to not realize that you both were demons," she said, trying to keep herself calm. "But I was not manipulated into anything. I asked him for help."

"Why the fuck would you do that? You could have come to me!"

"Come to you?" She couldn't believe it. "Why would I come to you? When have you ever offered me help?"

"I offered plenty of times." He stepped closer to her.

"Which time?" she said, losing her blanket as she poked a finger at his hard chest. "Was it the time you said you didn't trust me? Or the time you offered yourself to me, saying I could have done anything to you?"

He didn't respond, only glared at her.

"Or was it one of the times you mentioned killing me?" She was breathing hard now. "That seemed really helpful. Were you going to make it quick and easy, or toy with me before you did it?"

"I hadn't thought that far. It was only an idea; I wanted to see if your magic would finally explode."

"Wait," she said, raising her hands. "You're serious? I thought it was a joke."

Why would he want to kill her? He didn't even really *know* her.

"Of course, I didn't want to kill you," he said, looking angry. "But if I had to, I would have."

She felt the world drop from under her. "I don't understand," she said. "I haven't done anything."

"Not yet," he said, reaching for her, but she moved out of reach. "That's the thing, you haven't. How long do you think you can go before your magic consumes you and destroys everything? Do you even realize what could happen?"

"How do you know?" she said, stunned. "How could you know what I am?"

"I don't know what you are, Ellea," he said, reaching out a hand to push a piece of hair behind her ear. She didn't move this time. He kept his hand there, anchored behind her neck, and Ellea felt herself lean into it. "But I see it. All that power. You're being reckless, and I usually take care of rogue and reckless things."

Reckless?

"*Thing?*" she roared at him. "You just called me a fucking 'thing?'" She slapped his arm away. "Don't fucking touch me and then insult me."

TRICKY MAGIC

27

Ros

Ros had known it would come to this, all that quick anger she was showing. Yet Ellea was different. This wasn't a rogue group of water demons luring children to the water, it was only a girl with infinite power at her fingertips. It would be only a matter of time before she left destruction behind. But how much destruction? Maybe he could find out. He could force those powers to the surface, play a little, force her to do something.

Ros looked into her eyes, able to see the storm churning in their gray depths. He let his magic slither closer to the surface, teasing hers to attack. Hers instantly crackled in answer; he could see it sparkling in her eyes and by the way her skin pebbled at the feel of it. Her nostrils flared, and her breaths came quicker.

"Fine." The word came out on a rough exhale. "You want my magic to explode? Show you what I'm holding back? Let's see if you can handle it, old man."

And then she pounced.

The dock shook under his feet as Ellea's first attack of raw power hit him. He'd expected an illusion, something like their time in the woods, but he took each pulsing wave and smiled at the beautiful face that was scrunched in anger. A roar came from deep in her chest as wave after wave of power pulsed out of her. He leaned into it, forcing her to push harder. The trees closest to the lake began to sway on the heated wind that cascaded from her endless reserve of magic. The water rippled, and the nails in the dock began to shake out of place. He never broke her vicious gaze, making sure she didn't see the shadows slithering on the other end of the dock.

They struck at her like an asp, wrapping around her ankles and yanking her feet from under her. A pained breath whooshed out of her as she landed flat on her chest. Her hand was still outstretched, but no power flooded out of her.

That was easy.

Ros grabbed her hand and dragged her down the dock toward the shore.

"No need to ruin a perfectly good dock with your temper tantrum. I'm a little disappointed; I expected more."

His words ignited anger again, and she began struggling, trying to find purchase on the wood beneath them. Her foot caught on a loose board, and she steadied her feet. Yanking hard, she pulled him off balance, causing him to sway close to the water, but he had the upper hand. She couldn't get free in time, and they both toppled into the dark water. His height stopped him from slipping under the surface, and he looked down at her as she coughed and tried to stay above the waterline.

"I thought this would be harder," he said, smirking down at her. "You look like a cute drowning rat."

A guttural sound escaped as she kicked hard at the water. Her foot caught his thigh, and he didn't realize what she was doing until she was behind him and he was caught in a chokehold. He felt her lips curl into a smile against his cheek as she unleashed a wave of electricity.

Ros gasped for air as his body convulsed in the water.

"I'll show you a drowned rat, you brute," she snarled in his ear.

It was agony. He lost control of his body, forcing them both under the water. He hoped the lack of air would force her to stop her attack, but she held tight, and he slowly crawled to shore. It was difficult; each wave of electricity had his limbs violently shaking.

Ellea's head broke the water first, and she gasped for air. Her powers stuttered, and he took the opportunity to throw her as he broke the water. She flew twenty feet, landing with a thud on the sandy ground. He didn't give her a chance to stand before he rained his shadows and fire on her, smothering out her magic as swell after swell hit her. She drowned in it. Her crackles of electricity could barely be seen through the darkness. A wave of fire lit her face, and the look made Ros pause.

Ellea's mouth was slack in pure agony. She bellowed a scream, loud and long, causing something to shatter in his chest. That sound wasn't anger, it was absolute despair. Ros ran the short distance to her curled form as his magic quickly faded. Her shaking hands covered her face, and he grasped at her wrists, trying to pry them away, but she was so strong. He could see the horror through the gaps in her fingers, her eyes squeezed shut and her body racked with sobs.

"I'm sorry." It was a hoarse whimper. "I'm sorry, please stop. I'll try harder."

Ros didn't understand. His shadows and fire hadn't burned her. He was only trying to smother her, smother that destruction. Why was she sobbing? Was this not like the time in the woods? The realization that he'd harmed her in any way made him desperate. He pulled at her wrists harder.

"Ellea," he said over her continued apologies.

"Ellea!" Her hands came away from her face with a jerk. She looked up at him, bewildered, as though she'd forgotten he was there. Tears ran down her face, and he found himself suddenly wanting to kiss them away. When her mouth parted, her eyes searching his face, he wanted to kiss her lips. Then she scowled, and he had never felt so relieved to have someone look so mean.

The relief that came wasn't enough to erase the feeling that he may have made one of the biggest mistakes of his very long life. He would forever regret this. He was so dumb. Why couldn't he say the right thing? Why hadn't he gone about this in a different way? His heart broke as he remembered being in the same spot; his mentors drowning him in their own power until he would submit to them.

He brought her palm to his own face.

"I'm sorry." He pressed a kiss to her damp hand. "I'm so sorry. I was wrong." He closed his eyes as his chin dropped to his chest. "Please…" He couldn't finish.

A hand cupped the other side of his face, and he looked back at her. Stormy gray eyes held him there, their pull so intoxicating. That single vicious look had his body begging to be allowed to drown in their depths.

TRICKY MAGIC

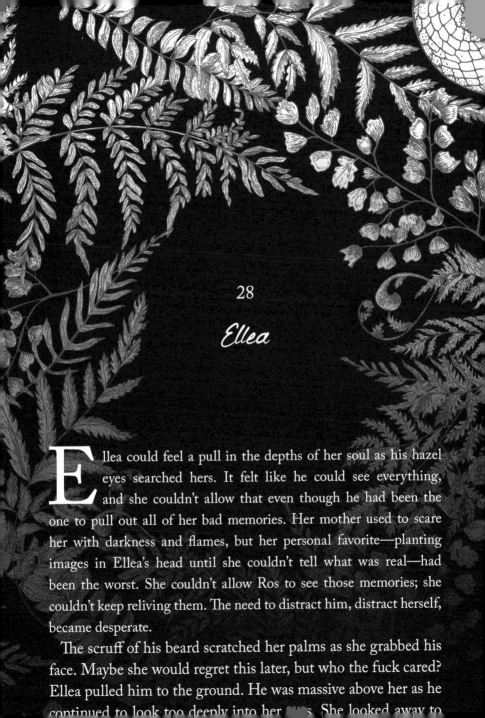

28

Ellea

Ellea could feel a pull in the depths of her soul as his hazel eyes searched hers. It felt like he could see everything, and she couldn't allow that even though he had been the one to pull out all of her bad memories. Her mother used to scare her with darkness and flames, but her personal favorite—planting images in Ellea's head until she couldn't tell what was real—had been the worst. She couldn't allow Ros to see those memories; she couldn't keep reliving them. The need to distract him, distract herself, became desperate.

The scruff of his beard scratched her palms as she grabbed his face. Maybe she would regret this later, but who the fuck cared? Ellea pulled him to the ground. He was massive above her as he continued to look too deeply into her eyes. She looked away to stop his search and bared her neck to him, inviting him to take whatever he wanted, to help her forget.

Ros only lasted half a moment before his mouth was on her skin. They both groaned as soon as his lips touched hers, and it was hard to know if she was pulling him closer or pushing him away. The fight was still in her, and the anger she felt was threatening to take over again. That was forgotten as his sharp teeth scraped along her neck. As he moved across her skin, tasting and biting, she melted into him. Their bodies melded together, and any idea of fighting floated away. He must have felt it too. He chuckled into her ear, a sound so dark with promise that she froze.

"Someone is quick to submit." His tongue grazed the sensitive skin behind her ear. Her hands moved through the thick hair at the nape of his neck, fingers tangling in the wet strands. She yanked hard. He hissed but still smiled down at her. "Are you ever going to not fight me?"

"I will always fight you," she seethed, and for good measure, kneed him in the stomach. "You're the one who was quick to give in."

He hunched over her in pain, but the asshole was still smiling, taking the closeness as an opportunity to lay on her fully, pinning her between him and the ground. They were nose to nose, sharing breath, but she still glared. He only grinned wider. His wet jeans were pressing in all the right—or wrong—places. She was so confused, and her body was giving her the worst signals.

Ellea knew Ros saw the battle raging as he stared into her eyes. His nostrils flared, and his eyes darkened with realization. He pressed into her a little more. She whimpered from the contact, and he dove back in, attacking her neck with his hot mouth and relentless tongue. The sharpness she felt as his teeth scraped her skin had her wondering what other demon things were going unnoticed. His hands explored her body, leaving goosebumps wherever he touched. He pulled at the collar of her shirt, freeing more skin for him to devour, and Ellea whimpered, grinding her hips into him.

Ros groaned, and she shuddered at the sound of it. His hands moved down her body and gripped her ass, pressing her into him harder, causing her to snap. It was too much and not enough. Her hands gripped him, moving him; she needed to taste him, bite him, anything to get closer. She yanked at his hair so he would bare his neck to her. And he did.

Her teeth and mouth were instantly at his throat. The taste of fresh water on her tongue and the taste of him were intoxicating. She was reminded of her favorite things as she explored his skin, perfect fall mornings, rich coffee, and the heavy taste of earth and heat. She couldn't get enough of it as she journeyed over every inch open to her.

As her tongue scraped against the hair on his chin, Ros broke. He tore Ellea's pants from her body. She gasped as cool air met her skin, and she only had a moment to look down to where she was bare against Ros' wet pants. He was already moving down her body, pushing her wet shirt up to have better access to her skin. He kissed and nipped every part of her, and as his hot mouth moved across her, she grew slicker between her thighs.

Ellea explored the best she could as he continued learning about her body. Her hands ran across his back, desperate to touch his skin. They raked through his hair and over his hands that held her. He freed one hand from her grasp and ventured down to her traitorous pussy that was calling to him.

He placed his big hand over her bare pussy; as soon as his palm touched her, she whimpered and sank deeper into the earth. He rested his head against her stomach and held himself still, just breathing and taking in the feel of her. Two fingers parted her, and he released a pleased sigh.

Ros didn't dive right in. He seemed to want to draw out his exploration; circling the wetness at her center and traveling to her clit, kneading and testing, feeling all of her. She grew frustrated, and her breath came out in pants. When Ellea looked down at the man who was torturing her, he smirked and inserted two fingers without warning.

She was ready for it. Hel, she wanted more. She matched his strokes, grinding into his hand the best she could. He growled as his mouth met her clit, and he held her there as she moaned to the night sky.

She felt power radiate through him where he held her down, his large hand splayed over her soft stomach, holding her there as he feasted on her. She couldn't hold her powers back, she couldn't even think when his tongue was doing that. It lapped from her entrance where his fingers curled and pumped to her clit where he circled and teased. His mouth devoured her, and she almost forgot how to breathe as the tingling crept up her thighs that were gripping his head, no longer fighting him. Her powers answered his, heating her chest and radiating out. She didn't even try to stop it.

She let it flow down her arms to her hands that were tangled in his hair. He growled in response. The vibrations of it sent her right to the edge of that cliff. He must have known it too; he smiled over her, taking just a moment to rest. He pressed a kiss to the inside of her thigh as his fingers picked up their rhythm. She began to shake, and he growled again, nipping where he was kissing.

"Are you going to fight even now?" he asked with a voice so thick and deep with lust. The tone of it made her moan and melt into the ground even deeper. His frustrating mouth hovered right above her sex, and she felt his hot breath caress her.

"Come for me, princess," he commanded.

She felt his power again—it met hers and twisted with it. There wasn't destruction. It danced and twined as she was kicked right off that cliff the moment his mouth clashed into her clit. She screamed as her orgasm ripped through her, losing control of her breath, her limbs, her powers. He held her to him through all of it and feasted on her release.

Moments or hours passed as she lay on the earth with his comforting weight on her. Her powers and orgasm gave one final flutter around his fingers, and Ros instantly stood. It was jarring to be free of his touch. She slowly adjusted and brought herself onto her elbows to look at him as he towered over her. He seemed feral as his breath picked up, and a darkness seemed to pass over his bright eyes. She let her gaze run down his body to where his cock was thick and hard, poking out of the top of his dark wet jeans. She smirked and reached for him, but he stepped back. Her brows drew together, and he took another step back.

"We aren't done yet," he growled before he turned and left her there. Pantless, wrung out, and wholly confused.

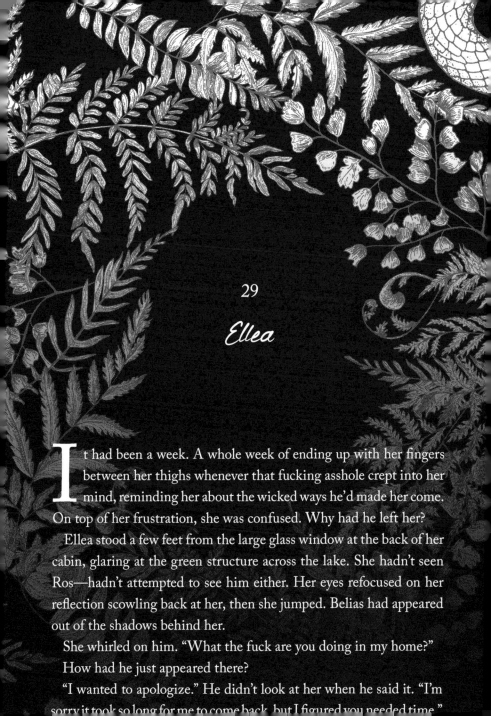

29

Ellea

I t had been a week. A whole week of ending up with her fingers
between her thighs whenever that fucking asshole crept into her
mind, reminding her about the wicked ways he'd made her come.
On top of her frustration, she was confused. Why had he left her?

Ellea stood a few feet from the large glass window at the back of her
cabin, glaring at the green structure across the lake. She hadn't seen
Ros—hadn't attempted to see him either. Her eyes refocused on her
reflection scowling back at her, then she jumped. Belias had appeared
out of the shadows behind her.

She whirled on him. "What the fuck are you doing in my home?"
How had he just appeared there?

"I wanted to apologize." He didn't look at her when he said it. "I'm
sorry it took so long for me to come back, but I figured you needed time."

"Time?" she scoffed, and he looked up. "I need a whole lot more than time to get over the fact that you lied to me."

"I didn't lie." He looked thoughtful. "I only kept what I was from you. Clearly, it was a smart thing to do with the way you reacted."

"Oh, please enlighten me, Belias. How should one react to finding out someone she trusted with her magic lied about who and what he was?" She couldn't believe him. How dare he show up inside her home and think the whole situation was nothing?

"Yes, I didn't tell you I was a demon prince, but what does it matter? What do you know of demons?"

Ellea rolled her eyes. Royalty meant nothing to her, and she didn't even know what a demon prince did with their life, but she knew demons were bad—even though she'd had one between her legs recently. She glared at him and realized he did look like a prince; clean, pressed clothes, raised chin, and a smirk that showed he got whatever he wanted. There was no way he and Ros were related. She waved her hand in the air, showing it didn't fix anything.

"What do you want, Belias?" She was still pissed about that lie too. She'd trusted him with her magic, and he couldn't even share his name.

"I came to offer you a proposition." Clasping his hands behind his back, he stepped closer to her, letting his chin and gaze lower. His dark eyes looked at her from under his lowered brows. "I want to offer you a spot in my court. Come home with me, Ellea, and let's really see what you can do."

Ellea's mouth dropped open.

"Excuse me?" It came out as a cough. He couldn't be serious. "Come home with you? Where?"

"To Hel, of course." He straightened as though he didn't understand why she was questioning this.

Suddenly, laughter bubbled out of her. She bent over with it, causing him to scowl at her.

"I'm being serious," he said over the hysterical giggles.

"I'm sure you're very serious," she said, wiping tears from her eyes. "Why would you think I belonged anywhere near your—what was it—court?"

Her laughs bellowed harder, and he rolled his eyes at her. He wiped his hand over his face, causing her to laugh more.

The laughter cut off as a zing of her magic shot up her spine. Ellea turned to her window, feeling a pull at her core. A wave of unease washed over her, and she looked back at Belias, but he didn't seem to notice what was creeping in her chest. Looking back at the window, she zeroed in on a clump of trees near Ros' cabin. They were swaying and falling too quickly to be someone chopping them down. A wave of something blasted them apart.

"Something isn't right," she whispered. Her feet moved toward the back door on their own, but Belias wrapped his hand around her upper arm, stopping her. She whipped a glare over her shoulder. "Let me go."

"I can't do that." It came out like a hiss, and there was something in his eyes she didn't recognize. Her magic reacted to his hold on her and scorched him through her shirt. He pulled his hand away roughly. "Stop that and listen to me."

"No, you listen to me." She created distance, stepping closer to the back door. "Something is happening, and I need to go help."

"No, you need to come with me." He reached for her, but she lunged away. "You don't belong here, you belong with me."

He tried again as a swirl of shadows appeared behind him. They were nothing like Ros' shadows, but she blasted some of her powers at it, at the void of endless nothingness. The dark tendrils dissipated as her shock of magic cleared them away. Belias glared at them. She took his distraction and swiped quickly at his foot. He landed on the floor with a thud.

An urgent wave of panic washed over her again, making her look over her shoulder to where she was being pulled.

Belias took advantage of her distraction and threw shadows that wrapped around her hands, her face, and then her feet. Again, the shadows were so different from Ros'. His were night and crisp darkness, these were suffocating. She fell to the ground, feeling weighed down and breathless. He dragged her across the floor, but she continued to fight.

What was it with males trying to drag her places?

Ellea cleared her mind, taking a shallow breath, and released her powers. They danced across her skin. Electricity zapped, and the shadows floated away. As her eyes cleared, she saw that Belias was trying to drag her to a doorway filled with shadows.

TRICKY MAGIC

30

Ros

At least forty demons caught Ros off guard. He hadn't seen so many in a group since he was in Hel. They were all different species but of one mind: to attack him. They were relentless and went wild with the taste of blood in the air—his blood, from a bite he didn't see coming. It was his own fault for going on a walk while letting his mind be occupied by the one thing he should try and forget about. This whole week, he could only think about Ellea. No matter what he did, he couldn't shake the vision of her under him, the taste of her on his tongue, the feel of her heated skin sliding against his. It was too much and not enough; he had gone too far. But there was no stopping it, as though the universe wanted them to join, to fight, and to fuck—but that wasn't fucking. It had taken every ounce of effort not to fuck her, especially when she looked at him with hooded eyes, sated from her release. And when she'd reached for him and he'd thought of her heat clenching around him like she had around his fingers…he'd used a feat of strength he didn't know he possessed to leave her on that bank.

He was so dumb for letting it happen—all of it, the attack and then what followed. Whatever they were, whatever the Gods were trying to make happen, it would be impossible. The whispers of his future were growing louder, and it would only be a matter of time before he had to go home and fulfill his duty. A duty that was cursed to leave him loveless and without a partner to rule beside him.

Fucking curses.

No matter the inevitability of it all, his mind always drifted back to her, and it had left him open to an attack. Even unprepared and without his weapons, he would get through it, but it would be bloody, painful, and take most of his magic.

Ros roared at the demon he clutched in his large hands, squeezing the last bit of rotten life from it. As it died, he pulsed a wave of razor-sharp shadows around him, taking down a few who weren't smart enough to duck. Then he attacked with fire and magic, blasting a group to his right so violently that they exploded into tiny pieces and the trees behind them lay burning on the forest floor. A creeping feeling pulled at his chest, and he looked back toward where the lake was, where Ellea was. The distraction left his right side open, and a demon took the opportunity. Its teeth clamped down on his shoulder, enveloping it wholly with its elongated mouth. Burning pain radiated from where its teeth sank into his muscle and bone. It felt venomous, but the pain wasn't enough to distract him from that pull that still grasped his heart. He grabbed the demon by the back of the neck, tearing it away. The demon smiled a bloody, razor-sharp grin, and Ros screamed at it as his magic answered, burning it from the inside out.

Ros turned, catching one of the slower groups with his flames, scorching them quickly and leaving twenty more. He picked up speed, heading toward Ellea's cabin where the draw to move was strongest. It became harder to breathe with every step as his injuries took over, his magic seeping from the wounds that wouldn't close thanks to the toxic bite.

Fucking demons.

31

Ellea

As soon as she saw Ros break through the trees, the suffocating anxiety dissipated. Even as she took in his blood-soaked body and followed the bloody stump of an arm he threw, she felt relieved. She spared his ragged look one more glance before heading deep into the cabin.

Ros crashed through her back door, panting, within a minute, and she couldn't help but smirk.

"Ellea!" It was a pained shout, his voice hoarse and tired. "Ellea?"

"Are you here to save me?" she called from the kitchen.

"Yes!" he yelled. "Please tell me you're okay. I will kill him if he hurt you."

She could hear his heavy footfalls as he searched for her. She wasn't sure how he knew it was Belias, but she scolded herself for not realizing he wasn't trustworthy from the start. Not that she would ever tell Ros that.

Ros paused in the doorway, his hand leaving a blood print against the wall that held him up. He searched her from head to toe, his gaze making her body come alight with awareness. She wouldn't call it *need*—why would she feel aroused by the brute of an ass, looking battered and eyeing her with utter relief? Of course, she was unharmed, she had never needed saving. His eyes shone with something she couldn't place. It was gone with one blink, his lips curled with anger as he looked down at Belias. Confusion flared across his face, seeing his cousin bloody and bound on her kitchen floor.

Belias had gained consciousness as soon as Ros stepped over the threshold. Looking up at the towering demon witch, he rolled his eyes once, and Ros swiftly kicked him in the gut. Both of them groaned, and Ros doubled over in pain, landing on the floor next to his cousin.

"Thank you for saving me." Ellea pressed her hand to her chest in mock praise before reaching down to haul Ros to his feet and into a nearby chair. "I don't know what I would have done without you."

He swayed in her grip but managed to get his feet under him, and she safely sat him at the small kitchen table.

Belias tried to mumble something through his gag, and Ros looked ready to lunge at him, but Ellea glared, forcing him to stay put. He settled into the chair with a groan and wiped at his face before pinning Belias with a murderous look. She headed to the sink, soaking two dish towels in warm water.

The extent of his injuries were covered in too much blood and dirt, so she took calming breaths, repeating the steps in her mind. Clean, assess, then heal. "What happened?" Ros asked, his voice cracking with pain.

"Well…" She released a breath, wringing out the wet towel. "Belias decided to pay me a visit and offer me a one way ticket to Hel." She slapped the towel to his face before Ros could get up and attempt to attack Belias again. "He wasn't happy with my answer, and I took care of it."

"I'm going to kill him," Ros mumbled through the towel, and Belias mumbled something in return. She groaned. Injured men were not going to be fun.

"Now your turn," she said, taking the towel from him and replacing it with a fresh one. He rubbed it along the back of his neck with his left hand, his right arm hanging at his side.

"I'm pretty sure this fucker"—he tried kicking Belias from where he sat—"summoned a horde of demons to attack me. Or distract me."

Had her magic pulled him to her? No, that would be ridiculous.

Maybe not too ridiculous; her Seer magic could pull toward those that needed help, it had nothing to do with Ros, a demon prince who had left her on the lakeshore after giving her one of the best—she shook her head. There was no need to think too much of it.

"Can you do something with him?" She toed Belias' bound feet, using the other demon prince as a distraction. "He doesn't do much for the room, and you are dripping enough blood on the floor for the both of you.

Ros gave Belias a pointed look. "I'm not finished with you, cousin."

He closed his eyes and gave a pained groan, then a black hole of shadows swallowed Belias. Ros panted heavily before peeling his eyes open.

"What do you need?" Ellea asked. Her voice was quiet and pained. She didn't know where to start; cleaning him had uncovered so many wounds. A bruise covered the side of his chin, and there was a large gaping wound through a hole in his shirt.

"Time. Maybe another towel? I will heal, but I used so much magic..."

259

He sighed, and his chin fell in defeat. "Do you have a first-aid kit?"

On cue, the home opened a cabinet, and on the bottom shelf stood a large red tote. Ellea reached for it. It held anything she could need to clean wounds, including potions and different dressings.

"Bring it here," he breathed. "I can fix myself up."

She looked over her shoulder at him. He was hunched in the chair with his eyes on the floor. How could such a powerful man look so ruined?

"Don't be stupid." It was pure sarcasm. "I can take care of you—of it." She stumbled on her words. "Just tell me where to start."

Hazel eyes met hers, and barely a moment passed before he reached for his shirt. She stepped toward him.

"Let me." It came out a bit shaky, but then he gave her one of his signature smirks, and she rolled her eyes. "One snarky word and you're on your own."

He raised his good arm in response, his smirk turned into a small smile.

Ellea held back on using her powers that could easily undress him. A random night by the lake didn't mean she trusted him, so she dragged the shirt over his raised arm, then his head. She gently pulled it down the arm that dangled at his side. Turning quickly, she threw the shirt in the trash and took a steady breath.

"I can't be that bad," he said.

She cleared her mind before turning back to him, taking in his injuries. Besides the gash on his side, he had several more peppering across his chest, his solid abs, and down to his left hip.

"If I didn't know any better, I'd say one of the demons was trying to get into your pants."

He chuckled softly before a pained look crossed his handsome face. Even under the bruise and the leftover blood, he was stunning. The definition of male with his heavy brow, strong jaw, and that scruff she wanted to run her tongue across. She cleared her throat and stepped toward him, ready to get to work.

Ellea pressed lightly against his good leg, leaning over his large body to hold his right arm still while she poured a cleaning solution into the deep gash at the top of his right shoulder. He hissed in pain and grabbed her thigh with his free hand. She scowled.

"Don't be a baby."

He only squeezed harder. After the blood and dirt were gone, she poured the healing potion into the wound. It was jagged, and she needed to press the skin together to help the magic work. Her eyes kept darting to his face, and with each stolen look, his smile grew.

"Don't move while it works."

As she moved to the wounds on his chest, he kept his hand on her, always touching, always looking at her. She only let herself look at him under her lashes, feigning that she was only focused on his care, not his hot and taut body under her fingers. A chill passed over her as he finally had to let go so she could kneel before him to get to the last wound. She took the moment to try and create distance, but the urge to keep touching him was unrelenting. The jagged gash across his hip wasn't enough to distract her from the feeling, especially when the wound continued under his tight jeans.

Don't think about his dick. Don't do it.

She told herself that this was purely medical as she pulled at the waist of his pants. It wouldn't budge.

"I wouldn't be surprised if you put this one here yourself just so I could get close to your…" She wouldn't say it, only waved at the prominent bulge in his tight jeans.

Ros choked on a laugh. "I know better ways to get you close to my cock, princess."

"If you can't behave," she said in a low voice, "I won't be able to finish this."

"There is only so much I can help," he said in a tone that matched hers. She reached for his button, and his eyes darkened.

"Don't look at me like that," she scolded. "I'm trying to get to the hole in your hip, and these jeans are skin tight. I don't know how you wear them." He held still as she reached for the button again.

The cabin was silent as they both held their breaths. The button coming free was so loud that it almost distracted her from his large cock that sprung toward her face. She choked on a breath, and he quickly covered himself with a clean towel. He wasn't fast enough for her to not see *all* of it; how he stood so hard with so many injuries was baffling, almost as baffling as the sheer size of him. A deep ridge extended up his thick shaft, and two large veins ran across the wide base. The skin looked tight and shiny, as if he had been hard this whole time. Thoughts of what it would feel like against her tongue ran freely through her mind. She imagined taking his rosy tip into her mouth and running her tongue around its edges. The taste of him...

She cleared her throat and begged the blush she felt crossing her cheeks to disappear.

"Did the demon that was trying to get into your pants also steal your boxers?" she asked, still trying to find composure.

"No," he growled. "I don't wear underwear."

His eyes traveled across her kitchen, looking anywhere but where she knelt before him.

"Are you embarrassed?" she asked. "I don't either, I was just surprised. I don't know any men who let their trouser snakes hang free."

A low sound came from his chest, and Ellea smiled as she got to work cleaning the last wound.

She held the skin closed to help the healing potion as it worked.

As she waited, her eyes wandered, no longer busy with the excuse of healing. Ros' hands grasped his cock hard through the towel. It twitched under her stare, and her mouth began to water.

"You can't seriously be enjoying this," she said as her eyes met his. They looked back at her, hooded and glazed over.

"I don't think any type of pain could stop me from enjoying the sight of you kneeling before me."

She suppressed the shiver that ran across her skin from the husky tone in his voice.

"But yes, I've always enjoyed a little bit of pain."

She couldn't respond. Images of what she could do with his cock to entice a reaction from him flooded her mind. She could let her teeth graze along the bottom of his hard shaft or rake her nails up his thighs as he hit the back of her throat. It would; there was no way it was fitting all the way in.

In all of her experience, she had never been overly rough, but now she wanted to see what his limits were. She doubted there were any with him, and another shiver of arousal ran down her spine. Her powers crackled at her fingertips. He didn't react to the light shock of it; his eyes grew darker as he continued to look down at her. It would be too easy to move the towel and take him in her hand, her mouth, her throat.

So she did.

Ros

Ros couldn't move. He couldn't breathe as she reached for his hand, the hand that was keeping pressure on his throbbing cock that wanted to be buried in any part of her. He could be missing a limb and bleeding out and it would still be hard for her. Especially as she looked up at him with those gray eyes, so dark with lust, the same shade as a winter storm.

Ros suppressed a growl as Ellea's tongue ran across her bottom lip. Her eyes never left his, and her grip was firm as she moved his hand. She placed it on his thigh, then removed the towel swiftly, as a street magician would reveal a trick they'd just performed. But it wasn't a trick; it was a cock that was hard for her, for the witch who had healed all of his wounds, the one who had let him feast on her after he made one of the worst mistakes of his life.

Her eyes roved over him greedily, and when sparks danced across her darkened gaze, he had to think about anything else, scared he may burst right there from her look alone. When she finally touched him, swiping her finger across the tip, where a drop of precum escaped and beaded on the slit, he forgot why this was a bad idea. When she put that finger in her mouth, groaning around the taste of him, he decided curses didn't matter. Responsibilities didn't matter, nothing mattered but being buried in any part of her.

"I should make you suffer for leaving me that night."

Please make me suffer.

She pulled his throbbing erection toward her, then released it. A wicked grin spread across her face as it bobbed between them, looking like a cat playing with its favorite toy.

Don't compare her to a cat, you dumbass.

He held his words; they would ruin this moment. She hummed to herself, tracing him one more time before she wrapped her hand around him. Her fingertips barely touched. He refused to blink as she brought her mouth to him, tasting him. The first feel of her hot tongue on his sensitive skin was complete and utter bliss, more than he ever dreamed of. Small licks on the small spot under his thick head had tingles forming up his thighs, and when she stroked him once, gently, then again with so much roughness—he couldn't help but jerk in the seat. She smirked as if saying *like that? Okay.*

She took her time, holding him roughly as she worked the tip in and out of her mouth. Slickness ran down toward her hand and she used it, moving her hand in time with her mouth. She moaned around him, and the vibration ran straight to his balls that were still held in his jeans.

He kept his hands fisted on his thighs as she plunged down on him.

His whole body twitched as he hit the back of her throat, and she paused there while her mouth puckered and her tongue did something magical to the underside of him. When she finally came up for air, letting her teeth scrape, he felt that telltale sign at the base of his spine. It was too soon. He didn't want this to end—he wanted to sit here forever.

He looked away and thought of demons and hairless rats—what were they called? Guinea pigs? Yes, guinea pigs, with their whiskers and creepy eyes. Guinea pigs in bikinis, dancing and frolicking. Ellea growled, forcing him to focus on her. She dug her nails in as her hand circled his shaft. His head snapped down to her, and she grinned up at him with the tip of his cock still in her mouth. Her eyes glittered as she smirked around him.

Seeming satisfied that he was paying attention again, she worked him harder. The constant pounding at the back of her throat and the tight grip wrapped around him that followed her rough pace undid any control he had. Releasing some of his hold, he began thrusting on his own, following her command. When she moaned around him, his vision began to blur.

"I'm going to…" He couldn't finish the words and wove his fingers through her hair, trying to gently pry her away. But she growled around him and buried him deeper in her throat. He couldn't help but tighten his grip when she sucked harder. As her tongue and teeth grazed along the underside of him, he erupted.

As he spilled into her, she moaned, swallowing all of him while he was still buried in her hot mouth, convulsing around him, gagging on his length. He thought he could come again if he wasn't utterly drained. She pulled free of him with a loud sucking *pop*. He panted as they stared at each other. There were no words, only boneless bliss. But when she audibly swallowed, he could feel himself hardening again. Ellea stood and wiped at the saliva and cum that beaded at the corner of her mouth. She continued to hold his gaze before turning on her heel, walking away. She stopped at the door frame and looked back at him.

He sat there, unable to speak, and she took one last look at him before saying, "You can let yourself out." And she left him there. Panting, spent, and utterly confused.

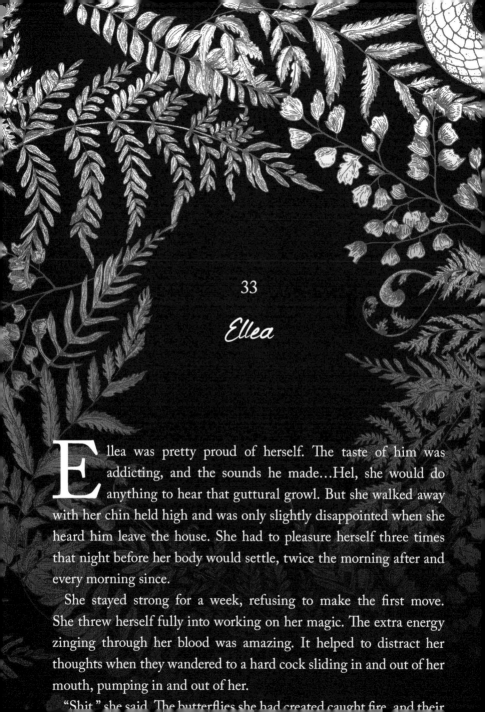

33

Ellea

Ellea was pretty proud of herself. The taste of him was addicting, and the sounds he made…Hel, she would do anything to hear that guttural growl. But she walked away with her chin held high and was only slightly disappointed when she heard him leave the house. She had to pleasure herself three times that night before her body would settle, twice the morning after and every morning since.

She stayed strong for a week, refusing to make the first move. She threw herself fully into working on her magic. The extra energy zinging through her blood was amazing. It helped to distract her thoughts when they wandered to a hard cock sliding in and out of her mouth, pumping in and out of her.

"Shit," she said. The butterflies she had created caught fire, and their ashes rained down on her head. Billy looked up from her sunning spot and rolled her eyes. "Don't look at me like that."

Celibacy doesn't suit you, Bug. She rolled over to sun her other side. *I would have chained myself to the man if he let me—or even if he didn't let me.*

Ellea ignored her familiar and summoned fresh butterflies. She felt a little guilty since they were real, not an illusion. Her magic and powers were cooperating so much lately, as long as she didn't let her mind wander.

"Do you think the things I create have feelings?" she asked the beast. Billy's eyes snapped open, but before she could answer, a knock sounded from the front door. Ellea took a deep breath, counted to five, and slowly walked to the front of the cabin. She didn't want to seem too eager, but her hand shook slightly when she reached for the door knob.

Deep breaths, he is just a man.

Yeah, keep telling yourself that, Bug. Billy laughed in her mind.

Ellea opened the door, and the butterflies flew over her head, escaping as late September sunlight blinded her. She didn't have time to take in the guy in front of her before she was lifted off the ground and brought into a rib-crushing hug.

She sighed as she took in the smell, like the forest with a hint of sandalwood and something beastly.

"Um," she said through a cut-off breath, still being squeezed. "Hi, Sam. Um, why are you rubbing against my face?"

It was weird, but she couldn't bring herself to swat him away. He was just as big as Ros, but his short beard was soft and he smelled like, well, the perfect day. It made her think of walking through the woods and easy conversations.

"Nothing creepy." He rubbed against her more. "Don't worry, it will piss Ros off later."

Mmmmm, I'm next! Billy called from her spot in the sun.

"Ah, the beauty that has had Garm running after her every night," Sam said to the familiar as he let Ellea's feet touch the ground. He still didn't let go of her.

"Okay," Ellea said, pushing away from Sam. "How is it you guys can hear her? Why could I hear Garm?"

Apparently, there were so many other things she didn't know, and it bothered her.

"And every night? Really?" she said, looking at her familiar. Billy only shrugged and smirked.

Sam didn't answer, he just let out a warm chuckle and said, "This is going to be fun."

34

Ros

Ros was slowly losing the ability to take a deep breath. He didn't fight it, either, since this was the only comfortable position for his raging and very hard boner. It was placed perfectly between two cushions as he lay face down on his large couch.

"Are you seriously trying to fuck your couch?" a gruff voice said. He hadn't smelled Sam as he came in, and he still didn't. He refused to move. "Come on, we have to get ready."

Oh right, tonight was Mabon. The past week had been pure torture. Not the endless work of setting up one of the largest bonfires or making sure the eldest supernaturals had a way to get to Sam's farm. The agony came from the constant thought of her, of her mouth, her tongue, her scent…

Her scent?

Ros shifted his face and took a deep inhale through his nose. "Ellea?" he asked and pressed up off the couch slightly, looking for her. Only Sam's laugh greeted him, and his friend walked closer to the couch.

"Oh." Sam laughed harder. "This is bad."

Ros narrowed his eyes at him. "Why do you smell like Ellea?"

"Why do you look like a nest of birds has been living in your hair?" he asked and made his way to where Ros laid. Then he sat on him, pressing his cock further into the couch. It was becoming painful. Sam felt a lot heavier than he looked.

"And I smell like Ellea because someone had to go over there and make sure she was invited to tonight." Sam leaned in closer to where Ros' face was pressed into the couch again. "I smell like her because she was all over me, and…"

He was cut off as Ros sent a stream of shadows to choke him and cover his mouth. Sam still laughed and fell to the floor as Ros stood over him, glaring.

"Excuse me?" he yelled.

Sam only raised an eyebrow as if to say *you are suffocating me and expect an answer?*

Ros bent over him and grabbed him by the shirt. His shadows disappeared, and Sam smiled up at him. He leaned to the side, glancing at Ros' bulge, and raised another eyebrow at him. "You've got it bad, buddy."

"What were you doing with her?" he seethed in his face.

"Okay." Sam raised his hands. "I misjudged this slightly. I only hugged her, aggressively. Nothing sexual, I promise."

Ros slowly released him and took a steadying breath.

"She's not even mine and I'm acting like an idiot. I can't even truly have her," he said, letting him go and running a hand across his face.

"She's coming tonight?"

"A Mabon gift just for you," Sam answered with a smile. "Don't let demon curses ruin my fun. It will work out. Now, let's try to find something for you to wear besides dark jeans and flannel."

Ros pulled at the dark sweater that Sam had made him wear. His hair was clean and brushed, his beard slightly tidy, and he still wore his signature dark jeans. Sam had attempted something called a 'blow out,' but when Ros threatened to strangle Sam's dick with the hairdryer's cord, he'd decided it wasn't needed. "I love the way your hair curls anyway," Sam had said.

He still didn't understand what the big deal was. If Ellea wanted anything to do with him, she would have visited, reached out to him, anything. But there had been nothing. Maybe it was a good thing she wasn't seeking him out; this wouldn't go as far as he wanted. He growled at himself as he sat in his truck in Sam's driveway. It was lined with cars, trucks, and bikes, and two horses grazed in the front paddock. Torches lined the dirt road since it was a new moon and the sky only held stars.

Ros found the courage to step onto the road and head toward the large field that already held about fifty of the town's residents. He took his time and stopped at the edge, looking through the treeline.

He loved it here. There were wolven, vampires, witches, shifters, and anything you could think of, all free to mingle however they chose. Children chased glowing butterflies nearby. Ros blinked; he had never seen butterflies like that before.

Ros' eyes followed them as they circled a head framed by long, loose curls. Their glow set off her freckles, and Ros forgot how to breathe. She wore a loose cropped sweater over a black paneled dress. She had on her black flat boots, and she looked...perfect.

"She got here about an hour ago and has been entertaining everyone with her magic," Sam said as he came up behind his friend. "Devon should be here soon. I can't wait for him to meet her."

Ros couldn't remove his gaze from her. He cleared his throat. "I still don't understand what her magic is," he said quietly. The butterflies shifted to bats that trailed flames behind their wings. "I have been here for over a thousand years, but I have never come across someone like her."

He tore his gaze away and looked at his friend.

Sam didn't answer; he was looking past Ros.

"I can't believe you couldn't pick me up at the airport," a new voice said.

He had such a unique accent; it could only be Sam's partner, Devon. Sam smiled wide and walked over to greet his long-lost boyfriend.

Devon was a few inches shorter than them but just as strong. He was a witch who had lived in every place imaginable. He had also chosen not to settle on one type of magic, refusing to only wield the magic inherited from his family. It only gave them another thing to hate.

"Well," Sam said, then planted a kiss on his cheek. "I'm sorry someone"—another kiss on his forehead—"decided to fly"—another kiss—"one of the worst airlines imaginable." Then he kissed him about five times on the lips. Ros cleared his throat.

"Don't even give me grief, princeling." Sam said to Ros. "I've had to be around your boner for the past month. Let me kiss my boyfriend in peace."

"A boner?" Devon's hiss was teasing. "Can the old man still get it up?" he said with mock shock as he left Sam's side and walked up to Ros.

"Welcome home, Devon," Ros said and smiled at him. He slapped him on the shoulder extra hard to make sure he knew that the old man he was poking fun at wasn't shriveled and in the ground.

Devon gave him a huge smile and slapped him back. "So who has you popping boners?"

"That one," Sam said, pointing a finger to where Ellea stood with even more children, taking requests and creating things from thin air. They were gathered around her and shouting for her to create every creature imaginable. Ros had never seen her with such a smile on her face.

"Fucking Hel," Devon cursed. His hand covered his mouth, and his eyes went wide. He even looked paler than before.

"She's hot, isn't she?" Sam asked with an eyebrow wiggle at Ros.

"No." Devon shook his head. "I mean, yes, clearly, but it's not that." He didn't explain, only walked right for her.

Ros and Sam exchanged looks and followed closely after him. The children were slowly leaving her and following the creatures she created.

Devon stalked right up to her, and Ellea's eyes widened at the intrusion.

"How are you possible?" he asked, searching her face. She didn't respond as she looked past him to where Sam and Ros stood.

"Um," Sam mumbled, "Devon, this is Ellea. Ellea, this is Devon."

"How?" Devon asked again.

"How what?" Ros said, moving to stand next to Ellea. She looked up at him with worried eyes.

"Well," Ellea started, looking down at the ground, "that lasted longer than I thought."

She looked so defeated. Billy came from around the pyre.

"You're a trickster witch," Devon stated. It wasn't even a question.

Ellea grimaced at the statement and looked up at Ros.

"I'm sorry," she said to him.

"Why are you sorry?" all three of them said at once.

Ros couldn't understand why she was sorry. He didn't fully understand what a trickster witch was.

"I've only heard about you in fairytales," Devon said with awe. "I thought your kind died out ages ago."

"I can't believe you know what she is," Ros said. "I'm ancient, and I've never heard of any type of trickster witch."

"I'm not sure, grandpa," Devon said with a smirk. "But they were in hiding after the seventeenth century and encounters were mostly overseas. I've never read about one being in this area."

"Can you not talk about me like I'm not here?" Ellea groaned. "Yes, I am a trickster witch. No, I don't know how I exist or my history. I got it from my father's side, but he never mentioned anything else about it."

"Is he here?" Devon asked, looking around. "Oh, it would be awesome to talk to him and learn more about it."

"No," Ellea said harshly. She didn't elaborate.

"Wait," Ros said, turning to her. "What are you sorry about?"

Ellea didn't get a chance to answer as Devon continued vomiting words.

"It's freaking cool!" he exclaimed. Ros and Ellea twitched at his screech. "I'm sorry, but it's super cool. You shouldn't exist, but here you are, making creatures with your magic. And you're freaking tiny. I thought you would be this big scary thing. Are you a princess? Do you know any other languages? What else can you do?"

He was breathless.

Sam shushed him. "Come on, Devon, let's go check to see where they're at with the fire," he said, directing his boyfriend away from a shocked Ellea. Billy looked up at Ellea. By the look on her face, they were communicating. After a few moments of silence, the familiar trotted off toward the woods without another look back, probably off to torture Garm some more.

Ellea was silent as she watched the beast disappear into the woods. Ros stepped closer to her, inhaling deeply through his nose. She turned slowly toward him, her eyebrows raised. She looked mortified. He liked that look better than how sad she'd started to look.

"Thank fuck," Ros said as he straightened. "You smell like you."

"I, um…" She fumbled with her words. "You're welcome?"

"I would have had to strangle Sam again if I smelled him on you," Ros said flatly. "He is one of the only people I like, and it would get quite lonely without him."

She rolled her eyes and began to walk away.

"Wait." Ros followed after her. "Where are you going?"

Her short legs were traveling pretty fast.

"I don't know," she said without turning. "But I don't want to bother you or the only person you like—or his boyfriend who was looking at me like a freak show." She sounded so angry. "If I wanted to be in a place where people hated me for what I was, I would have stayed in the city."

Ros ran a few short steps and grabbed her arm. "Wait." She whirled on him with fire in her eyes. "No one hates you, and that's not what I meant." She yanked her arm out of his hands and stood there, glaring up at him. "I really like it when you look at me like that," he said as a smirk grew across his lips.

"You're demented," she said before turning away from him.

"If you turn away from me one more time before I'm finished speaking to you"—he grabbed her again and held tight, bringing his face level with hers—"I will lift up that dress and bare your ass to the whole town, then spank you until you stop being a brat."

Her lips slowly parted with each word he spoke.

She was searching his face, and he could see her brain working on a reply. She smirked before opening her mouth to speak. He was ready for it, any reason to get a reaction that wasn't sad or discouraged, to watch her skin grow pink under his hand. She was cut off as the pyre behind them exploded into flames and everyone cheered.

TRICKY MAGIC

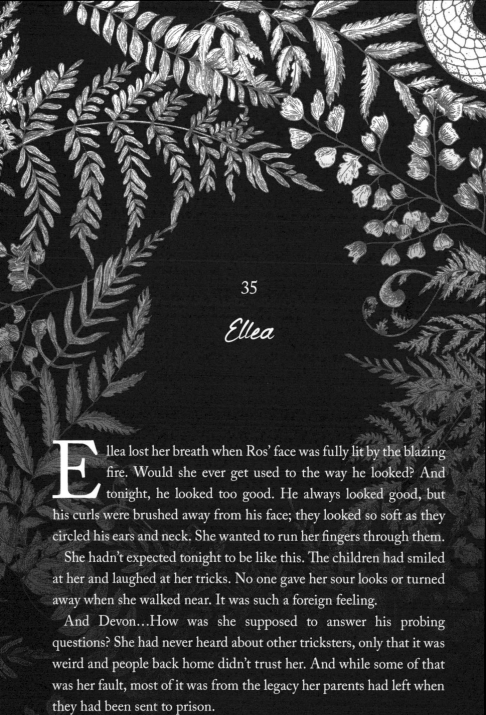

35

Ellea

Ellea lost her breath when Ros' face was fully lit by the blazing fire. Would she ever get used to the way he looked? And tonight, he looked too good. He always looked good, but his curls were brushed away from his face; they looked so soft as they circled his ears and neck. She wanted to run her fingers through them.

She hadn't expected tonight to be like this. The children had smiled at her and laughed at her tricks. No one gave her sour looks or turned away when she walked near. It was such a foreign feeling.

And Devon…How was she supposed to answer his probing questions? She had never heard about other tricksters, only that it was weird and people back home didn't trust her. And while some of that was her fault, most of it was from the legacy her parents had left when they had been sent to prison.

Ellea heard the crunching of grass behind her and turned to see Sam and Devon walking toward them. Ros groaned before he looked at her and reluctantly let go of her arm. "We aren't done."

"I'm getting used to that," she said with an eye roll. Something flashed across his face, and her heart skipped a beat. Would he ever actually do what he said? She suppressed a hopeful shiver.

Devon came up to her first. "I'm sorry for being an ass," he said with his hand on his heart. He gave her a small bow. "I didn't mean to vomit questions at you like that. I was very excited, and I acted like a fool."

He looked at her and smiled. His dark skin glowed in the light of the fire. He looked so young compared to the two brutes next to them. And his accent...she could see herself talking to him for hours and liking every moment of it.

"I brought you an 'I'm sorry my boyfriend is weird' gift," Sam said, and presented her a tumbler. "It's a Mabon Margarita, blood orange, cinnamon, and some of Ag's famous autumn syrup. Oh, and tequila, of course."

Ellea's heart melted. Margaritas spoke to her on a soul level. She sniffed the drink appreciatively before she tasted it.

"Oh, I could kiss you," she moaned as she took another sip.

"See, you beast," Sam said to Ros, "it's not that hard."

Ros only glowered at his friend and directed them toward one of the open blankets around the gigantic fire.

This wasn't like any celebration back in the city. It seemed everyone just enjoyed being around each other. The children played, and everyone else chatted or passed around food.

"Should I have brought something?" Ellea suddenly became worried that she'd done something wrong.

"Oh no," Devon said, patting her knee. "The wolven handles the snacks, Ros handles the fire, and everyone else just enjoys the night.

It's not like other witch gatherings, and that's why I love it."

"So," Ros said, clearing his throat. "Ellea, would you mind if Devon told us what he knows about tricksters?"

He looked at her, and it wasn't a pressing look, but an open one.

"Well, I don't know," Devon said warily. "It doesn't have a happy ending."

"None of them do," Sam cut in. "You know the story about the wolven, we are a bunch of inbreds with no brains who like to have sex with each other, blah, blah, blah." He finished by waving his hands.

"No." Ellea took a deep breath. "I want to hear it. Not much was shared with me growing up. My nana and uncle raised me, and they're seers, so I don't know my history."

She could feel Ros' eyes on her, but she wouldn't look his way. He saw too much as it was.

Devon cleared his throat. "Once upon a time..."

"Boo!" Sam said, and Devon rolled his eyes.

Ellea took a steadying breath and a few full sips of her drink. It was delicious and warmed her as it settled in her stomach. Devon gave both men a stern look before he continued.

"Once upon a time, a pretty princess traveled to distant lands to visit the royal family that ruled there. Her father had sent her to learn more about their customs, how they lived in those lands, and to possibly win herself a husband. She was beautiful, smart, and very cunning.

"When she arrived in the city that surrounded the castle, she was greeted with a parade. They showered her with flowers and gifts. Knights would lay down their swords in the presence of her beauty, promising to slay beasts in her name and win her hand. It was all very magical.

"But the princess had a secret. She had her own magic, and she was there on a secret mission. Yes, she was to learn their ways and how they did things. But she was also there to steal the crown.

"It only took her three months before she was crowned queen, and she didn't need one of the princes or the king to do it. Now as queen, she took control of their lands, their riches, and kicked the royal family to the curb. The people she ruled over revered her ways and welcomed her with open arms.

"One winter's day, a prince came home from war only to find his family nowhere in sight and a foreign ruler sitting on the throne. He was horrified and began his quest to avenge his family. He started small, spying when he could and whispering into ears. He bided his time and learned the whole story.

"The new queen was a witch, an evil trickster who used her cunning ways to take over the lands. The townspeople were horrified and accused her of working with Lucifer, the ruler of Hel." Devon's arms stretched out dramatically, and he gave an evil smile.

"Of course, he would show up," Ros said with a roll of his eyes. Sam shushed him. Ellea was thankful for the break. She'd had a feeling it would get to this, the part where all tricksters were bad and up to no good.

"As I was saying…" Devon cleared his throat and continued, "The townspeople were horrified. They revolted and threatened to string her up in the town square. And when it all became too much, the queen rained destruction onto all the lands. If she couldn't have the throne, no one could." Devon paused for a dramatic effect. "That launched the Newhope witch hunt, and that began the extinction of trickster witches."

Ellea's heart beat wildly as anxiety began to wash over her. It was hard to pull her mask down or calm her voice.

"And you wonder why I apologized for being what I am," she snapped at them.

"Oh, it's just a fairytale," Sam said with a wave of his hand. "Hey, do you think you're a long-lost princess?"

Ellea rolled her eyes and stood. She shook her empty tumbler as an excuse. "I'm going to find something else to drink."

She left without another word, but could hear them whispering behind her. They grew distant with each angry step. She had never heard anything close to that story, but it fit. Raining destruction and angry people, she knew a lot about that. Heavy footsteps followed her, and she looked up to ask the stars for strength.

"Hey," Ros said from behind her. She paused, plastered on a smile, and turned toward him.

"Yes?" The night had been going so well, and now she didn't know what to feel. Had anyone else heard the story? Did they all know? Were they just being nice to the new witch in town? She looked around and only saw people as they had been before, enjoying the night and each other.

"Stop that," he said and stepped toward her. "I'm sorry about Devon and that story. You should hear the ones about me."

Now she was curious. What stories were there? She couldn't stop her mind from wandering to the possibilities. She wished she knew what other secrets he carried and how many more demon qualities he had besides his sharper teeth and size. She shook her head from the thought.

"It's fine," she said with a sigh. "Honestly, I'm not surprised. I've spent my life living that story." She groaned inwardly. "You know what, never mind. I don't want to dull the night any more than I have. I'm going to go."

"What? No." His frown was so genuine. "Everyone loves you, and those kids"—he threw a thumb over his shoulder, and his huge bicep rippled along his black sweater—"it's the first time they haven't let a field of cows or goats into the celebration."

The brief distraction of his muscles rippling with any movement was overshadowed by her anxiety. Life here was different, and they had to be feeding the men something, 'cause no one should look like that. Maybe she was being stupid, but it was too hard to believe no one looked at her differently.

"Come home with me," he blurted out, and Ellea almost laughed. "I have a book you might like."

"Right, Ros," she said, crossing her arms. "If you want another blow job, you don't have to use such a lame excuse."

"No." He shook his head. "I do have a book for you."

"Sure you do." She stepped up to him and patted a hand on his hard chest. "What happened to the male that was threatening to turn my ass pink in front of the whole town?"

She cocked a brow at him as his eyes became darker.

"Devon will drive your car home in the morning." He grabbed her hand and headed for the front of the property.

The drive to Ros' cabin was short and quiet. He wouldn't even give her a moment to pet the horses on their way out, and she pouted the entire drive, thinking about how she hadn't said goodbye to the horses on her nana's property before she'd bolted from the city. Now, she stormed after him as she followed him up the stairs in his dark cabin.

"You're really wooing me here," she said to him as he turned at the top of the stairs.

"I'm not trying to woo you," he growled at her. "I'm trying to give you a book."

Ellea paused at the top of the stairs. Was she reading this whole thing wrong? Is that why he had been avoiding her? She stomped into his room.

"Look." She paused as he held a book out to her. "Oh."

"Yeah." He rubbed the back of his neck. "The morning after our first fight in the woods, I was curious about the magic you used, so I looked and found that in my library."

She took the book from his hands and looked down at the title. "It's in the old language. I can't read this."

She thrust the book back at him.

"Maybe Devon can help you with it," he said, refusing to take the book back. "He speaks it and a few other things."

"Do you speak it?" she asked.

"Yes," he said flatly.

"I had your cock in my mouth, but you can't help me read a book?" He cocked a brow at her, and that settled it. She needed answers. "Look, I'm getting mixed signals, and I'm too tired and over my life to deal with that."

"You're getting mixed signals?" He raised both brows at her. "You're the one that kicked me out of your home after you had my cock in your mouth."

"You're the one that 'attempted,'" she said with air quotes, "to kill me, then ate me out in the grass before you ran off."

He crossed his large arms over his massive chest and glared at her. "What are you asking, Ellea?"

Fine. He wouldn't say it, so she would. "Do you want to fuck me or not?"

Her heart raced as she waited for him to reply. This whole thing was messed up, but she couldn't deny what she was feeling. Her magic had finally settled down, and she could think somewhat clearly. But what if she was wrong and he didn't want that? What if he regretted what had happened?

"Of course, I want to fucking fuck you," he said, spreading his arms out. "I want to do more than that."

Ellea's heart skipped yet again, and heat pooled in her stomach. She felt like Billy, tongue hanging, drool dripping, as she took in the large man before her. The sheer size of him, body and cock. Her mouth watered as she remembered the feel of him sliding in and out of her mouth. How would it feel to have him inside her? Could she take it? She straightened and begged her knees to stop wobbling. Of course, she could.

"More?" She stepped toward him and smirked. "How could there be more than fucking? Is it a demon thing?"

She took another step and stood in front of him.

TRICKY MAGIC

36

Ros

Ros tried to grasp that Ellea was in his bedroom. It took him a moment to understand the weight of it. Yes, he'd admitted he wanted her, but she hadn't said the same in return. This could all be a game to her. He'd never understood women or men, and hadn't been with one in a few years; the last time had only been to see if he had a lick of humanity left. And yeah, he'd liked it. The woman had too, but they hadn't been in it for the same reason.

Now he had a woman in his room, but she still hadn't said what she wanted. He also hadn't asked yet. "What do you want, Ellea?"

He could smell the arousal on her, but he had to hear it.

"I want you to do everything you promised," she said in a voice full of lust. "I want to fuck you and to do what I want. I don't want you to hold back. I want you to spank me, punish me, and show me what 'more' is."

His knees almost buckled at that statement, but he held strong and took a steady step toward her. He bent and let his breath caress her ear. "What do you want right now, princess?"

She bared her neck to him, and he ran the tip of his nose along it, inhaling her perfect scent. It was spicy, soft, and laced with so much need.

"On your knees," she said breathlessly.

Ros obliged slowly. He let his teeth gently graze her neck, and the back of his knuckles brushed her breasts through her sweater. She shivered. He grasped her hips to steady his descent, not that he needed it. He would have crashed to the floor in front of her, but he had to hold on to some dignity.

Ros knelt in front of her. His hands moved to grasp her ass, and he squeezed hard. He couldn't wait to mark it. He looked up to her and cocked a brow, waiting for her next command.

Ellea took a steadying breath. "I may not know everything about being a trickster," she said before running her hands through his hair. Ros blinked once and her clothes were gone. "But that is one trick I know pretty well."

Ros stopped breathing. She was fully naked in front of him. In a mere second, her clothes were gone. He blinked a few times and finally found a way to use his lungs. He breathed out, "You're so fucking beautiful."

He grabbed her ass again and groaned, feeling her warm skin under his hands. He almost came in his pants at the feel of it.

She was beautiful, gentle curves and strong legs. He kissed her soft stomach and she moaned lightly, pressing herself into him. He nipped at her hip, and she placed her leg on the bed next to her, baring her pussy to him fully. Ros almost swallowed his tongue.

That night by the lake had been fast and rough. He hadn't taken the time to marvel at her. He would remedy that immediately. He took two fingers and ran them from her center to her clit, and they came back soaked. Looking up at her with a smirk, he put them in his mouth and sucked. His mouth watered at the taste. She gaped down at him, and he knew right then that he wanted to always surprise her like this.

Ros leaned into her and took as much as he could, letting his tongue roll around her center, lapping up her wetness. His finger slowly toyed with her, pumping in and out, one, then two. He would work to three, stretching her as he worked her clit.

Her panting turned into moans, and her legs began to shake. He turned her, and she fell back onto the bed. Giving her a break, he tore his sweater off, but she quickly stepped in and used her brilliant powers. He was fully naked without even feeling the pull of the clothes on his skin. His cock bobbed after being freed.

"I like that trick," he said to her. "Now open for me. I want you to come on my tongue before you come again on my cock."

She gave him a seductive smile and slowly let her legs spread wide across his bed, bearing herself to him fully. He lay before her, and as soon as he inserted his fingers, her legs began to shake again. He had to work her more before he could even think about getting his cock in there.

Ros slowed down, nipping at her thighs, her stomach, and her clit. She moaned, deep and low.

"Please," she begged.

He chuckled into her pussy. "Please what, princess?"

"Don't be a jerk," she whimpered. "Let me come, please."

He smiled against her thigh, keeping the pace slow before she let out a growl of protest. Curling his fingers inside of her and placing his mouth over her clit, he sucked hard, circling his tongue. She came instantly, and it was glorious.

He dragged it out the best he could, and she shook before him. The feel of her clenching around his fingers made his cock twitch against the bed. Her powers crackled across her skin with release, and he could almost see the sparks. His own powers answered to hers and began to swarm under his skin.

Getting to his knees, he grasped her thighs to drag her against him. Grabbing his cock, he rubbed it through her sex that was soaked with her release. She reached for him, wrapping her hands behind his neck and pulling him down. His elbows rested on either side of her head, and she opened her heavy eyes.

"Do you still want this?" he asked, searching her face. She answered him with a kiss, just one placed softly on his lips.

"Yes." She kissed him again, harder this time. "Yes, I want you to fuck me."

Ros' chest heaved with the feeling of her lips on his. They were soft and teasing. She nipped at him, demanding entrance, and he opened for her, letting her tongue explore. Her hands tangled in his hair, and she tugged hard.

"Please," she said again while rubbing herself against his length that waited between her thighs.

He felt he would die if he didn't give in to this pull toward her. His magic wasn't warning him of danger. It was warning him that he needed her, needed this. So he kissed her harder, letting his tongue dance with hers as he drove his cock home.

TRICKY MAGIC

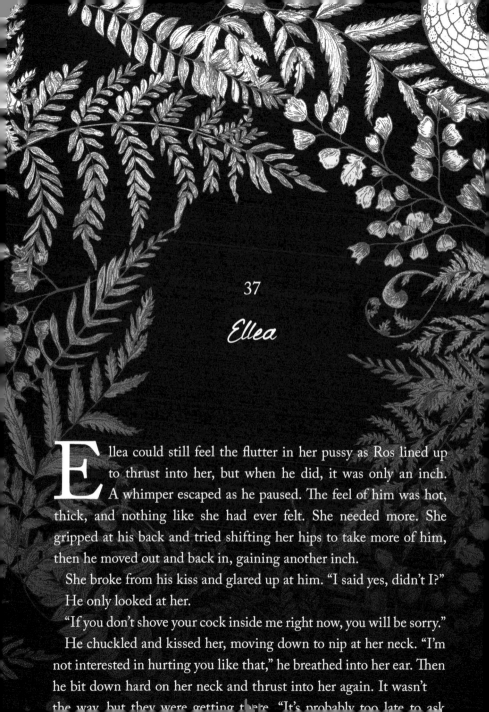

37

Ellea

Ellea could still feel the flutter in her pussy as Ros lined up to thrust into her, but when he did, it was only an inch. A whimper escaped as he paused. The feel of him was hot, thick, and nothing like she had ever felt. She needed more. She gripped at his back and tried shifting her hips to take more of him, then he moved out and back in, gaining another inch.

She broke from his kiss and glared up at him. "I said yes, didn't I?" He only looked at her.

"If you don't shove your cock inside me right now, you will be sorry."

He chuckled and kissed her, moving down to nip at her neck. "I'm not interested in hurting you like that," he breathed into her ear. Then he bit down hard on her neck and thrust into her again. It wasn't the way, but they were getting there. "It's probably too late to ask about birth control?"

She whimpered again as he pulled out, waiting for her answer. She clawed at his back and could feel his skin tear at the contact.

"I can't have children," she said and he moved to look at her face. "Honest."

Ros thrust into her again and she cried out. "We are going to talk about this later," he said to her as he slowly pulled out. "Hold tight, princess."

And then he drove his cock fully into her. She could feel him slide in and then resistance as her pussy clenched around him. He paused, kissing her hard, and when she relaxed, he began to move.

And, Gods, did he move. Slow, deep thrusts that had the tip of his thick cock hitting a spot she hadn't even realized she had. Heat radiated all around her, and she could have sworn she was going to come, but it was too quick, and it never happened with only a cock inside her. But it wasn't that. Instead, it was her magic building inside her, sparkling across her skin. She didn't feel the heavy dread that came with losing control of her powers. She felt lighter, and her heart fluttered with it.

Ellea gasped, and Ros abruptly stopped.

"What?" He searched her face. "Did I hurt you?"

"No," she breathed out. "What are your shadows doing?"

She watched them crawl up her legs and arms. They were a whisper of smoke compared to their usual blackness. They twined with the sparks of magic popping off her skin.

"I'm not..." He thrust into her again. "I've never seen them do that." He shivered on top of her. "I've never felt this. What is this witchcraft?"

She thought he was accusing her, but she quickly relaxed when he chuckled against her neck.

She couldn't find the air to speak; she only shook her head to say *this isn't me.* He swore, and his thrusts became more erratic; with each one, his shadows pulsed across her skin. They both shivered together as another wave of magic pulsed out, and when it passed, Ros snapped. He plunged into her in one hard thrust, and she yelped. A low growl escaped him, and he rose to look down at her. His eyes were feral, almost glowing as his chest heaved.

She felt wild with need and worried he would stop, that this was all too new for him, as it almost was for her. Her heart continued to flutter wildly in her chest, and she didn't understand it, didn't understand her magic. She reached for him, placing her palm on his face, running her thumb across his parted lip. *It's okay,* she tried to say without words, *I feel it too.*

A deep growl left him as he kissed her palm. He grasped her hips, leaned back on his toes, and brought her with him. A breath whooshed out of her at the feel of him. The deepness from this angle was right on the edge of pain. But she wanted it, needed it. She thought her heart would explode on that first thrust; its fluttering turned heavy in her chest, and her magic pulsed out again.

The crackle across her skin snapped like live lightning. Ros kissed her through it, tongues and teeth colliding. She twined her fingers in his hair, anchoring herself to him as he impaled her on his cock with deep, slow thrusts. He guided her with his large hands on her ass, up and down, again and again. There wasn't space between them as their chests, slick with sweat, heaved as one. The beats of their hearts were no longer their own, but each other's.

Another wave of magic began to crest, and it wasn't just hers this time. He shook as his shadows flowed out from him, twining again with her sparks. As it reached its peak, power radiated through the room, light exploded, and curtains swayed. As it fell, it brought Ellea with it.

An orgasm ripped through her so fast and sudden that she couldn't catch her breath. She roared against Ros' mouth, and when her pussy clenched around him, she could feel every inch of his hot skin inside her. He exploded after three long, hard thrusts, her walls fluttering around him, dragging out both their releases. It felt as though it would never end.

Ros held her to his chest as their breathing slowly became less erratic. He brushed her long hair away from her face and kissed her one last time before laying her on his large bed. They both groaned as he slowly pulled out of her.

Ellea grabbed one of his pillows and curled around it. She could feel his eyes watching her as she slowly came down from whatever had just happened between them.

A moment (or many moments, she couldn't tell) later, she heard a glass of water hit the table beside her and then the bed shifted. Ros grabbed her knee and pulled her away from the pillow. She grumbled at him, but he took a warm towel and gently wiped up the mess they'd both created. Once he was satisfied, he slid down next to her, putting his arm under her head and the pillow she clung to. Then grabbed her hip and moved her so she was pressed against him. He pulled a thin quilt over their bodies and settled into his own pillow.

"Just give me five more minutes and I will head home," she mumbled to him.

"You aren't going anywhere tonight," he said, kissing her shoulder, her neck, and the back of her head.

"Just five more minutes," she whispered.

"Sure, princess," he said. Ellea felt a curl of a smile against her neck before the heaviness of sleep pulled her closer to its depths.

"Whatever you say."

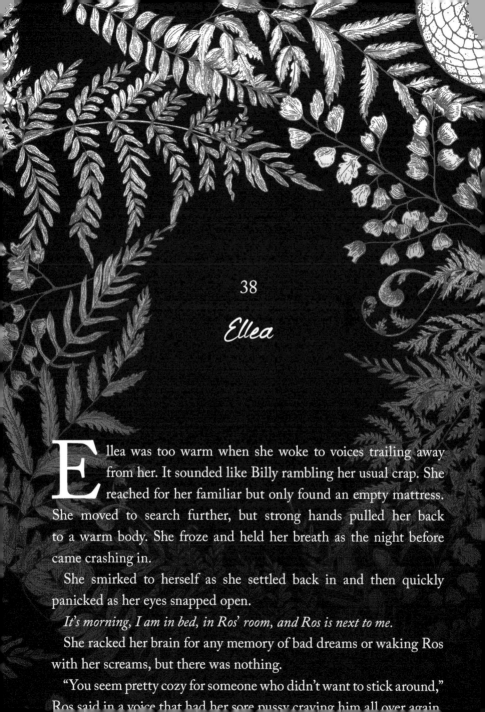

38

Ellea

Ellea was too warm when she woke to voices trailing away from her. It sounded like Billy rambling her usual crap. She reached for her familiar but only found an empty mattress. She moved to search further, but strong hands pulled her back to a warm body. She froze and held her breath as the night before came crashing in.

She smirked to herself as she settled back in and then quickly panicked as her eyes snapped open.

It's morning, I am in bed, in Ros' room, and Ros is next to me.

She racked her brain for any memory of bad dreams or waking Ros with her screams, but there was nothing.

"You seem pretty cozy for someone who didn't want to stick around," Ros said in a voice that had her sore pussy craving him all over again.

"I don't sleep with anyone besides Billy," she said and turned toward him. He wasn't letting go of her, and it made it hard to face him fully. She wished she hadn't. He looked adorable with his long lashes fanned across his still-closed eyes, sleep-tousled hair, and pouty lips. It wasn't fair. "I've never slept in the same bed with anyone besides her."

"Well," he said with his eyes still closed, pausing to yawn. He didn't even have bad breath. "Now you do."

"Now I do what?" She glared at his perfect face.

He opened one eye and smiled. "I can't say I've ever woken up to a female glaring at me like that before." He pulled her closer.

"Now I do *what?*" she asked again.

"Now you sleep with someone besides Billy. But I bet she wouldn't mind sharing a bed with us," he said.

I wouldn't mind at all! came Billy's voice from far away. Ros chuckled and settled into bed.

"That was a one-time thing," she said.

"Whatever you say, princess." He gave her a sleepy smirk with his response.

"Don't you need to get up and chop wood or something?" she said, trying her best to get out of his embrace.

"Someone is very grumpy after being thoroughly fucked last night," he said as he pulled her in tighter.

She tried to get out of his hold, and when she shimmied down, she was greeted with a very hard something pressed into her body. It twitched, and she suppressed a moan. Her pussy had to stay out of it. There were other pressing things besides a perfect cock and a good fucking. Like, how did she sleep through the night, what was with her powers, and why did she have so much energy coursing through her?

"Do you feel weird?" she asked.

"No," he said, and opened his eyes. They were so bright in the morning sunlight, the amber and greens sparkling at her. His cock twitched again. "I'm horny and hungry. Why?"

"Last night was..." She paused, searching for the right words.

"Magical? The best sex you've ever had?" He smiled.

"No." She frowned at him, and his face dropped.

Oh, the brute can be hurt.

"Stop; you know it was all of those things. But the magical part, that wasn't me and that has never happened before."

"How?" he asked, letting go with one arm and resting his head in his hand. "Don't all witches have some weird stuff happen during a new moon or holiday?"

"Not me," she said. "I have had plenty of sex during holidays and moons, and that has never happened."

"I would rather not hear about you having sex with other people," he growled, and his eyes darkened a shade.

"I'm sorry, does my partner count bother you?" she said with a scowl. "You're a billion years old; I'm sure you've slept with more people than me."

"It's not the count," he said with a soft expression. It turned aggressive before he said, "It's the thought of someone else touching you."

She didn't know how to respond to that. How could he be so territorial this fast?

"Oh, I see your brain working," he said and brushed hair behind her head. "Look, we have spent too many weeks dancing around things, not fully saying what we should."

"You mean like when you threatened to kill me?" she said with an arched brow.

He rolled his eyes.

"Yes, that, and other things," he said, and then held her gaze in such an intense way. "I am too old to dance around questions and feelings.

It didn't work for us the past few weeks, and I don't think it will work in the future."

The future. She didn't know how to respond to him. Thank Hel for Billy, who trotted in right when he seemed to notice her grasping for something to say.

I hate to break up this revelational love fest, but I need to talk to Ellea, Billy said.

Ellea kissed Ros fully on his non-morning-breath mouth before crawling out of his enormous bed. She stood there naked before him and had never felt so confident. He pushed up more and the blanket fell away from him, revealing his perfect tan skin, his broad chest, and abs that directed her to her new favorite thing in the world. Billy chuffed dramatically before nudging her out of the room.

Ellea summoned warm leggings and a light sweater as they headed out of Ros' cabin.

"Thanks for saving me," she whispered to her familiar.

I wasn't really saving you, just giving you time to think. But I do need to talk to you, Billy said to her. *Let's go for a walk?*

Ellea was concerned, but nodded. They headed toward one of the longer trails that would eventually loop back to her cabin. Billy looked up at her with big sad eyes, and Ellea was worried something was truly wrong.

I heard that story Devon told you last night, Billy said.

"Yeah, that was a real treat. But I'm not surprised," Ellea mumbled to her beast.

It's not the entire story, though, Billy said, sounding even sadder.

"Most fairy tales aren't," Ellea said, trying to keep her voice somewhat happy. She hated how Billy was acting.

The princess in the story, her name was Astrid, and she was a witch, just like you.

"Just like me?" Ellea asked in a whisper. "You mean..."

She was a trickster. But wholly trickster. You see, back then, it wasn't like it is now, with witches and mortals living side by side. Each had their own land and sometimes they would avoid each other or sometimes war would break out. But tricksters, they were feared far more than the other witches.

Tricksters were challenging. They fought against normalcy, constantly trying new things, and back then, new was never good. Everyone was so afraid of change or challenge. So when a trickster was discovered, they would be killed without warning. For most found, there was no trial, no test, just removed from the world. Others weren't so lucky. They would be tortured, forced to create things or to be experimented on. No one fully understood what a trickster could do, but they knew they didn't like it and they didn't want to find out—especially after Astrid.

She was a real princess, with a castle and a family who loved her. The king and queen ruled over a small island and kept their magic a secret as much as they could. They would hide other tricksters or any magical being that needed refuge.

When Astrid turned fourteen and it was time for her familiar to leave, her father asked it to stay. Asked me *to stay.*

Ellea stopped at the fork in the trail and bent down to her beast, her friend.

"Whatever you're about to say, it won't change anything between us," she said and rubbed the wrinkle between her deep forehead.

I know, Bug, but I need you to hear it.

Ellea nodded her head, and they continued walking.

Astrid had spent her whole life on the island, and as she became older, she became more restless. Her father asked me to stay for a year or two to accompany Astrid as she traveled away from the safety of the island for the first time.

So I did. I took my human form and accompanied her as we traveled for a few years. We traveled across the sea, through deserts and mountains. We saw mortal lands along with the good and bad that came with it. We saw secret supernatural territories, which were beyond amazing, but they also helped her understand why her parents hid her and the island for so long.

We traveled for three years and headed back after her seventeenth birthday. There were some small correspondences throughout our trip with her family, and no one ever said anything we would've worried about. But when we arrived home…the island was in ruins.

It was as if war had crumbled it in its ugly hand. There were no people left, no homes, nothing. Not even a way to understand what had happened. We salvaged what we could and left. After talking with a neighboring island, we learned that a royal family from the continent had come and destroyed everything four months before we came home.

Astrid was devastated. She had no family, no land, and no means to avenge what had happened. But she did have time, and she took it. The fairy tale you heard was true, but the time leading up to it, that was all her. She created a whole new identity and story in order to get access to the royal family that ruined hers. The middle part, with the prince coming home and learning what she was, that was also true. But when she destroyed the land and the townspeople, she burned with them, and I couldn't save her. I tried everything. I tried stopping her, protecting her, but she was too lost, too stricken with grief, and in the end, I don't think she wanted to live in a world where tricksters were no longer a part of it.

Ellea had tears in her eyes as Billy finished her story.

"But me?" she asked. "My father?"

I don't know, Bug. But when I heard your call and realized what you were, I knew it was meant to be.

"Is this why you've stayed with me for so long?" Ellea asked in a whisper. She would understand if it were true, to make sure she didn't follow in Astrid's footsteps.

No, not because of that, Billy said, reading her thoughts. *I mostly stayed because I want to make sure some of the last tricksters have a chance. But also because I love you the most, and I don't want any other witches after you.*

"Have I ruined you for anyone else?" she half-sobbed, half-laughed.

Of course not. Maybe I would have stayed if you had your own children. But when you chose to give up that part of you, I knew that was it for me too. And I don't blame you, please know that. It was fully your choice, and I support it.

Ellea couldn't speak. She couldn't form the words to tell Billy how much she loved her.

I know, Bug, I love you too.

They stopped in front of the cabin. Ellea crashed to the ground and embraced her familiar, her friend.

"Hey," she said, wiping at her eyes. "Why don't you ever take your human form with me?"

She had always known it was possible, but never thought to ask.

Humans don't get belly rubs from handsome strangers, and I like this form. I save my human form for Garm, Billy said with a wink, and Ellea laughed through her tears.

"Want to go watch Harry Potter and eat some junk food?" Ellea asked, rubbing at her eyes.

Like old times? Hel yeah!

They were halfway through *"Goblet of Fire"* when Devon showed up with Ellea's car. She had forgotten all about it, for obvious reasons, but was happy to have him there. Instead of handing her the keys and heading out, he heard what was playing and let himself in. The home had greeted him with a warm blanket, a bag of chips, and a hot cocoa.

"Um," Ellea looked at him, horrified, "it has never done that for me before."

"You don't have magical homes in the city?" he asked, shocked.

"I do, and I live in one, but this one," she said in a whisper, "is a freaking bitch and hates my guts."

As she said it, a cold breeze traveled across her face. Ellea scowled, and Billy and Devon laughed.

"I did come here for something, not just to couch-crash and steal snacks," Devon said as the laughter died down. "I'm sorry about yesterday; I hope I didn't make you uncomfortable."

"You did," she said with a smile. "But it's okay. I'm...working through some things." She looked down and toyed with a string fraying from the blanket on her lap.

"Well, if it helps at all," he said, placing a hand on her lap, "I think it's pretty freaking cool that you're a trickster."

"Yeah." She laughed lightly. "I kind of saw that last night. I'm not used to it, though. People back home hate it, have hated it for as long as I can remember."

"I totally get that," he said. "My family are all hereditary witches, and when I decided to not follow in their steps...well, I got shunned by the community. Don't even get me started on being gay." He shook his head. "There is nothing worse than an heir to a hereditary line choosing to not marry off and make little hereditary witchlings." He gagged on his words.

"You don't want children?" Ellea asked, hoping she wasn't probing.

"Oh, I do, but later. Much later," he said with a warm smile. "They won't be what my family wants, hopefully."

Ellea bet he meant little witch wolven children, and she smiled at the thought.

"What about you?" he asked. "Are you and Ros going to make little grumpy babies?"

Ellea's heart dropped, and Devon picked up on it.

"I'm sorry," he said, wiping at his face. "I really need to learn when to shut up."

"No," she said, hitting his leg lightly. "It's not that. I just…well, last night was…was last night." She smiled, and Devon smirked at her. "It's new, and no, I don't want children. I actually gave that up for immortality. It's a plus to not age, and I don't want to create monster babies. It's a fear I've had since I was a kid. I was far too young when my mother was already talking about the line I would create."

Devon's eyes widened, and Ellea's anxiety began to rise. Had she said the wrong thing?

"I'm sorry." She fiddled with the blanket again. "I guess I don't know when to shut up either."

"No," he said, sliding closer to her. "It's not that. I'm sorry about your mother. I just never knew a witch to do that."

Immortality in witches wasn't uncommon. In order to choose that path, you have to give something up—a part of your magic, a bit of your soul—or make a life-altering decision. Most would give up their lesser traits or something they loved, like their blue eyes. But the more you gave, the stronger your immortality would be. It was an easy decision to make when she turned twenty-five.

"I didn't want to give up my magic," she said, looking at him. "It was an easy decision, and the lack of wrinkles is a major plus. I shouldn't show signs of aging for at least five hundred years."

"That's badass," he said in awe. "I haven't made that plunge yet, but I still have time."

Ellea smiled at him, and when he gave her a true smile back, she fully relaxed.

"I also wanted to offer my services," he said. "I wanted to see, if you want it, help with learning more about your powers?"

Ellea thought about it. Belias came to mind, and she scowled inwardly, wondering where the dark ass-hat was. But Devon was different. She could feel it, and a whisper in the back of her mind pushed her.

"Yes," she said with a warm smile. "I would love your help." She glanced over to Billy, who gave her a nod in approval. "I would also like to introduce you to Princess Astrid's familiar."

Devon's eyes bounced between Billy and Ellea, and she couldn't help but laugh.

"You mean," he said, fanning himself, "that the story is true? I am in the same room as someone who knew her? I'm going to die."

Ellea worried this was too much and too soon for Billy.

It's okay, Bug. I want her story to live on, and I want you to have all the support you can get.

TRICKY MAGIC

39

Ros

Ros pulled into Sweet Betty's coffee shop. He had only been here a few times since his preference for coffee was black, boring, and something easily made at home, but he had a distinct feeling that Ellea took her coffee some fancy way. He wanted to make sure he greeted her with something other than an awkward "Hey, we fucked the other night, and I don't know what to do with my hands" this morning.

A chime rang overhead as he ducked through the doorway. Ros had barely stepped in before he was forced to stop. He scowled at the ten people before him, knowing he had no other choice but to wait. There were two girls working the counter and one working some mechanical hunk of metal that was shooting steam while grinding beans. The coffee shop was built into the first floor of an older house. The hardwood floors creaked under his boots as he shuffled his feet impatiently.

How were there so many people needing coffee?

Most of the chairs were taken up by people he knew. Some quickly grabbed their drinks and left to begin their days. He wondered if Ellea was up yet. Ros had grown worried after he hadn't heard from her all day and night, or when he woke this morning. She had been a little weird about waking in his bed the day before, and it made him wonder if he had done something else wrong. He groaned inwardly at himself as all the mistakes flashed in his head. Sam had saved him from his earlier spiral with a call to let him know Devon and Ellea fell asleep on the couch after watching some movie or show Ros couldn't name. The relief only lasted a minute before realization kicked in.

Where did they go from here?

The curse that haunted his family meant this wouldn't be forever, but they had time. He wanted to help her, teach her about power and what it meant, and enjoy her for as long as he could. But he would have to learn to let her go.

A tapping sound pulled Ros from his thoughts. He looked skyward, begging the gods for patience as the line before him barely moved. The sound became louder. He turned toward it and found a woman tapping her long black nails against the table she sat at. She was smiling directly at him, but it wasn't a friendly smile—it was wicked. Her amber eyes seemed to glow as they bored into his soul.

Why was she looking at him as if she knew him?

He had never seen her before, and her face was one he would remember. She cocked her head at him as they continued to stare at each other, her short, blunt hair swaying with the movement. It was a harsh black that swallowed up the light, and her rich tan skin reminded him of his time in the deserts a *very* long time ago. He searched her face, trying to remember if he knew her. She roughly kicked the chair out in front of her and nodded her head toward it. *Sit,* she demanded. Ros glared at her, and she rolled her eyes in response.

"I already ordered your coffee, handsome," she said and nodded toward the chair again. Her voice held a teasing tone he couldn't place, but he had heard it before. Tearing himself from the line, he headed toward her table.

"Do I know you?" Ros stood before her, refusing to sit. She leaned back in her chair, and a soft chuckle escaped her dark lips.

"Yes and no," she responded. Her long nails traced idle patterns in the wooden table. Their points were sharp, and they left a shallow indent in the worn wood. He broke the stare from her ethereal eyes and assessed her. Ink snaked up both arms and continued under the loose black shirt she wore. The details and the way the lines crossed and swirled in such an intricate pattern reminded him of the tattoos his family bore. Leaders and warriors inked their skin to match their weapons that were forged by the Gods. No two were the same. She leaned back further and stretched her long legs out from under the table in a feline manner. Bare feet poked out, and he noticed she was wearing loose faded jeans that were rolled up at the ankle. Her outfit was such a dramatic contrast to her features. They were fierce and strong, features he hadn't seen in quite some time.

"Like what you see?" she purred at him. He cocked an eyebrow in response.

"Why would you order my coffee?" Ros asked, crossing his arms over his chest.

"I ordered both of your coffees," she said, leaning forward. "I figured you wouldn't know what Ellea wanted."

"How do you know Ellea?" he growled.

"So protective," she mocked. "And she isn't even yours yet."

"I will ask you again," he said, placing his hands on the table in front of her—bringing his eyes level with hers. "How do you know Ellea?"

His powers began to build, ready to fight this unknown threat. Her eyes slowly squinted before a wide smile stretched across her face. Then she laughed, right in his face. Ros growled low and deep, and the table shook slightly under his hands.

"Oh, chills," she mocked with a shiver. "Sit, Rosier," she commanded, her rich laugh disappearing. "I won't ask you again."

"I'm not going to sit at a table with someone I don't know," he forced out.

"But you'll stalk a witch and threaten her life multiple times?"

Ros was stunned. How did she know so much? And that tone... Ros' mouth dropped open, and the female nodded her head.

"Billy," he whispered.

"Me," Billy answered.

Ros sat heavily in the chair as more questions popped into his head.

"How?" he asked. How was she here, like this? "How did you know I was going to get coffee?"

"We all have our secrets," she said, and Ros rolled his eyes at his own line. "We need to talk."

Talk? They talked already. Why was now any different from the times when she was screaming in his head about how nice his ass was?

"Rosier, don't make it weird," Billy said to him.

"Get out of my head," he scolded. "And since when do you use that name? It's always been 'hunk' or 'fine piece of ass.'"

"Since I fully understood the situation," she said seriously, but her eyes lightened. "And I will still probably call you those things." She dragged her bottom lip across her too-white teeth as her eyes roved across his body.

"Stop that," he said. "What did you want to talk about?"

"Don't play dumb," Billy said, meeting his eyes. "I need to know your plan."

"What plan?" he asked, more confused. "Get coffee and go see Ellea. Does she know you're here?"

"Not that plan. Gods, the pretty ones are always so thick-headed," she mumbled to herself. "What do you want from Ellea?"

"Want from her?" He was shocked. "I don't want anything."

"Oh, nice answer," she scolded. "First you wanted to kill her, then to mess with her, and now you share her bed?"

"It was one time." He looked down at his hands, questioning what she was getting at. Of course, he didn't have a plan, it'd been barely a day.

"She's special, you know," Billy said with so much love in her voice.

"I know," he answered.

"Then why the fuck did you think about killing her?" Billy barked.

"She was—is— dangerous."

"Is or was. Or does it matter now that you got her into your bed?"

"Got her into my bed?" Ros hissed. "How dare you?"

"How dare I?" Billy's lips pulled up in a snarl, reminding Ros that the creature in front of him was not just a pretty face. She leaned in close to him and her eyes glowed with menace. "She is too good and too special to be toyed with."

"I fucking know that now!" Ros bellowed, and the entire coffee shop silenced in the wake of his outburst. His chest heaved with the insult and everything Billy was throwing at him. Slowly, the sound of people and coffee being brewed picked up. Billy leaned back in her chair with a thick brow cocked at him.

"I know better now," Ros promised, lowering his voice.

"Do you?" Billy accused. "From what I hear, you like killing dangerous things."

"She's different," Ros growled.

"Different because she's prettier and accessible? Will you try to kill her once you grow bored or if she becomes too *dangerous?*"

"No," he said sternly. "She has always been different, I was just too dumb to see it."

"Finally," she said, clapping quietly. "You've finally said something true."

Ros rolled his eyes and took a breath. "Look, yes, I made a mistake, and I will live with that for a very long time."

"I'm not sure," she said, thoughtful. "You'll only get to live a long life if I don't slice your cock off with my claws the next time you threaten to kill Ellea." She paused, tapping her long nails on the table. "Or my mouth. That would be more fun."

She grinned at him wickedly. Ros scoffed, but closed his legs and turned them away from her.

"Ellea popped into my life at a weird time," Ros tried saying.

"That's not her fucking fault."

"What do you want me to say?" he demanded.

"I want to know why," she said, leaning into the table. "And I want to hear that it will never happen again."

"It won't," he promised. She gave him an accusing look. "In the past, it was easy to get caught up in 'kill first and ask questions later.' I acted naturally to her powers." Billy looked as though she wanted to claw his eyes out. "Again, I was wrong. Look, do you want me to explain?"

"Fine." She waved her hand. "Continue."

Ros took a steadying breath. "The line between stopping something before it happens or after it's too late is a hard one to dance on. I have too many regrets of those I couldn't save during my long life. And maybe even more regrets of those I've killed." Ros paused as guilt washed over him. He let his eyes meet hers and tried to put so much more into his look. "I want to help Ellea, and…I want to be with her."

He truly did. That night by the lake with Ellea may be one of his biggest regrets, and those screams he heard were ones he never wanted to hear again. Ros would spend all the time he had left to make it up to her.

"Good," she said as warmth crossed her face. "I would hate for you to lose your perfect cock."

Ros' shoulders relaxed as someone walked up to his right side. Billy looked at the person and smiled.

"Perfect timing," she said to the young woman who was holding two hot coffee cups. Billy gestured for her to leave them on the table.

Ros grimaced at the coffee shop employee as she retreated back to the counter.

"Ellea likes lattes with whole milk or cream," she said, sliding the cups toward him. "And any type of autumn syrup will do."

Ros choked on his words. "Thank you, Billy."

"You're welcome, stud muffin." She winked at him.

"Has Ellea seen you like this?" he asked, grabbing the cups and standing.

"We all have our secrets," she said without standing. "I'll be keeping an eye on things. I've always done so."

Ros only nodded and slowly turned to leave. He chanced a glance back at her, but she was already gone.

40

Ellea

Ellea waved as Devon and Sam drove down her driveway. She and Devon had woken up on her large couch about thirty minutes ago. She couldn't recall when they had fallen asleep, only that it was during their replay of *"Half-Blood Prince."* Ellea closed the door, ready for some coffee. She paused her steps when the loud noise of Sam's truck sounded outside of the cabin. Confused, she turned and opened the door to see not Sam's truck, but Ros'. She caught him grumbling to himself as he stepped out of the large vehicle. He was holding two coffee cups in his hands, and she groaned at the sight.

"Oh, I could kiss you," she said, walking across her porch to meet him.

"Don't say that yet," he said with such a sad look on his face. "I… so…I'm sorry."

"What's wrong?" Her heart dropped as too many possibilities flashed through her head. Did he regret sleeping with her? Was this an "I'm sorry, I'm not interested" coffee?

"So you see," he muttered, "I drank yours instead of mine. I didn't mean to!"

He paused, holding the cups close to his chest. "I took a sip of yours by accident, and then one thing led to another..." He trailed off.

"It's okay." She laughed nervously, scolding herself for jumping to conclusions too fast. "I'll drink yours." She reached for his, and he tried to take it away from her, but she was quicker. She stuck her tongue out at him before bringing the heavy cup to her lips. She quickly spit it out. "What the fuck is this?"

Ros closed his eyes. "I had a plan." He groaned. "This was supposed to go differently."

"What plan?" she questioned.

He stepped closer to her. "I don't know, something like 'here's a coffee and a reason to talk about the other night'."

Ellea's mouth opened and closed. "Oh."

"Yeah," he replied.

She searched his face, and what greeted her wasn't regret or harshness. Was he nervous?

She smiled up at him. "Let's go inside, and I'll make myself a coffee. Maybe I'll even make you one."

His eyes seemed to glint at the offer, and her stomach turned. It flipped the other way as he stepped toward her. With his free hand, he stroked her chin with his thumb and moved his fingers to grip the base of her neck. He tilted her head back gently and brought his lips to hers for a whisper of a kiss.

He slowly pulled away and whispered above her mouth, "Good morning, princess."

She rolled her eyes and glowered at him. His hazel eyes heated with her defiance, and her mouth dried. Clearing her throat, she directed him to the door, and he followed.

"I still don't know why you call me that," she called over her shoulder as she dumped the disgusting coffee down her kitchen sink. The dream she'd had about a mysterious man who also called her "princess" drifted to the surface. Had it been a vision?

"Because I can," he teased. He sat at the kitchen table in the same chair he'd sat in after Belias had tried taking her. The same chair she had sucked his cock in. She licked her lips at the memory.

"So, this coffee?" she questioned. "What were you trying to say with it, and how did you know what kind to get me?"

"I had help. You didn't seem too thrilled yesterday morning."

It wasn't that. She'd been more confused than anything else. And last night...She hadn't had time to process that either. Ellea grabbed her coffee supplies from the fridge and placed them on the counter. She paused and leaned into it, searching for what to say and what to think.

"That morning had nothing to do with that night with you," she said, distracting herself with working on their coffees. "And this morning with Devon—"

"What did you do with Devon?"

"Not that, you jealous brute." She sighed and decided on honesty. "I've never slept with anyone but Billy since I was eight. Well, except for you and Devon, now."

She didn't have to turn around to know that he was scowling. Ellea rolled her eyes.

"Okay?" He sounded puzzled and a little bit angry.

"I have nightmares—rough ones." She turned toward him with two finished lattes in each hand. His face was softer than she'd expected.

"We all have nightmares, Ellea," he said, and the sound of her name on his lips made her heart quicken. "You shouldn't hide yourself or think there is something wrong with you because of that."

"You have nightmares?" she asked, placing her mug down and turning to hand him his drink.

"Me? No, never," he said with a teasing grin. It quickly turned into a pout when she pulled the mug away from his reach. "Yes. Gods, yes. All the time. Now give that to me."

"Oh, so demanding," she mocked. "Especially for someone who has been drinking dirt for a billion years."

She slowly handed him his mug. He grasped her wrist before she could pull it away again. Grabbing the mug safely, he deposited a kiss to her palm before letting her go. Her hand tingled, and heat warmed her cheeks.

"I don't want you to be afraid to try something or do something," he said. "But you not wanting to sleep in the same bed or room as someone else? That's on you and your insecurities."

"Are you calling me insecure?" How dare he make fun of something that has haunted her forever? He grabbed at her free hand and yanked her. She fell in his lap with a low growl.

"We all have insecurities and demons. We all have things that haunt us," he said quietly, searching her angry face. "But trying to cope with them all on your own isn't always best." She rolled her eyes at him, and he glowered at her.

"Don't worry," he said with a wicked smile. "I'll get it through your thick skull one day."

"Are you calling me thick?" she teased.

"Oh yes." He kissed her swiftly. "In the best fucking way."

She laughed softly as she stood, needing her latte, and then yelped as he quickly smacked her ass. She scooted toward her chair and gave him a scolding look. He smiled at her and brought the mug to his lips.

She waited, worried if he would like it, but she was greeted with a low moan that made her think of wicked things. He took another sip and licked the foam that was left on his top lip.

"Oh," he moaned, "I'm going to fuck you later."

"Are you talking to me or your mug?"

"Both," he said with a smug grin. "But first, what are we going to do?"

"Do?" Ellea mimicked. "Do with what?"

It was too early for any more serious talk. She quickly sipped her latte, begging for strength and caffeine.

"Now. Today." He finished his drink in two more gulps and pouted at his empty mug.

"Oh," she said, glad it wasn't a loaded question. "I want to train."

She toyed with her mug in her hands, hoping he didn't think she was silly. She glanced up at him, and he had a smug look on his face.

"Then let's go train," he said. "But if I get handsy, it's not my fault."

Excitement bloomed in Ellea's stomach. She finished her drink and followed him outside.

This was going to be so much more fun than training with her uncle.

41

Ellea

Ellea ran her forearm across her forehead. She was drenched
in sweat and breathed hard as she tried to create distance
between her and Ros. She gripped the wooden dowels she
held in each hand and readied her stance.

"Again," Ros directed, and then he launched himself.

She had to use both dowels to block his blow. They crossed, and she
twisted him away, but he struck with his left, smacking her in the hip.
She yelped and glared at him.

"Ass."

"Use your magic."

They had been going for almost an hour, sparring with the dowels.
He was trying to force her to use her magic while her hands were
full, something she had never done and something that currently

seemed impossible.

Ellea had thought she would feel different after her night with Ros. Her magic had reacted in such a strange and powerful way. But right now, she didn't feel powerful. She felt like she had never been trained to fight or use magic.

"Again," he ordered, and she groaned as he took long strides toward her.

She feigned left and stepped right, catching him slightly off guard and smacking him in the ribs. He pivoted and whirled on her, sweeping her dowel out of the way and striking with both of his overhead. She blocked him again, but he was so much stronger. Her arms began to shake as he pressed down on her. She gritted her teeth and roared at him. The trees shuddered. Suddenly, she felt a yank on her ankle, and her back met the ground in a hard thud. His shadows slithered away from her feet, and she stuck her tongue out at them.

"Your magic is an extension," he said, hovering over her. "It's a part of you, but you have to let go of it. Don't control it, guide it."

She glared up at him, his large form blocking the sun. It was easy for someone as ancient as him; he'd had years to master his magic, and she had never tried.

"Do you expect there to be a time where I'm in the midst of battle with two swords in my hands?" she mocked, using one of the dowels to help her stand. Her legs wobbled underneath her. There was no way this would work.

"First"—he paused to wipe dirt from her leggings—"I would pay a lot of money to see you with two swords in your hands."

She grinned slyly at him, wishing she had the energy to do so.

"Second, I don't know what the future holds," he said solemnly. He placed her long braid over her shoulder and ran his callused thumb across her jaw. "All I know is I want you to be prepared."

Ellea didn't know how to respond to that. She could look into the future if she dared, but she already knew what awaited her. For him, though…she shook her head at the thought of it.

"You've shocked me before without your hands," he said, dropping the wooden poles and placing his hands on her bare arms. "Do it again."

"I wasn't controlling it." She sighed up at him and then smirked. "You were pissing me off—it was pure instinct."

He smiled down at her with a devilish look. "Would you like me to piss you off?"

"You already are, and clearly, it isn't—"

"Your coffee wasn't actually that good this morning," he interrupted. Her eyes widened at the insult as heat bloomed in her chest. Electricity radiated across her skin, and Ros yelped, jerking his hands away from her. He rubbed his fingers against each other and smiled at her.

"I'm never making you coffee." She glared at him. "Ever again."

"No." He grabbed her before she could walk away. "It was a lie, please don't say that."

Ellea held her chin up high as she sent another wave of electricity to where Ros' hand held her. He gritted his teeth and held on. She created a new wooden dowel out of thin air and whacked him in the shin. He yelped but held on, and when she went to hit him again, his shadows wrapped around it, halting it.

"Dammit," she cursed at his grinning face.

He let go of her arm only to snake his own around her lower back, pulling her in close.

"Please say you'll make me coffee," he pleaded quietly.

She ignored him, refusing to speak. He tried to kiss her, and she moved her head out of the way. He did it again, and again, kissing her cheek, her neck, and her hair. She couldn't take it, and swatted him away as a giggle escaped her lips.

"Fine." She groaned, and he landed a kiss on her lips. "I will still make you coffee."

"Thank you, princess," he said, kissing her one last time. "I will forever be in your debt."

She swatted his ridiculous comment away. "Can we be done, please?"

"That was barely an hour," he said, picking up the dowels from the ground.

"Well, I haven't sparred in ages." She rubbed at her sore arms as they walked toward her cabin. "And when I did, it was nothing like that."

"Who trained you before?" She noted jealousy rearing its ugly head again.

"Calm down," she scolded. "My uncle, Felix."

Ros relaxed instantly, and Ellea wondered if it would always be like that. It was too new for him to snarl at any mention of another male. It's not like she would do the same. *Would she?* She tried picturing him with someone else, and her throat instantly became dry. She shook the feeling the best she could. She was being ridiculous.

"You okay?" he asked. She nodded. "You know, I wanted to ask about him. I saw an article in the paper about a man being attacked by his niece."

"You're looking at her."

Ros didn't look at her with judgment, only openness, so she continued, "I got into an argument with someone and my uncle got in the way as my magic reacted. Reacted in a way you seemed to be worried about."

She guessed he was right about her. Eventually, she would cause destruction. "Well, let's make sure that doesn't happen again. Or at least make it happen on purpose, not with someone who accidentally gets in the way."

She needed to guide her magic; not contain it, but use it correctly.

Her brain felt fuzzy with thoughts of no longer hiding, feeling free.

"You okay?" he asked, looking too damn cute with his eyebrows furrowed in concern. How his face had so many expressions was crazy.

"Yea, I'm just thirsty," she half-lied, then her stomach grumbled. "And hungry, I guess."

Ros laughed lightly. "Come on, I'll make us lunch."

"You know," she started as he wrapped his arm around her, leading them toward his own cabin, "I think I had a dream about you before you began haunting my life."

"Oh yeah?" His smile was wicked. "Was it a sexy dream?"

Ellea groaned. Why did she open her mouth?

42

Ros

The forest floor under their feet was heavy with fallen leaves. Fall was here, and Ros enjoyed every chilly moment. He had convinced Ellea to go for a long walk instead of training today. They had been going hard for three days straight, and frustrations were high, particularly for her. Ros knew she was capable, but she held onto that control. And to think he had worried about how *not* in control she was. The power coursing through her veins was begging to be set free. If she would fully give in and let go, it would be a beautiful sight. Destructive, yes, but he would be there to help.

A twig snapped in the distance, and Ellea didn't pause or notice. Ros gave her one scolding look, and she rolled her eyes in response.

Such a brat.

He placed his hand by his ear to signal she should listen. Cocking her head away from her shoulder in a dramatic fashion, she listened. She slowed her steps, and he noticed her breathing steadying as she tried to hear whatever he had.

Another twig snapped, closer this time, and when Ellea whipped her head in that direction, her steps faltered and she toppled over herself. She cursed loudly as she tried to untangle herself from the fallen branches and leaves. Ros laughed as quietly as he could, but she turned on him quickly with a vicious glare.

"What's so funny?" she hissed at him. "You're the paranoid one making me listen for forest bunnies when we're supposed to be taking the day off."

Gods, she was cute when she was angry. "You can take a day off and still be on alert."

"There is nothing to be on alert for!" She was fuming.

Ellea continued to take her frustrations out on him, calling him everything from "ancient ass-hat" to "paranoid old man" while Ros stood there waiting for her to realize a giant gray wolven was barreling toward her.

"Why are you just standing there looking at me like that?" she screeched at him.

He only pointed behind her. She turned her head in time to see a wolven that was one stride away from attacking her. She screamed and rolled out of the way. The beast quickly recovered from his miss and headed for her again.

"Aren't you going to do something?" she yelled.

"Why?" he said, finding a tree to prop against to enjoy the show. "I'm just a paranoid old man."

Ellea blasted energy that the wolven easily dodged. She threw everything at it as she ran in a crazy zigzag pattern. She even tried hitting it with a tree branch, but it only snapped it in half with its large teeth.

Steps sounded behind Ros' resting spot, but he wasn't worried. Devon's scent had greeted him a half hour ago.

"How's it going?" Devon asked warily.

Ros only gestured toward the two creatures that were now barreling through the bushes.

"Ouch," he said with a chuckle. "She's going to be so pissed when she finds out this was your idea."

"I can't wait," Ros said with a wicked smirk.

"You two are really two sides of the same coin." Devon laughed.

Ellea escaped the bushes, the wolven close on her heels. It was actually Sam, and he seemed to be having too much fun. His tongue hung out of his large mouth, and the glint in his eyes was devilish. Ellea's foot snagged on a tree root, and she landed hard on her stomach. A whoosh ripped out of her, and she groaned.

Sam began stalking her slowly as she tried to crawl away. She rolled onto her back quickly and sent another wave of magic his way. He dodged it easily and pounced on her. She screamed as he pinned her arms at her sides, something Ros had specifically requested he do.

Sam had warned him this would not end up in Ros' favor when Ellea found out he had set her up. But she needed to learn, and he thought this was her best chance. Ellea had never seen Sam in his wolven form, and Ros was betting she would be scared enough to channel her magic the right way. He only hoped that Sam wouldn't get too hurt in the process.

Ellea screamed again as Sam snapped his teeth close to her face. She turned her head away from him, and Ros saw the change. Devon gasped, seeing it too. Her breathing became quick pants, but the smirk on her face was very deceiving. She slowly turned her head back to Sam. His head tilted to one side, ear quirked, before he was blasted away from her.

Sam's large form turned three times in the air before he landed on the ground. His large claws gouged out the earth as he stopped himself from sliding. Ellea stood gracefully and slowly walked toward him. Sam shook his large head and stalked toward Ellea, circling her. She summoned two large metal staffs, similar to the dowels they had been training with. She readied her stance like she had so many times before. Sam smirked at the tiny witch in front of him and attacked.

It was a trick, an illusion Devon and Ros had also missed. As Sam barreled toward Ellea, a massive, jet-black hound attacked Sam's blind side. It materialized out of thin air and was a beast Ros didn't recognize. It was similar to Garm, but the lower part of its legs were made up of iridescent black and green scales. Its long bald tail ended in a fork, and its eyes were a bright shade of green. It held a sinister grin similar to the one on Ellea's face.

Sam was able to dodge the attack from the beast, but Ellea followed through, sweeping one of her staffs through his legs, causing him to crash to the forest floor. Devon stepped forward, but Ros stopped him.

"One more minute," Ros whispered.

Devon groaned as the beast barreled into Sam as he tried to get up. It was a weak hit, and Ros knew it could be stronger. Ellea began to pant slightly, but she continued on. She took a few sloppy strides toward Sam as he lay there. Holding the staffs overhead, she went to strike, but he moved out of the way in time. The beast tried attacking, but Sam dodged him again.

"Enough," Ros bellowed. Ellea turned toward him with confusion on her face. Her steps swayed slightly, and the beast she'd conjured shimmered and then disappeared.

Devon grabbed a pair of pants from the pack he was carrying

and headed toward Sam. Ellea's confusion deepened as she looked at him. Looking back at the wolven, realization crossed her face, then pure rage.

"You!" She stomped toward Ros, who held up his hands. She swiveled back toward the wolven only to find a completely naked Sam standing there. "You. Oh, you're naked."

Ellea choked on her rage, but quickly recovered once she looked at Ros again.

"How dare you trick me?" she hissed at him.

"Me? Trick a trickster?" he said sweetly. Her glare intensified. "Look, I wanted to try something. So I did. And I think it worked."

Ellea wiped her hands across her face, and Ros quietly stepped closer to her. She looked exhausted, and he was a little worried. She had only been fighting Sam for maybe twenty minutes, but that beast had seemed pretty solid—and a lot larger than those little creatures she had been messing with before.

"Hey, are you okay?" he asked, brushing her messy hair away from her face and picking some twigs and leaves out of it.

"I'm so mad at you," she whimpered. "But I did it."

She smiled weakly.

"Yeah, you did." He rubbed her arms. "That thing was scary."

"I'm so fucking mad at you," she said again. "I could have hurt Sam."

"You can take it out on me later. And Sam is fine. But let's go get you some food and water. That took a lot out of you."

Sam, now fully clothed, and Devon walked up to them. Ellea cut Sam a heated glare and gave Devon the same. They both gave her a small smile but kept quiet.

"I heard 'food,'" Devon said. "Some of the wolven are barbecuing over at the farm."

Ellea's stomach growled in response.

"Sounds perfect," Ros said. "Let's go, little trickster, and you can tell me where you thought of that beast."

Ellea glared at him one last time, and the four of them headed toward the main road.

Ros reached his hand over and gripped Ellea's thigh. It was still a shock to have her in his truck, willingly next to him and not hating him. Well, mostly not hating him. She had spent most of the drive to the farm picking twigs and leaves out of her hair while mumbling about jerks and wolven.

"What's a wolven barbecue like?" she asked.

"It's like any barbecue," he answered. "Don't expect to see a wolven flipping burgers in its beast form."

Ros chuckled at the thought. They had arrived, and Ros put the truck in park. He turned in his seat to look at her.

She fiddled with her fingers in her lap. Ros grabbed them, his large hand able to hold on to both of them.

"What?" he asked, wondering why she was suddenly nervous.

"I've..." She hesitated. "I've never been to a barbecue before."

"Oh." He paused, trying to find the right thing to say. "Well, I'm glad to be with you for your first."

Ellea laughed lightly. "You probably think I'm ridiculous."

"Yes," he said truthfully. "But there is nothing wrong with the way you are."

Ros wondered what else she had missed out on. He thought about how she was at Mabon, how shy she'd seemed and how quickly she'd wanted to leave.

"Why haven't you been to any barbecues?" he asked.

"I'm not sure," she said thoughtfully. "I avoided most gatherings if I could. The only parties my family and I went to were for holidays or council things."

"Council things?" Ros wondered why she would be at those types of meetings.

"Yeah," she said. "My nana, Jadis, she's been on the council since before I was born."

Realization struck him. "Wow." Ros was a little shocked and slightly concerned. "Your grandmother sits in one of the witches' spots on the council?"

"Yes."

Ros' thoughts and line of questioning were quickly interrupted as their truck was assaulted by giant paws and yipping wolven. Ellea looked at him with concerned eyes.

"Don't worry, they're just happy I'm here," he said and opened his door.

"I highly doubt that," she said, following after him. "I don't think anyone would be excited to see you."

She had a teasing smile on her face as she slowly walked up to him and the wolven, who were already jumping on him. They were much smaller than Sam, but it was still a lot to take in. Devika slowly walked up to Ellea, sniffing the air around her. Ellea looked up at Ros, questioning what to do.

"They won't hurt you," he reminded her. She didn't seem so trusting.

Devika reached her nose toward Ellea's hand. She turned it toward the wolven to let her smell it better. Devika pressed her nose against Ellea's skin, then rubbed her face against Ellea's palm. A large grin spread across her face. Then the young wolven rubbed her whole body against Ellea's legs.

"Do I do something?" Ellea asked as her smile turned nervous.

"No, but Sam may be a little jealous. One of his betas is trying to call dibs," he said with a sly smile at Devika. She gave him an incredulous look with her bright green eyes.

"What's Sam going to be jealous of?" Sam called from his front porch.

Both men walked to meet them, somehow beating them to the farm.

"Devika," Sam said sternly. "You're supposed to be patrolling."

The wolven only blinked as she leaned her large body against Ellea's thighs.

"Devika," Sam said with a low growl, and the small black wolven seemed forced to bow.

"Don't be a bully," Ellea scolded him. She crossed her arms and stepped toward him.

"I know you're mad at me, but I'm not opposed to burning your burger if you try to deter my alpha business," Sam said.

Ros was having too much fun seeing Ellea focus her viciousness on someone else. Neither of them backed down for a whole minute, and a battle seemed to rage between them. Then Ellea gave Sam a cunning smile, and he seemed to falter. Sam looked over Ellea's shoulder toward the treeline. The large male swallowed hard and let his arms dangle at his sides.

"I'll take my burger medium, please," Ellea said to Sam, and he chuckled at her.

"Have you ever had a burger?" Ros asked, walking up to them.

Devika rubbed against Ellea one last time before walking toward the edge of the property. Sam looked shocked at Ros' question to Ellea.

"Yes," she grumbled at him. "I've just never had them off a grill...or outside."

Sam's hand rested against his heart, and he gasped. "You poor, sheltered girl," he said and wrapped his arm around her shoulder. "Let's go fix that right now."

43

Ellea

Sam's arm warmed Ellea through the sweater as he led her across
the worn porch to the back yard. She was thankful she'd had it
in Ros' truck; the shirt she'd worn during their "walk" had been
destroyed. She still couldn't believe he'd tricked her like that. Even
though it had worked, she was still pissed. Something had snapped
when Sam had her pinned against the forest floor. *Fucking assholes.*

She'd felt so helpless until a whisper came in the back of her mind,
telling her of freedom and power if she would only let it out. So she
had. A wonderful smell greeted her as they came to the back of the
porch. There were maybe fifteen people on the large lawn.

"What is that?" Ellea asked, pointing toward a gigantic black metal
thing that was smoking.

"A smoker," Sam answered. "We have all kinds of meats in there, chicken, ribs, and brisket. One of the guys started yesterday."

"It smells so good." She groaned as her stomach growled.

"It may be a little while before it's ready," Sam said, and then he turned her toward the far corner of the porch where two large tables stood, covered in different foods. "You can start there, and I'll go grab you a drink."

Ellea headed straight for that impressive table. It held chips, crackers, and so many other things—including cookies.

Oh, cookies, she groaned inwardly. She grabbed one and brought it to her mouth. It was rich and chewy. She moaned and took another bite before she'd even swallowed her first.

"You can grab more than a cookie," Ros said, coming up to her with a paper plate in his hand.

Ellea slowly took it from him and searched the table, unsure of where to start.

"You're acting like you've never seen food before."

Ellea rolled her eyes at him. She had, but never like this. "Of course, I've seen food before. It's always been given to me or served, never out in the open with so many random choices."

"I'll admit I was worried about your ability to take care of yourself or cook after seeing your fridge the other day," he teased.

She slapped him in his large chest with the paper plate. She knew how to cook, sort of. Being in the city meant she could order out every night if she needed to. But lately, it had been snacks, sandwiches, and a lot of coffee keeping her going. Seeing this magnificent spread had her feeling overwhelmed.

"You can come back for more," he said. "You don't have to make a final choice right now. Grab some food, and let's go sit."

She grabbed two more cookies, a small handful of cheese cubes, and some fried things that reminded her of egg rolls. Ros led her toward four cozy chairs at the corner of the porch. Devon sat in one and Sam stood next to him with two drinks in his hand. He handed one to Ellea, and when she took a sip, she was greeted with the same delicious margarita he'd given her on Mabon.

"You need water too," Ros scolded.

"I drank half a gallon on the way over here." She looked up to Sam. "Speaking of that, where's your bathroom?"

"There's one attached to the kitchen," he said, pointing to a side door. "You can't miss it."

"I'll show you," Ros offered.

Ellea arched a brow at him. "I can go by myself, thanks."

Devon chuckled at her attitude. "Actually, I'll show you. I have to grab something, anyway."

Devon led the way into the old house. Everything in it was wide and open, as if it had been built for the many large wolven that peppered the property. Every inch of the walls seemed to be covered in picture frames. Ellea paused at one that caught her eye. The photo was faded and in black and white. Ros, clad in camo, knelt in front of an ancient truck, with Sam next to him. They were both clean shaven with short haircuts. They looked so young, but the timing of the photo...

"What is this?" she asked Devon's retreating form. He turned and came to where she stood.

He looked at it for a moment and smiled warmly. "Sam and Ros."

"No shit," she said, looking up at him. "How long ago was this?"

"Mmm." He thought for a moment. "1944, in Newhope, after the war."

"But..." She did the math in her head. "But...wait, how old is Sam?"

"He turned one hundred and five this past summer," he said as if it was a regular thing. "That's where they met. They both enlisted, Ros when he was still an old man, and Sam when he was eighteen."

There was so much Ellea didn't know about…everything. "I'm going to go pee now and try to find a functioning brain."

Devon laughed and directed her toward the bathroom. Ellea headed in mindlessly. She had so much to learn about the world and her magic. Why had she never questioned what it was like for other supernaturals? Her earlier accomplishment was now being overshadowed by feeling like an ignorant, sheltered child. She sighed as she scooted off the very large toilet.

Ellea jumped when she caught her reflection in the old mirror. Her hair was free of twigs and leaves from earlier, but it was wild. She cursed Ros for not telling her. No wonder that wolven had been rubbing against her; she must have thought Ellea was some wild woodland creature. She conjured a hairbrush and got to work. It took ten minutes just to get it partially untangled. A knock came, and Devon's voice sounded from the other side of the door. Ellea opened it and grimaced.

"Oh," Devon mouthed. He grabbed the brush from her and turned her away from him. "You looked fine earlier," he scolded.

"Liar," she groaned.

"Well, let's hurry before Ros comes barreling in here," he said and got to work on untangling her long hair.

"Ros seems so quick to be jealous." It was easy to be honest with Devon, and besides Billy, he was the only one he could talk to about Ros. Sam would laugh at her and probably use it for fuel later.

"He may be ancient, but he didn't grow up like we did," he answered.

"I feel like I haven't grown up at all," she mumbled.

"What do you mean?" He placed the untangled parts of her hair over her right shoulder and started on the last section.

"I've never been to a barbecue, I don't know how long wolven live for, I didn't know demons were out in the world, and a number of other things."

Devon chuckled at her whining and finished her hair. "Do you want me to braid it?"

Ellea nodded and summoned a hair tie out of thin air.

"I don't know if I will ever get used to that," he said, easily braiding her hair.

"Me either," she said honestly. "There's a lot I need to get used to."

"That is why I left when I did," he said, placing the finished braid over her shoulder. "It's okay that you don't know a lot. What matters is what you do with your time. Listen and learn; there is so much outside of our bitchy circles."

Ellea sighed, playing with her braid. Finally, she nodded and looked up at Devon. His light blue eyes were so kind and open. She wrapped her arms around his waist and hugged him hard. He laughed, placing his arms around her back.

"Thank you for being my friend," she mumbled into his chest. "I mean, if you want to be my friend."

"We fell asleep watching wizard movies and hunky hunters, I think we're best friends."

Ellea let out a sob while buried in his chest and then Ros rounded the corner. She groaned and let go of her friend. She rolled her eyes and Devon chuckled as Ros' loud steps came toward them. He tugged on her braid before turning her toward the grumpy old man.

"She's ready for you, and she has *a ton* of questions," Devon said, and then he bolted off in the other direction.

Ros looked at him suspiciously as he quickly left through a side door. He looked back at Ellea and grasped her by the chin, searching her face. "What's wrong?"

"I'm fine, only feeling like a dumb child," she admitted.

"Child? You're twenty-eight?" he asked, looking concerned.

"Yes, but mentally, I feel like I'm missing so much." She sighed.

"Yeah, but…" He quickly kissed her scowl. "But you're learning."

"You're not one to soften the blow, are you?" She glowered at him.

"Nope." He grabbed her hand and walked her toward the door. "Let's go outside and see what you can learn tonight."

TRICKY MAGIC

355

44

Ros

Ros hated how Ellea was feeling. No one should ever feel as though things are being kept from them. From the little he knew about her upbringing, he worried that that was exactly what was going on.

Ellea had finished two burgers, five cookies, and some fried things she couldn't get enough of. He would keep feeding her just to hear her moan every time a new flavor hit her mouth. She now leaned back on the large outdoor couch she shared with Ros, cradling her drink in her hands. The sun hung low behind them, and the warm hue radiated off of Devon and Sam across from them, sitting in their own oversized chairs. Ros would have never guessed that this was where he would end up after Ellea came into town, with his friends, in comfortable conversation as the other wolven began building a small fire.

"Now that you're full"—Sam gestured to Ellea, who was melting into the cushions—"I hear you have some questions?"

"I don't even know where to start."

"She saw your photo on the wall," Devon said. "The one of you two after the war."

Ros couldn't help but answer the secret smirk Sam was giving him with his own.

"That was ages ago," Ellea said. "How long do wolven usually live for?"

"There isn't a set number," Sam answered. "Things are constantly changing, and with the numbers dwindling, the lifetime of a wolven has changed too."

"The numbers are dwindling?" Ellea asked with weighted concern in her voice.

Ros could remember a time when thousands of wolven lived in one area. Currently, it was in the low hundreds; everyone had their own theories about the decline, but both he and Sam agreed on one.

"Yes," Sam answered honestly. "Things aren't how they used to be." He paused, smiling at Devon. "Besides my ancestors having ten or twenty pups by the time they were my age, the world has changed. Technology rules and the Gods are gone."

"What Gods are gone?" Ellea asked.

"They aren't gone," Ros interrupted. "They're in Hel."

They had been since before he was born.

"Yeah, a lot of good that's doing for the supernaturals," Sam grumbled.

"In Hel? What Gods?" she asked.

"All of them." Even though Ros wanted to teach her about them, he didn't have the time and wasn't ready to visit that part of his life.

"I was never taught about Gods," Ellea said.

"But I've heard you curse them and Hel." Ros stared at her curiously.

"How haven't you heard about them?"

"Well, not specifically, and I think I picked that up from my nana," she said thoughtfully. "I guess I never thought about it. My history tutor only taught as far back as the Elimination period."

Devon groaned at her statement. "That is so ridiculous."

She looked at him with her brows bunched. "It's true."

"Sorry, I didn't mean to imply you were lying. I mean, well..." He growled. "Witches are so stuck in their own stupid, tiny circles. Not you, Ellea, those who raised us."

Ellea's brows raised at his comment. Ros knew where he was coming from, and he knew Devon's story well. As soon as he'd turned eighteen and was moments away from being forced into an early engagement, he'd left his family. He'd traveled for the past ten years, learning all he could; Ros was proud of the young witch, and he knew Sam felt the same way.

"What were you taught about wolven?" Sam asked Ellea.

She thought for a moment. "They're beasts who run around the forest and howl at the moon," she said quietly.

Sam laughed and Devon groaned. Ros saw the worried look on Ellea's face.

"What else were you taught?" Ros asked, trying to keep the conversation moving.

"Training with my uncle, basic remedies, potions, herbs, stars, and anatomy." She thought for another moment. "Oh, and seer stuff, of course."

"But never about your trickster magic?" Devon asked.

Ellea shook her head sadly. "Only to keep it under control. The small stuff and the illusions were always natural and came from... earlier times."

"But your father, he must have taught you something,"

Devon continued.

Ellea's breath shuddered, and she cleared her throat. "What he and my mother did…I wouldn't call that teaching. He left when I was young."

Ros cut in, not liking where this was going. "What about other supernaturals?"

"Same as the wolven; they are what they are and that's it," she said.

"But they aren't that," Sam cut in. "Supernaturals are no longer what they were; they just exist and they're ignorant to their past. Where do you think we all came from?"

"We're just here." Ellea looked stressed. Ros was feeling it too. How could she be so powerful and know so little?

"And what of Hel?" Devon asked. "What do you know about that?"

"Nothing," she groaned. "Well, that's where the bad people go."

Ros laughed a little. "That's where all people go."

Ellea sat up in her chair. "What?"

Devon and Sam settled in their chairs, ready for Ros to take over. He clenched his teeth, finding the right words. He hated talking about this part of his life.

"The short part of the long history of Hel—"

"You mean your homeland," Sam interrupted, and Ros rolled his eyes.

"Yes, I'm a demon, we all know," Ros growled. He noticed Ellea's little smirk. Clearing his throat, he continued, "Anyway, everyone goes to Hel. Well, most of Hel. One part is where the Gods dwell; it's where they've been since before I was born. Other parts are for the mortals and supernaturals. The worst people go to a different part."

"I used to daydream about being swept away by a prince when I was younger. I didn't think it would be a demon prince," Ellea teased.

"I'm only half demon," Ros growled.

"But all the good parts are demon," Sam taunted, reaching to flick his crotch.

"Flick my crotch one more time and Devon isn't going to have anything to play with," Ros snapped.

Ellea giggled so hard she hiccuped, then she groaned, rubbing her stomach. "I think I ate too much."

They all had, but Ellea had such a sleepy look in her eyes. He eyed Sam, who understood. He got up, grabbed their plates, and disappeared into the house.

"Would you want to go into town with me tomorrow or the next day?" Devon asked Ellea. "I could show you around and we can talk more about our lovely upbringing."

Ellea let out a huge sigh. "Yeah…I don't want to, but I need to know more. I should probably grab food too."

No shit. Her fridge was pitiful, and she needed to eat better. Snacks and coffee were not going to be enough with how much work she was putting in.

Sam came out with a few blankets in his hand. He handed one to Ros, who took it and spread it over Ellea. She gave him a small smile before grabbing a pillow. Resting it on his hip, she curled into a tiny ball and yawned.

"Tell me about you and Sam during the war," she demanded. "I'm swooning just thinking about you two in those early 1940s uniforms."

Devon chuckled and settled in with his own blanket. "Yes, please."

So Ros did. It had been a rough time in his long life, but with Sam there, he'd made some of his best memories. Ellea only made it five minutes into the story of how he and Sam met before she was fast asleep in his lap. He smoothed the hair that had escaped her braid before leaning into the chair. When he looked up, Sam and Devon were giving him a strange look.

"What?" he asked both of them. They only shook their heads.

"Keep going," Devon said. "This is one of my favorite stories."

361

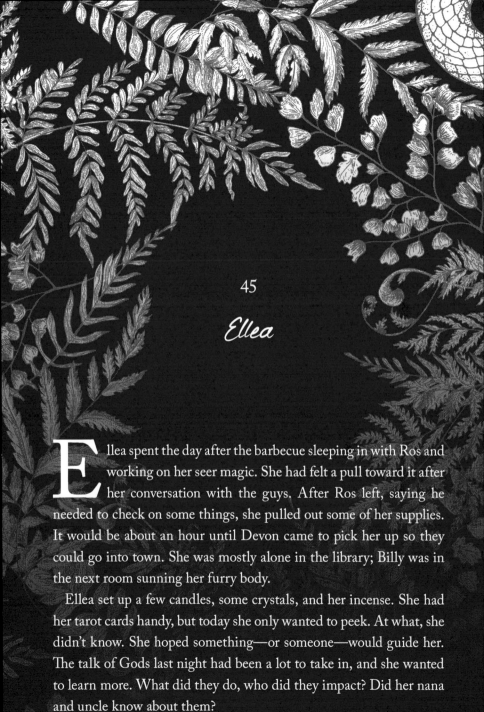

45

Ellea

Ellea spent the day after the barbecue sleeping in with Ros and working on her seer magic. She had felt a pull toward it after her conversation with the guys. After Ros left, saying he needed to check on some things, she pulled out some of her supplies. It would be about an hour until Devon came to pick her up so they could go into town. She was mostly alone in the library; Billy was in the next room sunning her furry body.

Ellea set up a few candles, some crystals, and her incense. She had her tarot cards handy, but today she only wanted to peek. At what, she didn't know. She hoped something—or someone—would guide her. The talk of Gods last night had been a lot to take in, and she wanted to learn more. What did they do, who did they impact? Did her nana and uncle know about them?

Clearing her mind, she lit her candles and then the incense. Spreading her supplies in a rough circle on the worn desk, she settled in. She had a slow grungy song playing low in the corner of the room. She took a long, deep breath and closed her eyes. The back of her hands rested on the hard surface. One more breath, and she felt the pull in her stomach. A weight pressed on her shoulders, and her head fell to the side.

The singing sound of a blade came first. The sight before her was a large soldier atop a brilliant chestnut horse. She reared at the top of the hill. The scales of her armor glinted in the smoky sun, and she seemed to breathe fire as she neighed along with her rider's roar.

Ellea took another breath, not forcing the vision but letting it carry her. The rider before her faded, and she was standing in a forest. The moon was huge, bigger than she had ever seen. Its white light shone brightly between the tall trees that surrounded her. She crouched low at the sound of crunching twigs. Wolven were creeping toward the large moon as if they hunted it, their hackles on edge. They didn't acknowledge her even though she was close enough to reach out a hand and touch their soft fur. The sound of battle sounded in the distance, and the wolven bolted. The air clouded as they chuffed and howled in the night.

Ellea didn't feel fear with this vision, only curiosity. She stood from her crouch as the last of the wolven left and turned her head toward the sound of her music playing. Before her was a vast lake, and she stood in it, up to her knees. As she turned her head again, Devon was standing in front of her, his back was toward her. She shifted to peek over his shoulder, and across from him stood a group of what could have been witches. They stood proud and almost haughty with their chins lifted in distaste. Devon turned away from them and walked through the water toward her. His eyes were set over her shoulder, and he had a smile on his face. She followed his line of sight and there stood Sam, with a pack of wolven behind him. Ellea turned back toward Devon and he was smiling at her. She jumped, realizing she was back in the library and Devon was actually smiling at her.

"Where did you go?" Devon asked with excited curiosity.

Ellea cleared her throat and that feeling of floating that came with drifting along visions. "A few places."

Devon cocked his brow at her. "I've only dabbled in seer magic, tarot, the stars, and a few other things, but I didn't find the gift to actually see things. I hear only the older families can go places."

"Supposedly, and I've never heard of non-seers trying seer magic before." It was unheard of. Well, from what she knew, which was turning out to be very little.

"Let's head out, and I'll tell you all about it," he said, blowing out her candles.

"Are you in a rush?" Ellea teased. He shook his head and headed out of her library toward the front of the cabin. "Jeez, slow down!"

She shuffled after him, grabbing a sweater and throwing her boots on. She called out to Billy to let her know she was leaving, and she only got a sleepy grumble in response.

He opened the front door and gestured to his old, black SUV. "Your chariot awaits, princess."

"Don't start with that," she scolded him.

"I don't mean it like Ros does," he said with a smirk. "But I'm pretty sure you're actually royalty."

Ellea laughed at him as she headed toward the SUV. It was open, and she got into the passenger seat. He got in and started it. "Isn't this a little large for you?"

"Nope. I can fit like four wolven in here," he said while pulling out of her driveway.

Ellea looked at the large back seat. "Only four?" It seemed like he should be able to fit way more than that with its three rows of seats.

"Have you seen how big they are?" Devon laughed. "And when they're drunk...Gods, it's a mess."

Ellea laughed at the vision of Devon trying to wrangle four drunk, Sam-sized men. "You poor thing."

Devon rolled his eyes at her and turned on the music. It was similar to what she'd been listening to earlier. She got comfortable in her seat and watched the colorful trees flash by her window.

"I figured we could grab coffee and walk before stopping at Ag's on the way back?" Devon asked.

"I will always say yes to coffee." She smiled, then remembered they would be exploring the town. "And, um, walking sounds fine."

"What's wrong with walking?" Devon pressed, obviously seeing through her.

"Nothing." He gave her a look, and she groaned. Honesty was key with the three new people in her life. "No one likes me in Halifax."

"We aren't in Halifax."

"Yeah, well, it's just what I'm used to," she said.

"I will say it again, we aren't there, and I'm sure you'll learn quickly that things are different here."

Ellea grumbled into her seat as they turned onto the Main Street of the small town. In the center was a small castle-type structure, and a roundabout circled it. Four small streets stretched away, and small shops and restaurants lined the stone sidewalks. Houses of every size sat on the outskirts of the small square. Some businesses seemed to be built into the old houses too.

There were a few people walking down each street; they all seemed to smile and greet everyone that passed them.

"Did we just step into one of those sappy movies?" Ellea asked.

Devon laughed. "It's still early; the night crew is a little rougher."

"Oh good, I was worried."

Devon parked at one of the parks under a large oak tree, its leaves fully turned orange and yellow. Ellea got out and anxiety instantly settled in her chest. An older couple was walking down the street close to them, and she readied herself for a sneer. Her face slipped into a mask of indifference.

Devon stepped onto the sidewalk, and the couple gave him happy hellos and shook his hand. The older female kissed him on the cheek before he turned toward Ellea, who hadn't moved a step.

"Ellea, stop that and come here." The couple looked at her eagerly. "Ned, Claire, this is Ellea."

Ellea stepped up to them and they gave her such warm smiles.

"My word, are you the trickster who has distracted Rosier?" the old man, Ned, said.

Ellea tried to smile but a grimace came instead. Claire gave a sweet laugh. "Ned, don't scare the poor girl. But my Gods, you're so pretty."

Devon's eyes widened at her, waiting for her to say something.

"Don't mind Ellea," he said to the too-nice couple. He leaned in and whispered, "She's from Halifax."

They nodded their heads in understanding.

"Welcome to Glenover, Ellea," Ned said sincerely. He grabbed her hand gently, and his cloudy eyes looked into hers. "We are truly happy to have you here, and we can't wait to hear what you and Rosier get up to."

"Ned!" his wife scolded.

Ellea actually laughed. "I'm sorry, but you sound like you like Ros? I thought only Sam and Devon put up with him."

Claire laughed. "Oh girl, we just let him think that."

"Such a big, scary man," Ned mocked, puffing his chest, and then laughed with his wife.

They said their goodbyes and headed into one of the shops nearby. Ellea turned toward Devon with wide eyes. "Well..."

"Well, nothing," he scolded. "People aren't out to get you."

"I just don't understand," she said, shaking her head.

"This isn't your typical witch community. It's a *supernatural* community," he said, grabbing her gently. "No one is here to judge you, and we have worse things than big, scary Ros and little tricksters that fake paying at a bar, and then make a wolven think his hands were ripped off."

Ellea's eyes widened even more, and her mouth popped open.

"Yeah, Ellea," he scolded her again. "Let's go get you coffee and make you meet enough people to forget the evil witches back home."

The rest of their time in town was the same. They grabbed coffee and walked down each street, visiting various shops and historic sites. Devon had introduced her to about twenty people, all of various species and ages. All of them had greeted her the same: warm, excited, and a little forward. Every single one of them was eager to learn more about her, or her and Ros. It had barely been a week. She didn't even know what she and Ros were.

Devon had explained how he'd practiced all sorts of magic outside of what he was born with. It was crazy to hear how he'd traveled to so many parts of the world, learning what he could and realizing the way they were typically raised wasn't the norm.

Ellea sighed as they pulled into Ag's parking lot. There was still so much she needed to understand. The store sat on the edge of town, closer to Ellea and Ros' area. There were a few quaint restaurants nearby, and Ellea's stomach growled at the thought of going to one of them. The chocolate pastry she'd had earlier was not enough of a lunch. Devon put the SUV in park and turned toward her.

"How bad was it?" he asked.

"Not as bad as I thought." She sighed. "You were right."

"I didn't mean that," he said quietly. "How bad was it back home?"

Ellea groaned. "Do you really want to know?"

"I would like to," he said. "If we're going to work together and continue to be the best of friends, I need to know your boundaries and what you've dealt with."

Ellea didn't know where to start or how much to tell him. She had spent most of her life shutting it out. She wasn't really up for bringing it back up again.

"You don't have to tell me anything you're not comfortable with," he said, seeming to read her mind.

"I want to work through things," she began. "But I've spent my whole life shutting it down, so it's hard to bring it back up."

"Start from the beginning," he said gently.

"Okay." She turned toward him and twisted her hands in her lap. "After my parents 'left,' I was prone to...outbursts. It got so bad that my nana pulled me out of school and hired tutors, but it wasn't soon enough. The other children remembered what happened, and so did their parents.

"If we were out at parties or shopping and we ran into another witch, they would hide their children or whisper about me. My nana thought I didn't notice, but I did."

"But most young witches are prone to uncontrolled magic," Devon interrupted.

"Did they cause buildings to explode and a hoard of angry rats, bugs, and snakes to attack a group of mean girls?" His eyes got wide, and she took a steadying breath. She hadn't told the next part to anyone outside of her nana and uncle, who already knew—and Billy, of course.

"My mother and father experimented with my magic as early as three." Devon's face paled. "I was able to summon illusions at the age of five, and by the time my nana and uncle got me, I could do worse."

"I'm so sorry," Devon said, reaching over to grasp her hand.

"So after that, things were your basic dramatic story. I went back to school in my teens, dealt with your typical mean girls, dumb boyfriends, and mean parents. Had another outburst at sixteen, got pulled from school, and the rest is history."

"What about your twenties?" he asked.

"That was okay; mean adults instead of teens and even dumber boyfriends, if I would even call them that," she grumbled.

"What did they think of your magic?"

"Did you also study psychology on your hunt for magic?"

Devon smiled sadly at her. "No, but I've had my own experiences."

Ellea searched his face and realized he wasn't trying to get a story out of her; he was trying to understand her, and maybe he did. She shook her head at the weird feeling.

"Some of them didn't care, others thought things would be different or fun since I was the 'crazy witch with the unknown magic.' Little did they know that I didn't even use that side of my powers." Isaac popped into her head, and she scowled. "Some saw me as a powerful thing they should obtain."

"You know Ros isn't like that," he interrupted.

"Of course not. He's way more powerful than me." She laughed. "Why would he need me for anything?"

Devon gave her a dubious look. "I wouldn't be so sure."

Ellea snorted at his comment. Why would he even think that? Ros was a freaking demon prince with some crazy magic, not to mention ancient. He was only interested in her ass, and now, her coffee.

"Can we go inside now, or do you have more therapy tricks?"

Devon's eyes softened, and he grabbed her hand again. "I'm not trying to piss you off. Thank you for sharing all of that with me. It sucks you went through it."

Her chin dropped. She was such an ass, and he was too nice for her.

"I'm sorry, I'm just a bitch and today was a lot."

"I know, but I'm glad we did it," he said, squeezing her hand and releasing it. "Let's go grab some stuff, and then I have a surprise for you."

Ellea looked up to the sky and took a breath. "I think I've had enough for one day."

"I don't know about that," he said with a wicked smirk.

46

Ros

Ros leaned against his truck, kicking at some rocks while grumbling about nosy mutts and their even nosier boyfriends. He didn't know what they expected of him, and this was a ridiculous task. His sweater was itchy and these jeans weren't as worn as he liked. But as soon as Ellea stepped out of Ag's, smiling at Devon, that all disappeared.

She was wearing a light gray sweater that matched her eyes, along with her typical leggings and her boots. Her hair was pulled into a ponytail, and he wanted to wrap his hand around it, letting her silken strands run through his fingers. He cleared his throat and shook away the thought before he got too distracted. He had to stay on task. She heard him, and a wide grin spread across her face that had his heart beating too fast.

"Ros, creepy as always." She smirked as she and Devon walked toward him. Devon stopped her and grabbed her bags.

"I'll drop these off at the house for you. I...need to get back."

"Oh, I'll come with you. Let me just see what the old, scary man wants," she said, and Ros' eyes rolled to the sky.

"No, I'll take you home," Ros interrupted. "Run along to your boyfriend, witch."

Ellea scowled at him, but Devon just winked and turned toward his SUV. She crossed her arms, stopping in the middle of the darkening lot.

"That was rude."

He walked up to her, taking up her space, and she craned her neck to look up at him. "And what are you going to do about it?"

She squinted at him, and he took his hand and grabbed her ponytail, holding her in place. Her eyes quickly heated at the pressure, and her lips parted.

Yeah, that's what I thought.

"What do you want, Rosier?" she whispered up to him.

"A lot of things, Ellea" he said, bringing his mouth close to hers. "But tonight, I want to take you to dinner."

"To dinner?" It was a squeak as she questioned him.

He gripped her hair tighter, and she bit her lip. "On a date," he said.

"A date?" Her gaze quickly switched from heated to confused, and when he grasped her lip with his teeth, she closed her eyes and leaned into him fully.

He released her lip and leaned back to take in her face. It was beautifully flushed, and her eyes glinted in the low light. "Yes, a date. To get to know you better. Talk and stuff."

"Talk?" she asked, and he cocked a brow at her constant questioning. "Is that what you want?"

"No. Well, yes," he stuttered.

"No? You don't want to get to know me better, or no, you don't want to talk?" She grinned at his scowl.

"I do, but right now I just want to bend you over the bed of my truck," he growled to her lips.

She kissed him swiftly, and it caught him off guard. It was too quick, and she leaned back the best she could with his hand still wrapped around her hair. "I'm starving."

"For food or my cock, princess?" he asked, tightening his grip on her. She whimpered as she melted into him, but then her stomach growled. He let her go. "You seriously need to eat more."

She rolled her eyes at him as she adjusted to not being held.

"Keep it up and I'll spank you after the first course."

"Promise?" she smirked at him.

Gods, she was trouble. He grabbed her hand and led her toward the sidewalk.

"Where are you taking me?" she asked, looking around.

"Over here," he said, pointing to a small restaurant two buildings behind Ag's. It was one of his favorites, and they had the best steak in the area. They had pretty much anything, so he was sure Ellea could find something she liked.

"Four Kings?" She looked at the small restaurant. "It looks closed."

Ros smiled at her questioning look. "It is closed."

Her face was priceless as he led her down the street and into the warm restaurant. He locked the door behind them, and she gave him another questioning look.

"I can always count on you to be creepy," she said with a grin.

"Welcome," a man's voice said, and Ellea jumped.

"Ellea, this is Lucifer," Ros said. She looked horrified. Both men chuckled. "Not that Lucifer."

"Hey, don't say that too loud; it helps keep the seats filled," Lucifer said with a sinister smile. He reached out to shake her hand. She eyed both of them before taking it.

"Nice to meet you," she mumbled.

"You too," he said respectfully. "Well, choose a seat, they're all open."

He winked at them and Ellea turned back to Ros with a confused look on her face as Lucifer headed to the back.

"I asked him for a favor," Ros said. "I figured you've had enough time around people lately."

Lucifer actually owed Ros a few favors, but this one was worth it. He would cook whatever Ellea wanted and then leave them to it for the night. Ros would lock up with the spare key when they were done.

Ros led her over to a table in the middle of the restaurant. It already had two glasses of water and a basket of warmed bread. He pulled the seat out for her, and she glared up at him.

"Get used to it," he scolded her.

"We really have the whole place to ourselves?"

"Yes," he answered, taking a sip of water. "Lucifer will leave once the food is served and we can take our time and enjoy the peace for once."

Ellea relaxed in her seat, and any anxiety Ros had disappeared. He handed her the menu and buttered a piece of bread for her.

"There's too much to choose from," she whined.

Lucifer chuckled as he came out of the back with two bottles of wine. "Is there something you're in the mood for?"

Ellea looked up at the older male. "Um…" She paused, expression thoughtful. "Something cheesy and fluffy?"

Lucifer thought for a second and then placed one of the two bottles of wine on the table. "I know just the thing. Would you like to know or be surprised?" he asked her.

"Surprise me." She grinned. "Honestly, if it's only cheese, I would be happy."

"Oh, you're a good one." Lucifer smiled fondly at her, and Ros cleared his throat. "Calm down, Ros, this one will be perfect." He motioned to the wine. Lucifer pulled the cork and poured them both a glass before heading to the back. Faint music began to play, and Ros placed the buttered roll on her small plate. She tasted the wine and moaned once it touched her lips. She took a big gulp and smiled at Ros over it.

"Don't look at me like that," she teased.

"Like what?" Ros mused.

"Like you want to bend me over this table while that very nice man cooks us food."

"What if that's exactly what I want to do?" It was what he wanted, and he didn't care if Lucifer was here. He hadn't slept with her since Mabon, and during his lowest moments, he worried she didn't want that from him. But then she would give him the most sinful look while they trained and he wanted to fuck her where they stood.

"I thought we were here to talk," she said, leaning back in her chair and popping a piece of bread into her mouth. She quickly grabbed another piece. He grabbed her wrist before she reached it and brought her fingers to his mouth, sucking on the tips and running his tongue along the pads. She shifted in her seat. The taste of her skin and the butter mingled in his mouth, and he answered her own groan with his. He released her with a pop of his lips and smirked at her.

"I do want to talk," he said, taking a bite of his own piece of bread. "But I want to do a whole lot of other things too."

Lucifer loudly left his kitchen with two soup bowls in his hands, whistling a cheerful tune. He placed them in front of Ros and Ellea and clapped once.

"Squash soup with a swirl of créme fraîche, and sourdough grilled cheese on the side," Lucifer said before heading back to the kitchen.

Ellea smiled at his retreating form before turning toward her soup. "So, what do you want to talk about?"

What did he want to talk about? Ellea brought a spoonful of the soup to her mouth and once again moaned at the taste of it. Maybe Lucifer's had been a bad idea.

"If you keep making that sound," he growled, "we aren't going to talk about anything."

"It's fucking tasty!"

She took three quick spoonfuls and kept quiet.

He tasted the soup, and a sound escaped him before he could stop it. She glared at him and he smirked at her. "Okay, you're right."

They both finished their soups and their sandwiches before another word was uttered. He really didn't know where to start, only that they needed to start somewhere.

"I haven't ever dated anyone," he whispered.

"That's impossible," she said. "You're a billion years old and, well, you."

"I'm barely fifteen hundred years old, and I'm being honest," he said through pressed lips. He couldn't call his past experiences dating. In the early years, he had messed with some of the women in court, but it hadn't been anything close to wanting to spend time with someone. "

Wait," she said, wiping her mouth and looking at him scornfully. "Besides that impossible fact, are you saying you want to date me?"

"Please don't make fun of me." He groaned. "Yes, I want to date you. You've danced around the 'future' conversation for a few days now."

This was so much harder than it should be, and she wasn't helping.

"Look," he started, then stopped, searching for the right words.

"You want to date me?" she interrupted.

"How many times do I need to fucking say it, Ellea?" Gods, she was such a brat. A smile crossed her lips, but before she could answer,

Lucifer came out of the kitchen once again.

"Oh, you liked the soup?" he asked.

Ros growled a yes and Ellea smiled with hers.

"Your dinner is almost ready." Lucifer grabbed the plates and headed to the back with another cheerful tune on his lips. Ros whipped his head back to Ellea.

"Before we get interrupted again…" she said, toying with her fork.

"If you ask me if I want to date you one more time…" He paused, trying to find patience.

"Ros," she interrupted. "I want to date you too. I don't know what that means, or what we do, but I want to try."

Lucifer whipped out of his kitchen, coming over to the table, and Ros was ready to curse the man where he stood, regardless of the amazing dinners in his hands.

"Dinner is served." He placed their plates in front of them. "Ros, your usual ribeye, honey potatoes, and asparagus. Ellea, darling, for you, I have sacchettoni. These little pasta purses are stuffed with sweet ricotta cheese, roasted mixed mushrooms, and poached pear. On top is my truffle cream sauce."

Ros eyed her plate, and she glared at him as if she would stab him with her fork if he dared to try and take some. She cut into one of the small fluffy pieces of pasta and brought it to her mouth.

"Fuck…" She moaned and brought another bite to her lips. Once she was finished trying her dish, she grinned up at Lucifer. "How'd you know this is what I wanted?"

He had never heard her sound so sweet.

"Aren't you going to see if I like my food, Lucifer?"

"You always like my cooking." Lucifer shooed him away. "It's one of my talents. The stove is off and everything is cleaned up. Leave your dishes in the sink and my morning staff will take care of them."

"Thank you so much, Lucifer," Ellea said sweetly, and Ros rolled his eyes.

"Yes, thank you," Ros said. "I'll make sure to lock up and check in with you tomorrow."

The restaurant owner waved goodbye as he headed out the door, locking it behind him.

"How do I get you to treat me like that?" he asked, cutting into his steak.

"Make me these little pasta things and I will be the sweetest thing you've ever met." She popped another one into her mouth and groaned around her fork.

"Is this what dating is like?" he asked, taking a bite of steak. His mouth watered at the perfection of it.

"Like what?" she asked, taking a sip of wine.

"Bribes with food?" he asked.

She laughed as she cut into her final pieces.

"Honestly"—she paused to take a bite—"I'm not really sure."

How could she not know? He knew why he didn't date, but how could a perfect woman like her not have experience?

"Men from your other home didn't want to date you?"

"They wanted to date me, sort of, but I didn't want to date them," she answered, pushing her empty plate away.

"I find that hard to believe."

"Well, believe it," she said, toying with her wine. "What do you think dating should be like?"

Ellea poured him more wine and watched him finish his food. Pushing his plate away, he eyed her over his glass, thinking.

"More of this?"

"Yes," she breathed. "This was perfect."

"Are you sure?"

"Of course!" She put her elbows on the table to lean closer to him. "No people, good food. What else could I need?"

"I could think of a few things," he said, toying with his lip. She gave him a questioning look. "What about dessert?

Her eyes glinted. "Your place or mine?"

"Why not here?" he asked, and she choked on a laugh.

"That's rude; he just served us some of the best food we've ever had and now you want to defile his restaurant," she scolded.

"Don't act like you don't have a few rude bones in that delicious body of yours."

He stood and cleared the table quickly. When he came back, she didn't dare move. He waited for her to deny what she wanted. She chuckled softly under his stare, but he saw the heat in her eyes and the beautiful pink color on her freckled cheeks. He put both hands on the arms of her chair and leaned into her. She leaned back and blinked slowly up at him, a small smirk on her lips.

"I sat here and listened to you moan around your fork," he said, leaning in to run his nose across her flushed cheek. "If you don't get your ass on that table and give me my dessert..."

"You'll what?"

"Oh, princess..." He chuckled softly and leaned into her one more time. He breathed against her neck, and a shiver ran down her body. "You're going to end up on that table whether I throw you on it or you get up there on your own like a good girl."

He licked up the column of her neck, and a whimper escaped her lips. She was fighting, like always.

"Why can't you just do what you're told?"

"Where would the fun be in that?" she whispered.

He growled and grabbed her by the hips. She half laughed, half shrieked and wrapped her hands around his neck before she fell back.

Ellea kissed him hard, demanding he open for her, and he did. He moaned as their tongues collided, twining and fighting for dominance. They hadn't kissed like this since Mabon, and he felt starved for her. He roughly placed her on the table. Leftover silverware clattered to the floor, and she laughed. She tore the sweater from him and leaned up to see where his cock was trying to poke out of the waistband of his jeans. Licking her lips, she reached for him, but he stopped her, pressing her back down on the table.

"You had your chance," he said and gripped the back of her leggings. She whimpered as he pulled them down to her boots. There wasn't enough time to untie them, he needed to taste her right now.

Ros grabbed a chair and placed it in front of her. She writhed on the table as he settled between her legs. He slid one finger through her, and it came back wet. Bringing it to his mouth, he moaned at the taste. She had begun to pant and they hadn't even started. He grabbed her thighs and yanked her to the edge of the table; she slid easily with the table cloth.

Ros kissed the top of her pussy, and she cursed and opened wider for him. He spread her sex and groaned at the sight, resting his head against her warm thigh. He couldn't wait to bury his cock in her again, all that silken wetness teasing him. He unbuttoned his pants to give himself more room and got to his treat. He ran his tongue from her opening to her clit, and she shivered in response.

"Oh Gods," she begged.

"So ready," he groaned into her, lapping her up and circling her clit.

"Please," she panted, "I need more."

He chuckled at her politeness. But he delivered on her request, circling two fingers at her opening and slowly sliding them in. He did it again and again, circling her clit with his tongue while giving her teasing strokes. She arched off the table when he curled his fingers deep inside of her. When he nipped roughly at her clit, he felt the flutter around his fingers as she let out a long, languid moan. He did it one more time, but she wasn't allowed to come yet. He slowly pulled out, and she leaned up, blinking at him.

"Not yet," he commanded, and her bliss turned to a scowl.

"Sick demon games," she growled.

"You haven't seen my demon games yet." He stood between her legs, and her eyes widened at the sight.

His cock was fully out of his jeans and stood hard and ready for her. The tip was already dripping. Gathering it on his finger, he brought it to her mouth. She instantly opened for him, letting her tongue jut out to taste him. A glint showed in her eyes as she grabbed his wrist and sucked hard on his finger, letting her teeth graze the pad and groaning around it. He twitched in response and tried to yank his hand free, but she held on, smirking. He grabbed his cock with his other hand and ran it through her soaked center.

"You dirty little witch." She squirmed below him as he sunk slowly into her. She released his finger on a loud moan. He slid his hand under her shirt and bra and bunched it around her breasts. Her pale skin glowed under the restaurant's lights, and a blush crept along her chest where he held her.

Sinking further, she tried to open for him, but her pants were in the way.

"Use your magic," he commanded, and she did. It took her a moment while he sunk further into her, but she freed herself from her clothes and lay fully naked on the table.

Ros plunged into her fully, and she screamed while her pussy clenched around the intrusion. He paused, waiting for her to relax as he slowly kissed up her ribs and her breasts, circling one nipple with his tongue. She shivered, and her pussy tightened again.

"Oh, you like that?" he murmured against her breasts. She didn't answer, but when he circled her other nipple and then tugged on it gently with his teeth, she groaned low and guttural. "Yeah, I think you do."

Ros slid out of her, only an inch, before pressing into her again. Slowly, he felt her relax around him, and he rewarded her with a kiss on her lips. She nipped and growled, urging him to go faster, harder, and when he pulled away, she glared at him.

"Hold on," he growled at her and grasped her raised thighs.

Grasping the table's edge, she smirked at him. "Do your worst."

Heat radiated through his body at the offer. He gripped her hips as he slowly pulled out of her and then plunged in, hard. A whoosh left Ellea's mouth but she tried grinding her hips, asking for more. He gave it to her; again and again, he thrust into her. The table moved an inch every time, and he cursed himself for not choosing a better spot.

Ellea's chest heaved as she moaned loudly. He could feel her orgasm building, and he lifted her more to go a little deeper. Her stomach flexed instantly, and she lifted her head to watch him plunge in and out of her.

"Oh, fuck..." The words were drawn out, and when she glanced up at him, when his eyes met hers, he saw so much demand. A wicked smile crossed her lips, commanding him to unleash himself, so he did, no longer holding back. She threw her head back and roared as an orgasm ripped through her. He could have sworn the windows shook, but he was too distracted as she clenched around him.

He swore as heat built around his cock and tingles crept up his thighs. Gripping her hard enough to bruise, he lifted her a little more and then he was lost in the feel of her, the flutter of her pussy as her orgasm continued. She whimpered and swore, cursing him, and he knew then that he would never tire of this. She lifted her head one last time, glancing to where his cock disappeared into her perfect pussy and then up at him.

"Please, I want to feel you cum." That request and those gray eyes had him losing all senses.

An orgasm ripped through him instantly, and he exploded into her. She smiled at the feel of it. A "yes" escaped her lips, and when he slowed, still twitching inside of her, she let her head rest on the table, smiling sleepily up at the ceiling.

PART FOUR

Excuse me? Which level of Hel is this?
- Unknown

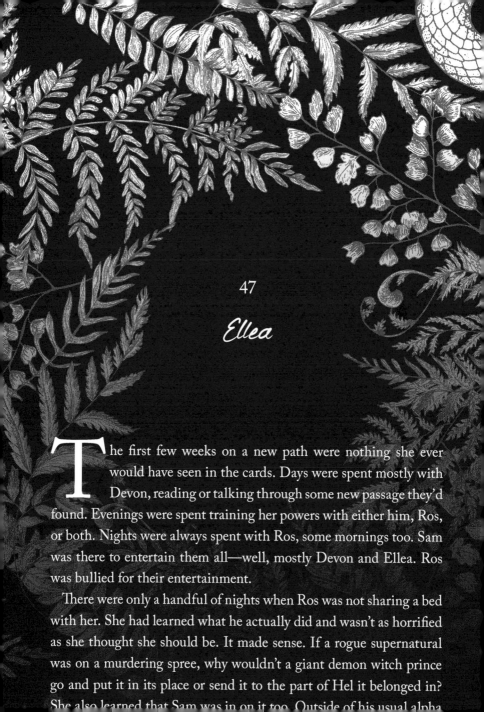

47

Ellea

The first few weeks on a new path were nothing she ever would have seen in the cards. Days were spent mostly with Devon, reading or talking through some new passage they'd found. Evenings were spent training her powers with either him, Ros, or both. Nights were always spent with Ros, some mornings too. Sam was there to entertain them all—well, mostly Devon and Ellea. Ros was bullied for their entertainment.

There were only a handful of nights when Ros was not sharing a bed with her. She had learned what he actually did and wasn't as horrified as she thought she should be. It made sense. If a rogue supernatural was on a murdering spree, why wouldn't a giant demon witch prince go and put it in its place or send it to the part of Hel it belonged in? She also learned that Sam was in on it too. Outside of his usual alpha duties, he would accompany Ros or go on his own missions. Ellea wouldn't admit it made her feel better when Sam tagged along with Ros. She knew they could take care of themselves, but it was always nice to have backup. Right now, Ros was her backup.

They had been walking for an hour and Ellea was thankful for all those mornings spent running after the giant brute in front of her. Ros had gotten word that a single demon was in their part of the woods and had been asked to take care of it. He'd tasked Ellea to take care of it.

After Mabon, her powers had manifested into something more. They became less erratic and easier to control. She was able to conjure full objects, some creatures, and transform them into something else. They were constantly finding new things to try.

Ros had found a passage during their research that described a trick, and he wanted her to test it on the demon. Ellea smiled to herself as she remembered that the particular passage came before she got tired of reading boring books and decided to suck Ros' cock instead.

They'd been in bed, and when she'd turned the page to find more dull text instead of something smutty or with dragons, she'd decided to make her own smut. Ros had been sitting up against his headboard, looking adorable and sexy with a small book in his large hand. Ellea had gotten on her knees next to him, pulled him out of his sweatpants without warning, grasped him hard, and sucked him into her mouth. He'd been rock hard almost instantly. The book in his hand had dropped to the floor with a smack.

Ellea had scraped her teeth along the tight, sensitive skin, and he'd rewarded her with such a hard smack on the ass that she'd yelped and fell face first onto his cock. He'd grabbed her hips and moved her so that she was on full display with her ass in the air. Slowly, he'd pulled her leggings down and he groaned at the sight.

"Does sucking my cock make you wet, princess?" he'd asked with his sinful voice. She hadn't needed to answer; her wet pussy had been on display for him to play with. She'd smiled as he ran a finger through her slit, and swallowed down until his cock was hitting the back of her throat.

Smack! Ellea found herself on her ass, an old oak tree in front of her and an ache in her forehead. Ros was laughing a few paces away from her.

"You should pay attention, princess," he said with a chuckle.

Scowling at him from the ground, she got up quickly and swiped at the leaves now stuck to her damp leggings. A crunch sounded, and her eyes snapped to Ros. His eyes calmed her, *it's okay,* and he pressed his finger against his lips.

Crunch, crunch. It sounded about fifty feet away. Ros moved closer to her on silent feet. She had no clue how he did that with how massive he was. The sound of crunching footsteps staggered with their uneven steps.

"Are you ready?" he asked her quietly, and she nodded her head.

Ros clapped his hands loudly, and the sounds stopped. Then the steps became erratic and fast as they headed right for them. Ellea steadied her breath and remembered everything they'd practiced. If she could make things, she could unmake them or alter them.

The demon came through a line of trees, and Ellea froze. All the practice could not prepare her for what was before her. It didn't look human at all, besides the fact that it had arms and legs. The skin was jet black and oily. It had no eyes, and its mouth seemed to extend to its ears—or where ears should be.

"Ellea," Ros warned.

She readied her magic. As the demon got closer, she unleashed it, but nothing happened. She tried again...nothing. It was so simple on objects and things she had conjured, but unmaking something that hadn't been formed by her powers felt impossible.

"Fuck," she groaned. The demon was so close that she could smell its foul scent. She tried again and nothing happened.

Well, use what I know.

As the demon lunged for her, she swiped at its feet and knocked it on its back. Its arms windmilled and sliced at her arm with its jagged nails.

"Bastard." Anger radiated through her as pain shot through her shoulder. She rallied her magic again, but instead of going for the demon, she created a sword out of thin air. Its hilt grasped tightly in her good hand, she swiped it over her head once. As the demon sat up, she swiped clean through its chest, slicing it in half. Blood sprayed her and the surrounding trees as the demon thudded to the ground, no longer moving. Ros walked up behind her and looked down at the demon that was now split in two.

"Nice swordsmanship," he said. "But I was hoping for more of a magical touch than brute force."

"Well." She winced in pain. "I worked with what I had." She poked the sword into the very dead demon and looked over at her shoulder. "Fucking thing...I didn't even realize it had claws."

"You'll learn to pick up on it," he said, examining her arm. He peeled her sweater off of her and took a better look at her arm. "You'll also learn the different types."

"Why do you think this one was here?" she asked up at him. He seemed satisfied with her wound, but his nostrils flared once.

"I'm not sure," he said, looking around. His eyes bounced around them, looking for something. "Sometimes they slip out, and sometimes someone lets them slip out."

"Hey," she said, grabbing his arm and forcing him to look at her.

"What's wrong?"

"I'm not sure," he said, searching her face. "Are you okay?"

She rolled her eyes at him. "Yes, I am fine."

"You just killed something." He grasped her face, forcing her to keep her eyes on him. "Have you ever killed anything before?"

"No," she said. Now she wondered if she shouldn't be okay. But no remorse or worry crept in. "It did attack me."

He smirked down at her.

"We'll keep working on it." He kissed her once. "Let me know if you start not feeling okay, okay?"

And he kissed her again, deeper this time, and moaned against her lips.

"Are you getting a chub because I killed something?" she asked as he kept kissing her. She dropped the sword and wrapped her arms around his neck. She loved how freaking tall he was.

"Yes." It was a groan against her lips, and he lifted her off the ground. Her legs instinctively wrapped around his hips. "I get a raging boner any time I think about you punching me."

"You're demented," she said as he assaulted her neck.

"And now I have a vision in my head of you with a sword in your hand," he moaned into her ear, and shivers crept down her spine.

"It was a small sword," she said breathlessly as he ground his hips into her.

"It was still sharp, and you sliced that thing in two like it was nothing." His hand moved down the small of her back, sliding under her pants to grab her ass. "What do you want, princess?"

She whimpered into his mouth. He broke from her, wanting a response.

"More," she said roughly. "Do some demon thing."

His eyes darkened, and he smirked at her. "Do that thing with the clothes and I'll show you a trick of mine."

So she did; in the blink of an eye, they were naked in the forest and their clothes hung from a nearby tree. They still stood wrapped around each other, her back against a tree. She smirked up at him. "Your turn."

He kissed her softly on the lips and pulled her hands away from his neck, reaching them over her head.

"If you tell me to stop, I will stop." He kissed her lightly again. "Okay?"

She nodded yes. She was too excited to speak.

"Let me hear you say it." He tugged on her arms.

There was resistance, and when she looked up, her wrists were coiled in shadows. She tugged and they didn't budge. They kissed lightly at her skin but didn't hurt like ropes or chains would. Her heart raced as she looked back at Ros. His eyes had gone wholly dark and wild with lust.

"Yes," she breathed out.

He smiled and stepped out from her legs. She hung there by her wrists. Her feet were dangling a couple feet above the ground, and excitement vibrated through her. A cool autumn breeze caressed her bare skin, and she shivered.

"I've wanted to do that to you since the night you kicked my ass in the woods." He walked around her and the tree, not touching her.

"You let me kick your ass."

"Mm," was his only reply as he stopped his circle and stood in front of her.

The wait was torture. She wanted to be touched, needed to be touched.

"Are you going to do anything?" she asked with a smirk. "Or just stand there?"

He arched a brow at her, and she felt something creep along her ankle. She couldn't see it from where she hung, but she could feel it winding around her. It made its way around her calf, her thigh, and when it got to the apex of her thighs, it caressed her sex, sliding through it in a long, slow sweep. Her moan was more a gasp of shock at the feel of it. Then it continued winding up her body, her stomach and then her breasts. She looked down to see a ribbon of shadow dancing along her peaked nipples.

Her breath picked up as she felt another shadow wind around her throat and then a third weaving around her thighs, running through them and caressing her continuously. The constant cool touch against her heated flesh was the best kind of torture.

"To see you strung up like this," he said as he let his hand travel across his stomach. He grasped his cock in his hand and slowly pumped it. "To see my shadows dance across your pale skin. It's too hard to take."

"Oh fuck," she moaned, watching him.

"Do you like watching me fuck my hand while you can't do anything?" He continued to slowly jerk himself, and her mouth went dry, watching his abs flex, seeing how hard he gripped himself.

She began to shake as she felt two shadows grasp her ankles, bringing them up so she was open and bare before Ros. He stopped his hand as he took in the sight.

"Please," she asked breathlessly. The shadows around her neck were not restricting her breathing, but they held her there. The thought of what they could do made her desperate with need.

"You seem to become so polite when you are desperate for my cock." He slowly jerked himself again and took a step toward her.

She needed him inside her, but only a shadow danced harder through her, kissing at her soaked entrance.

"Look how wet you are," he moaned as he pumped himself hard again. "I bet you could take all of me in one thrust with how much you are dripping."

She nodded as best she could as the shadow around her neck

held her still.

"Would you like that, princess?" He took another step toward her. The shadows picked up their pace, and her legs shook. "Would you like me to shove my cock into that pretty pussy and see how much you can take?"

She nodded violently as she felt a tingle caress her thighs. She was going to come from only his dirty words and his shadows. He took another step toward her, and she felt herself clench, desperate to be filled.

"Will you look at that..." he said. "Are you going to come? And only from my shadows dancing through your wet pussy." He grasped her face with his free hand, and his breath danced across her lips. "You naughty little witch."

He kissed her hard as his shadows dove inside of her. She came hard, her pussy clenching around his shadows, desperate to be filled with his heated erection. The need for him was only there for a moment as he plunged his cock inside her in one thrust. She screamed into his mouth and he kissed her through it. Her orgasm dragged out as he fucked her with feral abandon. After only a few minutes, he came inside of her with a roar, thrusting hard, filling her with everything. And when he was done, when she was spent, he stepped back while she still hung there, strung up by his shadows, and watched both their releases drip out of her.

TRICKY MAGIC

48

Ros

They had been walking for thirty minutes, and visions of what they had done were burned inside his mind. Ellea's pale skin flushed with need, her chest heaving with desperate breaths...the way she'd screamed into his mouth when his shadows fucked her, and when he'd buried his cock inside of her, her wet heat consuming him...He would never get the beautiful image out of his head, ever.

"Stop it." She smacked him on the arm. "If you keep that up, we will never make it back."

The past few weeks had been something out of a book, a life he never could have imagined for himself. It was almost enough to suppress the darkness that crept through their lives, almost enough for him to forget that it would come to an end. It was only a matter of time until this happy bubble broke.

All of it was pushed to the back of his mind as he thought about the demon in the forest. How did it get here? Was Belias behind it? It sure as Hel felt like it. Add to that the vampire attacks last week, and it was undeniable that things were ramping up and getting too close to home.

Ellea broke him from his spiral. She asked, "What's it like in Hel?"

They hadn't talked much about it; she seemed to want to live in the happy bubble too.

"It's like... Hel." He sighed. "The shorter version is that it's like any dark kingdom you've read about in a book. Big black castle, different areas to rule over, asshole rulers, and their bratty kids."

"You're only a little bit bratty." Her smile was warm and teasing. "But how are both you and Belias 'princes?' I'm still not convinced you're one."

"Trust me, I don't want to be one." He took another breath. He hated talking about this part of himself. He had been topside for over a thousand years, and he felt more human than demon. "With Hel being split into its four parts, each realm has a ruler. So Belias comes from one part, and I come from another."

"Do you have other cousins like Belias?"

"No one is like Belias," he said with a frown.

"You're right about that, cousin." The dark voice slithered to his ears before Belias appeared in front of them. Ros instinctively moved to stand in front of Ellea.

I really need to stop saying his name out loud.

Ellea peeked around his bicep and scowled at him. "I would like to remind you that I took care of myself last time he was here." She took a step to stand next to Ros.

"What do you want, Bel?" He hated that he was here and near Ellea, but he wasn't too surprised. Where demons lurked, Belias would be too.

"I've come to give you one last chance to accept my deal," he said with his hand on his chest. "I offered it to Ellea too."

"What deal?" Ellea asked. Belias began to speak, but Ros stopped him with a band of shadows around his mouth.

"No deal, Bel. I am not interested in whatever you're planning or working with you," Ros said as Belias tried to get the shadows away from his mouth. He didn't want Ellea anywhere near Hel or his family.

Belias magicked the shadows off of his mouth and scowled at Ros before turning to Ellea. Ros took a step to cover her again, and she pushed him out of the way. "Ellea, my offer still stands."

"No." It was stern and final.

"Are you sure?" Belias asked with a raised brow. "You may find you like some other...tricks that Hel can offer. I would hate to see you tied to this place."

"No." She took a step and pressed herself against Ros' side. "I'm fine where I am."

Anger flashed across Belias' face for a moment before it was replaced with boredom.

"Fine. See you two around." He stepped back into a mass of shadows and disappeared.

"Yeah," she said with a shiver. "No one is like *him*."

Ros shook his head and sighed, guiding them toward home while his thoughts whirled with darkness. "I hope you never have to meet the rest of my family."

Leaves rustled nearby, and Ros stepped in front of Ellea again. "I swear to the Gods, if you do that one more time, I'm really going to kick your ass."

Ros didn't care, he wasn't taking any chances, especially with his magic on edge. It had been all day. The rustle sounded again, followed by heavy breathing. Billy bounded around a corner, running toward them like her tail was on fire.

Hurry! the beast yelled. *Vampires, wolven compound, a lot of vampires.* She was panting hard and her eyes were wide. *Garm and Devon are there too. We have to hurry.*

They were only a few hundred yards from Ros' cabin as they began to run. They whirled on his truck, ripping open the doors. Ros slammed the door and reversed quickly, gravel and dirt flying. He heard Ellea send up a quick wish as her magic began to crackle across her skin.

There was chaos everywhere as they pulled up to the farm. Ellea and Billy jumped out of the truck before it even stopped, heading right to the fight. There were two wolven for every three or four vampires. Devon was using every type of elemental magic he could. Water drowned a vampire who was stalking a wolven, then fire flowed to another before it could get to one of the betas. Garm ripped the head off of one and shimmered into shadow to attack another one fifty feet away.

"Go for the head!" Ros yelled after Ellea as she threw herself into the fight with Devon at her side.

Billy had fully shifted into her beast form, tripling in size and headed straight for Garm, protecting his back.

There had to be over a hundred vampires, but luckily many of them were already dead. Ros searched for Sam and found him closer to the treeline in his wolven form, with Devika at his back. His deep gray fur was splattered with dark blood and his muzzle was caked in it. Where he would attack, Devika would be right there with the follow up.

"Sam!" Ros shouted to his friend, then he signaled with his hand to listen. Ros sent a thought to Garm, who spread it to Sam, Ellea, and Devon. They had to create a wall and corral the vampires into a group.

Ros caught a vampire getting close to Ellea, stepping through his shadows in time to grab it by the throat. Ellea didn't even notice as its claws swiped through her hair. Ros roared as the vampire burned from the inside, and Ellea turned with a surprised look on her face. Ros didn't give her a chance to react; instead, he turned to see if his plan was working.

Sam worked with the other wolven, picking off vampires where they could and forcing the rest toward the center of the clearing. Devon created a wall of water that forced those retreating to circle back. Ellea sent a wave of electricity through it, shocking those trying to get through the thick wall.

Once the group of vampires was clustered closer together, Ros sent a blade of shadows and fire slicing through them. He pulled it back toward him, slicing off the heads of those who had ducked. Silence hung heavy as they all looked around, searching for anyone that may have gotten away. Devika howled to the sky, and a few calls from further away answered back.

The breath Ros was holding shuddered out of him. Everyone seemed to be in one piece. The wolven began dragging those killed into the center of the clearing with the rest. They would need to burn the bodies before anyone came looking or the smell took over.

"What happened?" Ros asked Sam. He shifted into his human form; skin replaced fur and he stood before them fully naked. Ellea whistled long and low before Ros glared at her. She rolled her eyes and conjured a pair of sweats on Sam.

"Thanks, El." He smirked at her before turning a serious face to Ros. "One of my betas was patrolling the woods when she caught the scent of this hoard. They weren't locals, so she sent word to us. They attacked within the hour and, well"—he swept his arm, showing the mess before them—"all of this."

"I don't understand," Devon said. "Vampires don't attack wolven just for fun."

Ros thought for a moment, thinking of Belias and the demon. "I think this is something else."

Sam gave him a knowing look. "Do you think this was part of what we have been watching up north?"

"It might be," Ros said, rubbing at the back of his neck. "I think we need to head up there and check on things."

"I'll go with you," Ellea said as she walked up to him.

"No," Sam and Ros said together. She glowered at both of them.

"Sam and I will go, Garm too," Ros said, looking toward his hound.

"I need the rest of you to stay here and keep an eye on things," Sam said, looking toward Ellea, Devon, and his wolven. "Once cleanup is done, I want everyone to patrol the whole town and make sure no one is lurking. We will leave in the morning."

Sam looked to Ros, who nodded back at his friend.

TRICKY MAGIC

49

Ros

Cleanup was pretty quick thanks to Ros' fire and Devon backing him up with his own. Once word came that the town was clear, Ros and Ellea headed for her cabin. Her shower was bigger, and if they were lucky, the home would cook them dinner, but only if Ros asked. Ellea was still pissy about how much the home liked the guys more than her. She seemed pissy in general as they crossed the threshold to her empty cabin. Ros sent a wave of magic through it to make sure no one was lurking in the corners.

"What's with the attitude?" he asked as she stormed toward the stairs.

"I don't understand why I can't go with you." She whirled on him, crossing her arms over her chest. "We've been working so hard, and you know I can take care of myself."

Her lower lip pressed out in a pout, making it hard for him to stay serious. Yes, he knew all of those things. He didn't have to worry about her fighting or being safe. But he didn't want her to see what went on when monsters were truly monsters.

"Yes," he said, pulling on her lower lip with his fingers. "You're a big, scary witch who can take care of herself. And you're still staying here."

Her eyes grew vicious, and he knew she was ready to argue. "Don't lie. If you thought I could take care of myself, you would let me come with you."

"I'm not arguing with you about this."

"Stubborn brute," she hissed.

"Yes, I'm a brute; and I'll turn your ass raw if you don't stop the attitude." He let his tone drop so she knew what she was in for. "I know you can handle yourself, but the answer is still no."

Ellea scowled at him, and he grabbed her chin before she could turn away.

"One. More. Look. And I am going to fuck you senseless. After I beat your ass raw with my hand and before you're allowed to shower." He breathed the warning over her lips. "I dare you."

She lowered her chin as much as she could in his grasp and looked up at him through her lashes. Her eyes darkened as she stuck her tongue out at him with a *fuck you, do your worst* look written on her face. Then she kicked his feet out from under him and turned to run up the stairs. He landed with a thud on his ass and a growl escaped him.

He counted to ten before stepping into the shadows and into her bedroom. She screamed in surprise. "I didn't know you could..." Ellea choked on her words and swallowed hard. "Why don't you do that all the time?"

He watched a flush creep up her neck as her breaths came in quick pants.

"I'm old-fashioned." He sauntered toward her, and she backed away from him until her legs hit her bed. "Now, are you going to make this easy or hard?"

Ellea steadied her breath and cocked an eyebrow at him. He knew it meant hard, and he wouldn't want it any other way. She swung at him as he stepped closer to her. He caught her clenched fist and turned her, pinning her arm behind her back.

"You know the rules, princess," he said over her ear in a whispered growl. "You say stop, and I stop."

Her only reply was to stomp on his foot and hook his leg with hers. They both crashed to the ground, and Ellea took the opportunity to crawl away on her hands and knees, but he grabbed her ankle and yanked her back.

"You're such a fucking ass," she screeched out.

He smacked her ass once and pinned her legs under his. She kept trying to crawl away from him. It was adorable.

"Now, now…" He ran his hands up her covered legs. "Take your punishment, and you'll be rewarded later."

She shivered under his touch but held tight to her fight. "Shove the reward up your ass."

"Maybe next time, but I'm going to take my time with your ass." He gripped her perfect backside, his large hands making indents as he squeezed her through her leggings. She shimmied it in front of him, and he knew it was on purpose. "You know, I love when you make these disappear with that little trick of yours, but do you know what I love more?"

"No," she said breathlessly.

"This." He grasped her leggings in his hands and tore them from her skin. Ellea was bare before him, and his cock twitched against his tight jeans. "No underwear."

The feel of her bare skin sent waves of arousal through him, but he had work to do. Their time in the woods had been quick and rough, now he would drag it out, make her wait. She yelped as he smacked her on her right ass cheek, her pale skin quickly turning pink. He smacked the other, and she moaned into the floor. She arched into him, her arms stretching as she gave him better access. He knew she wanted him to slip his fingers a little lower, a little deeper into her sex that was probably wet and waiting. Instead, he smacked her again and again. Her moans turned into whimpers as she began to rub her thighs, fighting for friction.

"Will you stop being a brat?" He rubbed at her welted skin.

She scoffed into the carpet before she turned her head slightly. He could see the small smile that formed on her mouth.

"No." It was a taunt.

She had never given in, never told him to stop no matter how far he pushed. Her fight was something to revere, and he wondered if she was made for him and the harsh life he was destined to live. He shook the thought and slapped her one last time, causing her to shake with pleasure. He leaned over her, pressing his body to hers, and turned her head, kissing her cheek and breathing in her beautiful scent.

"Do you know how strong I know you are? How capable?" he asked with a growl.

She moaned as his breath caressed her ear.

"Yes," she breathed out.

"Good girl," he said, and he kissed her gently on her cheek.

He rolled her over slowly. She gazed up at him, her face flushed and imprinted from the floor. He caressed the mark and kissed her softly. She answered with a whimper. He knew her ass was raw and probably stung as his weight pressed her into the floor. He smiled against her lips before slowly making his way down her body.

Ros peeled her shirt away so she was fully naked under him. She grabbed at him, trying to take his clothes off. He grabbed her hands and held them to her sides, shaking his head. She groaned as he brought his mouth before her, his hot breath caressing her soaked pussy. He licked her once, and she opened for him.

"So responsive to being punished," he growled into her hot skin. She lifted her hips, trying to get him to continue, but he took his time, needing her to learn patience, even if she would be quick to find release.

Ros took one finger and ran it down her, halting at her entrance. She twitched at the movement, and when he inserted it inside of her, he could feel her walls already fluttering around it. Then he inserted another and just held it there.

"Please," she mewled. Her fingers twined in his hair as she tried pulling him toward her. He chuckled, slowly pumping his fingers in and out of her. She cursed his name and threw her head against the floor.

Ros curled his fingers deep and brought his tongue to her clit. In a few short passes, she was screaming out. Her breasts heaved with the release as she shook, crying out words no one would understand. She pulsed around him, and his cock strained painfully against his jeans. He tried moving it out of the way, but it was no use. This was about her, and it would have to wait.

Ros continued to lick and pump as she came down for her orgasm. When he wouldn't stop, she pulled at him, but he continued to work her. When she clawed at him, he loved it and decided he wasn't done.

"One more." It was a command, and he loved how her wide eyes looked down at him.

"I can't." It was breathless, but she didn't tell him to stop.

"You will."

He delved into her deeper, adding a third finger that had her throwing her head back with an unrestrained scream. Focusing on that spot deep inside, he pumped in time with his mouth sucking on her clit. She submitted fully, widening her legs more and thrusting her hips.

"Come for me again." It was another command, only breaking from his rough sucking and licking to utter his filthy request. "I want to feel you soak my fingers and face. I want you to come so hard, so much, that I'll taste you for days."

A whimper was her only response as her stomach flexed and her legs shook. She curled around where they met and roared as her second orgasm ripped through her. The way she clenched, the way she gushed around his fingers and mouth, he thought he would spill in his pants at the feel and the taste of her. But he held on to his sanity and slowly pulled out, not rushing it and letting her adjust to the emptiness that it would leave. He licked her clean before trailing kisses up her thighs, stomach, and breasts.

Ellea smiled sleepily at him as he peeled away the hair that was plastered to her face. He sent a silent plea to the home, and the sound of running water came from the bathroom.

"Bitch," Ellea cursed. Ros chuckled and slowly picked her up off the ground.

"But you?" she asked, wrapping her arms around his neck. She didn't even open her eyes.

"Bath, food, and then we can talk about me." He kissed her on the forehead and walked into the warm bathroom.

TRICKY MAGIC

50

Ros

Over the past few months, Ros and Sam had been hunting a vampire group, one that worked with demons and was kidnapping mortals instead of killing them like they usually would. They had only been able to get close once, but even then, they'd barely made it out alive. He knew the three of them wouldn't be enough, so this was only a scouting mission to see if they could get any info on what they were planning. He wanted to see if these were the same vampires that had attacked the farm. But Ros found himself distracted, part of him left in Ellea's driveway. When they'd left, she had walked him to the end of the driveway with her hair a beautiful mess, her eyes hooded with sleep and a bratty pout plastered on her face. Ros had never felt so happy and sad as when he saw her waving in his rearview mirror.

They had driven north for eight hours and spent another day on foot. They'd made camp close to the compound that loomed in front of them. It had been a month since Ros was here last, and it had doubled in size. Something would have to be done soon whether or not the council stepped in or Belias was involved.

They were using an old military fort as their base. The night before, they'd watched a dozen trucks enter; now, they watched the same trucks leaving. They weren't able to get too close with the magical perimeter around the base, and Ros was utterly frustrated. All that could be done was to send Garm in. Ros could have gone as well, but they'd all decided that wasn't a good choice. If Belias was in there, he would know the moment Ros crossed the perimeter. They may not be blood related, but their demon powers answered each other's, and without proper shielding, he would be found. Garm going was already a risk, but it was one they had to take.

Ros and Sam took a breath as Garm shimmered into shadows.

"And now, we wait." Sam sounded so solemn.

"Now we wait," Ros replied, bringing his campfire coffee to his lips.

"So what are you getting Ellea for her birthday?" Sam smiled widely as Ros spit out his coffee. His mood change was bound to give him whiplash.

"What the *fuck* do you mean?" He wiped at his mouth. "When is her birthday?"

"You didn't know?" Sam's smirk said he knew the answer. "Devon and I already have her gifts wrapped."

"You asshole." Ros glared at his soon-to-be-dead friend. "How long have you known?"

Sam pretended to think hard. "A few days after Mabon. She and Devon had talked for hours and it came up."

"And when is her birthday?" Ros was so angry that all of his worry about the mission was gone.

"Samhain." Sam's smile grew.

"That's in two weeks." Anxiety quickly washed away the anger. He was most definitely getting emotional whiplash. "Why did you wait to tell me?"

"To see this look on your face."

Why hadn't he thought to ask her? Was it too late?

"What do you get the witch you are madly in love with after only knowing her for a minute?"

"I'm not madly in love with her," Ros said, looking horrified. "We're just..."

He paused, not knowing what they were.

"Fucking constantly and giving each other heart eyes when you're not trying to kill each other." Sam paused. "Don't forget you guys share a bed when you have never slept with any man or woman before. Ever. Garm doesn't count, and I'm still mad about that one time you snuck out of my bed."

"You're crazy," Ros said.

"Yes, but you're also crazy." Sam punched him lightly in the arm. "Crazy about Ellea. I almost threw up in my mouth when I watched you kiss her adorable angry forehead before we left."

"I'll get her flowers and chocolate. She loves chocolate," Ros said, ignoring Sam's comments.

Sam fell over laughing. "Yeah, do that, and please let me know when you do so I can watch her cut your balls off."

What the fuck would she want? What did she need? His head fell into his hands, and Sam patted his back.

"You'll think of something."

Ros groaned, but his anxiety dissipated as Garm appeared before them. *The place is empty,* he said. *I think they left in those trucks this morning. You're not going to like what I found.*

"What is it?" they asked at the same time.

Before Garm could answer, Ros' chest heaved in pain. His heart felt as though it would beat out of his chest, and he doubled over, breathless.

What's happening? Garm's voice was a worried ring in his head.

"I don't know," Ros groaned, still bent over. It was a heavy feeling, like a fist gripped his ribs.

He took deep, steadying breaths as his friends looked at him with worry. The pain lessened, and he tried shaking the feeling of something being utterly wrong.

"Do we need to go into the compound?" he asked, wiping the sweat from his face.

No, we should go home. I can tell you on the way, Garm said seriously.

"Tell me!" Ros demanded.

I smell war.

TRICKY MAGIC

51

Ellea

I t was the third morning since the men had left. Ellea's anxiety
had grown to a tipping point when she woke this morning, and
Billy answered the pressure in her chest with her own whine.
"It's fine." Ellea smoothed the wrinkle that formed between her
familiar's glowing, amber eyes.

Sure, Bug. Let's go see if Devon is awake.

Devon had spent each night in Ellea's cabin. They were supposed to
spend the past few days training. Instead, they started their mornings
reading and it transitioned into Supernatural or Harry Potter
marathons, binging on snacks, and eating all of the worst dinners.
They either fell asleep in a pile on the couch or Devon would spend
the night in one of the spare rooms. Ellea was thankful to have him
nearby; Billy wasn't enough to fill the gaping hole the brute had left

when he drove away.

Ellea grabbed one of Ros' shirts she had stolen and a pair of thick socks. They headed down the hall and knocked lightly on Devon's bedroom door. His sleepy voice rang from the other side of the door. "I'm up."

Ellea cracked the door open and poked her head in. Devon was still under the covers in the massive bed. She was thankful her nana and uncle had furnished this house with big cozy things. He lifted the blanket, and Billy rushed past her to jump in the bed with him. Ellea followed behind and got under the covers.

Billy's nose poked out from the thick blanket and her body warmed both of them from her place sandwiched between them. Ellea toyed with her velvety ear before looking at her friend. His intuition was almost as good as hers, and she wasn't ready to see what he was picking up on.

"Are you as anxious as me?" His light eyes flickered as he studied her face, and Ellea nodded. "They should be home today or tomorrow."

"Can I be honest with you and you won't judge me?"

Devon rolled his eyes but his smile was warm and open. "Yes, you can be honest with me. Tell me all you are feeling; I probably already know."

He probably did. Both he and Sam always had that *no shit, Sherlock* look anytime she asked or brought something up. She had said it to herself a million times, but life was different and nothing like what she expected or prepared for.

"Things are too good," Ellea said in a whisper.

"No, things are how they should be."

"It feels like the other shoe is about to drop, I wasn't prepared for this, but now that I'm here, I don't want it to end. But I feel like it's going to end."

"No matter what happens"—Devon paused and reached for her hand—"I will be here. Sam too. And you couldn't get rid of Ros if you threw him off a cliff."

"I just hate not knowing." She took a deep breath.

"Um…" A sly smile spread across his face. "Aren't you a seer?"

Ellea rolled her eyes, mostly at herself. She had been so focused on her trickster magic that she hadn't needed to tap into her seer side. She sat up, and Devon followed. Billy buried herself further under the covers and immediately went back to snoring.

Smoothing out the blanket in front of her, she conjured her favorite deck. The worn black velvet felt smooth in her hands. She gently took out the black and gold cards and took a steadying breath. Devon was quiet next to her, a solid weight of comfort.

"Let's see what the cards have to say," Ellea said and shuffled them five times.

"How many are you going to pull?" Devon asked.

Ellea took a breath. "Three."

Flipping the first card, they both exhaled together. It was the Devil. The black card showed a gold male with a goat's head, his hand extended from the arm of the throne and his pointer and middle finger pressed together, pointed toward the sky.

"Could be worse." His grimace was saying something else.

Ellea glared and flipped the second card. They both groaned together. The ten of swords shone bright in the morning sun. The light glinted off all ten swords that were stabbed into a man lying in a pool of his own blood. She shot Devon a look that told him to keep his mouth shut.

Ellea waited five breaths before she flipped the last card, but she knew it wasn't good. Her magic knew, and her hand shook as the Tower showed upside down. The lightning bolt glimmered menacingly at her from the worn card.

"Fuck," they both said together.

Ellea pointed at the first card, The Devil. "Negative in both positions, and I can't do anything to fix what is to come." She grimaced and pointed to the middle card, the ten of swords. "A fight is on the horizon." She groaned as she looked at the third card.

"The tower," Devon said sadly. "Reversed, it usually means complete and utter destruction."

Ellea looked at her friend, who was trying to look strong as he said, "Maybe it's just a bad pull?"

The door downstairs opened and she glared at him.

"Zaza?" a familiar voice called from downstairs.

Ellea got to her feet quickly and ran to meet her uncle. She took the steps two at a time and rounded the corner, crashing into his chest. She wasn't the adult witch who had harmed her uncle with an outburst, she was a small child, happy to see one of her favorite people.

"Uncle Felix!" she exclaimed. She squeezed him around his waist in a brutal hug. "I've missed you! What are you doing here? My birthday isn't for a couple weeks."

Felix embraced her hard before grasping her shoulders and pushing her away to look at her. He searched her face, looked her up and down, and gave her a sad smile.

"Ellea," Felix said and paused. Her heart dropped. He rarely called her that.

"Is Nana okay? Where is she?"

"Mom is fine," Felix said, and she felt she could breathe.

"The council?"

Was he here to take her in? So she could answer for all the mistakes she had made?

"No, they won't be a problem." She couldn't find a way to be elated about his answer when he still looked at her with so much worry. "It's your parents."

Ellea felt the floor crumble beneath her. "What is it?"

Felix held to her tightly. "There was an explosion at the prison."

"Are they dead?" Ellea was hopeful. Yes, it would mean he lost a sister, but then there would be two less horrible people in the world.

"They escaped," Felix said.

Ellea forgot how to breathe, and stars popped at the edges of her sight. Her ears rang, and her heart battered in her chest as her body fought for oxygen. Felix's face became blurry. As blackness swallowed her whole, she thought she saw Ros barrel through her front door.

Ellea woke up in her own bed as a late autumn sun shone through her window. She stared at the rays for a moment, wondering why it was so late and why she was still in bed. Turning, she found Ros sitting in a chair in the corner. He looked exhausted and a little angry—or was that sadness? She blinked a few times. Angry was his natural state. They stared at each other for a moment before they both spoke at once.

"Hi." The simple word seemed to weigh heavy in the space between them.

Ros stood and strode over to her before the thought of getting out of bed crossed her mind. She pulled back the covers, inviting him to lie with her. He crawled in beside her and dragged her into his side, pressing her head to his chest and wrapping a leg around her so that she was fully pressed to him. She breathed in his scent, earthy embers and bergamot, and felt herself relax.

"Your uncle left an hour ago," he said, pressing a kiss against her hair. "He will be back in the morning with your grandmother."

"How long have I been out?"

"Most of the day. Do you remember what happened?"

"I'm trying not to." It was mumbled into his chest. "How much do you know?"

He took a deep breath. "All of it." And he kissed the top of her head again, breathing her in. "I had heard the story before, when it happened. It was the disaster that shook the continent." He was quoting the headlines. "I never realized it was your parents."

"You wouldn't; I was never mentioned and they kept the details quiet. Only the council knew."

"I think I've been ignorant for too long," he said with a sigh. "I've lived a quiet life, ignoring the signs and ignoring my responsibilities."

Ellea pulled away to look up at him. "But you already do so much."

"Small missions, just a regular hunter taking care of rogue supernaturals. There is a lot more going on in the world, and I have been blind to it."

Ellea searched his face. "What happened?"

Ros sighed and buried his face between her and the bed. "We were too late, but we saw enough."

Ellea shifted, pulling his face away from where it was tucked in. "Don't hide it from me. What is it?"

Ros took a deep breath and looked her in the eyes.

"I can't fully blame Belias for it; I don't even know if he's the one that did it. But there have been whispers. One too many demon sightings, way too many vampire attacks, and all the missing people." He paused, seeming to try and find the right way to say it. "Over the past year, more and more people have been going missing. I came across a group of women and children being herded into large semi trucks, but I was alone. I couldn't save them." He closed his eyes as guilt washed over his features. "Vampires and demons have joined forces, and they are planning something big. I don't know what, but something is going to happen."

"Don't blame yourself for this." She ran her hand over his rough beard, the scruff tickling her skin. He was so strong, did so much, and he didn't see it? "You can only do so much."

He laughed darkly. "I can do a whole lot, but I've been holed up in my happy little town."

"Are you saying you regret our time together?" She couldn't stop her face from scrunching in pain. "Could you have been saving the world instead of dealing with me and my crap?"

"I could never, would never, regret you," he said, taking a finger and smoothing out her brow. "I have loved every minute of these past few months. My head was buried in the sand way before you barreled into my life." He paused, searching her face. "I've missed you so much."

It had only been three days, but she hated the thought of ever separating from him again.

"I've missed you too." She kissed him gently, trying to put as much into it as she could, trying to lift him up a little bit. "So what's the plan now?"

"Now?" he said, thoughtful. "Right now, I plan on fucking you enough to make up for three days. Then, we have a birthday to plan."

He returned her kiss with one of wild hunger, as if their three days apart had been years. She almost missed the mention of 'birthday.'

"Now is hardly the time for fucking and birthdays," she said, confused. A prison had just exploded and two of the most evil people in the world were on the loose.

"One evening isn't going to stop us from saving the world," he said, kissing along her jaw and pausing at her ear to whisper. "We can save the world tomorrow. I want to bury myself so deep in you that I forget all my problems. Let's start the birthday fucking now."

He squeezed her ass, pressing her into his already solid erection, but she punched him in the chest. He only laughed and began kissing her neck. "Was it Sam or Garm who spilled the news?"

The way his tongue and teeth ran across her neck was so distracting. She was sure Billy had told Garm during whatever it was they did, and Devon had used his adorable smile and easy way with conversation to magic it out of her. So, of course, he'd told Sam.

"Ugh, that hound is on my shit list now too," he said against her neck.

She yelped as he nipped her hard this time, then she moaned as his hand traveled down to her bare pussy. She was still in only his shirt. He cupped it, letting one finger play in the wetness that began gathering there. "I guess one night of fucking won't hurt too much."

TRICKY MAGIC

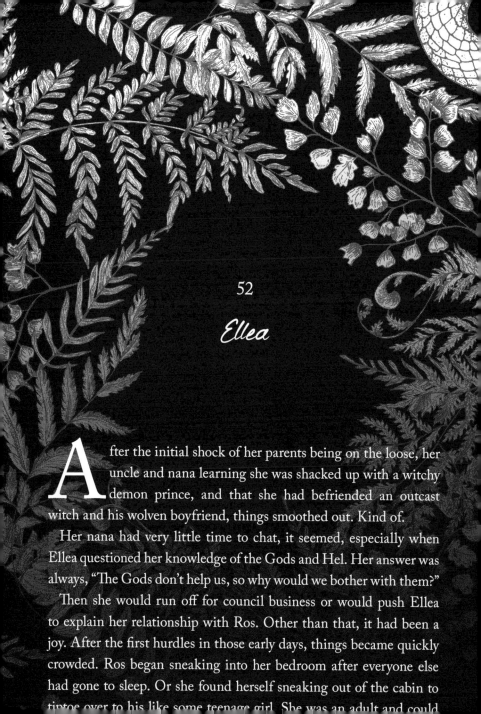

52

Ellea

After the initial shock of her parents being on the loose, her uncle and nana learning she was shacked up with a witchy demon prince, and that she had befriended an outcast witch and his wolven boyfriend, things smoothed out. Kind of.

Her nana had very little time to chat, it seemed, especially when Ellea questioned her knowledge of the Gods and Hel. Her answer was always, "The Gods don't help us, so why would we bother with them?"

Then she would run off for council business or would push Ellea to explain her relationship with Ros. Other than that, it had been a joy. After the first hurdles in those early days, things became quickly crowded. Ros began sneaking into her bedroom after everyone else had gone to sleep. Or she found herself sneaking out of the cabin to tiptoe over to his like some teenage girl. She was an adult and could make her own decisions, but Ros was being *old-fashioned*. She tried explaining to him that it was fine, it didn't matter that her nana was on the council or that her last relationship was with multiple partners. That was a mistake.

Ros looked like he'd swallowed his tongue. Ellea rolled her eyes as he spluttered. Once he recovered, his chest seemed to puff out, and she rolled her eyes the other way before he spoke.

His raised, defiant chin could not hide the blush that crept along his cheeks. "At the same time?"

"Yes, Ros." She sighed and leaned into his bed, ready for whatever ass-hat argument he was going to start.

"Do you still want that?" He turned away from her, striding around the room slowly before picking up a book and examining it. The bored act wasn't working.

"And if I do?" she asked with a raised brow.

"And if I don't want to share?" It was a snarl as he whipped his head around, but her pussy clenched at his tone.

Something was so very wrong with her. She really wanted this anger to continue, to have him take it out on her. But with the way their life was at this moment, with everything going on, she chose a calmer approach.

"Come on, you're a billion years old and you're telling me you never had multiple partners? At once? In the same bed?"

He seemed to consider it for a second before taking slow, even steps toward where she lay on his bed.

"Of course, I have." He knelt before her, slowly crawling over her and enveloping her body with his large one. He pressed her into the mattress and brought his mouth to her ear. "But I didn't like them the same way I like you."

His nose trailed along her neck, breathing her in.

"You like me?" A shiver ran down her spine, and she opened her legs wider for him.

"Yes, I like you." He trailed his tongue along the column of her neck before biting her ear. "But I like you alone."

"It could be fun."

"It could be," he said, but it was an angry growl. "We could get Sam in here, but Devon may put up an argument."

"I'll smooth things over with him." It came out as a whimper. She was naked and he was only in his jeans. The rough fabric rubbed against her, but she wanted his heat, his hard length that would make her mind go blank and stars spark across her skin.

"I can see it," he said with a groan in her ear. "Two men worshiping you, three if Devon were into females."

Ellea couldn't speak as visions popped into her head.

"Would you want Sam to take you from behind while I slide into your sweet, wet heat?"

She shivered as he whispered the filthy words in her ear.

"Having you pressed between us, moving as one."

She stuttered when she replied, "I-I've never done it like that before." She was quickly losing her bravado. She'd been with multiple men, but they had never done that.

"There is nothing quite like taking it from behind while also being pleasured in the front." He drove his hips harder into her.

"You sound like you're speaking from experience."

"I am speaking from experience, princess," he said, pulling away from her neck to look into her eyes. "How is it you had men worshiping you but ignoring some vital areas?"

She was having a stroke. She had to be. The images of Ros having sex with multiple partners were delicious. But the vision of him being with another male, enjoying it, them writhing in pleasure while he slid his perfect cock into another female sent a pang of jealousy through her. Ros saw it all play on her face and smirked at her.

He rolled her so they were both on their sides, and she whimpered at the loss of contact. He kissed her scowl, then her face and her neck, and she began to pant with need again. "We have to remedy your lack of experience."

Her brow scrunched at the remark. He wouldn't call Sam.

"I'm not lacking in experience," she said. It wasn't like she was some young virgin. "I'm sorry I'm not old as dirt and my sexcapades don't range from all sorts of demons, beasts, and partners."

"Don't judge me for who I've slept with."

Why didn't he deny her mention of demons and beasts?

"You've had sex with demons?" she asked quietly.

"Ellea, I *am* a demon." His brow arched, and so many visions flashed through her mind. "But the things I've had sex with isn't the point."

He grabbed her face and kissed her hard, smothering her remark.

She felt shadows caress her spine, her thighs, and then...

"Oh," she gasped, breaking the kiss as they slid down her backside and through her wet slit.

"I may not be up for sharing." He said it with so much lust in his voice that she wondered if he was actually up for it. "But right now, we can add something new to your list of experiences."

Ros managed to shimmy out of his jeans so he was wholly naked as he lay next to her. He grabbed her leg and hiked it up to rest on top of his, giving him better access to rest his cock at her entrance. It pressed into her, hot and thick, and she reminded herself to breathe. She trusted him fully but didn't know what he had planned. How would she react? Would she like it?

The shadows slid over her clit and circled his cock where it sat ready, then another set ran up her ass and over the tight entrance. She shifted away from the foreign feeling, and her movement pushed him deeper inside of her.

"You're shying away after boasting about multiple men in your bed?" It was a tease, but she couldn't think.

"I didn't boast," she began to say, but it was quickly cut off with a shocked moan as the shadows toyed with her, slipping in slightly and back out to caress her. They continued, demanding further entry.

Ros moved with them, slow, shallow thrusts that had her pussy clenching to be filled. Other parts of her began to tighten, and a hot shiver ran across her skin. It was too much. She kissed him hard, begging for something rough to bury all the sensations she was feeling.

Would this have happened with the guys? Could this happen in the future? Ros and someone else? Thoughts ran through her mind as pressure built and built. She didn't know where he began and where his shadows ended. It felt like they were entwined with her soul, teasing and caressing, then rough and heavy. She came to the conclusion that she would be happy if it was just Ros and his naughty shadows.

Sweat beaded on her chest and back as Ros and his shadows continued to fill her. There was so much pressure that she knew she couldn't orgasm—there was no way.

"Relax," Ros breathed in her ear. Then he growled and bit hard on her neck, forcing a shiver out of her. The shiver turned into an orgasm she hadn't expected, one she couldn't handle. She felt herself clench around his cock and his shadows. "Look at me."

It was a demand, one she didn't know she could answer as her release continued to barrel through her. She managed it, and he rewarded her with a wicked smile as he watched her come undone.

It still rolled through her, but she found the strength to push Ros down so she straddled him. His shadows gently caressed at her back side, and she rode him hard. She could feel her walls clenching around him, and with each pulse, with each aggressive rise and fall, he lost control. He gripped at her hips hard enough to bruise and their thrusts became so erratic, neither knew which one was in full control.

His cock hit that special spot deep inside of her and a new orgasm crested as a smug look crossed his face.

"Are you going to come for me again, princess?" he asked, every bit of him a smug male.

She growled, and his smile grew. He wouldn't win this, so she took a breath and leaned into the crook of his neck. Her teeth grazed across the hot skin under his collar bone. She made herself clench around him as she bit down on his flesh. She was rewarded with a feral moan, and when her powers flowed through her hands, crackling across his chest and neck, he bucked into her and roared with pain-filled ecstasy. He swelled inside of her, and a wicked smirk crossed her face as he writhed in bliss under her. As soon as he found his release, filling her, she let go and came a second time.

TRICKY MAGIC

53

Ros

One night had turned into ten. During that time, no disasters struck, there were no attacks, and no sign of Ellea's parents. The explosion at the prison had been a distraction and someone had slipped them out. Thankfully, no other high-security prisoners had escaped and there weren't any casualties. Ellea's uncle and grandmother had stayed with them for three nights. On the third night, Jadis had been called back into the city. She had to begin plans for a task force, what safety measures had to be taken, and a bunch of other important crap.

He didn't mind Ellea's family, but it was hard to share her with them. Never in his years did he think he would meet a woman's family, let alone one that sat on the council. Jadis was sweet and open about the two of them, but he worried that she knew something more. Felix was the wary one, not fully trusting their relationship, whatever it was. Ros couldn't blame the man.

Felix and Jadis tried talking Ellea into going home with them, but she flat out refused, even though it meant that they would be apart for her birthday. Her uncle had seemed ready to stay until Jadis gave him a stern mother look. They both left the next morning.

Sam and Devon took care of planning Ellea's party while Ros continued to hunt down the perfect gift. The plan was to have a sunset party with the wolven. Since Samhain fell on the mortals' Halloween, the families in town held their own celebrations instead of the usual big gatherings.

A bell rang overhead as Ros entered Ag's shop. She greeted him with a warm smile as he walked to her counter.

"Perfect timing," she said.

"And three days to spare." Ros smiled at the shop owner. "I will never be able to thank you enough."

"Oh, I'm sure you will," she said with a laugh. "And then we will do it all over again next year."

Next year.

His heart skipped at the thought of a whole year with Ellea. Would she want to still be with him? Would he get a whole year with her? It was so hard to think about the future with so many disasters looming in the shadows and his own destiny. Ag grabbed his hand and turned his palm over. Tracing a finger over the deep lines set in his large hand, she shook her head before smiling up at him.

"Yes." One word, one knowing word, and then she placed his hand back on the counter before bending down to pick up a long, heavy package. "Here they are. They're already wrapped."

He cleared his throat, trying to shake the weight of that "yes."

"I don't get to inspect my order?"

"Ellea will be extremely happy." She raised a brow and pushed the package toward him.

"Thank you." He headed to the door with a lighter gait.

Ros had never bought a birthday present for someone he cared about. He used to make things for his mother, but that wasn't the same thing. In the early days of living in his father's court, gifts were used to impress and bribe a person. That was a lot easier to do than painstakingly searching, worrying, and choosing the right gift. There was no impressing Ellea. She could conjure anything she wanted, especially now with her powers growing. If he chose the wrong thing, she would probably make fun of him for being an old man with no taste. Or what if she read too much into it? Did he want her to read too much into it? Life was so much easier when he was killing things and living on his own. But he smiled to himself as he climbed into his truck and put the gifts in the passenger seat. He wouldn't change a thing.

54

Ellea

The ground was cool under her feet as she took a late-autumn walk. Ellea had hoped the fresh air could wash away the nightmare that had woken her. She had fallen asleep after Ros left her, saying he had to run an errand. She knew he was picking up a gift for her even though she'd told him a billion times to not bother with it, but she still fell back into bed with a giddy smile on her face. And then she'd woken up screaming.

She could still feel the skin of the different beasts and creatures she had been trudging through. Scales, feathers, and pebbled skin rubbed against her as she clawed through the endless bodies. It was a nightmare she'd had once before. The beasts were vicious, wild with need to kill. And she recognized the cavernous room made of black stone and the throne at its center.

The beasts fought over a man sitting on the throne. She refused to believe it was someone she knew. The monsters' grotesque bodies created a mound over him as he struggled to break free. She did her best to save him, to get to him before he drowned in the endless attack. But she'd woken up before she could reach him.

She needed to stop worrying about it. There was already enough to think about, like her birthday.

Her birthdays in the past were always quiet affairs spent with Billy, her uncle, and nana. This would be one of the first ones without them since her parents were put in prison.

Her parents.

The forest hushed around her as a small snap of twigs sounded in the distance. Ellea froze and waited. Was this it? Would they catch her alone in the woods? If she were a smarter witch, she would have stayed at home and waited for company; instead, she was alone with only her magic to defend her. Or was this what she wanted? All of this waiting and looking over her shoulder was exhausting. Every day was spent holding her breath and then celebrating another day of survival that night with Ros. It was only a matter of time before they came to collect her—their prized possession, their greatest creation.

A black fox slowly stepped out of a nearby bush, and a small twig snapped again. It was only a tiny and cute animal, not her evil parents. The fox took her in, its small, sparkling eyes assessing her from head to toe. She dared not move since; she had never seen a creature in these parts (unless Ros counted).

The fox took one sniff in the air before it walked off and disappeared. Ellea let loose a breath and continued on her walk. The steep climb up the hill brought her to the abandoned third cabin, the one she and Belias had visited. She had been meaning to visit this place again after a dream she'd had. In it, she had walked the halls, the land,

and the greenhouse with a companion she didn't recognize. She only remembered the feeling of being shown something important, and she'd woken up before finding out what it was.

Ellea didn't dare go into the house, but the property was fine to walk. It was still overgrown, still run-down, and she wondered if Belias was actually going to move here. Was it all a game? He had said his aunt would have loved it, and she had a feeling he meant Ros' mother. He never talked about her. She wouldn't press him about it. He never brought up his father, either; if she asked, he would grumble and change the subject. There was still so much for them to learn about each other, but they had time. Well, she hoped they had time.

Ellea sighed, and her breath clouded before her in the crisp air. It was about to get crowded again with her party. She hadn't asked for one or anything, but Sam and Devon had gone a bit overboard. Now she was along for the ride, and poor Ros was being dragged along with her.

55

Ellea

Ellea was slowly dragged from sleep as Ros pulled her into a tight embrace, kissing her hair.

"Good morning, princess," he said with his beyond-sexy sleepy voice. "Happy twenty-ninth birthday."

His shadows abruptly opened the curtains, and a bright autumn sun peeked through the windows.

"No." She angrily stretched, trying to burrow deeper into the bed. "I'm twenty-five and will be that age for a while."

He ignored her comment and dragged her up, swiftly kissing her on the lips.

"I have you all to myself for a few hours before you get swept away," he said, pushing her messy hair away from her face. "Will you go somewhere with me?"

"Only if you tell me when your birthday is." She had been trying to get it out of him for weeks now.

"Fine." He pulled her on top of him and sighed. "I was born on the twenty-first of December."

"You would be born in winter," she said, sitting up and poking at his ribs. "Now, where are we going?"

"It's a surprise." He pulled at her pouty lip with callused fingers. "First things first."

He held her with one arm while he leaned over and dragged a package from under the bed.

"I told you no gifts." She rolled her eyes and took the outstretched package. It was heavy and dense.

"Open it." He looked so nervous, and her heart melted. "If you hate it, I can get you something else."

She slowly tore at the corner of the black and gold paper. The first thing she saw was leather, and she cocked a brow at him. He only nudged her to keep going. She peeled away the wrapping paper completely and was greeted by six leather-bound books. They looked ancient and thick. They were smaller than books printed now, and they had gold foil on each cover. She carefully pulled out the first book and squealed when she saw the cover.

"Fucking shit balls, Ros!" She took each one out and squealed louder as she read all the titles. "How?"

It was the complete series from an author who had been banned for centuries. Ellea only had one of her books, and the pages were almost see-through from the amount of times she'd read it. Now she had the complete series, and...

"First editions," she whispered, running her fingertip over the gold Roman numeral on the spine. Then she ran it over the embossed title of the first book. It was one she had only heard in whispers in the bookstores. *Bear and My Heart* by C. Clair.

"Ag said it was something called a reverse-harem shifter series?" Ros said. "I thought that you would maybe want the hardbacks since you carry around that disheveled paperback. Is it okay?"

"Ros…" She couldn't find the words. "This is too much."

She looked down at the books in her lap, and they became blurry with tears.

"If you want something else"—he lifted her chin—"I can bring these back and get you something better."

"You are so annoying." She wiped at a tear that escaped. "These probably cost a fortune, and they shouldn't even exist."

"Do you like them?" He still looked worried.

"Of course, I like them," she said, slapping his arm with the book and then quickly cradling it to her chest. "I fucking love them."

"Good." He quickly pecked her on the lips and then got out of bed. "Let's go."

"Where?" She tried to suppress her whine.

Ellea hated surprises. She would have rather had breakfast in bed and maybe Ros for breakfast dessert, then spend the day reading. Instead, he was picking out a pair of jeans, her boots, a sweater, and a jacket for her to wear.

She reluctantly got out of bed and got dressed as he ignored her pout and whine.

"I really wanted to spend most of my birthday naked," she said, cocking an eyebrow at him as he buttoned her up in the jacket he'd chosen. "And also reading."

She looked sadly at the books on the bed.

"We are going for a ride to my favorite spot in the whole town," he said as he pulled her in for a rough kiss.

"Ride?" She was curious.

"Motorcycle ride." He grinned at her and grabbed the first book, placing it gently in his large pocket.

Ros looked so young with that grin on his face, all white teeth and a glint in his eyes. She forgot how to think. It was so different from his smirk, his quiet smile, and the grimace that he wore most hours of the day. Swallowing hard, she nodded at him, and he dragged her out of the cabin.

Ellea was thankful for Ros' massive size as she sat behind him on his motorcycle. He blocked most of the harsh wind as they rode through the winding roads. Her arms clung to his waist and hid in his pockets. She had only groped him a few times before her fingers began to freeze.

The morning sunlight shining on the autumn leaves was beautiful. With each hill they climbed, the sights changed. There were rolling hills with horses peppering the fields. They rode past dense forests where beasts and creatures raced alongside them as they sped down the roads. The road narrowed as the ground leveled out. The trees connected overhead and blocked out the sun so much that you would think it was twilight.

Ros slowed and Ellea relaxed her grip on him. She sat up straighter and looked up at the trees. They were massive and old and made her feel as though she was traveling through an ancient tunnel, one that led to an unknown land filled with dragons and old, wild magic. Ros tapped her leg and pointed ahead. The sun shone through again as they neared the treeline, and her heart picked up. Once her eyes adjusted, she gasped.

They were at the top of a valley. Glittering lakes, orange and gold forests, and endless scenery lay before them. In the distance, she could see the small town center. Ellea couldn't peel her eyes away from the view as Ros pulled his motorcycle off the road and stood it next to a low rock wall. He helped her down before grabbing a blanket, thermos, and small tote from his saddle bag. He grabbed ahold of her hand and led her over to a clearing.

The sun warmed her face as Ros spread the blanket and sat. He spread everything out and motioned for her to sit. As she did, he poured her coffee. Her mouth watered; she could smell her homemade syrup, and it looked like he'd put in just the right amount of cream. Then he pulled out two chocolate pastries that were somehow still warm.

He was being so quiet, and she couldn't bring herself to break the spell of it. The coffee was perfect, and as soon as she'd wiped the crumbs off her hands, he reached into his pocket and pulled out her new book. She could have jumped him right there if she wasn't so eager to read. She placed a quick kiss on his lips and gave him a winning grin, then she settled her head on his lap and opened to the first page.

56

Ros

Today was a dream. It had to be. Ros would never get over waking up next to Ellea. No matter how pouty or tousled she was, he would always want to wake up to her. And her present… He would build her a library to hear her squeal like that all the time.

He'd been worried that she wouldn't enjoy the ride to the top of the valley, but she did, and the time spent up there was unbelievable, so simple and quiet. They spent the morning reading, and once he heard her stomach growl for the third time, they'd taken the bike into town for lunch. Pumpkins and Samhain decorations filled the town, and most people waved as they rode by. Some even wished Ellea a happy birthday. She blushed each time, and he couldn't get enough of it.

Ros rode with one hand on her arms that were wrapped tightly around him.

They slowed as they neared the edge of the wolven farm. Tonight would be spent at the far edge of the property. There was an old hunting cabin and a spot for a decent bonfire. It would be nothing compared to the Mabon one, but big enough to keep them warm in the cool autumn evening.

The sun hung low in the sky and the fire was already lit. Laughter could be heard as he and Ellea walked hand in hand to the edge of the clearing. She stopped him and stood there.

"Thank you for today," she said, looking up at him. "It was the perfect day."

She sounded almost sad. Before he could answer, Sam came bounding up to them and picked her up. He spun her until she was breathless and laughing.

"Put her down, you beast," Devon called, walking toward them. He grabbed her by the shoulders and gave her a kiss on each cheek. "Happy Birthday, Ellea."

Garm and Billy followed Devon, and a *Happy birthday* rang in Ros' head from the two beasts. She smiled at all of them and reached for Ros' hand. He saw the glint in her eyes, but he wouldn't dare point it out. They walked toward the fire, and each one of the wolven in their human forms greeted Ellea with birthday wishes. A few howls came from the woods where some were patrolling. Ellea blushed for the hundredth time that day, and Ros felt as if his dark heart would explode.

Someone handed out drinks and music played from the cabin. Ros watched the evening play out full of laughter and dancing. He joined in on the laughter, but kept far away from any dancing. As the sun set and the evening turned colder, Ros realized he had never felt so settled. It shook him, and he suddenly felt the need to hunt down more firewood. He found a large pile settled at the edge of the forest. Before he could grab any of it, a shiver crept up his spine.

Belias stepped out of the shadows, and Ros let out a brutal snarl. His cousin only regarded him with a bored look. Ros could hear the patrolling wolven creep closer, aware of the threat and ready to step in. Ros gave one glance toward Devika, and it was enough to tell her to stand down.

"You are really turning into those wolven you love so much," Belias said.

"What are you doing here, Bel?"

"Came to give my wishes to the birthday girl."

Ros blocked his way to the crowd. He wasn't allowed near her. He wanted to rip out his eyes to stop him from even thinking about her.

"No."

"I'm only here to say hello." He lifted his shoulder nonchalantly.

"I don't know why you bother lying. Come out and say it."

But Belias said nothing. He only grinned as another creeping feeling ran down Ros' back. His heart picked up as it sensed the danger lurking in the shadows. He heard a fearful gasp leave Ellea's lips in the distance and he rushed to stand by her side. Billy and Garm stood next to her as she stared into the forest, her hand covering her mouth. Two people stepped out of the shadows near the edge of the property, and Ros snarled. He knew who they were because of the way Ellea shook beside him. The older woman smiled at Ellea. The man almost flinched, but seemed to steady himself.

The wolven in both forms stepped up to protect Ellea, but as soon as they came close, they hunched in pain. Whining and screaming filled the air, and Ros threw his hand up to stop them from stepping in any further.

"Daughter," the woman said, looking Ellea up and down. "You've gotten...thicker since the last time I saw you."

"Cerce," Ellea said, raising her chin to her mother. "The last time you saw me, I was eight and you locked me in the basement."

"Don't you dare talk to me like that," she said with pure venom on her tongue. She snapped her fingers once, and Ellea flinched. Nothing seemed to happen until Ellea crashed to the ground. A sound Ros had only heard once, the one he had never wanted to hear again, bellowed from Ellea.

She lay there with her hands clutched to her face.

"Not real, not real," she moaned to herself between the screams of agony. Billy snarled next to her as she tried to shield her from her mother.

Cerce stepped closer, and Ros shot up a wall of shadows that was blown away instantly. The block had to have come from the man; the woman wouldn't have such magic. Ros tried to step in again, but was instantly blinded. No, not blinded—he was somewhere else. Everything was burning, and the cries of the injured sounded from all around.

He looked up at where Cerce stood, hissing horrible words to her daughter who was writhing on the ground.

"The vision you have always feared, dear daughter..." She bent over Ellea with a menacing sneer spread across her face. "You will never outrun us. We will always stand at the top of the hill with our destruction laid before us."

Ros looked around again. He felt he had been here before. He didn't have enough time to place it before the vision disappeared.

"That's enough." Ellea's father stepped forward, forcing his wife to stand down.

Snarls sounded around them, and Sam, in his wolven form, stepped up to protect Ellea. He nudged her with his nose and let out a whine as Ellea lay there, panting. Her hand still covered her eyes as she clung to the ground, helpless and hurt. Ros' vision began to shadow as anger clawed at his chest. His powers splintered under his skin, and he lunged for her father.

Ros threw a knife made of shadow and the man waved his hand. Electricity cut through him, and he sent another wave of electricity at Ros' chest, but he dodged it in time. Ros slowly gained ground on him, ready to send up a wall of shadows to trap him, but the vision of the hill and fire blinded him. He was alone, and the sound of burning and death was deafening. He heard Cerce's laugh ringing through the world, an evil cackle, and Ros roared into the nothingness before him.

He no longer felt the cool autumn night, but fire and the heat of destruction. It burned through his boots, and he looked down to see his hands were bloody. This was a nightmare, one he'd had before, but how could that be?

The vision you have always feared, dear daughter. Cerce's words rang through his mind. If this was what Ellea saw, how had he seen it all those months before? Ros turned and he found Ellea on the ground. She was covered in mud and blood. She wasn't moving. He rushed for her, and the vision disappeared again.

57

Ellea

"Cerce," she heard her father scold. "That's enough."

A cold, wet nose nudged her again, and Ellea peeled her shaking hands away from her face. The first thing she saw was Ros crawling toward her, his eyes blank, and she knew her mother was sending visions into his mind.

"Stop," Ellea croaked from the ground. Her father gave her a pained look, and Ellea flinched away from it. He took one step toward her before Sam attacked.

Sam lunged for her father, and as his large teeth snapped inches away from his face, he sent his electricity through the wolven. She screamed with Devon as Sam crashed to the ground.

"That's enough." Her father's voice boomed through the clearing. "Cerce, go wait with the prince."

The prince? Why would she wait with Ros? Ellea looked toward Ros, whose eyes were now clear. He blinked a few times as he continued to crawl to her, surer with each step. He ran his hand across her face when he reached her, searching her eyes. Ellea looked up and saw her mother head toward the shadows of the forest.

"Ellea," her father loudly addressed her, and her head snapped to him. "It's time you came back with us. No one will be harmed if you obey now."

Ros snarled at him from her side. She took a moment to glance over toward Devon, who knelt next to Sam. She saw a giant heave of the wolven's chest, and Ellea suppressed her sob of relief. He was still alive.

"We will be back if you say no," her father said. "We will not be as kind."

Ellea couldn't let anything else happen to her friends or her family. They didn't deserve to be punished for who she was, for what her parents wanted. She went to move and Ros held onto her. He gathered her into his arms and held her as he knelt on the ground.

"Don't you fucking dare," he growled into her ear.

Her father stepped closer to them, and Ros moved to hide Ellea from him. But he bent toward them and whispered,

"I'm so sorry, daughter. Please come with us. I can't protect you for much longer."

Ros cursed his lies as Sam stirred from the corner of her vision, but she couldn't take her eyes off of her father and the sadness painted across his face.

"Come with us," her father pleaded again. "Please."

She'd never seen him like this, so desperate and afraid.

"Please, Ellea, don't leave me with her. We can figure something out," he begged quietly, gripping at his own shirt.

Don't leave me with her? she thought. What was this? Memories flashed before her eyes. *Her father showing her control and her mother stepping in, pushing her to use more magic, generate more chaos. Her father gripping at his shirt as her mother laughed in his face for being too soft. Him shielding her from one of her mother's episodes. Him walking in while Ellea was curled in a ball, shaking and afraid of what she'd created. Her mother torturing her until she used so much of her power.*

Had it been her all along? She looked past him to where her mother stood at the end of the forest, Belias at her side.

"I won't," Ellea hissed to her father.

Ros cradled her against his chest, shielding her from anyone that wanted to cause her harm. His voice was low and vicious as he said one final word to her father. "Leave."

Ellea glanced at her father over her shoulder. He straightened and gave her one final, sad look before he plastered boredom across his pale face.

"Let's go, Cato," her mother called. "She had her chance, and she failed us once again."

She failed us once again. It kept ringing in her head. She knew she hadn't failed her parents, but she had failed her friends. Sam had been attacked. Would the wolven ever look at her the same? Would they still be kind?

Devon said Sam would heal; he said it to her a hundred times as she cried over his body. He was still unconscious when Ros had grasped her by the shoulders and directed her out of the farm house.

Billy and Garm had left earlier to help patrol, wanting to make sure there were no other attacks. Before Billy left, Ellea made her swear she would stay near Sam until he recovered. Garm agreed to do the same.

The faint sound of wolven howling followed her as Ros rode back to his cabin. She didn't say another word and clung to him the whole way there. Ros pulled into the driveway, and tears continued to fall silently down her face. He kept a hand on her as she got off the bike and made her way to the front door.

Ros scooped her up after a few steps and brought her straight to her room, where he undressed her slowly. He grabbed one of his clean shirts and placed it over her head, letting it fall down her naked body. He pulled the covers back, and she crawled into bed without another word.

He only left her to grab water and undress himself. She lay there with her eyes staring at nothing, and when Ros returned, he crawled into bed next to her. She took one look at him before rolling over to face away. He grabbed her and pulled her into him, fitting his body around her protectively.

You failed them.

58

Ros

Ellea had fallen asleep around two in the morning, and Ros hadn't slept at all. He laid there with her through the night, counting every breath, holding her through each nightmare. When morning broke, he continued to hold her through the darkness and the fear that weighed on her like a heavy blanket.

She'd gotten up once to use the bathroom, and he'd used that minute to call Devon. Sam had woken up and was fully healed. He was only a bit tired, and worried about Ellea. Ros told Ellea the news, and she only nodded before crawling back into bed. Ros drew a hot bath and woke Ellea. Part of him wanted to let her keep sleeping, but she'd slept half the day, and she needed to take care of herself. When he gently shook her awake, she jumped, and a panicked look crossed her face. Ros soothed her.

"It's okay," he said. "But it's time you woke up."

Ellea tried protesting, but Ros stripped her of her shirt and carried her to the bath. He got in with her and sat her between his legs. She sat there in the water, curled around her knees. Ros took his time, washing her hair and body, and when the water began to cool, he heated it for them. There was a moment when she finally relaxed slightly, and Ros took it as a gift.

Once he'd pulled her from the bath, he took his time drying her. Ellea kept her eyes to the ground the whole time. Ros grasped her by the chin and made her look him in the eyes. He kissed her softly.

"I'm going to kill them," he said, and Ellea's eyes darkened at his promise.

"I wish it were that simple," she said quietly. "She's strong, and my dad—"

"I'm going to kill him too. And she isn't strong. Your mother fears you," Ros said. Ellea began to protest, but he shook his head. "She fears you because you are stronger than her. Don't let her put fears into your head. They aren't real."

She frowned. "I wish it were that easy."

He kissed her again and reached for a hairbrush. "Me too."

A smile broke across her lips as Ros fought with the tangles. He didn't know why he'd started to brush it in the first place, but he was too stubborn to give up. When he cursed the hairbrush another time, she gave him a soft giggle.

Ros paused for a moment to take it in. They were here, Sam was okay, and they would be okay. He let loose a deep breath. He could feel an apology forming on Ellea's lips, and he glared at her. *Don't you dare,* he said to her without words.

Ellea let go of an equally heavy breath and reached up to him to kiss him. The kiss was real and deep, and Ros melted into it. He dropped the hairbrush to grasp her by the ass and lift her to him. She wrapped her legs around his waist. The kiss deepened, and they both groaned. Ros sat her on the bathroom vanity and tangled his hand in her long, wet hair. Wrapping it once, he tugged gently, baring her neck to his mouth. The taste of her was electric, and his cock twitched against her wet skin. He needed to feel her, her heat, her fight.

Her fingers tangled in his hair as she held him against her neck. She rubbed her wet pussy against his hardening erection. He yanked his mouth away from her delicious skin to look her wholly in the face. He searched her eyes, her expression. "Are you sure?"

"I'm always sure." She reached for his cock that was straining between them, wet from her, and stroked him roughly. Need shivered through him as he watched her hand move up and down his length. Her eyes sparkled with mischief as she grasped him tighter, letting her nails scrape against his tight, sensitive skin.

A growl sounded low in his chest as she did it again and again. He grasped her knees and spread them as wide as they would go, baring her to him. She whimpered under his stare, and her strokes became erratic.

Ros slowly inserted both fingers, and her head fell back as a moan escaped her lips. He only pumped a few times, curling his fingers inside of her, and she rode his hand. He grasped her by the back of the head and forced her to look at him. He needed her fully present. He needed her here like he needed her to be whole, to be okay. His gaze bore into hers, and she whimpered. When he inserted a third finger, sparks danced around her gray depths. He watched them go fully dark except for her power shining, desperate to escape as he took his thumb and circled it across her clit. His hand became soaked; she was only moments away from finding her release. He could feel it with each hot flutter of her pussy. He needed his cock inside of her. He wanted to feel her come around it, soaking him.

Ros pulled out of her, and a vicious look crossed her face as he robbed her of a quick orgasm. He loved that look. And he loved it even more as her mouth dropped when he brought his soaked fingers to his mouth and sucked on them. She reached for his cock, and he stepped away from her, out of her reach. She scowled again, and he saw the heat blaze in her eyes. He wanted her back, needed her to be herself. So he left her.

Ros turned and headed out of the bathroom, leaving her dripping on the vanity. It was torture for him, but it was only a moment before a sharp *thwack* sounded from the hairbrush she threw at him. He turned, and she bounded after him, throwing herself at him and wrapping her arms around his neck.

Ros smiled and took one step toward the bed and then he threw her on top of it. She landed with an angry squeal. He grasped her by the ankle and dragged her so that she was flat on her back. She tried kicking at him, but he grabbed that ankle too. Spreading her wide, he crawled between her legs, kneeling before her. He grasped his cock in his hand and pumped it once, twice, a third time, and her eyes grew heated as she watched.

"Are you going to be polite and ask nicely, princess?" he asked her, ready to play a game.

She placed one arm behind her head and let the other trail down her chest, around her breast, and then slowly down her stomach.

"I don't know, princeling," she said, using Sam's nickname for him. Then she took two fingers and ran them through her center. She moaned as she circled her clit.

Ros' hand faltered around his cock. He forgot what he was doing as he watched her toy with herself, plunging a finger inside of her, gathering up more wetness to circle around her clit. A flush crept across her chest, and Ros bit at his lip so hard that his sharp canine drew blood. He let out a hiss as she plunged two fingers into her sweet pussy, pumping hard. When he ripped his eyes from where her fingers plunged in, he saw the smug look on her face. She knew she had him.

Ros broke. If she wanted to play, they would play. He flipped her and then smacked her swiftly on the ass.

"Do you enjoy seeing me undone?" he snarled into her ear. She shook her head into the mattress, and he heard a suppressed giggle. "Don't you dare take your fingers away from your clit."

Smacking her ass again, she yelped, but he saw her shift and reach between her legs. He widened her knees and sat back on his heels to watch. Her touch was slow and teasing, her pussy clenched around nothing. He slid two fingers inside of her and she moaned against the intrusion.

"Harder," he commanded. She did, and after a few rough passes, her pussy clenched again. "Do you want to be filled?" he asked, and she nodded. "Do you need to be filled?" She nodded again. "Say it, princess."

"Yes," she panted. "Please, I need more. I want your big demon cock inside me."

She moaned as he curled his fingers inside of her and then swiftly removed them. He grasped his cock and circled it around her entrance. She pushed back, trying to rush him, but he held her still.

"Don't be impatient," he scolded her.

What sounded like a growl escaped her as she rubbed at her clit harder.

"Please," she panted. "I want to come around your cock."

Ros groaned as the dirty words left her mouth. "As you wish, princess."

He slowly entered her, and she moaned as each inch gained entry. When he was fully inside, he paused, holding still. Ros thought he would come just from the pulse and flutter of her pussy.

"Move," he commanded, and she did. He held still as she impaled herself on him, pulling almost to the tip and then slamming against him again and again. She continued rubbing her clit in rough passes, and he felt her heat and pool around him. She was close, but they both needed more. Pulling her hips up, he rammed into her anew, hitting that spot deep inside of her that had her roaring into the mattress. She cursed him, the Gods, and his demon cock. As her powers sparked across her skin, shocking him where they met, he found his own release.

They had sex two more times before night took over and sleep stole them. That morning, after a sleepy shower, Ros made Ellea a full breakfast. After that, she stayed curled on the couch around one of the books he had given her. They weren't out of the woods yet, but he felt the change. There were still moments when darkness shadowed her gray eyes, but he was there, and he wouldn't leave her. They would get through this.

He kissed her softly as he grabbed her plate and headed to the kitchen to clean up. He heard her get up, and when he peeked around the corner to check on her, she was heading toward her stack of books. "When you're done with your next book, let's head to Sam's to check on him," he called from the kitchen. "He might even like it if you read him the dirty wolf-shifter one you were telling me about."

He laughed a little at the thought. Ellea didn't answer, so he peeked around the corner again. The dish in his hand dropped to the floor and shattered.

Ellea stood there in his living room, a book held to her chest. Her eyes were wide as she looked at Ros. Asmodeus, his father, had Ellea by the shoulders and was looking right at him.

His father blinked once and gave him a knowing smile. Ros couldn't speak, couldn't move, and his father nodded at him.

"I'll see you soon, son. But until then, I will be taking her with me." He stepped backward into a shimmer of shadows, taking Ellea with him.

EPILOGUE

Time and space whirled around her as the weight of a man's hands held firm atop her shoulders. Darkness shimmered in front of her eyes and then stopped as she appeared in the middle of what seemed like a library. The ceiling was domed and molded with an intricate design that looked like feathers and scales. The far wall held shelves and shelves of black books. To her right was a massive paned window, where a faint glow shone through the glass. She whirled to the man behind her. He was dressed in a black suit and black tie. An emerald-colored silk square sat in his jacket pocket. His hair was dark and peppered with gray. He was as broad as Ros, but not as tall.

"Who?" Ellea croaked out. Her mouth had gone dry. "What?"

"I am sorry for the intrusion," he said to her. "But it seems the easiest way to my son is by you."

Son? That meant that this man in front of her was Ros' father, and that meant he was also a king of Hel. She swayed on her feet, and he reached out a gentle hand and grabbed her elbow. His skin was surprisingly warm as he steadied her.

"My name is Asmodeus, and it is time my son stepped into his responsibilities." He made sure she was steady before removing his hand. "He has been having fun for far too long."

"Fun?" She scoffed at him, finding her strength. "He has been saving lives while your nephew has been causing destruction."

"I will deal with my nephew after I deal with my son," he snapped at her. He smoothed his hands down his jacket, and a cool look spread across his face.

"Why not deal with your son on your own?" she asked, trying for a steady tone. She realized she was standing in the middle of Hel wearing only an oversized shirt. "You're a king of Hel, aren't you?"

"I am," he said as his chest puffed with pride. "But I'm getting old, and I prefer to avoid any conflict. I only want my son to come home."

He turned away from her and stepped toward the window at the back of the room. Ellea matched his bravado, trying not to fidget when she remembered what she could do. She didn't know if her powers would work here, but it was worth a shot. While he continued to look out the massive window, she conjured a simple black dress and a pair of heels. She wasn't sure what a proper outfit was while in the presence of a king, but anything was better than a t-shirt.

Asmodeus turned toward her as if he'd sensed her powers. He only nodded. "I hope you know that I'm not blind or deaf. I have heard the whispers, and I know what my son sees in you."

"I don't understand," she said honestly, continuing to try and stay calm.

"I think you do, or you will," he said as he walked toward her. He examined her face, her body, and she thought he may be sensing her magic. "I want to show you something."

She raised her chin and held his stare. "And I would like to go home."

He chuckled at her. It didn't sound evil, only honest. She rolled her eyes at him. "It was worth a shot."

"I knew I would like you," he said with a cool smile. "Come, let me show you the legacy my son left behind."

He raised his hand toward a door she hadn't noticed before. She stepped through it and stood before a hall that was blacker than the darkest night. There was only one way to go, so she stepped forward.

Asmodeus trailed behind her as they entered a room of black obsidian. The cavernous walls extended so far up; there was no end. There were no decorations, no furniture, just stone and a carved throne. It sat in the center of a circular room. On the floor leading up to it were claw marks of every shape and size. The throne seemed to be built from the very depths of evil as it loomed in front of her.

Ellea's heart raced as a vision passed before her eyes. She had been here, crawling through scales and burnt flesh. She'd crawled to get to Ros. She realized that she was always meant to get to him.

The story continues.
See you in Hel.

A SCENE FROM

TRICKY PRINCESS

How do I get to her?" The question was a growl as he sank the blade further into the demon's chest. Blood gushed from its mouth. "How do I save her?"

Each stab became more desperate, more feral, as he slipped further and further into the depths of his dark soul. He would live in the pits of shadows and death if it meant he got the answers he needed.

"I can't…" It was a pained groan as it tried to get the words out. Ros ripped the blade from him only to plunge it in again. "I told you—"

The demon's words were cut off by his own sobs, tears mixing with the blood that coated his face. They always got to this point, losing all their vile pride, their disgusting comments turning into cries for mercy. Soon, he would beg for his life, but it didn't matter. This one had nothing more to give; even if Ros got the answers he sought, it would end up dead in the end.

Slowly, Ros sunk his obsidian dagger into the commander's chin, its sharp point breaking through bone and tissue with a sickening crunch. The sound mixed with the demon's final rattling gurgles. Then there were only the heavy breaths that heaved through Ros' chest as visions of Ellea's frightened face flashed before his eyes.

An empty glass dangled from his hand as Ros glared out the window of Ellea's library, the too-small chair biting into his tired muscles. Muscles that had hunted and killed for the past seven days.

Seven fucking days without her.

He brought the glass to his lips for another sip, but growled when no amber liquid was there to wash away the taste of rage that coated his mouth. He stood only to stumble a few shuffling steps before he caught the wall by the fireplace, the rough-cut stone grating on his hand. He steadied himself but couldn't help the urge to throw something. The house intervened—probably tired of the messes he'd made in his countless fits of rage—and filled his glass.

"Good house." He blinked slowly as he brought the glass to his lips. His mouth instantly watered. The drink had a light, earthy taste with a hint of citrus and lime. "A fucking margarita?"

His lip curled, and the emptiness of the cabin washed over him. His powers answered with a splintering rage. Ellea was in Hel, alone, and only the Gods knew what she was going through. Shadows crept up the walls as he relived each of the last seven days and his failed attempts to save her. His shadows curled around him, trying to hide him as his eyes burned with shame and frustration. All of this power, and he couldn't get to her.

He whirled and threw the drink into the fireplace. It was her favorite drink, and that was enough to set him on yet another spiral. The flames erupted as a roar came from deep in his chest, and the house shook around him. He forced a breath down; demolishing the house wouldn't help. Another breath, and the lights stopped their shuddering. A tink sounded in the empty room as a glass appeared before him.

"This better be bourbon."

Silence answered as he hesitantly brought the glass to his lips. A deep oak flavor exploded in his mouth and warmed his still heaving chest. "Better."

Ros had been throwing things all week, more so since Felix and Jadis left two days ago. They'd been brought here as soon as Ellea was taken. Well, as soon as Ros had realized he couldn't portal directly to Hel to save her from his father. Ros had gone straight to her family with help from Billy. He was able to portal to Halifax, but not to Hel. It should have been easy; that dark realm was a constant pull on his soul. With a single thought, he should have been able to step into his shadows and out into the castle he knew too well. The connection now felt severed, its edges frayed and impossible to piece back together. If his father wanted him home so desperately, he was making it hard.

Jadis and Felix surprisingly didn't blame him. They were upset, beyond upset, and had stayed as long as possible while planning and learning all they could about Hel. Like most witches, they hadn't been paying attention to the old ways or any other supernaturals. The council eventually called them back to meet about the situation, not that it would help. He was the only one who could do anything about it, or so he thought. Ros shifted his shoulders as more rage washed down his back. He finished his drink in an angry gulp, and the home instantly filled it before he could put it down.

Taking a smaller sip, he paced. There had to be another way, a spell or a demon he hadn't thought about, one he hadn't killed. Garm was no use either, his own abilities blocked. He internally cursed the hound even if it wasn't his fault.

A door slammed open. "Speaking of the bastard." Ros readied his glare as the sleek black body of his oldest friend crossed the threshold, his lover trotting close behind.

Fucking Hel, Billy cursed inside his head.

Both beasts slowly walked into the library, matching Ros' glare with their own as they sniffed the air. Garm grimaced, his large sharp teeth showing as his lips curled.

Who did you kill now? Garm asked. And when was the last time you showered?

Ros looked down at himself, wondering why Garm sounded so judgmental. His hands were clean, but everywhere else was splattered with black blood.

"I summoned one of Beelzebub's lower commanders." He paused to shake his empty glass in the air. It slowly filled, and he gulped most of the contents before continuing on to explain what his uncle's commander had had to say. "Questioned him for a bit, tortured him for a bit longer, and he finally spilled some minor details."

They watched him drink down the rest of his glass. He swayed where he stood, and Billy rushed to push a chair under him before he fell.

Enough! Garm commanded, and the house listened, refusing to fill his glass. Ros glared. Get on with it, boy. What did the bastard say?

Ros rubbed his face. He had been drinking for the past hour to try and forget what the vile piece of shit had said. His laughter still rang in his head, along with the sound of his final moments. It was the only demon out of the twenty or more he'd hunted that had news or a whisper of Ellea.

"Ellea is still alive, but she won't be able to evade them for much longer. The fucker said something about the demons in my father's court keeping her preoccupied."

Billy's snarl shook the frames that lined the wall. Her wild anger answered his own.

Did he say anything about our powers? Garm growled.

"No, he only laughed and said, 'Good luck getting to the princess.' Then I stabbed him until he couldn't utter another word."

The princess? Garm questioned. Why would he call her that?

"He was probably trying to piss me off," Ros growled. "Using my nickname for her."

Billy gave Garm a look before walking closer to Ros.

We have an idea. She nudged him, forcing his hand away from his face.

"If it's killing more demons"—he looked down into her amber eyes that glinted at his comment—"I'm in."

She had hunted beside him a few times. Not only did her anger match his, but she was utterly bloodthirsty. He had come to realize that she could be ridiculous as much as she could be deadly.

No, she scolded. Well, we can always kill more demons. I'm talking about the road to Hel.

"The road to Hel is fucking blocked." What did they think he'd been doing this whole time? "Garm and I cannot enter Hel."

You can't enter your usual way. I'm talking about a literal road to Hel, Billy said.

Ros stared down at the beautiful beast; she looked so serious. All he could do was laugh, a deep, hoarse laugh. "That's a myth," he choked out. "If there was a road to Hel, why wouldn't people hop into their cars and try to visit those they lost?"

"Try" being the key word. You couldn't disturb a soul who had found peace.

You ignorant idiot, Billy snarled.

She's right. Garm stepped in before Billy could snap at him again. The road is as old as time and as old as the Gods. It's a journey, one you can't drive, and at the end there is a gate to Hel.

Ros stared at the two beasts. He had heard about the road but never thought it was real. Why would he? Until now, he hadn't needed any other way to get into Hel.

"How hard could it be?" Ros asked.

Hard, Garm answered.

"Why?" Ros shook his head. "We were born in Hel. We should be able to get in easily."

This road doesn't follow the same rules.

I've taken it many times, Billy said with a distant look in her eyes. It won't be fun, but we can do it.

"Let's go!" Ros yelled, trying to stand. "What are we waiting for?"

Garm rushed to him, but it was too late. As Ros stood, his long legs tripped over themselves, and his large body crashed to the ground. He groaned into the wooden floors and burped unceremoniously.

"How about you sober up first?" came a gruff voice from the door frame. Sam slowly walked up to Ros with his nose pinched between two fingers. His sharp features and angular eyes softened as he took him in. "And shower."

Devon leaned against the door frame; he and Sam had walked in with no one noticing. Devon looked as rough as Ros, cleaner, but he still had that hollowed look in his eyes. His usually bright blue eyes were cloudy, and his rich skin was pale. They were all looking and feeling rough since his father had walked out of the shadows and taken someone they cared about. Devon had been reading day and night, trying to find ways to get to Ellea. He'd even gone as far as contacting his family to see if they had any idea on what to do. They didn't, and neither did the books he read. Ellea was in Hel, and it seemed the only way to get to her was this road Garm and Billy spoke of.

Devon cleared his throat and pushed off the wall. "Sam, take Ros up to shower."

Sam looked up at his boyfriend, appearing slightly shocked by the sternness his voice carried. "And what are you going to do?"

"Billy, Garm, and I will talk about the plan to get to this road," Devon said, crossing his arms and walking toward the desk. "And then to get to Ellea."

"How much did you overhear?" Ros mumbled into the floor.

"Enough," Sam and Devon said together.

Billy seemed ready to protest, but Devon gave her a stern look. She returned it with a smirk.

Yes, Billy said. Take the princeling and hose him off. We will begin planning and talking when he's more sober.

Sam easily gathered Ros under his arm and steered him toward the door. The sound of running water could be heard from the upstairs bathroom thanks to the magic of the house.

"Come on, Ros," Sam said. "Let's get you cleaned up, and then we can plan the snacks for the road trip."

The two men navigated through the lower level of the cabin. Their large bodies melded together, and Ros took up so much more room as he stumbled under his friend's care.

"We need to get her, Sam," Ros grumbled.

"I know, buddy." He squeezed him a little tighter. "We'll get her."

"We will," he agreed and began carrying more of his own weight. "Then I'm going to burn my father's kingdom to the ground."

ORDER

TRICKY PRINCESS

OUT SEPTEMBER 13, 2022

Nothing would stand in his way of saving Ellea,
not his father, not Hell, and not the Gods. The funny thing is,
he would be reminded once again that she never needed saving.

AUTHORS NOTE

Tricky Magic has been one Hell of a journey. I'll be honest…where we are now, is nowhere near where we started. The two MC's that have consumed my mind and soul popped into my head during a long drive home from spooky St. Augustine in February 2021. Ros was supposed to be a Wolven, Billy was supposed to be a vulture, and El was always meant to be a badass Witch. But here we are and I just want to fucking say THANK YOU! From the bottom of my weird heart, I can't believe I did this and I can't believe you've read this. Look at us, doing things.

WANT MORE?

Facebook: Lexi L. Campbell
Facebook Group: L.L.'s Wicked Witchlings
Instagram: @readsbylexi
Tiktok: @readsbylexi
Patreon: patreon.com/readsbylexi
Sign up for my newsletter for exclusive awesomeness!
Website: readsbylexi.com

ACKNOWLEDMENTS

Girls…Ash, Jess, Gabbie, and Britt…I'm not going to cry. This is all for you and I will never, ever, be able to thank you enough! Ash, thank you for the endless voice messages, Dean gifs, listening to my ramblings, and helping bring Ros to life. Jess, your support has meant so much. Thank you for fixing all my flaws and never letting me feel dumb. I owe you so fucking much. Gabbie, you're the freaking best! Thank you for hyping me up, listening to me when my imposter syndrome was at its lowest, and for loving these characters. And last but not least, Britt. You're a badass and you still supported me while you were already consumed. Thank you for loving me, this book, and and batting away all my internal negative questions.

Big thank you to Genesis for swooping in and helping with editing. Seriously, THANK YOU! My Alphas, Laura, Reva, Teddi, and Leez. Thank you for all your help! You're the FUCKING best! To my Beta and ARC readers. Thank you for giving this thing a chance.

To my street team…you all give me life and please don't ever stop! Thank you so much for sharing and supporting Tricky Magic.

To all four of my parents who have always supported my creativity, crazy ideas, and have always said I could do anything. Look mom! It's printed! Thank you for all the love and I really hope you didn't get this far.

what is to come...

what is to come...

turn worlds...

upside down...

what is to come...

mortal terr

purgatory

ruler: Belizbub
dwellers: the malevolent
description: entless waste,
the pits, fire, and pain

southern territory

supernatural te

ruler: Leviathan
dwellers: supernaturals only

ruler: Sonneillon
dwellers: mortals only

ory

gods territory

itory

ruler: Asmodeus
dwellers: the gods and
those who no longer
wanted to dwell with the
living or dead.

Printed in Great Britain
by Amazon

10125593R00285